P9-CRN-838

In truth, the bite hadn't hurt. It had
even been pleasurable . . . at least
until she'd seen his fangs and realized
what he'd done. That thought made
her frown. He'd had a reflection.
Vampires weren't supposed to have
one. Maybe he was just a freak and
the fangs were glued on. That made
more sense than that he might be a
vampire. A freak was better than a
vampire, wasn't it?

*There was no way
she was going anywhere
with this man.*

"Inez? You were here all day and perfectly safe. If I'd wanted to harm you, I could have done so first thing in the morning. Instead, I drew you a bath and ordered you breakfast—"

"And then you bit me." Inez had luxuriated in that bubble bath, thinking what a wonderful, sweet man Thomas Argeneau was. She'd looked down at his sleeping face and pondered how wonderful it would be to have a handsome, thoughtful man for a mate.

She'd imagined him greeting her at the door with a kiss, the smells of scrumptious cooking drifted to her as he kissed her hello, his hands moving over her body, stripping away her clothes one at a time . . .

Right up until he woke up and bit her.

By Lynsay Sands

VAMPIRES ARE FOREVER
THE ACCIDENTAL VAMPIRE
BITE ME IF YOU CAN
A BITE TO REMEMBER
A QUICK BITE

Coming Soon

VAMPIRE, INTERRUPTED

LYNSAY SANDS

Vampires Are Forever

AN ARGENEAU NOVEL

AVON
An Imprint of HarperCollinsPublishers

AVON BOOKS
An Imprint of HarperCollins*Publishers*
10 East 53rd Street
New York, New York 10022-5299

For David F. Jackson.
Thank you for all the help,
especially since you "don't read romance." <grin>

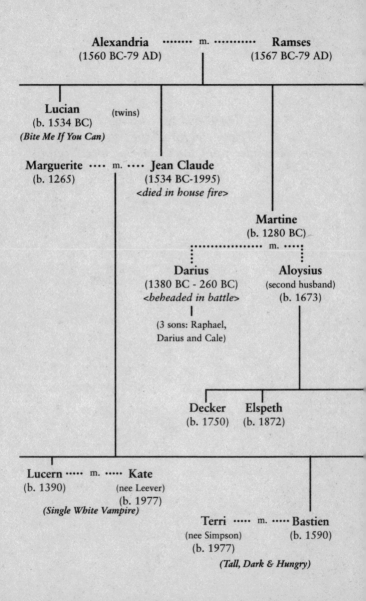

Argeneau Family Tree

Armand
(b. 1100 BC)
m.

Susanna
(1430-1449)

Althea
(1775-1798)

Rosamund
(1888-1909)

Inez ···· m. ····· **Thomas**
(nee Urso)   (b. 1794)
(b. 1979)

(Vampires Are Forever)

Jeanne Louise
(b. 1909)

Marion ···· m. ···· **Victor** ···· m. ···· **Elvi**
(1301-1695)   (b. 230 BC)   (nee Black)
<burnt at the stake>   (b. 1946)

(The Accidental Vampire)

Jackie ···· m. ····· **Vincent**
(nee Morrisey)   (b. 1590)
(b. 1976)

(A Bite to Remember)

(twins)
Julianna **Victoria**
(b. 1983)   (b. 1983)

Etienne ····· m. ····· **Rachel**
(b. 1689)   (nee Garrett)
            (b. 1972)

(Love Bites)

Gregory Hewitt ····· m. ····· **Lissianna**
(b. 1965)   (b. 1798)
(A Quick Bite)

Prologue

"You'll be flying over in one of the company jets. It should be ready and waiting by the time we get to the airport."

Thomas Argeneau nodded, but his attention was on the clothes he was ripping from hangers in his walk-in closet and shoving into his knapsack.

Etienne watched briefly and then burst out, "Why hasn't Mother called?"

Unable to answer the question, Thomas grimaced and shook his head. He found the whole situation upsetting. After seven hundred years as a housekeeper, Marguerite Argeneau had decided to start a career. But she hadn't eased her way into the workforce with a secretarial job or some other mundane career. Instead, she'd decided she wanted to be the next Sam Spade, or Samantha Spade as the case may be. The woman, who had rarely left her home before this, had taken on a job as a private detective and flown off to Europe to locate the mother of a five-hundred-year-old vampire.

While Thomas understood her desire to have a career to fill her time, he wished she'd chosen something a little less exotic, and preferably one that could have been done at home in Canada.

"She called every evening for the first three weeks; sometimes twice in a night. And then, *bang*, nothing at all. Something must have happened," Etienne muttered.

Thomas glanced over his shoulder, noting that his fair-haired, usually mellow cousin was anything but mellow now. Etienne was pacing behind him in the small walk-in closet, his face marred by lines of concern. It was an emotion the entire family was presently suffering. Marguerite Argeneau had been out of contact for three days now. Normally, that wouldn't be cause for concern, but Lissianna, her only daughter, was in the last month of her first pregnancy. That was why Marguerite had been checking in so regularly. Everyone knew she'd intended to drop everything and fly home at the first sign that Lissianna was going into labor, which made this sudden silence very disturbing.

"Thomas." Etienne stopped pacing and suddenly touched his arm. "I really appreciate your flying over to check on her like this . . . and so does the rest of the family."

"I care about her too," Thomas said with a stiff shrug and then turned back to his packing, knowing he'd just spoken the biggest understatement of his life.

Biologically, Marguerite Argeneau might only be his aunt, but she'd raised him and was the only mother Thomas had ever known. He loved her as much as her daughter and sons did.

"I wish I could come with you," Etienne added fretfully, beginning to pace again. "If I didn't have this deadline . . ."

Thomas didn't comment. He knew Etienne, as well as the rest of the family, wanted to go and look for the missing woman as much as he; they simply weren't able to on such short notice. However, he also knew they were making arrangements to follow as soon as they could. Thomas was sincerely hoping that wouldn't be necessary. He hoped to arrive and find her alive and well and with some silly, simple explanation for the lack of phone calls.

The sudden electronic ring of a phone made both men pause. Thomas watched Etienne slide a cell phone from his pocket and place it to his ear. His hello was followed by silence as he listened, and then he said, "Okay," and put the phone away.

"That was Bastien," Etienne announced. "He's managed to book you a room at the Dorchester Hotel in London. It's where Mother was staying before she disappeared."

"London?" Thomas asked with a frown. "I thought Aunt Marguerite and Tiny were in Italy. The case they're working is for some guy from Italy. Nocci or something."

"Notte," Etienne corrected, pronouncing the name *No-tay*. "And he *is* Italian. At least on his father's side, but apparently he was born in England so that's where Marguerite and Tiny started their search."

When Thomas merely stared at him doubtfully, he added, "Bastien arranged the plane for Mom and Tiny and he says they went to England."

"So, she's in England not Italy," Thomas muttered and began dragging out the white linen pants he'd been stuffing in the knapsack, replacing them with jeans and a couple long-sleeved shirts to go with the packed T-shirts. It was early fall, the evenings would be cooler in England.

Once he'd stuffed as many clothes into the bag as he could, Thomas shifted the bulging knapsack past his cousin, and hurried out of the walk-in closet.

"Has Bastien heard from Jackie? Has she heard from Tiny?" Thomas asked, hurrying to the dresser drawers to find socks and underwear. Jackie Morrisey was the owner of the Morrisey Detective Agency, and Tiny and Marguerite's boss. She was also the lifemate of his cousin Vincent.

Etienne grunted in the negative as he followed. "He still can't reach Jackie. She and Vincent are in the wind. They're probably locked up in a secluded cottage somewhere enjoying each other. I know, Rachel and I didn't leave the house for several weeks after we finally got together."

Thomas nodded as he crammed socks into the bag. He'd watched as each of his cousins found their lifemates, and everyone had disappeared for weeks afterward . . . all except Bastien. The head of Argeneau Enterprises hadn't felt he could take the time away from the family company. In truth, he might as well have. The man had been working at half his usual efficiency ever since his lifemate, Terri, returned to him. While the others had disappeared for a month or so and returned able to at least hold an entire conversation again without having to rush out of the room to be alone with their lifemate, Bastien's not taking the time to get it out of his system had just seemed to drag out the length of time during which he was easily distracted.

Thomas gave up trying to cram any more into his bag and began to zip it up. Finally admitting it was too full, he grimaced and pulled out the underwear he'd stuffed in, deciding he'd just have to go commando until he bought more in England.

"Greg tried to call mother at the Dorchester when Lissianna started having labor pains, only to be told that she'd checked out," Etienne said unhappily.

Thomas nodded as he slowly managed to work the zipper closed. Lissianna's lifemate had already told the family that when they arrived at the house en masse to keep him company while Lissianna gave birth to their beautiful baby girl. Their kind couldn't go to the hospital and risk having their otherness revealed. Most immortals gave birth at home with only an immortal midwife to aid them, but Lissianna had asked Etienne's wife, Rachel, to attend her. The woman might work in the local morgue, but she was also a doctor and had done a fine job of bringing the latest Argeneau into the world.

"Disappearing like this just isn't like her," Thomas said with a sigh as he finally got the zipper closed.

"No," Etienne agreed. "Especially when she knew Lissianna was so close to giving birth. She made me promise to call if there was any sign that the baby was coming."

"She made me give her the same promise," Thomas

admitted. "I suspect she made every one of us promise that."

They both fell silent, contemplating what could possibly keep Marguerite Argeneau from contacting her family, or at least calling to check on her daughter. The answer was simple; death or physically not being able to call were the only things that could have kept her from doing so.

Pushing that thought away, Thomas swung the knapsack over his shoulder, snatched up the binder lying on the bedside table, and headed for the door.

"Are you composing something?" Etienne asked curiously, following him out of the room.

The question made Thomas's hand tighten on his binder. He'd grown up in a home filled with music. Aunt Marguerite had loved all forms of music and had ingrained that same love in him as well. He had very fond memories of falling asleep as a boy to the sweet sound of her playing various piano concertos. When he'd expressed an interest, she'd taught him to play piano and guitar. He'd gone on to learn several other instruments since then.

Thomas was fourteen when he'd started his first clumsy attempts to write music. Unfortunately, Jean Claude hadn't appreciated music and had belittled his attempts. It hadn't taken long for Thomas to decide to keep his efforts a secret to save himself the heart ache of the old bastard's taunts. Afraid his male cousins would take his efforts no better, Thomas had kept what he was doing a secret from them as well. Aunt Marguerite, Lissianna, and Jeanne Louise had always known, however, and praised him when the music he wrote began to get published and gain popularity back in the early nineteenth century. They'd been very upset at his insistence on publishing the music anonymously and keeping the knowledge of what he did from the others. But they'd honored his wishes. Or he'd thought they had, but now . . .

"Which one told you? Lissianna or Jeanne Louise?" he asked grimly. He'd sworn both women to secrecy over his career and didn't appreciate their breaking the promise.

"Neither," Etienne answered. "Mother told me."

Surprise made Thomas stop walking and peer around.

"You didn't think you could keep what you were doing a secret from her, did you?" Etienne asked with a laugh, and then added dryly, "She reads all our minds and knows everything about all of us."

Thomas grimaced, but said, "I knew she knew. Who do you think taught me to read and write music? I'm just surprised she told you. Bastien and Lucern don't know, do they?"

Etienne shook his head. "Your reputation as a useless loafer is safe from them, cousin. As far as I know she hasn't told them a thing about it. In fact, she made me promise not to tell them either. She said you'd tell them when you were ready."

"Hmm." Thomas nodded with relief at this news, but then said, "It makes one wonder why she told you."

"It was an accident actually. She caught me humming 'Highland Mary' back when it was popular and said it was her favorite of your musical compositions to date. Of course, I hadn't a clue what she was talking about and made her explain it, but then she swore me to secrecy."

"And you're breaking that promise now?" Thomas asked with amusement. "Why?"

"I didn't realize how long I'd have to keep the secret. It was almost two hundred years ago, cousin, and you're showing no signs of revealing that you're a musical composer any time soon." He shrugged and then asked curiously, "Why *are* you keeping it a secret?"

Thomas continued up the hall, muttering, "It isn't secret to everyone. Besides, Bastien and Lucern would just think it was a 'cute little hobby' and tell me to put away such childish efforts and go to work at the family business."

"That sounds like something Father would have said," Etienne commented quietly.

Thomas merely shrugged. It *was* something Jean Claude Argeneau had said, and it had hurt enough at the time that he wasn't interested in hearing it again from Bastien and Lucern.

"There you are." Rachel smiled at the pair as they joined her in the apartment's large living room. "Thomas, is this your mother?"

His gaze slid past her to the portrait over the fireplace and he nodded slowly. Althea Argeneau had been a beautiful woman, but he had no memory of her. Marguerite had presented the painted portrait to him on the day he'd moved out of her home and into his own. The painting was the only connection he had to the woman who had given him life. His gaze now slid to the portrait on the opposite wall. It was of his Aunt Marguerite and he hoped to God it wasn't now his only connection to the woman who had raised him. He had to find her alive and well.

"So . . . is she any closer to being able to have that next baby yet?" Rachel asked with amusement, drawing his attention back to the portrait of his long-dead mother.

When he peered at it and then turned a blank gaze to Rachel, Etienne reminded him, "The first time you met Rachel was at the Night Club. She thought you were younger than Jeanne Louise. You told her she was wrong, and then said your mom had wanted more children but had to wait another ten years or so because of the hundred-year rule."

"Oh." Thomas smiled wryly as he recalled the conversation in question. The comment had been a throwaway line one would give to a stranger. He'd hardly wanted to explain about his family tragedies to her then, that there was no "mom" and Jeanne Louise was only his half sister by his father's *third* marriage.

The fact was Thomas's father seemed to be cursed when it came to wives. They just kept dying on him, a difficult occurrence since they had all been immortals. In response, the man had grown bitter and angry over the centuries, shunning any real contact with his son or daughter. It was a sore subject for Thomas, and one he preferred to avoid, which was why he'd made that comment at the time rather than explain that Jeanne Louise was only his half sister and that Marguerite Argeneau was the only mother either of them had known.

However, it looked like he'd now have to explain himself. "I—"

"It's all right, Etienne told me the story after we were married," Rachel interrupted quietly and then crossed the room to run a hand soothingly over his arm. "I was just teasing. I'm sorry if I brought up bad memories."

Thomas shrugged the matter away as if it weren't important and then turned to lead the way to the door. "We should get moving. The sooner you drop me at the airport, the sooner I'll get to London, find Aunt Marguerite, and set everyone's minds to rest."

One

"This is as close as I can get, love," the taxi driver announced apologetically. "That'll be fourteen pounds."

Inez Urso frowned as she noted they were at least three sets of doors from the gate she wanted. Unfortunately, there was a long line of cars waiting to collect arrivals and the driver couldn't get any closer. Knowing she had a jog ahead of her, Inez handed him the money, managing not to grimace at the expense.

It isn't coming out of your pocket anyway, she reminded herself. *It's a business expense*. That was the only reason she was here. Only a direct order from Bastien Argeneau would make her suffer through forty-five minutes of London traffic in an airless taxi during one of the hottest Septembers in history. If she'd had more warning, Inez would have had one of the company cars take her to the airport to meet Thomas Argeneau. She also would have gone to bed earlier last night. But she hadn't had more warning. Bastien Argeneau, head of Argeneau Enterprises and her boss, had called at five o'clock in the morning, waking her from a dead sleep to ask her to pick up his cousin at the airport. Worse yet, he'd called a very short forty-five minutes before the plane was supposed to land.

Knowing it would take that long to get to the airport from her flat, Inez hadn't even taken the time for a shower or cup of tea, but had dragged on her clothes from the night before with one hand as she'd rung for a taxi with the other. Still doing up buttons, she'd grabbed her purse and run downstairs, rushing outside just as the taxi had stopped in front of her apartment building.

Inez wasn't at her best. No makeup, hair a mess, unshowered, and wearing her day-old clothes, she wasn't likely to impress anyone. Fortunately, Thomas Argeneau wasn't someone she felt she had to impress. She'd only met the man once. After being promoted to vice president of UK operations several months ago, she'd gone to New York to tour the company's head offices. That was when she'd met Thomas, or at least seen him. They hadn't been introduced. She and several other top executives had been in a meeting in Bastien's office when Thomas had sauntered in—unannounced and without knocking—to spout a lot of gobbledy gook that Inez hadn't quite been able to catch except to note that it seemed to be sprinkled liberally with "yos, dudes, and dudettes."

Inez had seen enough movies to know he was talking like a stereotypical 90's California surfer. She somehow doubted the old terms were still used, but it didn't matter since he wasn't from California and—as far as she knew—there wasn't much surfing done in Southern Ontario. She'd decided it was all an affectation. He was just a lazy layabout youth, taking on this surfer lingo in a misguided attempt to impress someone.

It had turned out that Bastien had called for him to deliver something to one of his brothers. Thomas was nothing more than an errand boy, she'd realized, and that had simply confirmed her assessment of him. He was an Argeneau, but rather than get a degree and take a position in the company, he delivered things and talked like a stoned idiot.

Which meant, Inez thought now, *that she'd been dragged out of her bed at five in the morning to pick up a man who had no importance, and probably didn't have a good reason to be in the country other than to loaf on new shores.* It made him nothing more than an annoying pain in the arse in her mind.

Unfortunately, the request had been made by Bastien, and he was someone she *did* want to impress. So Inez snatched the receipt the taxi driver handed her, said thanks, and then flung the door open and hurled herself out of the cab to charge toward the Arrivals entrance.

A glance at her watch as she raced through the pneumatic doors and into the milling people said she'd made it to the airport five minutes after Bastien had said the plane would have landed. Inez felt a moment's panic, but then assured herself that he couldn't have got through customs yet.

Reaching the busy arrivals section, she took a moment to orient herself, and then made her way quickly along the row of glass windows toward the gate where Bastien had said she should meet Thomas.

Inez was perhaps twenty feet from where she needed to be when she saw the doors slide open and the man she was there to meet walk out. Forcing a pleasant smile to her face, Inez picked up speed and called out breathlessly, waving a hand to catch his attention.

Her call had been faint enough, Inez didn't think he'd hear, but Thomas did glance her way as he proceeded forward. He even seemed to notice her waving at him, yet he simply continued forward and out of the airport through the pneumatic doors in front of his gate.

Shocked at the apparent snub, Inez stared after him with shock, and then cursed and burst into a run as she saw him walking toward the row of cabs waiting out front. Tossing apologies left and right, she jostled her way through the crowd to the doors and rushed out onto the concrete just in time to see the cab he got into pull away.

Inez stared after the black cab, disbelief giving way to anger. She'd been dragged from her bed and rushed out here only to have the ignorant idiot hop in a taxi and ride off on her.

"Do you need a taxi, love?"

Inez glanced around at the question, and then sighed at the sight of the same smiling cabby who'd brought her to the airport. The man had burbled happily on about this and that and nothing at all the entire ride out from the core of London where she lived. Now she would no doubt get to enjoy the same happy burble all the way to the Dorchester hotel where Thomas was staying.

"What I *need* is a tea," she muttered, then sighed and nodded and moved to where the man held the taxi door open. Inez didn't see the dark-haired, thin-faced man approaching the cab until they were both nearly to the door. She hesitated in surprise. He didn't. However, before he could slip into the open door, the taxi driver stepped in front of it.

"I'm taking the lady," the cabby announced firmly. "I brought her out, and I agreed to take her back."

The man didn't even glance her way, his attention focused on the driver. Inez had no idea what he said, but suspected he must have promised extra money, because the driver suddenly stepped out of the way for him to get in, closed the door, and got in the driver's seat without another word, or even a glance in her direction.

Once again, Inez was left gaping after a departing taxi.

"Diya need a taxi, lady?"

Inez glanced around with a start as a younger driver hailed her. Mouth tightening, she rushed forward, not willing to allow another ride to be stolen from her. Reaching the car unimpeded this time, Inez slipped onto the backseat, forced a smile, and muttered thanks as the driver closed the door behind her. She then sagged wearily on the seat, thinking she really needed that tea now. Unfortunately, it would have to wait until after she got to the Dorchester and made sure Thomas Argeneau had everything he needed. That had been Bastien's order. "Collect Thomas, take him to the hotel, and see that he has everything he needs."

And that was what she would do. She would make sure Thomas Argeneau had every single thing he needed . . . right after she gave him a piece of her mind for riding off without her. Then she could have her tea.

"Thanks, just set it there on the table," Thomas said as the bellhop followed him into the suite's sitting room. When the man did and then turned, mouth opening to inform him of all the amenities on offer, he waved him to silence.

"I'm good, thanks," Thomas assured him. Offering the man a tip for seeing him to his suite and carrying the knapsack, Thomas urged him toward the door.

"Thank you, sir." The bellhop's lips spread into a grin that he quickly softened into a more businesslike smile. "Just ring the desk if you need anything. Ask for Jimmy and I'll get you whatever you need."

"I will. Thanks again," Thomas murmured.

Closing the door behind the bellhop, he then turned and stepped back into the sitting room of his suite. Classy, luxurious, tasteful . . . Nothing less than he'd expect. Aunt Marguerite always had shown good taste.

Moving forward, Thomas collected his knapsack and headed for the door leading into the rest of the suite, intending to place it in the bedroom. The ring of his cell phone made him pause, however.

Dropping the knapsack back on the table, he pulled the phone from his back pocket and flipped it open as he dropped onto one of the love seats.

"Yo?" he said lightly, already knowing who it would be.

"You arrived all right, then?" Bastien asked.

"Of course, dude. The flight was smooth sailing."

"And Inez had no problem finding you at the airport?"

Thomas's eyebrows rose. "Inez?"

"Inez Urso. I called her to meet your plane and take you into the city."

Thomas could hear the frown in Bastien's voice, but ignored it, his mind on his arrival in Heathrow as he suddenly recalled a little, dark-haired woman running through the airport waving. Thomas had noticed her, but Etienne hadn't mentioned there being anyone to meet him so he'd just assumed she was there to collect someone behind him and kept walking. Now that Bastien mentioned Inez, however, he recalled the pristine and tucked-up little miss he'd met some months ago in his cousin's office. But the woman who had been waving so frantically at the airport that morning had been less than pristine and tucked up. She'd looked like she'd just rolled out of bed.

"Thomas?" Bastien said impatiently. "Did she not show up?"

"Yes. She was there," he answered truthfully, a knock drawing his gaze to the door of the suite. Standing, he moved to answer it.

"Good," Bastien was saying as Thomas opened the door. "She's very efficient as a rule, but I did wake her up at five in the morning to collect you and I worried that she hadn't made it there in time."

"Yes, she—" Thomas stopped abruptly as he recognized the woman at his door. His gaze slid over her limp, dark curls, her slightly wrinkled clothes, and her makeup-free face with its irritated scowl. Inez

Urso. A very angry Inez Urso, he added, noting the fire flashing in her eyes.

When her mouth opened, Thomas instinctively slammed the cell phone to his chest to prevent Bastien's hearing the tirade he suspected was coming. He wasn't wrong. The phone had barely hit his chest when a barrage of words shot from her full, luscious mouth and poured over him. Unfortunately, very little of it was in English. Portuguese would have been his guess. He gathered that was her mother tongue and the language she slipped into when upset, and Inez Urso was definitely upset.

When she began to move forward, Thomas automatically backed up, allowing her into the room. He was too distracted to do otherwise, finding it fascinating how a woman who had looked perfectly plain on first sight could become almost beautiful as she berated him. Her eyes were flashing, her cheeks were flushed with anger, her lips flapping so rapidly they were almost a blur. She was also waving a finger angrily under his nose, something he normally found vastly annoying if the women in his family tried it. But coming from this short woman, he found it kind of cute and couldn't help the smile that tugged at his mouth.

Big mistake, Thomas realized at once. Inez Urso did not like his amusement and her rant took on some real energy. Unfortunately, that's when he became aware of the chittering coming from the phone.

Thomas scowled down at it, and then glanced toward the door closing behind the little barracuda still lecturing him, judging whether he could get her back out of the room long enough for him to deal with

Bastien. It didn't seem likely, at least not without being rude and Aunt Marguerite had raised him better than that.

He held up a hand for silence. Surprisingly—she obeyed the directive, her tirade ending at once, but then he supposed she'd been close to winding down. At least, her eyes had lost some of their heat, becoming more subdued. Inez was still breathing rapidly from her anger, though, and Thomas found his eyes falling to her slightly heaving chest, noting that with every inhalation, her blouse was stretched tight, threatening to pop a button.

A sharp inhalation drew his gaze back up to her face. Her dark brown eyes were flashing again, her mouth opening to go at him once more. Thomas didn't blame her at all . . . really . . . it was perfectly rude to stare at a woman's chest. Aunt Marguerite would be pissed at him too. Still, he didn't really have time to apologize properly, or let her vent with Bastien's voice still squawking into his chest, so Thomas said, "Hold that thought."

Inez blinked at the order, but closed her mouth and Thomas gave her an approving smile before whirling away. He hurried through the small dining area and continued on into a small hallway with two doors leading off of it. The first led into a spacious marble bathroom, the second a bedroom. Knowing the bathroom would have a lock, Thomas slid inside and then locked it for good measure lest the woman follow to finish her lecture. He then took a breath and raised the phone back to his ear. "Bastien?"

"What the hell was that about?" his cousin growled.

"Oh, I . . . er . . . sat on the remote control and accidentally turned on the television. Some foreign film was playing and I couldn't figure out how to shut it off," Thomas lied blithely.

"Right," Bastien said with open disbelief. "What was the name of this movie?"

"The name?" Thomas echoed and then scowled. "How the hell would I know?"

"I don't know, Thomas. I thought maybe you caught it before you turned it off. It sounded terribly interesting. I quite enjoyed it when the woman called the man an idiot for making her drag her butt out of bed at five o'clock in the morning and haul herself down to the airport without either tea or a shower only to have him ignore her and march out to get in a taxi and take off to the Dorchester Hotel."

Thomas closed his eyes on a sigh as he recalled Bastien spoke several languages, including Portuguese.

"Hmm," Bastien added now. "That's the same hotel I booked you into. What a coincidence."

"All right, all right, so it wasn't the television," Thomas muttered irritably and then asked, "Did she really call me an idiot?"

An exasperated sigh came through the line. "How could you walk right past her, Thomas? *Why* would you? For Christ's sake! I called her to make things easier for you and you just—"

"You didn't mention that anyone was picking me up at the airport," Thomas interrupted grimly. "Neither did Etienne. He said you had a plane waiting at the airport and had booked a room at the Dorchester. That's it. There was no mention of anyone waiting for me at the airport, so I just hopped in a taxi."

"Well, when you saw Inez—"

"Bastien, I met the woman once for about three minutes in your office almost six months ago," Thomas pointed out dryly and then acknowledged, "I *did* see her waving and rushing toward me at the airport, but didn't recognize her. I thought she was there for someone else. How was I to know otherwise when *no one told me she would be meeting me*," he ended, emphasizing every word.

"All right, I get the point. You didn't know," Bastien said.

"Right," Thomas sighed.

"Okay." A moment of silence passed and then a sigh slid from the phone and Bastien said, "I should have contacted you myself and told you she would meet you rather than counting on Etienne. You'll have to apologize to her for me."

"Are you sure you told Etienne?" Thomas asked.

"What?" Bastien asked, his voice short. "Of course I did."

"Of course you did, because you wouldn't ever make a mistake. Those are for lesser immortals like Etienne and I."

"Thomas," Bastien said wearily.

"Yes?" he asked sweetly.

"Never mind. Look, she's there to help you. Let her. She knows London and she's a damned efficient woman. One of our best employees. She gets things done, that's why I decided to have her help you."

"You mean that's why you decided to have her baby-sit me, don't you?" Thomas asked dryly.

There was a brief silence on the other end of the line, then Bastien took a breath, but before he could speak, Thomas said, "Don't worry about it. I know you think I'm useless. Me, Etienne, and anyone under four hundred years old. So don't worry about it. I'll apologize to her and let her help me."

He pushed the end button on the phone before Bastien could respond and tossed it irritably on the marble counter as he headed for the door. He'd grasped the doorknob when a thought made him hesitate. Releasing the doorknob, Thomas turned back to briefly pace the room.

He didn't want another berating by Bastien's underling. While it was cute and he'd found it fascinating to watch the fire dance in her eyes as she'd spat words rapid-fire at him, it would have been more entertaining had he understood some of it. Besides, he didn't know London and this woman obviously did and while he'd like to be able to find his aunt all by himself and be the hero of the moment, the main concern was *finding* Aunt Marguerite. Common sense said he would probably get farther faster with help, and Inez was the only help on offer. But she was, no doubt, in a really rotten mood right now and he couldn't blame her. Bastien might owe her an apology, but Thomas felt he owed her something too. He might not have known she was coming to collect him, but the woman went out of her way to do so and was ignored and left behind for her trouble.

After pacing the room twice, Thomas reached for the hotel phone on the bathroom's marble counter. He punched the button for room service and quickly placed an order, then hung up and moved to the tub. His cell phone rang as he pushed the button to drop the tub's stopper into place, but—knowing it would be Bastien with more orders and instructions—he ignored it and grabbed the bottle of bubble bath off the counter. Thomas dumped a generous amount of the liquid in and turned on the taps, then sat down on the side of the tub to wait for it to fill.

Inez dropped wearily to sit on one of the love seats situated on either side of the fireplace and scowled at the knapsack on the table in front of her. The man couldn't even bother with proper luggage. He was staying in a five-star hotel and checked in with a knapsack. It was the only article of luggage in the room and the only thing he'd been carrying when she'd seen him at the airport.

She glared at the offending article and then realized what she was doing and shook her head, her eyes closing in dismay. She was losing it. Inez never lost her temper, yet here she was not just glaring at luggage, but she'd greeted her boss's cousin by berating him like a harridan and cursing him in two different languages. Her boss's cousin!

Dear God, she hadn't just lost her mind but probably her job too once Bastien heard about this. Thomas Argeneau was probably on the phone in the other room right now complaining to him.

The rude little pillock, Inez thought unhappily. She still couldn't believe he'd looked right at her and then just marched happily off and hopped in a cab. *What kind of idiot—*

Her thoughts died abruptly when the phone on the end table beside her began to ring. Inez switched her scowl to that, waiting for Thomas to answer it. It rang three more times before she recalled that he'd actually had a cell phone in his hand. Supposing he was still on that and couldn't talk on two phones at once, she heaved a sigh and picked up the receiver only to get a dial tone.

Too late, Inez realized and dropped it back in its cradle with a shrug. She hadn't wanted to play secretary for him anyway. She was the vice president of U.K. productions for Argeneau Enterprises Worldwide, for heaven's sake. He could answer his own damned phone. As well as his own door, she added mentally when someone knocked on it.

Inez glanced toward the door Thomas had disappeared through, expecting him to appear to answer it, but there was no sign of the man.

"Room service," a deep voice called as the knock came again.

Inez glanced toward the door again and then rose impatiently to open it, stepping out of the way as the bellhop began to roll a trolley into the room.

"Thank you, miss." The man smiled as he passed. "Where would you like it?"

"What is it?" Inez asked rather than answer. Her gaze was fixed on the small teapot on the tray, but kept drifting to the silver-covered plate. Delicious aromas were drifting up to her nose, making her stomach rumble with interest.

Eyebrows rising, the man lifted the silver cover. "A proper English Breakfast. Eggs, bacon, baked beans, sausages, fried tomatoes, mushrooms, black pudding, hash browns, and a fried slice," the man rattled off.

"The full Monty," Inez murmured, her eyes roving over the food until he replaced the cover.

"And, of course, tea," the man added. "So? Where shall I put it?"

Inez shook her head helplessly. She hadn't a clue where Thomas wanted it, but *she* wanted it in her stomach. Right then. Dear God, breakfast *and tea*. The very idea made her want to weep, the actual sight of the food made her moan silently in her head. She was starving and could have killed a cup of tea, but had no doubt this was all for Thomas. He was probably going to eat it all right in front of her too, the—

"Oh, good. It's here."

Both Inez and the bellhop glanced toward Thomas Argeneau as he entered the room. The bellhop was smiling. Inez was not. Her eyebrows drew down in displeasure as she eyed him. If he'd just taken a little more time she might at least have pinched a sausage before he came out.

"Roll it in here please . . . Jimmy, isn't it?"

"Yes, sir." The bellhop smiled and promptly followed him with the cart.

Inez watched the food roll away with a little sigh. Just a small sip of tea even would have been nice, but the man hadn't even bothered to think of her when it came to that. There had only been one teacup on the trolley.

Her thoughts were disturbed when the bellhop returned. The man threw her a wide smile and wished her a good day as he crossed to the door and left.

Inez scowled after him. Sure! *He* was happy. He'd probably eaten and even had half a dozen cups of tea by now. He'd probably also got a big tip from Thomas.

"Inez?"

Her gaze moved resentfully to the open door to the rest of the suite. "Yes?"

"Come here, please."

Inez frowned at the request and hesitated. Come here? Come where? To his bedroom? It would be just her luck if the man was a pervert and thought one of her duties as an employee of Argeneau Enterprises was to "service" relatives.

"Not gonna happen," Inez muttered under her breath.

"Please?" Thomas called.

Throwing up her hands with exasperation, Inez headed for the door. She'd go see what he wanted, but if he tried anything, anything at all . . .

Inez stepped through the door into what she'd thought would be the bedroom and found herself in a dining area. However, neither Thomas nor the food was in there, and it just made her suspicions increase regarding his motives. Continuing on through the dining room, she stepped into a small vestibule leading to three more doors. Thomas was calling from the room on the right.

Inez stepped into the marble bathroom, taking in the trolley of food, and the bathtub brimming with bubbles and then Thomas pushed a stack of towels at her.

"There you go. Enjoy."

Inez blinked in confusion at the fluffy white stack she held and then turned toward the door he was now exiting through.

"Wait!" she cried, taking a step to follow him. "What is this?"

He turned back, surprise on his face. "I'd think it was obvious."

Inez frowned, her eyes narrowing as her mind returned to the pervert possibility. Did he plan to feed her, bathe her, and expect her to perform for him? Wishing she wasn't holding the towels so that she could prop her hands on her hips, she growled, "I think you'd better explain."

Thomas eyed her for a moment, and then said, "Bastien forgot to tell me that someone would be at the airport, that's why I hopped in a taxi. He says he dragged you out of bed at five A.M. and that—from what you said earlier—you rushed to the airport without either breakfast, or tea, or even a shower." He smiled crookedly as he added, "Bastien asked me to give you his apologies. They are duly given, Bastien is sorry."

Inez waved the apology away and nodded to acknowledge it at the same time.

"This"—he continued, gesturing around the bathroom with the full tub and trolley of food—"is *my* apology. Slip in the tub, eat your breakfast, and drink your tea, and when you're feeling better, come back out and we'll start to work."

"Work?" she asked uncertainly.

"On the search for Aunt Marguerite," he explained and when she looked blank, shook his head and said, "Bastien said he'd arranged for you to help me, that you knew the city and—" He paused suddenly, muttered something under his breath about Bastien and his sudden forgetfulness, and then sighed and explained, "Aunt Marguerite is missing. She flew to England about three weeks ago, stayed at the Dorchester a couple nights, and then headed north. She and Tiny were investigating— That's not important. Basically, she was traveling all over England her first three weeks here and then stayed at the Dorchester again for a night. She apparently checked out the next morning, but we don't know where she and Tiny went after that and neither of them have reported in since. I'm here to find her."

"I see," Inez said slowly.

"Bastien said he wanted you to help me, so, I thought we'd start with calling hotels to see if they just moved to another one for some reason. Failing that, we'll try calling rental agencies, train stations, and so on to try to get a lead on where they've gone."

"Oh," Inez said blankly.

"Right . . . Well, don't worry about that now. Enjoy your bath. We'll talk about it after." He started to pull the door closed, then stopped and added, "And don't worry about rushing. I'm going to catch a couple z's on the couch in the suite's living room while you're in here. Soak as long as you like." He started to close the door again, and then paused once more and turned the inside lock, locking himself out once he pulled the door closed, which he immediately did.

Clutching the towels and housecoat to her chest, Inez stared at the closed door for several minutes. Her mind was a blank. Well, not really. Her mind was awhirl with myriad thoughts and feelings, mostly amazement. She couldn't believe he'd gone to all this trouble and effort for her.

Her gaze slid to the bath he'd drawn and then to the trolley of food. Hers. It was all hers. And it was all so sweet. So thoughtful and considerate . . . Not what she would have expected from Thomas Argeneau or anyone for that matter. She tended to expect the worst from people so was always surprised by a kindness. And Thomas Argeneau had definitely surprised her.

Inez frowned at her own thoughts. Really, she hardly knew the man so shouldn't have any judgment of him yet. Her prejudgment was made up of one meeting and the fact that the few times Bastien Argeneau had mentioned his cousin Thomas, it had been with a tone of exasperation.

From those two small things, Inez had assumed Thomas was a shiftless, lazy, thoughtless spoiled rich relative. She should have known better. Assumptions were bad, useless, a waste of time. But she had assumed, which made her an ass if she went by that old saying. And at that moment, it seemed to her the saying was true. She really did feel like an ass for making such obviously erroneous assumptions.

Inez sank down on the side of the tub with a little sigh, her mind turning to the fact that he wasn't there to loaf as she'd thought, but to find his aunt . . . and he seemed to expect her to help, but all she'd been instructed to do was collect him and see him to the hotel. She was just wondering what she should do about that when a phone began ringing.

Standing again, Inez followed the sound to the counter, eyes landing on the cell phone lying there. Thomas's. He'd obviously set it down and forgotten about it.

She glanced at the digital display and bit her lip when she saw Bastien ID'd as the caller. After a hesitation, she set down the towels, picked up the phone, flipped it open, and put it to her ear as she headed for the door.

"Hello Mr. Argeneau. This is Inez. Just give me a minute and I'll take Thomas his phone so you can talk to him."

"No, that's all right. I don't need to talk to him," Bastien interrupted quickly. "I really wanted to talk to you anyway."

"Oh." Inez leaned against the door rather than open it.

"Did Thomas explain and apologize for me?"

"Yes," she assured him, straightening away from the door and beginning to pace the room, her footsteps echoing on the marble floor. "He apologized."

"Hmm, but probably not properly," Bastien muttered.

Inez frowned at the words as her gaze slid over the food trolley and then to the bathtub brimming with bubbles. Perhaps it hadn't been her fault she'd made her assumptions. It seemed obvious Bastien underestimated his cousin.

"Actually, he did do it properly," she said firmly, feeling a need to defend the younger Argeneau, and then added, "more than properly."

"Oh?" Bastien queried. "How is that?"

Inez hesitated, and then admitted, "He drew me a bath, ordered tea and breakfast from room service, and suggested I make use of both to feel better. He's being quite nice about all this, sir."

"He ran you a bath?" Bastien asked with surprise.

"And room service," she added defensively, suddenly uncomfortable and wishing she'd kept her mouth shut. "And then he went out to nap while I clean up," Inez added quickly in case he was thinking anything was amiss. She bit her lip and then said, "I probably won't take the bath, of course, but—"

"No, take the bath. That's fine," Bastien said quickly. "It will make me feel less guilty about rousting you from your bed. Besides, it isn't like the two of you can do any looking for Mother right now. Thomas will need to sleep and then there's the sun and so on. You may as well clean up first."

"So you did want me to help look for your mother?" she asked with relief, glad to have the matter cleared up.

"Yes," Bastien said and then there was a short silence, followed by a curse, followed by, "I forgot to mention that part, didn't I?" A wry laugh came down the line. "I'm sorry, Inez. I'm a little distracted at the moment. So much has been happening, what with Lissianna having her baby, the trouble with Morgan, and then Mother going missing . . ."

Inez raised an eyebrow as she heard him blow out a long, calming breath. She had no idea who this Morgan was he spoke of, but knew Lissianna was his sister, and had met his mother while in New York. Marguerite Argeneau was a beautiful woman who didn't look a day over twenty-five. It was very difficult to believe she was the mother of Bastien Argeneau who she would guess was in his mid to late twenties himself.

"I guess I owe you another apology. I know you have a lot to do, but I want you to put everything aside for now and help Thomas find my mother," he explained grimly.

"Okay," Inez said slowly, then cleared her throat

and said, "Sir? Wouldn't it be better to hire a private detective and—"

"She *is* a private detective," Bastien interrupted impatiently, and then said, "Well, not really. She's just started into the career, but Tiny, the man she's with, *is* a proper private detective. A very good one, in fact, and he's missing too."

"Oh," she murmured.

"Look, I know this isn't part of your job, but we're all quite worried about my mother. Thomas knows her habits, but has never spent much time in England. You know it better than he and you're the most organized, details-oriented person I know. Between the two of you, I think you can track her down. It's probably just a case of her getting wrapped up in the case and forgetting to call."

Bastien didn't sound as if he believed what he was saying, but Inez didn't question him on it and merely said, "Okay. I'll do what I can, sir."

"Well . . . good. I really appreciate your assistance with this, Inez."

"Yes sir, but . . ." Inez hesitated and then said, "you mentioned Thomas and the sun. Is he allergic like you are?"

She shifted, uncomfortable in the sudden silence that came from the other end of the phone, and then explained apologetically, "I only ask because if he is, I should probably arrange to use the car with the treated windows that you use when you are here and need to travel in sunlight."

"Yes," Bastien said finally. "Yes, he has the same allergy. It runs in the family. You'd best arrange for my car to take you around."

"Okay."

"Now I'd best let you get to your breakfast before it gets cold. Would you put Thomas on the phone? I've just recalled something I forgot to mention to him."

"Of course. Just a minute." Lowering the phone, Inez moved to the door, unlocked it, and slid out into the hall. She hurried through the dining room and found Thomas in the sitting room, seated on one of the two love seats facing each other in front of the fireplace. He was apparently writing something down in a binder.

"Bastien wants to speak to you," she said quietly, as she approached holding out the phone.

"Oh, thanks," Thomas muttered, not looking at all pleased at the interruption. He set the binder on the coffee table between the love seats, and accepted the phone. "Now, go have your bath before it gets cold."

Nodding, Inez turned away, but not before glancing curiously at the binder to see that he hadn't been writing at all, at least not words. The binder held pages with musical tables on them, scored with musical notes scratched in bold black. He'd been writing music.

Inez pondered that and listened absently as Thomas greeted his cousin in impatient, irritated tones as she crossed back to the door. She had nearly passed into the dining room when Thomas suddenly yelped, *"What?"*

Inez turned back with concern, but Thomas glanced her way with wide eyes, and seeing her still there, pulled the phone from his ear and slammed it to his chest.

"It's all right. He just surprised me. Go on, have your bath."

Inez hesitated. His tone hadn't sounded surprised so much as shocked, perhaps even horrified, but he was waving her away, obviously wanting privacy for his call, so she turned away to return to the bathroom.

It was none of her business, Inez told herself as she crossed the dining room. Besides, her bath would get cold if she didn't hurry. Bastien had said to take the bath and enjoy it and he was the boss, she told herself a smile slowly spreading her lips. Breakfast in the bath . . . how decadent was that?

She was about to find out.

Two

"You have got to be kidding me," Thomas said into the
phone the moment he heard the bathroom door close.
"You arranged for someone who doesn't know about
our people to help me find Aunt Marguerite? What
were you thinking?"

"I—"

"Besides, I thought all the senior executives in Argeneau Enterprises and Argent knew about our kind,"
Thomas interrupted with a frown. "Isn't Inez a vice
president or something? She should know."

"Yes she should," Bastien agreed quickly. "We
bring anyone promoted to an executive position to
Canada or New York under the pretext of a tour of
the head offices. We then reveal the truth to them and
read their minds repeatedly over the next week to see
how they accept it. If they are able to accept the in-

formation and keep the secret, all is well and they are promoted. If not . . ."

Thomas grimaced, actually able to visualize his cousin shrugging. "*If not . . .*" meant the person's memory would be wiped and they didn't get the promotion. In fact, they'd most likely find themselves working for a different company shortly after that, hired away by a headhunter who suddenly noticed how brilliant the individual was . . . with a little help from an immortal. It was hard to work with someone who was horrified by what you are.

"Right," Thomas said dryly. "So how did Inez get promoted without the indoctrination?"

"Where did you meet her, Thomas?" Bastien asked quietly.

"In New York," Thomas answered.

Bastien rarely spent much time in the New York office, keeping Canada as his main base to work from, but the whole family had been there for Lucern and Kate's wedding. It was where Bastien had met and briefly lost his lifemate, Terri.

"The afternoon Inez arrived, I knew she'd be tired from the flight," Bastien informed him quietly. "So we just had the meeting to introduce her to everyone— the meeting you walked in on—and then I sent her to her hotel. I intended to indoctrinate her the next day, but Terri arrived from England and . . . I got distracted by her turning and everything and . . ." He blew his breath along the phone line. "I ended up just telling Inez she was promoted and sending her back. I called Wyatt in England and told him to just keep her away from any information that was too revealing and I'd fly over and indoctrinate her at the first chance, but then there was the trouble in California with Vincent's saboteur, then Morgan cropped up to cause his own difficulties, and now Mother is missing and I'm trying to arrange the wedding, but now it's a double wedding with Lucian and Leigh, and Donny is driving me absolutely mad, and—"

"Bastien," Thomas interrupted his ranting. "I get it. Despite all outward appearances, you're not perfect, dude. You screwed up. Get over it."

Another long, drawn-out sigh slid down the phone line. It was followed by a quiet, "Thomas?"

"Yeah?" he asked with amusement, hearing the annoyance in his voice.

"Never mind," Bastien muttered and then asked, "Do you have any ideas on how you're going to find Mother?"

"A few," he admitted reluctantly. "I thought I'd call the other hotels in London to make sure she hasn't just booked into another one. If that doesn't turn up anything, we'll have to check car rental agencies and trains and flights . . ."

"That's a hell of a lot of calls. Even with the two of you working at it, it could take forever. There are hundreds of hotels in London," Bastien muttered unhappily.

"Yeah," Thomas agreed quietly, his mind returning to an idea he'd had on the flight over. He hesitated over mentioning it, sure Bastien would think it was stupid, but then sighed and admitted, "I had a thought on the plane."

"What's that?" Bastien asked hopefully.

"Well, I read an article a couple months back about tracking cell phones. If I can track Aunt Marguerite's cell it might be the fastest way to find her."

"They can track phones?" Bastien asked with interest.

"Yeah. Maybe it's only when a nine-one-one call is placed from the phone in the states and Canada, though. I'm not sure, but I'm going to check into it and see if it's possible. I have a techie friend who just moved back to England last year who should be able to help me with that. If it can be done, I'm going to try to track her that way."

"That's a good idea," Bastien said.

Thomas scowled at the surprise in his voice and said dryly, "I do have the occasional worthy idea, Bastien. I know you and Lucern think I'm a loafer and an idiot, but—"

"We don't," Bastien interrupted. "We know you're intelligent and creative and—"

"Yeah, right," Thomas interrupted with amused disbelief.

"We do. Really, we—" He released a slow breath and then he said, "Look, Thomas. Lucern and I know about your music."

Thomas stiffened at the bald announcement and then asked warily, "You do?"

"Yes. Vincent mentioned it. He didn't know it was a secret," Bastien said, answering the unspoken question.

Thomas grimaced. He'd been composing music for Vincent's plays for decades. It hadn't occurred to him that now that Vincent and Bastien were talking again, Vincent might mention it to him.

"Why didn't you tell us?" Bastien asked quietly. "Why the big secret?"

"It wasn't a secret," Thomas said quietly. "Aunt Marguerite and Lissianna have known all along. So does Jeanne Louise and Mirabeau. And Etienne," he added.

"So only Lucern and I didn't know?"

"Well, dude, you never asked what my interests were, or what I do with my time when I'm not at Argeneau Enterprises," he said simply.

There was silence for a minute, and then Bastien said, "And only Lucern and I get the dude business."

Thomas grimaced, but didn't say anything.

"I know you only talk like that to annoy Lucern and me."

"What makes you think that?" he asked with amusement.

"The first clue was that Lissianna gets this really amused look when you do it, Greg just looks curious, and you slip up all the time and forget to stick in the 'dudes' and 'dudettes.' I've overheard you have whole conversations with her and others that don't include a single 'dude,' which means you only do it with us, and since it does annoy us, I'd guess that's why."

"Hmm," Thomas muttered.

"Look, I know over the centuries, Lucern and I have sometimes acted like we think you're a snot-nosed kid. But it's just . . ." Bastien paused and when he spoke again Thomas could hear the frown in his voice as he tried to explain, "You're like our younger brother, Thomas. When you were growing up you worshipped Lucern and me and wanted to do everything we were doing."

"Well, worship is kind of an exaggeration, but I did look up to the two of you," he admitted wryly.

"Yeah, well, we reacted like typical older brothers, being annoyed and condescending to you."

Thomas was silent as he realized it was true. They really had treated him like a younger brother, the same way they treated Etienne.

"However, you're well past two hundred now and I suppose we have to acknowledge that you've grown up some. So if you'll try to cut out the 'dudes' and 'dudettes,' I'll do my best to be less condescending and older brotherish."

Thomas felt his eyebrows rise at the suggestion.

"Deal?" Bastien asked quietly.

"Deal," Thomas echoed.

"Well, now that we have that out of the way . . . Since you're going to be spending the next few days with Inez anyway, and will be right there to read her reaction, why don't you just explain about us to her and—" He stopped when Thomas burst out laughing.

"No thanks," Thomas said. "Nice try at dumping one of your problems on me, though."

"I thought it was worth a shot," Bastien conceded with a laugh.

Thomas smiled faintly at his admission, and then said, "Surely, there is someone at the company here who could take care of it?"

"You would think so, wouldn't you?" Bastien asked dryly. "But no one will do it. I've always done it and they expect me to continue to do so."

"Nice," he said dryly

"Yeah." Bastien sighed. "Okay, look. Just do the best you can to keep her from finding out. Wipe her mind if she sees or overhears something she shouldn't, and I'll bring her over for the indoctrination right after you find Mother."

Thomas nodded silently, and then remembered Bastien couldn't see him and said, "Yeah sure."

"Good. Call that techie friend and then catch some sleep while you can. But, call me back if he is able to track her phone."

"Okay. Later." Thomas's gaze landed on the open binder on the table as he pressed the button to end the call. Scowling, he reached out and flipped the book closed. The music he was working on was for a comedy, and he wanted the music to be light and bouncy to reflect that. Unfortunately, it was difficult to write light, bouncy music for Vincent's play when his mind was full of worry and concern for Marguerite. Despite his best intentions, Thomas doubted he'd get any work done until he found his aunt. Fortunately, Vincent didn't need it right away.

Turning his attention back to his phone, Thomas opened the digital phonebook to find his techie friend's number.

Herbert Longford was his name. An immortal who'd lived in Toronto for a while during one of his breaks from his homeland of England. Thomas had met him several years ago while delivering blood, something he occasionally did when Bastien's couriers got behind, or one was off on vacation. The two had got talking and a friendship had formed. Herb was British, 280 years old, and even more of a computer geek than Etienne. If anyone would know if Marguerite could be tracked by her cell phone, Herb would.

Pushing the button to call his number, Thomas sank

back on the love seat, mentally preparing an apology for waking the man during daytime hours when he, like most of their kind, was no doubt sleeping.

Thomas was dreaming of music when the irritating ring of the phone woke him. Despite the circumstances that had brought him to Europe it was a light and sweet refrain and was still playing through his head as he snapped his eyes open. His gaze shot to the binder on the table and Thomas automatically snatched up the pen that lay beside it as he sat up. He was already scribbling the notes on paper as he reached for the phone and flipped it open.

"Yeah?" he said absently, his attention on getting the music he'd dreamed onto paper.

"Thomas? I'm guessing by the fact that you didn't call that Mother can't be tracked by her cell phone," Bastien said, sounding unhappy. "But I called just to be sure and to let you know that I've arranged for blood to be delivered to your room. It should arrive at sunset or shortly thereafter."

"Sunset?" Thomas asked setting down his pen with a frown. "I won't be here by sunset, I should think. And, yes, they can track her cell phone. I did call the penthouse to tell you that, but I got your answering machine."

"I've been in my office all morning waiting to hear from you. They tracked her?" Bastien asked eagerly.

"Yes. You won't believe where she is, though," Thomas said with a wry laugh.

"Where is she?" Bastien asked, a frown evident in his voice.

"Amsterdam."

"Amsterdam?" Bastien echoed with disbelief. "No. That can't be right. Have them double check—"

"I did have it double checked, Bastien," Thomas assured him with annoyance. "Both times it came back Amsterdam, though from two different locations in the city," he admitted reluctantly.

"Amsterdam," Bastien repeated, obviously not pleased with the results of the tracking. "Italy I would have believed, and anywhere in England, but Amsterdam?"

Thomas could picture Bastien shaking his head as he said the word. He spoke the name of the old city as if it were tantamount to Babylon. Rolling his eyes, he pointed out, "She and Tiny are here in Europe looking for Christian's birth mother. Maybe the woman lives there now."

"That's possible, I guess," Bastien said reluctantly. "So, you need me to arrange a flight—"

"I've already done that," Thomas interrupted with exasperation. "I figured the company jet would have returned to Canada after dropping me here, so when the second tracking confirmed she was in Amsterdam, I booked myself a flight over."

"You did?" he asked and then grumbled, "Well you should have called me, I could have arranged the flight for you."

"Bastien, I am not helpless. I can book a flight," Thomas said grimly. "I leave at six-fifty P.M."

"I know you're not helpless, but I could have booked it through the company. You're doing this for the family. You shouldn't have to foot the bill alone. I could have— Did you say six-fifty?" Bastien suddenly interrupted himself to ask.

"Yeah," Thomas said with amusement. "Why?"

"Isn't England five hours ahead of Toronto? I'm sure it's—"

"Yes. England is five hours ahead of you guys back there in Canada," Thomas said patiently, wondering what time it was exactly. Inez was supposed to wake him after her bath so it couldn't be much after eight in the morning. Actually, he'd taken so long about his calls earlier that when he'd finally laid down he'd felt sure he'd barely drift off to sleep before she was waking him.

Turning slowly, he peered around the room, searching for a clock. Thomas never wore a watch. It wasn't usually a problem, but at that moment he wished he did. He'd just spotted the clock on the mantel over the fireplace when Bastien squawked, "Then it's four-thirty there, Thomas!"

"Yeah, I see that," Thomas muttered, wondering why Inez hadn't woken him after her bath. "I'd better get off the phone and get moving. It's an hour to the airport and I have to be there an hour before the flight leaves."

"But the blood isn't there yet," Bastien protested. "It isn't to be delivered until sunset."

Frowning, Thomas walked to the curtained windows lining one wall of the room and tugged the heavy material aside to peer out, wincing as late afternoon sunlight splashed over him. He let the drapes fall quickly back into place. "Well, it won't be sunset for another couple hours by my guess, so unless you can arrange it to get here in the next twenty minutes, I'll just have to go without."

"There's no way a courier could get across town

to the Dorchester within twenty minutes. Not with London traffic the way it is. And you are not going without."

"Bastien, if you can't get blood here before I leave, I have little choice. My flight leaves at six-fifty. I have to leave here by four-fifty if I want to get there on time," he pointed out patiently, but wasn't terribly happy to say so himself. He normally had three or four bags of blood a day, and there had been a full mini fridge of blood on the company jet that had brought him to England, but—distracted with his worry for Aunt Marguerite—he'd only consumed one bag. Now Thomas was feeling the hunger.

"Well . . ." Bastien hesitated, and then asked, "Is Inez still there?"

"Inez?" Thomas echoed with confusion, unsure what one thing had to do with the other. Turning, he walked through the suite, checking each room for the woman as he went. "No, I don't think so. I expected her to wake me up when she got out of her bath, but that would have been hours ago."

"I presume you didn't tell her about the search moving to Amsterdam. She probably decided to let you sleep while she arranged for my car with the treated windows."

Thomas grunted at this news as he crossed the dining room. The car hardly mattered now since he was headed to Amsterdam.

"It's a shame she isn't there," Bastien continued. "I was going to suggest you feed from her before heading to the airport."

"What?" Thomas gasped, coming to a halt outside the bathroom door.

"Don't sound so shocked," Bastien said with irritation. "You have to feed."

"Yes, but, this is hardly an emergency situation yet," Thomas pointed out. "The council would have my head if I—"

"You're in England, Thomas," Bastien reminded him. "The European council has different rules than us. A lot of the older immortals reside there. They like their traditions and dislike change. Many of them refused to even consider banning feeding off the hoof. It's still allowed there within reason."

"Yes, but *our* council—"

"Can't penalize you for behavior that's completely acceptable where you are," Bastien said firmly. "And you're going to have to feed."

Thomas frowned with displeasure at his words. "Can't you get blood to me in Amsterdam?"

"Yes. But that's hours away. Thomas, I don't like the idea of your being on a plane full of people when you're hungry."

"I'll be fine."

"You only had one bag of blood on the plane."

Thomas grimaced. "Checking up on me?"

"Never mind that," Bastien said, sounding uncomfortable. "The point is, you only had one bag and if Inez isn't there—"

"I wouldn't have bitten Inez anyway," Thomas assured him.

"Why not?" Bastien asked and Thomas frowned at the interest in his voice.

"Because she seems nice," he answered vaguely.

"Nice? She berated the hell out of you when she got to the hotel," Bastien said with amusement.

"Yes, but she looked cute while doing it," Thomas muttered, and then added, "Besides I somehow don't think that's under her list of duties in her job description."

"No, it isn't," Bastien agreed on a sigh. "And I normally wouldn't even consider it, but Mother is missing and the longer the delay . . . Besides, it wouldn't harm Inez. And it is kind of an emergency." When Thomas didn't say anything, Bastien sighed in defeat and said, "You'll have to rebook a later flight."

"No," he protested at once. "I'll be all right, Bastien. I can hold out until I get to Amsterdam."

"What if you have someone afraid of flying seated beside you?" he asked. "They'll be nervous and sweating, their smell taunting you. And what if the stewardess cuts a finger or something? Hell, what if someone in the airport itself has a bloody nose while you're waiting to board your flight? No. It's too risky, Thomas."

"Bastien," Thomas began grimly, but paused as a light popped on in the bedroom. Frowning, he took the two steps necessary to bring him to the door of the room and peered in. His eyes widened as he saw Inez seated at a small table in the dying light of the day. Obviously, she'd worked by sunlight until now, but that was dimming as the sun slid lower in the sky and she'd turned on the lamp on the table to better see what she was writing as she spoke rapidly on the hotel phone.

"What?" Bastien asked.

Inez glanced toward the door and spotted him, offering a smile as she spoke. Thomas forced a smile in return, and then spun out of the doorway and took several steps away. "She's here."

"Mother?" Bastien asked with sudden excitement.

"No, Inez," Thomas explained.

"Oh . . . Well . . . Good. Feed off her. Just enough to make it through the flight without being tempted to feed off a seat mate," he added quickly before Thomas could protest again. "And then wipe her memory and head for the airport."

When Thomas was silent, he sighed and said, "I know you don't want to do it, Thomas. But you know better than to surround yourself with mortals when you hunger."

"Right." Thomas sighed, giving in. "Okay."

He didn't wait to see if Bastien had more to say, but snapped the phone closed and then simply stood there, considering what he had to do. Thomas actually found himself grimacing at the idea of biting Inez. He was a vampire. He used to feed off the hoof all the time before blood banks had come into existence, but that had been a good fifty years ago. All of his meals since then had been bagged and he found himself nervous at the idea of having to bite someone now. Not the actual doing of it, but enjoying it.

Thomas very much feared he would enjoy it. Bagged blood was cold and pretty much tasteless compared to the real thing. It had none of the scent of the owner, none of the individuality, and none of the pleasure of warm, pulsing blood pouring into your mouth and body. It was rather like the difference between the much-loathed airplane food compared to a home-cooked meal.

Oh sure, his kind could go to the Night Club to get specialized drinks that still bore some of the characteristics of the donor. Diabetics had sweet blood and so on, but it was still cold and really not as flavorful as blood from the source . . . And it had been a long time. What if he drank too much, or had lost the technique to share the pleasure and prevent her feeling pain?

"Thomas?"

Turning abruptly, he found Inez standing in the doorway to the bedroom peering at him curiously. When her eyes widened at the sight of his expression, he suspected that his guilt was plain to see there and tried to replace it with a smile.

"I didn't know you were still here," he said to distract her from what he suspected was a sickly smile, and then changed it to a scowl as he added, "You were supposed to wake me after your bath."

"Yes, I know, but I thought you were probably exhausted after your flight. Besides, we couldn't both use the phone at the same time, so I let you sleep," she explained. "I've spent the day making calls; first trying the various hotels in the city to find out if Marguerite didn't just move to another hotel, and when that didn't turn up anything, I started on the car rental agencies, but there's been no luck yet."

She frowned. "It occurred to me, though, that they might have booked under the name of the man she's working with, but all I know him as is Tiny. I didn't know his last name, and I didn't think that was probably even his real first name so couldn't ask about him."

"Actually, his first name really is Tiny. He's Tiny McGraw. At least I think that's his name," Thomas said with a frown, wondering if the Tiny was really just a nickname.

"Oh. McGraw?"

Thomas blinked the thought away and glanced to Inez as she suddenly whirled to rush back across the bedroom and out of sight. Frowning, he stepped into the doorway to see that she'd returned to the table where she'd been working when he'd spotted her earlier. He hesitated briefly in the doorway, and then followed.

Thomas stopped a step behind Inez, his nose quivering as her scent hit him. She wore no perfume, having had none here to use after her bath. The only fragrance masking her natural scent was the faint whiff of the hotel soap and bubble bath, but it was a very faint scent after the whole day spent making calls in the hotel room. Most of what was reaching his nose was her natural scent, a sweet musky aroma that made his nose quiver.

His gaze slid over her back and up to her neck as she bent over a notepad and scribbled Tiny McGraw's name and added a note beside it. Her hair had fallen to curtain her face, leaving him a peak of just a bit of the back and side of her neck. The skin there was smooth and unblemished, a perfect swath of skin stretched over the muscles and veins of her throat. It was the vein though that caught his interest. He could almost see it throbbing with the blood rushing through it.

When Thomas realized he was licking his lips hungrily at the sight and smells hitting him, and that the hunger in him was ramping up just at the thought of biting her, he knew Bastien had been right. He couldn't travel in a busy airport, or sit on a crowded plane, with countless mortals and not be tempted to lure one to a quiet corner for a quick bite. It was a foolish thing even to contemplate in this day and age of security cameras and watchful eyes everywhere on the lookout for possible terrorist activities.

Inez straightened suddenly and stepped back from the table, stiffening with surprise when her back pressed into his chest.

"Oh." Stepping away, Inez turned swiftly, eyes wide as she peered up at him. "I'm sorry, I didn't realize. . . ."

Her words faded as she peered at his face. Thomas knew his expression was probably hungry, so wasn't surprised by the sudden uncertainty that flickered on her face and the way her heartbeat sped up. It was a natural response to a predator, and he was definitely that, he acknowledged. The very fact that he was suddenly aware of her heartbeat spoke of the fact that his old predator instincts were kicking in. The extra sensitive hearing his people enjoyed was a useful skill when on the hunt, but he normally blocked out much of the sounds it brought him, or had since blood banks had come into existence.

Now her heartbeat played like a concerto in his head, the dance of the hunted. He couldn't resist stepping closer again and invading her space. Thomas found himself smiling as her heart fluttered and skipped a beat, and then settled into a rapid tattoo. He saw her eyes dart nervously toward the huge king-sized bed before skittering away, and he smiled as her scent changed. The pheromones coming off of her now were a combination of the sharp tang of fear and the deep musk of desire. Inez was nervous of him, but she wanted him and the two emotions were battling inside her.

"You haven't had your tea yet."

Thomas raised his eyebrows as Inez suddenly blurted that statement, then she was hurrying away across the room. He immediately followed, her scent making it impossible for him not to stalk her. She was a doe on the run, and he was the wolf, instinct sending him after his prey. Thomas allowed her to think she was fleeing toward freedom until she was out of the bedroom. Her anxiety level dropped a great deal the moment she was out of sight of the bed and that's when he caught her arm and drew her back around.

Inez gasped in surprise and opened her mouth to speak as Thomas swung her back to face him, but she never got the chance to say the words of confusion burbling on the edge of her mind. Her mouth was suddenly covered by his, his lips and tongue moving over her. She caught at his arms to keep her balance and stiffened under the onslaught, her mind a confused jumble, but then his arms closed around her. He pressed her body against his with one hand firm on her backside even as his other hand slid into the wild mane of curls at her head and tilted it to a better position as he kissed her.

Inez moaned as her resistance melted away. He was overwhelming her senses. She was breathing in his scent through her nose, tasting him on her tongue and her body, was soaking up the touch of his like an eager sponge.

Groaning deep in her throat, Inez slid her own

hands up around his shoulders, allowing the fingers of one hand to dive into his soft, dark hair, and curl closed around a handful of it. She then held on for dear life.

Inez had never had this strong or swift a response to a man before. Her body was tingling everywhere, liquid desire already pooling low in her belly.

Normally cautious and constantly assessing every situation, Inez was incapable of it this time. She didn't care that this was her boss's cousin, or that she could be involving herself in something that might be ultimately damaging to her career. Her body was humming, her mind bouncing around inside her skull like a useless rubber ball as he slid a thigh between both of hers and rubbed it against her core.

When Thomas broke the kiss, she moaned her disappointment and then gasped as his hand on her behind lifted her slightly so that her thigh pressed against the hardness between his legs even as she rode his own. Then his lips slid across her cheek and tarried briefly at her ear before dropping down over her throat. Inez groaned and let her head drop back and to the side, her eyes blinking briefly open.

A flash of surprise slid through her as she found herself peering straight through the open bathroom door and at their reflected image. They stood sideways to the mirror, and there was something erotic about seeing their bodies entwined. Inez just wished she could see more of Thomas's face as his lips moved down her throat. A shudder went through her as his teeth scraped over her sensitive flesh and Inez let her eyes drift closed as passion washed through her, and then she stiffened and clutched at him with surprise as a needle-sharp pain struck her neck. Before Inez could quite grasp that pain or respond to it, the unpleasant sensation was gone, replaced by a wellspring of pleasure and passion that exploded in her mind, blanketing every thought.

Inez was aware she was panting, could hear a soft keening and knew it was her own as her body shuddered and writhed in his embrace. She wanted to tug at his hair and pull his face back to kiss her again, but couldn't seem to move. Like a kitten picked up by the scruff of the neck, she was paralyzed in his arms, her body able only to experience the pleasure trembling through her.

It was only the ringing of the phone that roused her from the fever passion. Blinking her eyes open with confusion, Inez found herself peering at their reflected image in the mirror again. The sight of their embracing bodies ratcheted her need up another notch despite the annoying sound of the phone, and then Thomas eased his hold on her and began to pull away. His mouth was open as he lifted his head, and for one brief second she caught a glimpse of two, long, blood-stained fangs protruding from that open mouth and then they seemed to slide away and disappear and he closed his lips. Her eyes shifted immediately to her own throat, but his mouth had been working on the side of her throat away from the mirror. She couldn't see it, and then Thomas was easing her back to her feet on the floor and shifting his hands to either side of her head, holding her still as his gaze focused on her face.

No, not her face, Inez realized with confusion. He seemed to be staring at a spot in the middle of her

forehead, as if he could see into her mind. She'd barely had that thought when he began to frown. Thomas
gave his head a shake, and refocused his attention on
her forehead again, but she could tell by his expression that something was wrong. Not that she cared
what he thought was wrong. Now that he was no
longer embracing her, her mind was beginning to
function again and it was going a little wild. She had
seen fangs. Like a Vampire's fangs. *Bloody* fangs. Her
blood? Was Thomas Argeneau a vampire?

The thought was a mad one, Inez knew, but suddenly she was seeing some things in a different light.
Thomas had an "allergy" to the sun, and while he'd
ordered breakfast for her that morning, he hadn't got
himself anything, not even a cup of tea. But Bastien had
an allergy to the sun as well, she realized. While her
boss would attend day meetings with the higher-ups of
other companies if he couldn't schedule it later, other
than that, he worked at night. And she'd never seen
Bastien Argeneau eat. Oh, he toyed with and picked at
food when it was brought to the few business meetings
she'd been to with him on his infrequent trips here to
England, but she never really saw him eat more than
a bite or two. And then there was Marguerite's not
looking a day over twenty-five, but with four grown
children.

None of that really mattered, Inez acknowledged.
The facts were that Thomas had fangs and she was
pretty sure he'd bitten her. That said *vampire* to her.

Inez's mind immediately tried the rational route,
reminding her that vampires were mythological crea-
tures that existed only in movies. But it carried little

weight when she was becoming aware of a burning
sting in her neck at exactly the point where Thomas
had been concentrating his attention.

"What the hell?" Thomas whispered the words
with a sort of horrified amazement and Inez gave up
her thoughts and scowled at him, thinking he really
didn't have any right to either emotion at the moment. *She* was the one who had been bitten. Maybe.

Wanting to know for sure, Inez pulled free of his
hold and rushed into the bathroom. Standing before
the mirror, she tugged her hair out of the way and
stared at her throat. Sure enough, there were two
nasty holes in the skin.

"Inez?" Thomas asked, his voice sounding worried
and uncertain.

She immediately whirled from the mirror to glare at
him. "You bit me!"

He opened his mouth, but rather than say anything,
snapped it closed looking for all the world like a lost
puppy. The man was a ravening vampire, but honest
to God he was standing there looking at a complete
loss as if he didn't know what to say or do.

For some reason that infuriated her. Probably because some part of her wanted to give him a hug
and tell him everything would be all right. A foolish
response. That was what *he* should be doing to her
right then, she thought with irritation. She immediately burst into a rant, hardly even aware of what she
was saying as she waved a finger under his nose and
began to back him out of the bathroom.

His cell phone began to ring again as he backed
into the hall, and Thomas reached for it almost with
relief.

"That will be Bastien," he said over her words, his own definitely relief soaked. "He'll know what to do."

Inez stopped her rant and stared at him with amazement. "What to do? What to do? You *bit* me!" she snapped furiously, and then slammed the door in his face and locked it.

Three

Thomas ignored the ringing phone in his hand and stared at the wooden door Inez had just slammed in his face. It was as blank and featureless as the wall he'd run up against in her mind. He'd tried to slip into her thoughts to erase them once he'd fed enough from her, but much to his amazement, he couldn't.

He'd redoubled his efforts, but had come up against a solid wall in her mind. The graffiti on it read "Bugger off! No Entry here." He couldn't read Inez Urso.

The phone stopped ringing, only to start up again a moment later and Thomas glanced down at it with a sigh. Spotting the caller ID stating it was Bastien, he flipped it open and lifted it to his ear.

"Thomas?" Bastien asked.

"Yeah."

"Did you feed from Inez?"

"Yeah."

"Good, good. Are you on the way to the airport?"

"No."

There was a moment of silence. "Why?"

"We have a problem," he muttered.

"What kind of problem?" Bastien sounded wary.

"I can't wipe her mind."

"*What?*" Bastien asked with disbelief.

A crash sounded in the bathroom as something was knocked to the floor. It made Thomas back away so Inez wouldn't overhear his conversation. "I can't get into her thoughts to wipe the memory of the bite from her mind."

There was another pause and then Bastien clucked and snapped, "Dammit, Thomas! Inez is one of my best employees."

He pulled the phone away from his ear to peer at it with disbelief, and then slapped it back to his head. "What the hell has that got to do with anything?"

"Well, if you had to find your lifemate, couldn't it have been someone *else's* employee. I'm going to lose her now. She'll want to be with you and come to Canada and—" Thomas heard the sound of material rustling and knew Bastien had pressed the phone to his chest while he spoke to someone else. Etienne, he supposed, and guessed he was explaining things to the other man.

The whole family would know by sunset, Thomas realized and rolled his eyes.

"Never mind," the older immortal said apologetically. "I'm just tired and cranky. Congratulations."

"Congratulations?" Thomas echoed with disbelief.

"Yes, congratulations, Thomas. You've just met your lifemate."

"I've just *bit* my lifemate," Thomas snapped. "And she's now locked in the bathroom, probably fashioning a cross and a stake out of the soap bars and anything else she can find in there."

"Oh crap."

"Yes, oh crap." Thomas snarled. "*Bite her* you said. *Feed off of Inez so we don't have to worry about you being tempted on the plane.* Brilliant, Bastien."

"Well, hell, Thomas, how was I supposed to know she would turn out to be your lifemate? Couldn't you have tried to read her *before* you bit her?"

"Why the hell would I do that?" Thomas snapped. "I had no idea she was my lifemate."

"Okay, okay," Bastien said quickly. "Let me think." Thomas rolled his eyes, but remained silent.

"She's locked in the bathroom?" Bastien asked finally.

"Yes."

"Have you tried to talk to her?"

"What would you like me to say Bastien? *Oh, I'm sorry, Inez. I didn't mean to bite you, my fangs slipped.*"

"You could try reassuring her. Maybe explain about what we are."

"I think she's realized what we are," Thomas pointed out dryly. "And judging by the fact that she's locked in the bathroom, she isn't happy with the realization."

"Give her the phone, maybe I can explain."

"What part of *locked in the bathroom* aren't you

getting?" Thomas asked with exasperation. "I *can't* give her the phone."

"Okay . . . Just a minute," He covered the phone again and conferred with Etienne.

Thomas shook his head and paced the small space of the little hallway between rooms.

"Thomas?"

"Yeah?" he turned his attention back to the phone.

"You're going to have to try talking to her."

"What do you suggest I say, Bastien?" Thomas asked wearily.

"Ask her if she's all right."

Shaking his head, Thomas lowered the phone and moved to the door, pressing his ear to it before speaking. All he heard was breathing, a fast, shallow panting. The woman was either on the verge of having an anxiety attack or she was jogging on the spot in there.

"Inez?" he called through the door, trying for a soothing tone. Judging by the scurrying sound of her shuffling away from the door, it didn't have the desired effect. Grimacing, he asked, "Are you all right?"

A spate of Portuguese sounded through the door.

Frowning, Thomas lifted the phone to his ear. "Did you get that? What the hell did she just say?"

"I don't know, I couldn't hear," Bastien admitted unhappily. "Put the phone to the door and ask her to repeat it."

Muttering under his breath, Thomas moved the phone to the door, cleared his throat, and said, "Er . . . Inez, do you think you could repeat that? I don't speak Portuguese and Bastien couldn't hear you."

"You bit me!!"

Thomas waited to see if there was more, but when silence followed, he lifted the phone back to his ear. "Hello?"

"That wasn't Portuguese," Bastien said at once.

"Well, hell, Bastien, I know that. It was Portuguese the first time."

An exasperated sound came down the line and then Thomas heard Etienne say something in the background.

"What did he say?" Thomas asked with a frown.

"He said apologize and just keep apologizing. It's the only way to handle a woman," Bastien told him, and then added, "It works with Terri."

"Apologize," Thomas muttered, taking the phone away and moving it back to the door in case Inez responded in Portuguese again.

"Inez? I'm sorry I bit you," he said with sincere regret, and then inspiration made him add, "Bastien made me do it."

"What?" Inez screeched, and the word was echoed by Bastien on the phone.

"Well, you did," Thomas pointed out, placing the phone back to his ear. "You told me to bite her. I didn't want to do it but you were going on and on about flying while hungry. I never would have bit her otherwise. You *made* me."

Thomas heard Bastien curse on the phone, but he was already moving the phone back to the door. Inez had started ranting again in Portuguese. It ended with English again, this time it was, "I work for the devil!"

"Yes, well, you should try being his cousin," Thomas muttered. Inez must have heard him. She was suddenly terribly quiet. Bastien wasn't, however, Thomas could hear him squawking away over the phone, his voice not dissimilar to the squeaky voice of a mouse in a cartoon at that distance. Sighing, he placed the phone back to his ear.

"What did she say in Portuguese?" he asked, cutting off Bastien.

"She said you're a soulless vampire, a blood-sucking fiend, and she has a cross and knows how to use it," Bastien translated dryly. "Look, I'm going to hand you over to Etienne and use my cell to call the office there in London and have someone sent over to wipe her memory."

"No! Don't do that!" Thomas said sharply. He didn't know why, but the idea of another immortal messing with Inez's brain made him cringe. Taking a breath, he said, "Look, just give me a minute. I can fix this. There's no need to wipe her memory."

He didn't give Bastien the chance to argue the point, but lowered the phone and stepped closer to the door. "Look, Inez, I'm sorry I bit you. I really am, and I really didn't want to. Like I said, Bastien insisted on it. I shouldn't have given in, but . . . It didn't hurt, did it?"

Inez scowled, her suspicious gaze fixed on the bathroom door. In truth, the bite hadn't hurt. It had even been pleasurable . . . at least until she'd seen his fangs and realized what he'd done. That thought made her frown. He'd had a reflection. Vampires weren't supposed to have one. Maybe he was just a freak and the fangs were glued on. That made more sense than that he might be a vampire. A freak was better than a vampire, wasn't it? She pondered the matter, but really wasn't sure which would be worse.

"What are you?" she asked suddenly. "Some sort of gothfreak vampire wannabe?"

"No, I—" His voice died briefly and then she heard him muttering, "No, Bastien. I don't want you to have her memory wiped. Just give me a minute here."

Inez frowned in the silence that followed, wondering what he meant by having her memory wiped. While she wasn't sure what it was, it didn't sound like something she wanted either.

"No," Thomas repeated on the other side of the door. "She's *my* damned lifemate, Bastien, and *you* aren't having her wiped."

Inez's eyebrows rose. She was his damned lifemate? What did that mean? Was she literally damned now that he'd bit her? Frowning, she turned to peer in the mirror at the marks on her neck. Was she a vampire now too? She didn't feel soulless and dead. And she did still have a reflection. What—

"Another five minutes isn't going to make much difference," Thomas snapped on the other side of the door. "You're the one who said she was the best damned employee you've ever had. She's smart and sensible. I can make her see sense. Instead of calling Wyatt and ordering him to come here and wipe her, call the damned airport and book a seat for her on the plane to Amsterdam."

Inez frowned at the mention of Wyatt. He was the president of UK development for Argent, the British division of Argeneau Enterprises. He was her boss.

She had always liked the man, but now recalled that he too had an allergy to sunlight. In fact, most of the upper echelon of executives did, she realized.

Dear God, she worked in a nest of vampires! How could she have worked with them all so long and not realized?

She was realizing now, of course, and noticing other oddities; like the fact that few of the upper echelon of the company ate food or drank alcohol or even tea or coffee. They were all friendly, and nice, intelligent people, but didn't do the usual social things like going out for drinks together after landing a big contract, or attending the Christmas parties and other celebrations the underlings at the company held. In fact, only the day workers attended such functions, she realized with dismay.

"Yes, we *can* still make the flight to Amsterdam," Thomas insisted on the other side of the door. "Just let me talk to the woman without you interrupting me."

Inez couldn't hear Bastien's response, but supposed he must have agreed when Thomas cleared his throat and said close to the door, "Look, Inez, I got a hold of someone who was able to track Aunt Marguerite's cell phone. It turns out she isn't here at all. She's in Amsterdam, so I have to fly over there. In fact, I'm booked on a flight for six-fifty and I have to leave soon to catch it."

"Okay. You go ahead," she suggested and heard him sigh on the other side of the door.

"I can't until we fix this."

"There's nothing to fix. I'm fine," Inez lied glibly. "You go on and fly to Amsterdam."

"I can't. I want to explain everything to you so that you won't be afraid or freaked out anymore," he said quietly.

"I'm not freaked out," she lied again.

"Right," he said dryly.

"Okay, maybe I'm a little freaked out, but I'll be fine," Inez assured him and then held her breath, praying he'd just go away and leave her alone. She'd slip out and call the police . . . No, she couldn't do that, they'd think she was mad. Maybe she should go to her church. Surely the church knew about the evil living in the bosom of London?

"Inez, I can't just go away."

She closed her eyes at his unhappy words, and then opened them again and suggested, "Okay, so explain."

"I can't do that either. Not right this minute anyway, it would take too long and we have to catch that flight to Amsterdam."

"We?" she echoed with alarm.

"Yes. Won't you please come out of there and fly to Amsterdam with me so that I can explain matters to you? I promise not to bite you again."

Inez didn't say anything, but she was shaking her head with certainty. There was no way she was going anywhere with the man. He'd bit her, for cripes sake. Asking her to accompany him was like asking her to get in the back of a van with a rabid dog. How stupid did he think she was?

"Inez? You were here all day and were perfectly safe. If I'd wanted to harm you, I could have done so first thing this morning when we were alone in the suite, but I didn't, did I? Instead I drew you a bath and ordered you a breakfast, and—"

"And then you bit me," Inez snapped, interrupting him before his words could remind her of the kinder feelings she'd had for him earlier in the day. And she had most definitely had kinder feelings all day for the man. She had luxuriated in her bubble bath, thinking what a wonderful, thoughtful, sweet man Thomas Argeneau was. She'd eaten her breakfast, every bite giving her fonder and fonder thoughts of the man. And the tea? The first sip of the golden nectar had nearly convinced her Thomas was a God among men.

After her bath, Inez had gone out, looked down at his sleeping face and noticed just how handsome and sweet he looked in sleep. She'd wanted to touch his soft, dark hair and brush it away from his chiseled features softened in sleep. She hadn't, but she also hadn't had the heart to wake him, and had set up shop in the suite's bedroom to avoid disturbing him as she made the calls, first arranging for the car to be brought into the city from the warehouse, then calling hotel after hotel, and then car rental agency after car rental agency, stopping only to walk out and moon over the pretty man asleep on the sofa and ponder how wonderful it would be to have a handsome, thoughtful man such as he in her life.

Every time she'd been placed on hold as she made her calls, Inez had found herself sitting there, fantasizing about what it would be like to have a man like him to come home to at the end of a long hard workday. She'd imagined him greeting her at the door with a kiss, the smells of scrumptious cooking drifting to her as he kissed her hello, his hands moving over her body, stripping away her clothes and then caressing every inch of skin revealed . . .

Oh, yes, Inez had woven a lovely little fantasy in her mind and had been happy when he'd woken up and come to join her . . . right up until he bit her.

"I won't hurt you," Thomas said solemnly through the door. "I could have broken down this door if I wanted, but I haven't, have I? I don't want to hurt or frighten you, Inez. Once we leave this suite, you'll be surrounded by people in the hotel, the taxi driver in the car, the people at the airport and on the plane, and you'll have your own room at the hotel. You only have to see me in public where you feel safe so I can explain everything. Surely you're curious to know about us?"

Inez scowled at the door, cursing herself for being tempted by the promise of an explanation.

"Please," he said quietly, and then added, "You've worked for Bastien for . . . how long now?"

"Eight years," she admitted reluctantly.

"Right. Eight years. And he says you're one of the best employees he's ever had. He wouldn't let anyone hurt you."

"You just told me not five minutes ago that he told you to bite me," she pointed out dryly.

"Yes, but he didn't think it would hurt you, or that you'd even remember it. I was supposed to wipe it from your memory."

She snorted at that.

"Look, Inez. If you don't come with me and let me explain things, he's going to send over someone to clean up this mess."

Inez frowned at the door. "Clean up this mess?"

"Yes. He'll send an immortal to come here and remove this incident from your memory."

"Like you were supposed to do?" she asked dryly.

"Yes."

She ignored the fear that quivered through her at the thought and said, "You couldn't do it. What makes you think anyone else could?"

"I'll explain that too, but we really don't have time right this minute. I have to head to the airport. So make up your mind. Do we wait here for someone to come remove this whole incident from your memory, or do you come with me, memory intact and perfectly safe?"

Inez hesitated, considering her alternatives, and then Thomas added, "If they remove your memory, they'll probably remove the memory of everything from the day you were promoted on. You'll go back to being whatever you were before being promoted to vice president."

"What?" she squawked with dismay. While Inez wasn't completely sure she wanted the job anymore, she wasn't sure she wanted to give it up either. This whole working for and with a nest of vampires rather sullied things. But Inez had worked for Argeneau Enterprises for eight years and enjoyed her greatest triumphs there. She'd also worked long and hard for that promotion. She'd neglected her own social life, forsaking dates for work and pouring all her energy and time into it, building a career and climbing the corporate ladder to her vice presidency. She'd worked too damned hard and given up too much to let anyone take it away.

"That's the only alternative," Thomas explained. "Either you come with me to Amsterdam and allow me to explain things, or we wait here for Wyatt to come wipe everything from your memory."

"But just the memory of the bite," she protested. "He wouldn't—"

"He'll wipe everything from the last few months," Thomas responded firmly. "Bastien was supposed to explain about our people to you when you were promoted. In fact, you shouldn't have been promoted without it. You were sent to New York to be told about us. If you'd been able to accept it and agreed to keep the secret, you would have been promoted. If you hadn't, what he'd told you would have been wiped from your memory and you wouldn't ever have been promoted.

"Unfortunately," he added dryly, "Bastien was a bit distracted at the time. He'd just met his lifemate and there was a lot going on. He promoted you, but sent you back to England without doing the rest of it. Wyatt was supposed to keep you from any jobs or information that might give us away until Bastien could fly to England and take care of you. If you can't accept us and our explanations, Wyatt will wipe everything from your memory, including your promotion."

Thomas let that sink in and then said, "So what is it going to be? Are you going to fly to Amsterdam with me and allow me to explain? Or do we wait for Wyatt, let him wipe your memory and return you to whatever job you had before the promotion?" He waited a beat, and then added, "At least until they find another job for you and remove you from the company altogether."

Inez didn't have to think long. Her career had become her life. She wouldn't give it up easily. In fact, they'd have to take the key to the vice president's office from her dead, clutching fingers before she'd give it up. Still, she hesitated, her eyes on the doorknob, but her fingers refusing to reach for it.

Finally, she raised her hand to her throat. A golden cross hung from a fine gold chain around her neck. It had been blessed by the pope during a trip to Italy. It should have double power, but had been tucked inside her blouse when Thomas had bit her. Now, she pulled it out and held it up before her like a shield with her left hand as she unlocked the door and tugged it open with her right.

"Back up, Nosferatu!" Inez snapped, covering her fear with anger as she glared at Thomas. Much to her relief, he backed up at once.

His hands were raised—the cell phone in one—in a gesture that might be used to soothe a wild horse, but a smile tugged at his lips.

"I knew you'd come out," Thomas said, and much to her amazement he sounded proud, as if she'd done something praiseworthy instead of incredibly stupid.

"Tell Bastien not to send Wyatt. We're on our way to the airport," she ordered, holding the cross higher.

Nodding, he raised the phone to his ear. "We're on our way. Make sure there are tickets waiting for both of us."

Thomas didn't wait for Bastien to respond, but then snapped the phone closed and turned away to head through the dining room.

Inez hesitated, and then moved quickly back into the bedroom to snatch up her purse before moving more slowly—and cautiously—back through the hall and into the dining room, holding the cross out in front of her as she walked into the living room. Spotting him by the love seat, she positioned herself by the door of the suite and silently watched as he gathered his knapsack and shoved his binder and pen into a side pocket, then moved to join her. The moment he headed in her direction, she skittered backward, reaching behind her with her free hand to open the door. She then preceded him out into the hall, never turning her back to him.

"You can stop flashing that at me," Thomas said calmly. "You're kind of drawing attention holding it up like that."

Inez quickly glanced in both directions to see that there was a maid and two couples in the hall, all staring at them curiously, and did lower the cross closer to her chest. She didn't release it, however, but held it tightly in her sweaty hand in case he suddenly pounced.

Heaving out a sigh, Thomas gestured for her to precede him down the hall. "After you."

"No," Inez said, and then cleared her throat and said more firmly, "After *you*."

Thomas shrugged and led the way to the elevator. She followed at a safe distance, watching narrow-eyed as he nodded at the first couple they passed in the hall. Inez hardly even glanced toward them herself, her attention wholly focused on Thomas as he led her to join the older couple waiting by the elevator.

"That's a lovely cross, dear."

Inez glanced nervously to the older woman who had spoken. She managed a weak smile and then glanced sharply back to Thomas as she said, "It was blessed by the pope."

Thomas raised an eyebrow at the claim and asked

with interest, "Which one? The new one or the one before him?"

Inez hesitated, wondering if one had been holier than the other, and then lied and covered her basis by saying, "Both."

Thomas gave a little laugh and shook his head, murmuring, "It's going to be a long trip," as the doors opened and he followed the older couple on board the elevator.

Inez followed, thinking that he was right. She felt like she'd aged ten years in the last few minutes. It was going to be a long flight indeed.

They rode down to the main floor and crossed the lobby in silence. It wasn't until Inez had followed Thomas into the back of a taxi that he spoke again, and then it was to mutter, "We'll have to buy you some perfume when we get to the airport."

Inez's eyes sharpened on him suspiciously. "Why?"

"Because I can smell your fear, Inez, and it's making me want to kiss and comfort you," he admitted easily.

Inez's eyes widened, her mind dragging up memories of his arms around her, his mouth on hers, the passion coursing through her as he'd kissed and caressed her and then the overwhelming pleasure and excitement as he'd bit her. She was hard-pressed not to slide across the seat and plaster herself to him as the memories assaulted her. She'd enjoyed his touch and even his bite until she'd realized he *was* biting her.

Shaking away the memories, Inez focused on him again, suspecting he was somehow putting those thoughts and sensations in her mind, somehow *mak-*

ing her want him. This was a much more dangerous trip than she'd first realized.

"London Gatwick Airport," Thomas instructed the driver and Inez watched him silently as she sank back in her seat. When she saw him inhale, his nose quivering slightly, she frowned and wondered if he still smelled fear, or if he could differentiate that from the desire that had shot through her as she recalled their earlier embrace. When she saw the small smile that tugged at his lips and noted that his eyes—normally a beautiful silver blue—now flared more silver, as if filled with fire, she felt herself blush, sure he had picked up on her desire.

Her eyes widened with alarm when Thomas eased a little closer on the seat until his hand brushed lightly against the side of her upper thigh. The light touch immediately sent up a clamoring in her body that was alarming in its strength.

"Get your soulless butt back on the other side of the seat," she hissed, glancing nervously at the back of the driver's head. Surely he wouldn't try to bite her right here with the driver in front of them?

"Sorry," he murmured. "I thought . . ."

Thomas didn't finish the sentence, but moved away and turned his head to peer out the window, as if he was trying to ignore her presence in the car. She decided to wait until they reached the airport to ask for the explanations he'd promised her. For now she was content to let him ignore her. It was incredibly disturbing to realize she was lusting after a dead, soulless thing.

Frowning, Inez peered over him, taking in his strong, pale features. He wasn't pale like the dead, but pale like a man who spent little time out in the sun. There was a healthy pink glow to his cheeks and she wondered grimly if it was her blood that had given it to him.

She stiffened as his nose quivered again and he glanced her way so that she caught a glimpse of the silver fire in his eyes. Inez shrank back into the cushioned seat, feeling like a cornered cat. Fortunately, he immediately turned his gaze away again and she was able to relax a little.

Watching him warily, she decided his idea hadn't been a bad one. The first thing she was going to do when they reached the airport, was visit duty free and buy a bottle of perfume. Inez didn't want him being able to tell what she was feeling. Especially when she was beginning to experience more desire than fear now that they were out in the relative safety of the public. Yes, she was definitely buying perfume. It would be easier to ignore her desire if he wasn't so obviously aware of it.

Four

Thomas was twisted around in his seat, watching a group of rowdy Brits at the back of the plane with fascination. They were all men, but one of them was in a short nurse's costume with pink fishnet nylons covering his hairy legs, a blond wig, high heels, and a very bad makeup job on his bearded face. He also wore a piece of paper taped to his back that read *I'm getting married. Kick me.*

The rest of the men in the group were all laughing and taunting the groom-to-be, and every one of them seemed to be three sheets to the wind. It was obviously a stag party on the way to Amsterdam to kick it up for the weekend, and Thomas shook his head, wondering why they didn't do things like that in Canada. He'd have taken great enjoyment in seeing Lucern dressed like that. Not that he'd probably agree to do it.

Thomas was smiling faintly at the idea, when Inez suddenly said, "Explain now."

Sighing, he gave up watching the group milling about the back of the plane. The stewardess was having trouble keeping the half a dozen or so men in their seats. They kept stumbling into the aisles to talk to the others in their group. The men weren't being rude or annoying, and most of the passengers were watching their performance with amusement, but they were keeping the stewardesses busy.

Turning back in his seat, he glanced at Inez, noting that she wasn't wearing the indulgent amusement of most of the rest of the plane. Instead she was watching him with narrow-eyed displeasure.

Sighing, he glanced around at the people seated around them, and then shook his head. "I can't. There are too many people here."

That just made her sweet little mouth compress a bit tighter and her eyes go cold. The woman was a bundle of passions—one moment angry, the next flaming with desire. His senses were alert to every change, reading the scents rolling off of her in waves and fluctuating between desire and guilt as her mood changed.

Inez had headed straight for the duty-free shop once they'd checked in at the airport and purchased a bottle of Paris. Unfortunately, they hadn't given her the perfume then, but told her she could collect it when she boarded the plane.

Inez hadn't been pleased. Trying to distract her, Thomas had steered her to a small pub-and-grill in the airport waiting area and they'd both ordered and eaten a meal.

Inez had been openly surprised that he ate food. Thomas had been a little surprised himself. Not so much because he was eating, but because of how enjoyable it was for a change. He'd grown tired of food the last decade or so, finding it all tasted the same and was something of a bother, but that meal in the restaurant had been bursting with flavor and texture and he'd gobbled it up with relish. Thomas knew he shouldn't be surprised. Eating and enjoying food was one of the signs of finding a lifemate, as was not being able to read the individual. It seemed there was little question that Inez was his lifemate.

While her curiosity had been obvious, the loud talking and music in the establishment had prevented her questioning him. Not eager to start into explanations, Thomas had insisted on remaining there until they were called to board. Inez had been given the bag with her purchase of Paris when they boarded, but had merely tucked it away in her purse rather than use it in such an enclosed space.

Thomas was kind of glad about that. While the roller coaster her emotions were taking was forcing him to roller coaster with her, he was enjoying the ride. After decades of experiencing little in the way of emotional stimulation, he was eating up the highs and even the lows, enjoying each nuance. Although, the truth was, he was enjoying her passion more. Thomas's interest in women had started to wane of late as he grew bored with even sex. It was the thing that had bothered him most over the last few decades.

"Thomas?"

Hearing the annoyance in her voice, he realized he was just staring at her, unspeaking as his thoughts crowded in his mind. Now, he cleared his throat and said, "Not here. We'll be overheard."

"You said we would be in public all the time so I would feel safe while you explained," she pointed out grimly. "If you can't explain in public, how—"

"All right," Thomas said at once, ending her irritation. He glanced around again, relieved to see that everyone seemed to be paying attention to the men at the back of the plane, and then turned back to her. Thomas hesitated and then reached out and caught her cross in his hand. As she watched wide-eyed, he closed his fingers around it, holding it for a moment, and then opened his hand to reveal the golden pendant lying in his unharmed hand.

"The cross didn't keep me from harming you, Inez. I did. You are safe with me," he said quietly, then smiled wryly and added, "And the Caeser's salad with extra garlic that you ordered at the airport restaurant was completely unnecessary. Garlic does not harm us either."

She flushed at his words, but didn't say anything.

Releasing the cross, Thomas continued, "We aren't dead. We aren't soulless. We aren't cursed."

Her eyes widened with each claim. "Well then, how—"

Thomas held up a hand and she immediately fell silent. Nodding approval, he said, "I'm going to tell you a story."

Inez tsked with irritation. "I don't want to hear a story. I want—"

"Work with me here, Inez," he said with exasperation and gestured to the people around them.

She glanced around, noting that while no one appeared to be glancing their way, they were certainly close enough to hear. Biting her lip, she nodded in understanding. "Tell me the story."

"I was reading this book about Atlantis," he began, peering at her meaningfully.

Her eyes widened, but she remained silent.

"In this book, Atlantis was an isolated civilization that held a much more advanced society than the rest of the world at that time. More advanced than even we are now."

Her eyebrows rose slightly.

"And in Atlantis, scientists discovered a way to combine bioengineering and nano technology to create little nanos that could be shot into a mortal's blood stream and carried through the body where they repaired damage and killed off illness in the individual as well as regenerated new cells where necessary. These nanos were programmed to shut down and disintegrate once the repairs were made."

Inez nodded her understanding, her expression fascinated.

"But what the scientists hadn't taken into account was that the mortal body suffers constant damage from sunlight, the environment and even aging, so the nanos never shut down, but continue to repair and regenerate, even replicating themselves to continue the work they had been programmed to do."

"So you—"

Thomas caught her hand, bringing her to silence so he could continue. "These nanos, however, use more blood than a mortal can produce. In Atlantis, this wasn't a problem. They had blood banks and those mortals in Atlantis who were now immortals, because the nanos kept their bodies at the peak stage between about twenty-five and thirty-two years old, were simply given transfusions every morning."

"Where did they get the blood?" Inez asked.

"From mortals," Thomas answered, and then explained, "Not everyone in Atlantis had these nanos in them. I don't know the exact sequence of events or how many it was tested on before they realized the nanos weren't dying off as expected. All I know is that my father's parents were among those who had the experimental treatment before it was stopped. It's how they met. And then, of course, all their children were infected, the nanos passed into them through their mother."

"I see," Inez murmured. "And these nanos gave them fangs and—"

"No. They had no fangs in Atlantis. As I said, they had blood banks and got transfusions. The fangs weren't necessary . . . but then the day came when Atlantis fell."

"Fell?" she asked curiously.

Thomas nodded. "It was a combination of earthquake and a volcanic eruption or something. Atlantis fell into the sea, I think. Anyway, most if not all of the mortals were killed in the fall, and even some immortals, but some managed to escape and survive. They spread out over the face of the earth, but what they found was that while their society had been sheltered by the mountains surrounding it and their people had advanced, the rest of the world was way behind them technologically. Primitive even." He cleared his throat, and added, "This was around 1500 . . . BC."

Her eyes widened incredulously. "What?"

When he simply nodded solemnly, Inez frowned in response. "But that means they were *worlds* ahead of the rest of the world. Why? How?"

Thomas shrugged. "They stuck to their own and didn't share their technology."

"But why?" she repeated. "Why stay so isolated? Why did they never travel beyond the mountains surrounding them? If they were as advanced as that, surely they had the ability."

"I'm sure they did," Thomas agreed and then shrugged. "But I don't know why they remained so isolated. My cousin once said something about an age-old feud with a neighboring clan and a peace treaty guaranteeing that neither people would cross the border of the mountains separating them."

"But they did when Atlantis fell?" she murmured and he nodded.

Inez considered that and then asked, "How did they survive when they suddenly found themselves without the blood banks and so on?"

Thomas saw the realization on her face even as she asked the question, but answered anyway, "At first it was bad. They needed blood, but had no way to get it. There were no blood banks outside Atlantis. But the nano's job was to do what was necessary to repair and regenerate the body and they needed blood to do it." He shrugged. "Their response was to make the teeth come on, I guess. Plus, the survivors also became faster, and stronger, and able to see better in the dark."

"Why the dark?" Inez asked at once. "If you aren't cursed and soulless, why can you not walk in sunlight?"

"*They* can," Thomas said, as he glanced nervously

around to be sure none of their flight mates were paying attention. "They can walk in sunlight, but sunlight does the worst damage to the body, which means they have to consume more blood. They avoid sunlight to avoid the necessity of feeding more often."

When she frowned, he added, "Mortals weren't too happy to be considered cattle by immortals. Many Atlanteans were killed or at least injured horribly when they were discovered feeding on mortals. It was better for them to avoid sunlight as much as possible and live, sleep, and hunt under cover of night. Of course, the other abilities help with that."

"Being faster, stronger, and having night vision?"

"That and the ability to read and control the minds of mortals, as well as erase their memories so that they don't feel the pain of the feeding or recall it afterward. If not for that, it would be impossible to hide their existence. They would be hunted and eventually eradicated," he said quietly and then pointed out, "Mortals could defeat us—I mean, them, by sheer numbers alone."

She frowned, opened her mouth, then closed it and leaned forward to whisper, "But you didn't erase my memory."

"No," Thomas agreed quietly. He could see the question in her eyes, but shook his head. He wasn't explaining that to her here. He wasn't at all sure how she'd take the news that she was his lifemate and he didn't want her freaking out on the plane. Trying to steer her away from that subject, he said, "The older ones prefer being called *immortals* to vampire, though they aren't completely immortal. They can die, but not from illness, and not even by most injuries."

"How?" she asked.

Thomas hesitated. What she was asking was a dangerous question to answer. If she decided she didn't think mortals should have to suffer immortals living amongst them, she could use this information to hurt them. Unfortunately, he couldn't read her mind, so couldn't gauge how she was accepting this information. She didn't look as afraid as she had. In fact, if anything, Inez appeared more fascinated than anything else. . . . Still . . .

"Is it the stake in the heart like the mythological vampire?" she asked abruptly.

"That can stop the heart," he admitted carefully.

Her eyebrows drew together. "But it won't kill them."

"Not if it is removed quickly enough," he admitted.

"Then, how—"

"The only thing you need to know is that now that there are blood banks again, they do not need to hunt to feed," he said quietly.

"But you bit me."

Thomas glanced around again. No one seemed to be paying attention, but as he turned back toward Inez he glimpsed the woman in the seat in front of Inez through the slight gap between the two seats before them. The woman's head was turned sideways, her ear close to the gap. Narrowing his eyes, he focused on her thoughts, relieved to be able to read them until he realized she had indeed been listening avidly. And she suspected it wasn't just a story he was telling Inez. Thomas immediately began erasing her memories, replacing them with the thought that she'd slept through the whole flight. He then took a moment to put her to sleep for the rest of the flight before turning back to Inez.

She was glancing between him and the seats before them with suspicion. "What did you just do?"

"I bit you because the cooler of blood Bastien was having sent to me at the Dorchester hadn't yet arrived," he said in a near whisper, ignoring her question. "I was distracted by my worry for Aunt Marguerite on the flight to England yesterday and only had one bag of blood. Bastien was concerned about my getting on the flight hungry and possibly being tempted to feed from someone at the airport or on the plane and being discovered."

"How much blood do you normally have to have a day?" Inez asked in a whisper, a frown on her face.

"Three or four bags as a rule," he admitted reluctantly.

"Three or four bags?" she asked with amazement. "That's like what? Three or four pints?"

"Something like that," he muttered with a shrug.

"You had one bag yesterday and none today, so you were about seven pints low when you bit me?" she asked.

"Something like that," Thomas repeated uncomfortably.

Inez stared at him for a minute and then said with certainty, "You didn't take that much from me. The human body only holds something like eight pints of blood, doesn't it?"

"No, I didn't take that much from you," he agreed. He had no idea how much blood the average person had in them. It wasn't something he normally considered.

"What happens when you don't get enough blood?"

Thomas hesitated and then admitted, "The nanos will leave the blood stream and go into the organs and skin in search of more blood to fuel them."

"Is it painful?" she asked, her expression solemn.

"Like acid traveling through your body," he muttered, shifting uncomfortably in his seat. Afraid of misjudging and taking too much blood after so long without feeding off the hoof, Thomas hadn't taken much blood from Inez at all . . . just enough to soothe the worst of the cramps at the time. It hadn't taken long for his body to run through the small amount he'd consumed and the pain and cramps of hunger had quickly returned. They'd grown more unbearable with the passing time, but he'd mostly managed to ignore it by distracting himself with the sights and sounds around them. However, now that they were discussing the subject, he was having trouble ignoring the pain. It would be a great relief when they reached the hotel in Amsterdam and he could raid the cooler of blood Bastien had promised to have waiting there.

Inez worried her lip as she peered at Thomas, her feelings pitched somewhere between relief and worry. She was very relieved to know that he wasn't some soulless, dead, bloodsucker like the fictional Dracula and his cohorts. That would have been a nightmare. She couldn't have accepted that even to keep her job. But the rosy cheeks she'd noted after he'd bitten her had been a temporary state. Staring at him as she had in the taxi, Inez had actually been able to see the pink glow fade from his cheeks during the hour-long ride to Gatwick Airport. By the time they'd arrived and checked in at the terminal, there was no glow left and he'd been terribly pale . . . unhealthily so.

Inez hadn't been too concerned at the time, but now that she understood just what he was she was beginning to be concerned. From what he'd explained, it seemed obvious that Thomas was really not much different than herself and other mortals . . . except that he had a certain longevity. He did have some special abilities that most humans didn't have; the added strength and speed he'd spoken of, the ability to see better in the dark, and the fangs of course. But he also had some rather terrible weaknesses, even afflictions. The man couldn't survive long without blood without suffering terrible pain. She could see the lines of pain gathering around his mouth and eyes. The first of those lines had begun to appear shortly after they'd arrived at the airport and had become more obvious by the time they'd boarded the plane.

Much to her shame, they hadn't concerned her overly much at the time. She'd rather thought it served him right since her neck was still a bit tender to the touch, but now that he'd explained how he was the way he was . . .

Inez stared at him silently, fighting the urge to offer to let him bite her again. Had it been a wholly altruistic urge, she might not have fought it so hard. She did hate to see others in pain, and really now that he'd explained, she wasn't so angry about his biting her. She didn't care for the idea of being "cattle" for an immortal as he'd put it, but it was really no different than donating blood to the blood bank, or for a friend. Except for the delivery of it . . . and therein lay the problem and the reason she was struggling with the offer. It wasn't wholly altruistic. Inez had enjoyed the experience; his kisses, his touch, his scent, the passion that had flooded her, and part of her was eager to experience it all again.

If this was how she was going to react to the man biting her, she really needed to work on getting herself a social life, Inez thought with self-disgust. Obviously her lack of one had made her desperate if she was willing to be bitten just to enjoy the passion that went along with it.

She heard Thomas take in a deep breath and glanced his way to see that he was letting it out slowly through his nose. Inez recognized at once that it was an effort to ease the pain he was suffering and opened her mouth, the offer to let him bite her again trembling on her tongue when the seat belt sign suddenly came back on.

"We're losing altitude," Thomas said as he did up his seat belt. "We'll be landing soon."

Inez closed her mouth on the offer she'd been about to make and quickly ducked her head to peer around for her seat belt. There was no need to make the offer if they were nearly there. Part of her was relieved. Another part was disappointed indeed.

Schiphol Airport in Amsterdam was just as busy as Gatwick had been, but Thomas had less patience for it. The crowds shifting around him ramped up the cramps he was suffering. Eager to escape the press of bodies, he rushed Inez through the airport to platform one, relieved when he saw that a train was pulling in. Pausing at a ticket machine, he waited impatiently for the young man already there to finish his purchase, then bought their tickets and hurried Inez onto the train, boarding just before the doors closed.

The main floor was three-quarters full, crowded to Thomas in his state of mind. When Inez moved toward a pair of empty seats along one wall, he urged her past them and to a set of stairs leading to the second level. As he'd hoped, the upper compartment was much less busy. Thomas steered Inez to an empty table for two and dropped his knapsack on the floor by his feet as he sat down.

"I'm surprised Bastien didn't arrange for a car to collect us," Inez said with a breathless laugh as she dropped into her own seat.

"He offered to," Thomas admitted. "But the train is probably faster. Besides there isn't a lot of car traffic in Amsterdam. Most people walk or travel by bike. We'll take the train into the city, and then catch a tram to the hotel."

Inez nodded, her gaze sliding out the window to watch the passing scenery as they moved out of the train station. There wasn't much to see. It was night, and dark with a scattering of lights. That was all. Apparently no more enchanted by the sight than he'd expect her to be, she turned back to glance at him and asked curiously, "Have you been to Amsterdam before?"

Thomas nodded. "Many times. You?"

The way she quickly shook her head made him smile and he suggested, "Scared off by its reputation?"

Inez smiled wryly and nodded.

"It isn't what it's famous for," Thomas told her quietly.

Inez tilted her head and raised her eyebrows dubiously. "Pot isn't legal here and there is no Red Light District?"

"Well, yes, and yes," he admitted with a grin. "But that's just one aspect of the city. It's really a lovely place. There aren't a lot of cars in the city. Most people walk or bike around, and then there are the trams and buses. The lack of cars keep the pollution down and the buildings are older than you'll find in London, very picturesque. I think you'll like it."

"We'll see," she said noncommittally.

Thomas nodded and glanced out the window, then back to her to say, "Bastien was having some clothes and necessities delivered to the hotel for you."

When her eyebrows rose, he shrugged. "I reminded him that you would be flying without luggage."

"That was thoughtful," she said quietly, her expression solemn.

Thomas waved the compliment away and said lightly, "I'm a thoughtful guy."

"Yes, you are," she agreed and he was made uncomfortable by how seriously she said so. He was made even more uncomfortable when she asked, "How old are you?"

Thomas grimaced. Because of the way Bastien and Lucern always treated him, he usually felt like the baby in the family even though his sister Jeanne Louise was younger. Now, however, knowing that Inez couldn't be more than thirty, he was embarrassed by how old he was. Finally, he simply said, "I'm old."

"How old?" Inez persisted and then grinned and explained, "I only ask because they say men become more considerate as they get older and you're *very* considerate."

"No more than most men," he argued, and she snorted with derision at the words.

"Thomas, you are definitely much more considerate than every other man I've met in my life." When he opened his mouth to argue, she began counting facts off on her fingers. "First you drew me that bath and ordered me tea and breakfast when you found out I had rushed out to collect you without, and now you've seen to it that I am not without clothes while here in Amsterdam. You always take my arm to walk me about, open doors for me, and—aside from the jog through Schiphol airport—generally measure your stride to mine," she pointed out and then arched one eyebrow and said, "If consideration in men is commensurate with age, that must mean you're at least a thousand years old."

Thomas smiled at her teasing. "I was raised by my Aunt Marguerite. Her daughter, Lissianna, and I are only four years apart. They taught me consideration."

"How old?" she insisted.

He frowned, briefly searching for a way to change the subject without answering, and then realized that if she was going to be his lifemate, he'd have to fess up to his age at some point and reluctantly admitted, "I was born in 1794."

Inez blinked at this news, stared at him for a moment, and then blinked again before finally asking with disbelief, "Seventeen? *Seventeen* hundred and ninety-four? You're over two *hundred* years old?"

"Old, huh?" he asked apologetically.

Inez was silent for a moment and then sat back in her seat and tried for a nonchalant shrug and simply said, "Well, two hundred is better than six hundred."

"That would be my cousin, Lucern," Thomas said, glancing out the window again as the lights outside began to grow in number.

"Your cousin is six hundred?" Inez asked with disbelief.

Thomas smiled at her horror and nodded, then collected his bag and stood up. "Come on, we're here."

He led her off the train and to the ticket and info office to buy them both passes for Amsterdam's public transport.

Once they were on the bus headed for the Amstel Hotel, Thomas pulled out his cell phone to call Herb. He planned to check in to the hotel, down two or three bags of blood, and then head right out to try to find Aunt Marguerite. To do so, he'd need the co-ordinates for where she was. He hoped if he called Herb now, by the time they'd checked in and he'd fed, Herb would have Marguerite's present coordinates for him.

Thomas watched Inez as he waited for his call to be answered. She was busy taking in everything, her eyes flying over the older buildings and the walking people, and he wished he could read her mind to see what she was thinking. Amsterdam was one of his favorite cities in the world, and he was curious to see if she would like it.

He let his curiosity go and turned his attention to his phone as his call was answered. Inez seemed enraptured by the passing scenery, so he was taken by surprise when he finished his call and hung up and she suddenly turned back to him and asked, "Who is Herb?"

"He's a friend," he answered as he slid his phone

back into his pocket. "He's the one who tracked Aunt Marguerite's cell phone here to Amsterdam."

"And he's tracking it again now?" Inez asked.

"Yes. I want to head out and look for her as soon as we're checked in. It takes a few minutes to track the cell, so I thought if I had him start on it now, he'd have the new coordinates when I'm ready."

Inez accepted that with a nod and then asked, "Why couldn't you read my mind or erase my memory?"

Wholly unprepared for the question, Thomas found his tongue suddenly glued to the roof of his mouth.

"You said that the nanos allowed you to read the minds of others, control them, and even wipe away the memory of what had occurred, but at the hotel you said you couldn't erase my memories," she pointed out. "Why?"

Thomas let his breath out slowly. He hadn't expected this to become an issue so soon. He'd hoped to have a little time to woo her before approaching the subject of lifemates and so on. He somehow didn't think Inez was ready for that discussion.

Immortals quickly accepted that the person they couldn't read was their lifemate and acted accordingly. Mortals, on the other hand, were a bit trickier. Some accepted the idea of being a lifemate without difficulty, others didn't seem to trust the idea and needed a long courtship, while still others simply wanted nothing to do with immortals or being one of them. He couldn't just announce that they were lifemates and expect her to go along with it. Thomas wasn't yet sure the news would be well received, and would rather avoid the conversation until he had some idea how she would take it. Would she be horrified by the very thought of being his mate? He, himself, rather liked the idea that she was his mate and found himself warming to it more with every passing moment they spent together, but how would she feel about it? She was no longer staring at him as if he was the Devil's spawn, but that didn't mean she would agree to settle down and play house with him . . . for the next several centuries.

"Thomas?" she asked insistently.

He opened his mouth, but couldn't think of a thing to say to change the subject. His gaze slid desperately out the window and his breath whooshed out with relief as a bell rang. "We're here."

Standing abruptly as the bus slowed to a stop, he hurried off the vehicle, for once not taking her arm to usher her along. She was right behind him, however, and he almost laughed out loud when she muttered, "Saved by the bell," in sour tones.

Schooling his features into a suitably innocent expression, Thomas took her arm to lead her into the hotel. She walked along docilely enough until they stepped through the front doors. Then she came to an abrupt halt and simply stared around the huge lobby. Despite having been there before, Thomas paused and peered around with her.

Built in 1867, the hotel was stately and elegant. It had a large white lobby, the center stretching up two floors with a carved wooden staircase leading up to the secondfloor balcony with its arches, columns, and carved railings. It was all quite impressive, Thomas thought as he took Inez's arm to lead her to reception. He checked them in, politely refused help with his bag, and then led her to the elevator.

"So?" Inez said as soon as the doors closed on them.

"Why couldn't you read me or erase my memories?"

"Who says I couldn't?" Thomas muttered evasively, dismayed by her persistence. "Maybe I just didn't want to."

"I heard you talking to Bastien through the bathroom door. You said you couldn't erase my memories. Besides, everything would have been a lot simpler for you if you'd just made me forget everything that had happened. So, why couldn't you read me or erase my memories? Are there many you can't do that with?"

Thomas grimaced, wishing she'd forgotten her question at least until after he'd got to his room and consumed a couple bags of blood and his brain was in better working order again.

"Thomas?" she asked insistently.

"No, there aren't many mortals an immortal can't read, control, or wipe memories from," he admitted grimly.

"But you couldn't do any of those things with me?" Inez asked with a frown.

Thomas nodded, his eyes slipping to the elevator lights. They were almost to their floor.

"But you said Wyatt could and Bastien would send him over to do it for you if I didn't come with you to Amsterdam and allow you to explain," she pointed out and then asked, "Is Wyatt an older, stronger vampire? Is that why you thought he could do it when you couldn't?"

Before Thomas was forced to come up with a lie, they arrived at their floor and the elevator doors opened. Nearly gasping with relief, he hurried off the elevator, glanced at the sign pointing out the direction to take to reach their room numbers, and hurried that way.

"You really aren't comfortable with this conversation are you?" Inez asked dryly as she hurried up the hall behind him.

Thomas knew he was being rude not measuring his pace to hers, but he was almost desperate to get to their suite. He was sure if he could just slap a bag or two of blood to his teeth his mind would clear and he would know exactly what to say about lifemates and that she was his own.

He'd just stopped in front of the door to their suite when his phone began to ring. Tugging it from his pocket, he handed it to Inez.

"Say hello to Bastien," he growled, turning his attention to unlocking the door as she flipped the phone open.

"Hello, Bastien," Inez said cheerfully. "Why can't Thomas read my mind or control me and why is he so rattled by the question?"

The door clicked open, but Thomas hardly noticed, his attention had turned to Inez. The woman's eyes were sparkling with amusement. She was aware of and enjoying his discomfort over the matter. Women! He would never understand them. They were supposed to be the softer sex yet took great pleasure in tormenting a man.

Leaving her to follow as she liked, he strode into the room, relief pouring through him the moment he spotted the A.B.B. cooler on the table in the sitting room of the suite.

Thomas felt his teeth shift and slide out in his mouth as he strode quickly across the floor to the cooler. Flipping the lid open, he reached in, grabbed a bag, and promptly popped it to his teeth. The bag was nearly empty, the blood soaking into his system and easing the cramps at once when he realized Inez had gone very quiet. Suddenly anxious, he turned with the bag at his mouth and peered toward her. She had followed him into the room and now stood by the sofa, her expression grim as she listened to whatever Bastien was saying. Obviously, she wasn't pleased at his explanation of lifemates, or perhaps she wasn't pleased that she was *his* lifemate.

Shoulders slumping, Thomas turned back to the cooler and pulled out a second bag, holding it in his hand as he waited for the one in his mouth to finish draining. He was about to switch bags when Inez suddenly appeared at his side.

"He wants to talk to you," she said, holding out the phone.

Thomas pulled the now empty bag from his mouth, dropped it on to the table, and reached for the phone.

"Thank you," he murmured.

Nodding, Inez turned and moved off, heading straight for the door leading into the rest of the suite. No doubt in search of her room, he realized with worry. Her expression had been terribly solemn when she'd handed him the phone, all the amusement drained from it. In fact, she'd looked rather pale to his mind. Now he really wanted to know what Bastien had told her.

Sighing, he lifted the phone to his ear, his eyes slipping to the full bag of blood he still held. He absently read the label on the blood as he opened his mouth to say hello, and then stiffened, dropped the full bag to the floor, and reached for the empty one on the table, reading that label with growing horror.

"Thomas? Thomas are you there?" Bastien was asking over the phone.

"Oh shit!" was his answer.

Five

It was only nine o'clock at night, but Inez was exhausted by the events of the day when she entered the first bedroom of the suite and peered curiously around.

Thomas had said that Bastien was arranging to have some clothes there for her, but she didn't see any evidence of that. The room was neat and tidy and absent of anything personal that she could see. Inez was about to back out of the room, when she suddenly thought to check the closet.

Crossing the room, she opened the first door she came to and found herself peering into a huge, beautiful bathroom. She spotted the toiletries at once and moved forward, her eyes sweeping over the items lined up on the marble countertop. There were at least three lipsticks in varying shades and a mirage of other cosmetic items, half of which she didn't even recognize.

Inez had never bothered much with makeup; a bit of face powder, a little lipstick, maybe some blush, and she was good to go. She rarely bothered with eyeliner, and shadow, and all the other things she saw laying there, at least not for work. Still, they'd been provided, as had a brush, a comb, and various hair supplies. Anything she might want appeared to be there all lined up and ready for use.

Turning away, Inez moved back into the bedroom and found the closet, not terribly surprised to open it and find the hangers full of clothes, including a couple of nightgowns and a robe. A quick check reassured her that they were all in her size. Stepping back, she glanced down to see a variety of shoes; slippers, running shoes, casual shoes, and high heels. Something for every occasion.

Shaking her head, she turned away and moved to the drawer beside the bed, nodding when opening it revealed a selection of panties, bras, socks, and stockings.

Inez didn't bother to check their sizes, knowing they would all be her size too. Bastien Argeneau was a man with an attention to detail. She wouldn't be surprised to hear he had the size and color preferences of every member of his staff on file somewhere, just in case. It was either that, or the man had sent someone from the company to get her landlord to let him into her flat to check the sizes on her clothing.

Inez turned to survey the filled closet again and shook her head. There were enough clothes there for a two-week stay, but then the Argeneaus didn't do anything by halves.

Sighing, Inez sat on the side of the bed and then fell back on it and closed her eyes. She was exhausted, she was also still annoyed. The clothes and other goodies had not lifted her mood. Bastien had refused to explain why Thomas couldn't read or control her, insisting it was something Thomas would have to explain himself when he was ready. But from his reaction to her questions, she suspected Thomas wouldn't be ready to answer them for some time.

Inez grimaced. She had never been a very patient person, and hated feeling ignorant. Being left in the dark on this matter simply made her think it was important and something she really should know.

Frowning as she became aware of a pounding coming muffled from the next room, she stood and moved to the door to the sitting room, her eyes finding Thomas still standing by the table with the cooler on it. His back was to her and his shoulders hunched as he listened to whatever Bastien was saying on the phone and made notes on a notepad on the table.

Her gaze slid to the door to the hall as the pounding continued, and then back to Thomas, but if he heard, he didn't care that there was someone at the door. He was now hissing rather urgently into the phone in tones too low for her to hear. Worried that Bastien may be giving him bad news about Marguerite, she frowned with concern and moved to the door to the suite to bring an end to the pounding. At this rate, whoever was at the door was going to have the people in the neighboring hotel rooms calling hotel security.

Irritated at that possibility, Inez was scowling when she opened the door. She only opened it a little ways, an effort to keep whoever it was from seeing Thomas, the cooler and the empty bag of blood. She didn't want to upset housekeeping or whoever it was. However, the man on the other side of the door was already upset, his expression a strange mixture of worry, apology, and relief as she opened the door.

"Yes?" Inez asked, relaxing a little as her gaze slid over the black nylon jacket he wore with the A.B.B. logo on it. The same logo that was on the cooler he carried as well as the one on the table in front of Thomas. A.B.B., Argeneau Blood Bank; it was one of the companies under the Argeneau Enterprises umbrella. It was also a company she didn't know much about. Inez had always been kept away from anything having to do with A.B.B. Now she understood why, of course.

Her gaze jerked back to the man's face as a spate of Dutch was spat at her in anxious tones. Inez shook her head with a small frown. "I'm sorry, I don't——"

"Ah! English." The man nodded. "I have made a mistake. I delivered the blood here earlier."

"You didn't leave it with the front desk, did you?" Inez asked curiously, wondering how they would explain why a cooler of blood would be delivered to one of their hotel rooms.

The man blinked, obviously not expecting the question. Still, he answered, "No, of course not. I found out the room number, brought it up, and found a maid to let me in to leave it. But I made a mis——"

"Mind control?" Inez asked.

He peered at her, his expression confused.

"Did you use mind control on the maid to let you in?" she explained.

"Oh, yes," he was frowning now, and becoming a bit annoyed. "But I left the wrong cooler. The one I left was to go to the Night Club."

"The Night Club?" she asked curiously.

The man snapped his mouth closed and stared at her, and Inez blinked in surprise as she felt a slight ruffling on the edge of her mind. It was so faint that if the man weren't concentrating so hard on her and she knew nothing about immortals and what they could do, she didn't think she'd even have noticed it.

"You're reading my mind," Inez accused and then frowned. "But Thomas couldn't read my mind."

Whatever he read in her thoughts seemed to make him relax. He even smiled and said lightly, "Lucky him."

"Why lucky?" she asked warily.

The man grinned and said simply, "Who would not think him lucky? He has found his lifemate."

"Lifemate?" Inez echoed the word slowly. She'd heard the word before. Now that the man had said it, she distinctly recalled overhearing Thomas talking on the phone through the bathroom door and saying something about biting his lifemate. She tilted her head and asked the man, "Not being able to read me means I'm his lifemate?"

"Yes." Now he was frowning too. "Has he not explained things to you?"

"No," she admitted and glanced to where Thomas still stood talking into the phone before turning back and asking, "Do you think you could?"

He hesitated and then said, "It's probably something he should explain."

Inez scowled at the suggestion, knowing Thomas wouldn't explain.

"Besides, I really have to trade coolers. The Night Club is waiting on this delivery. They were very upset that I got the coolers mixed up."

Inez considered him silently as her business side-kicked in telling her that she had something he wanted and he had something she wanted.

Before she could speak, his eyes grew sharp and he threatened, "I could control you and move you out of the way to get what I want."

Her eyebrows flew up. He'd obviously read her mind again, though Inez hadn't noticed the earlier flutter again. She considered her options and then asked, "Can you control Thomas too?"

When he hesitated, she added, "I'm the vice president of the UK division of Argeneau Enterprises and we oversee all the European operations. In effect, I'm your boss."

A slow admiring smile crossed his face. "You play hardball."

"I didn't get to be vice president by pussyfooting around," she said with a shrug and then stood waiting anxiously as he decided whether he would take control of her, get what he needed, and get out—which she definitely didn't think she'd like—or if he was going to answer her question.

Much to her relief, he gave a low chuckle and said, "Okay, guarantee I won't get in trouble for this mix up and I'll play. This could be interesting."

Beaming at the man with gratitude and relief, Inez

nodded. "Agreed. I'll talk to your boss. Now, explain lifemates to me."

He shifted the cooler he held from one hand to the other, and then said, "Lifemates are exactly what they sound like, a life partner, the one who matches you, whom you can live with and love and exist with happily."

Inez frowned as she considered his words and then asked, "And not being able to read someone is how your kind recognize a lifemate?"

"We also start eating again, but not being able to read or control them is the most important attribute."

"Why?" she asked curiously.

He frowned and then said slowly, "We can control and read most mortals. Actually, all mortals except for a lifemate."

"All?" she asked with amazement.

"If you can't read them, they are a lifemate," he said simply. "For some that is a once-in-a-lifetime occurrence, others are lucky enough to find another if they lose the first, but there are often centuries between one and the other, centuries of being alone. It's not a horrible circumstance, but it isn't a happy one either. Everyone needs someone they can share the centuries with, someone with which to enjoy life's pleasures and sorrows."

"So," Inez said slowly, "while Thomas can't read or control me, every other immortal can?"

He nodded. "I could shut you down, move you out of the way, and wipe this from your memory if I liked."

Inez cringed at the very idea. She was someone who liked to be in control at all times.

"I kind of picked that up about you right off," he announced with a grin. "You have control issues."

Inez scowled as she realized that he was still reading her mind despite her not sensing it. "Please stop reading my mind."

"Sorry," he said, however, there was little sincerity behind the words. "But that's my point. If Thomas was able to do this to you . . . Well, it hardly makes for an equal relationship, does it? Even if an immortal cared for someone, it would be hard to resist the temptation to take control to get what you wanted when you wanted it. Those sorts of relationships don't work. An immortal needs someone he can't read and control and who can't read and control him or her. It allows them to relax and let down their guards."

"Guards?" Inez asked curiously.

"Immortals can often read other immortals too. It's harder if the immortal is older than you, but if they get distracted, we can even read them. To prevent that, we have to put up guards in our minds and keep them up. But at home, with a lifemate who can't read our thoughts, or control us, we can relax and not worry about such things."

"So it's better to be with someone who can't read or control you," she acknowledged, and then added, "But just because you can't read or control them, doesn't guarantee a happy relationship. What if you met someone you couldn't read or control but who was completely unsuitable to you? What if their personality doesn't suit yours?"

"That doesn't happen," he said with a shrug. "If you are lifemates, you will suit each other."

Inez frowned at his simple assurance and said with

disbelief, "Surely just because you can't read each other doesn't guarantee a happy relationship?"

"Yes, it does." When her mouth pursed with disbelief, he assured her, "I am only a hundred years old, but I have never heard of any true lifemates who didn't suit each other and have a happy union. Oh, certainly they have occasional disagreements, but that is it. They are made for each other."

"But how is that possible?" Inez asked with amazement.

"I don't know," he admitted, not sounding too concerned. "Perhaps the nanos recognize something in the individual that compliments their immortal and prevents their being able to read or control the other so they can be happy together. Or perhaps God makes a perfect mate for each individual and then puts them in their path. I have no idea, but does it matter? Why question something if it works?"

"You believe in God?" she asked with surprise.

His eyebrows rose slightly. "Don't you?"

Inez reached up unconsciously to clasp the cross around her neck and he smiled as if she'd spoken aloud and then said, "If you're done with your questions, I really need to switch coolers and get the other one to the Night Club."

Sighing, Inez nodded. "I'll get it for you."

Turning away from the door, she headed across the room. A million questions were running around inside her head, but she had some thinking to do before she would ask them, and if she asked them of anyone, she thought it should be Thomas. She understood enough now to be going on. Thomas couldn't read her. That made them lifemates. Simple. No muss, no fuss.

Actually, it was the perfect arrangement for a woman who didn't have time for a social life, Inez thought as she reached the table and the cooler sitting on it. She glanced to Thomas, opening her mouth to explain about the cooler and mix-up as she saw that he had apparently finished his conversation and was closing the phone, but before the first word was more than formed on her tongue, his phone was ringing again and he was returning it to his ear.

Shrugging, she picked up the bag that lay on the floor and replaced it in the cooler. She spotted the empty bag on the table and hoped the delivery guy wouldn't be in trouble for being a bag short. She'd definitely have to call and talk to his boss now, Inez supposed. She'd promised.

Closing the cooler lid, she carried it back to the door.

"I'm afraid he had one," she announced, handing over the cooler and taking the one he held out. "I hope that's not a problem."

His eyebrows flew up, and a perfectly filthy grin lifted his lips. "Not for me, but you're in for one hell of a night."

Thomas moved quickly back to the table to write down the latest coordinates Herb was giving him, said thanks, snapped his phone closed, and straightened to glance around just as Inez closed the suite door. He'd heard her speaking to someone, and been half aware of her moving to the table and back to the door, but hadn't paid her much attention as he talked to first Bastien and then Herb. He'd actually been too stressed out to speak much to Bastien. With everything that was going on, the man's constant calls were becoming something of a nuisance. Knowing the calls were due to his worry about Marguerite, Thomas hadn't snapped at him like he would have liked to do, but merely told him he'd called Herb for new coordinates, would head out as soon as the man called back with them, and would let Bastien know the moment he'd found Marguerite. He'd then hung up on him only to have the phone ring again as Herb called to give him the updated coordinates. It was yet another locale. She, or at least the phone, was obviously on the move. The location was supposed to be accurate to within fifty feet since it was in the city. Hopefully that was close enough that he could spot Marguerite if she hadn't already left the area by the time he got there. The quicker he got there, the better the chances he'd arrive before she moved on . . . which meant Thomas had to move.

"Oh, you're off the phone."

Thomas focused on Inez, noting the feline grace to her walk as she crossed the room toward him. She was short, curvy, and had a seductive smile. Her lips were the kind that gave a man ideas.

Realizing he was allowing himself to be distracted, he growled, "Who was at the door?"

"The A.B.B. delivery guy," she answered. "He said he dropped off the wrong cooler here. You got what was meant for the Night Club. He came back to switch coolers."

"I hope you gave him an earful," Thomas muttered, moving to what he now realized must be the replacement cooler. It looked the same, but when he opened it he saw that it was just straight blood in this. Several bags of A positive.

"An earful?" Inez sounded surprised. "Why? Is there a great deal of difference between the other blood and this?"

"Oh yeah, there's a difference," Thomas muttered with disgust as he picked up a bag of the cold liquid. The moment he touched the bag, he felt the teeth in his mouth shift and begin to extend. Much like Pavlov's dogs, his body responded to what it knew was coming. He suspected he even salivated as the dogs did at the sight of their food arriving.

Inez was peering curiously down at the bags in the cooler, but glanced up just as he opened his mouth and popped the bag to his fangs.

"Your fangs aren't there all the time," she said with surprise. "I saw them slide out of your upper jaw."

Thomas didn't comment. He couldn't with the bag in his mouth, but he wondered that she hadn't noticed that he didn't always have fangs. It would be hard for immortals to hide what they were if they walked around flashing fang all the time.

"So you don't even have to taste the blood?" Inez asked curiously.

Thomas shook his head, his nose flaring as she moved a little closer and he caught a whiff of her scent. Damn, he'd found it enticing in the hotel in London, but right now it was positively intoxicating. Stupid delivery guy, he thought impatiently, and stupid him too for not reading the bloody bag before slapping that first one to his teeth on arriving in the suite.

"That's good," Inez announced, drawing his attention away from his thoughts. "I don't imagine blood tastes good."

Thomas stared at her silently, his nostrils flared to take in as much of her scent as he could. His skin was now tingling a little. He could actually feel the body heat coming off of her. It made him want to move closer . . . so he took a step back. This was going to be hell, he realized with dismay. He had to get away from her.

"S.E.C . . ." Inez said and he noted that she'd picked up the empty bag on the table, the one from the first batch of blood. She'd examined the label, apparently noting the initials under the blood type. Large and bright red on the white label, those initials were the only difference from the other bags. But Thomas hadn't stopped to read the label. He'd been too hungry to take the time to do so and had slapped that first bag to his teeth without hesitation. It was only Bastien's call that had prevented his slapping the second bag to his mouth, and pure luck that he'd glanced down and noticed the initials.

"What does S.E.C. stand for?" Inez asked as he tugged the empty bag from his teeth.

"Sweet Ecstasy Concentrate," Thomas muttered and promptly slapped another bag to his teeth before she could ask what that was. He knew she would the moment he finished with this bag, though, and had no intention of telling her. He felt like a complete idiot for not reading the label and getting himself into this fix. And what a fix! He had a full bag of Sweet Ecstasy swimming around in his body and—he realized as she stepped closer and he felt the sweat break out on his forehead—he was already starting to feel the effects. The first bag was making its way into his system. Soon he would be hard-pressed to keep his hands off Inez if he didn't get away from her.

His eyes slid over her body in the wrinkled slacks and blouse she'd been forced to re-don that morning in her rush. She still looked delicious to him and he found it hard not to stare when he noted the way the silk of her blouse was pulled tight at her breasts, the material pulling the slightest bit open with every indrawn breath and then relaxing closed with every exhalation. It was just the tiniest bit, hardly noticeable, but he was noticing and his body was responding as if it were a full-body peep show.

Giving his head a slight shake, Thomas decided he needed some distance and quickly. He hooked his free arm through one shoulder strap of his knapsack, then managed to snag two more bags of blood in that hand before heading out of the sitting room in search of his bedroom.

The first bedroom door was open, the lights on and Inez's purse lay on the bed. Her room. Thomas bypassed it and moved on to the next room The second bedroom was in darkness, but he didn't bother with the lights at first. Walking inside, he set the blood on the bedside table, and let the knapsack drop onto the mattress before turning back to flip on the light. Much to his relief, Inez hadn't followed, or if she had, she'd stopped when she realized he was going to his room.

Pushing the door closed with his foot, Thomas turned back to the bed and then realized the second bag of straight blood affixed to his teeth was empty.

Pulling it from his fangs, he set it on the bedside table and quickly rifled through his knapsack in search of a clean shirt and jeans. He hadn't taken a shower or changed his clothes since leaving Canada. He might as well take a quick shower while he finished off the next two bags of blood. It was the only way he could manage it. He had to get out there and find Marguerite.

Thomas took the clothes and blood into the bathroom, set them on the counter, and then stepped into the small room-sized shower and turned it on, quickly adjusting the temperature. He then began to strip, deciding that he wasn't even going to go back out to the living room and tell Inez that he was going out, but would slip out through the door in his bedroom instead. It just wasn't safe to be around her at the moment. He didn't think she'd appreciate his slavering all over her and jumping her bones this early in the relationship. He might know they were lifemates and be perfectly all right with it, but she had no idea. Coming on so strong so soon in the relationship was likely to bring it to a grinding halt.

Grimacing, Thomas ignored the erection now waving around between his legs, grabbed a bag of blood, and slapped it to his teeth as he walked to the shower. This was perfect irony, he supposed as he stepped under the spray of water. It was probably fate paying him back for giving Rachel and Etienne Sweet Ecstasies at the Night Club while they were courting. He deserved every miserable moment he was going to suffer.

Unfortunately, fate hadn't seen fit to find a way to give Inez the Sweet Ecstasy too, so he was definitely going to suffer alone . . . if he could avoid her. The warm water dropped down on his erection in a soft rainfall that was almost a caress and Thomas groaned and turned his back to the spray. Yes, the first bag of blood was definitely hitting his system now, and it would only get worse and probably very quickly. It was a swift shower for him and then a rush into his clothes and out through his own door without risking even seeing Inez again. He'd left the coordinates Herb had given him in the other room, but didn't really need them, he had perfect recall and avoiding her was the best idea until that first bag of blood had left his system.

Inez heard the shower turn on in Thomas's room and frowned. Obviously, she wasn't going to get any answers from him for now. Pacing impatiently to the window, she glanced out, surprised to find herself looking out over a stretch of water as her mind went over what she'd learned from the delivery man.

Lifemates were life partners who matched an immortal and whom they could live with, love, and exist with happily.

Inez played the words through her mind slowly and then played them again. A life partner . . . live with and love . . . happily. And she was that for Thomas . . . which she supposed meant that he was that for her too . . . A life partner . . . and a special one, chosen for her by nanos or God or by some other mysterious manner. However it came about, they had been chosen for each other. It was just the way it was. They'd met, he'd bit her, tried to read her but couldn't, and to his kind that meant they were lifemates.

She didn't know whether to jump up and down for joy, or run back home to England like a scared bunny.

On the one hand it was like a dream come true. Actually it really *was* a dream come true since she'd spent most of that day fantasizing about coming home to the man. And who wouldn't jump at the possibility? Thomas was handsome, intelligent, and so incredibly considerate . . . not to mention dangerously sexy.

But it was scary too. After all, the man was handsome, intelligent, and sexy and she was just . . . well . . . herself. A little below average height, a little heavier than was considered attractive by today's standards, and while her features were passable, her nose was just a little too sharp to be pretty, her cheeks a little too round, her hair a little too wild . . .

Of course, that was the physical aspect. Inez feared she didn't have the looks to hold a man such as him. The other side of the issue was that he seemed intelligent and considerate . . . and that was all she knew about the man. She didn't really know him at all. She had no idea what he liked or didn't like, what his interests were, or his ambitions, did he have any? And yet, according to the delivery guy, none of that mattered. They were lifemates and so would work well together, were meant to be together.

It was a tempting idea; a lifemate with whom to share life's joys and troubles, someone to come home to at the end of the day and relax with; a lover, friend, and partner. She'd never feel lonely again. Not that Inez felt that way a lot now. Usually she was too busy to feel lonely, but her family was far away and on those rare occasions where she had a little time to herself she was aware of how alone she was. As a lifemate to Thomas, she would never be alone again. And the best part was that, according to the delivery man, it couldn't be a mistake. He couldn't be the wrong man and she wouldn't later end up struggling to disentangle herself from a bad relationship. If he couldn't read her, she was his lifemate and lifemates worked out. Period.

It was almost too good to be true, like fat-free ice cream or calorie-free chocolate and yet if it was true, it was the most wonderful thing she'd encountered in her life and she wanted to believe in it. She wanted Thomas. Inez had never had such a quick attraction to a man. Usually, she had to get to know them and like them before she even started thinking of them in a romantic way, but Thomas . . . Well, after he'd presented her with the bath and breakfast and explained that he hadn't meant to snub her . . . she'd pretty much been lost.

Goodlooking and sweet too? The man was walking, talking cheesecake. Irresistible. And, apparently, hers. All those fantasies she'd had earlier about his greeting her at the door when she got home, kissing her and stripping away her clothes to make love to her, suddenly seemed possible and she shivered in anticipation at the idea.

Suddenly impatient for Thomas to come out of the shower, Inez turned away from the windows, her gaze sliding over the room and stopping on the empty blood bag.

"You're in for one hell of a night." The delivery man had said and the memory of his expression brought a frown to her face. Obviously there was something different about the blood in the first cooler and the first bag Thomas had consumed, but she had no

idea what. Thomas had said the S.E.C. on it stood for Sweet Ecstasy Concentrate, but what was that? She wished he'd told her before disappearing into his room, but he hadn't and now she was terribly curious. Impatiently so. She wished she'd asked the delivery man what it was, or that she knew someone else who could tell her—

Blinking, Inez suddenly whirled away and hurried into her room to retrieve her purse. Digging inside, she pulled out her cell phone and punched the speed-dial number to call the office. Her call was answered on the second ring and she immediately asked to speak to Wyatt.

"Ms. Urso," his secretary said with surprise, obviously recognizing her voice, "I thought you had flown to Amsterdam to help Mr. Argeneau's cousin."

"Yes, I did and I'm calling from there," she said calmly. "*Is* Wyatt in?"

"Yes, of course. Just one moment."

Inez paced the length of her room as she waited, her footsteps slowing when she heard the click of the phone being answered on the other end.

"Inez. How is Amsterdam?" Wyatt Kenric, Inez's direct supervisor, asked jovially.

"Fine, fine," Inez said and shook her head, finding it hard to believe the good-tempered man was an immortal . . . and that she'd worked with him so long without realizing it. She should have realized there was something fishy. He worked evenings, leaving her to run things during the day. How many company presidents did that? Sighing, she pushed the question aside and dove right in, saying, "Look, Wyatt, we got a delivery of blood here at the hotel, but I think there might be something wrong with it. What does S.E.C. stand for under the blood type?"

The sudden silence on the line didn't surprise her. She'd expected as much and now forced a light laugh and said, "Oh, I'm sorry. Of course, you don't know. I'm Thomas's lifemate. He's explained about Atlantis and everything."

Inez actually heard his breath *whoosh* out over the line. He sounded both relieved and startled as he said, "Really?"

"Yes. He couldn't read or control me. In fact, they almost called you in to wipe a memory from my mind, but then Thomas explained everything and . . . well . . . here we are in Amsterdam."

"Well, congratulations, Inez. I'm happy for you. Tell Thomas I'm happy for him too," Wyatt said.

"I will. He's in the shower at the moment. Actually, that's why I called you rather than bother him. I was hoping to have this all cleared up before he got out."

"Oh, yes, the blood delivery," he murmured, sounding a little less jovial. "S.E.C. you say?"

"Yes," Inez murmured. "I don't really know enough yet to know if that should be there or not. It might be perfectly all right, but the other blood he had didn't have that on it, and it's in bright red letters, so I wondered . . ."

"You did right to wonder," Wyatt said seriously. "S.E.C. stands for Sweet Ecstasy Concentrate. You don't want him drinking even one bag of Sweet Ecstasy, at least not in the concentrated form."

"Sweet Ecstasy," Inez repeated, hoping she sounded

as if she'd never heard the term before. "What is that? Would it hurt him?"

"Sweet Ecstasy is the immortal version of a Viagara/Spanish fly mix," he explained. "It's blood full of oxytocin, dopamine, norepinephrine, phenylethylamine, and various other hormones and pheromones. The donor blood has been dehydrated, removing at least half the liquid so that it's a concentrated chemical mix. It's then used to make Sweet Ecstasy drinks, where the concentrated blood is combined with a sweet soda as a mixer and served in a glass. One bag of the concentrate is used to make several drinks, at least four, sometimes six if the owner of the club is cheap. If Thomas drank a straight bag of the concentrate it would be the equivalent of four to six drinks of the cocktail."

"I see," Inez said quietly.

Wyatt gave a chuckle. "It's a good thing you noticed the S.E.C. before he had any. If he'd just slapped a bag to his mouth without checking you'd have your hands full."

"My hands full," she echoed, wondering what that euphemism meant. Was Thomas suddenly going to turn into some kind of ravening, horn-dog vampire, dry humping every piece of furniture in the suite? Or did problem mean—?

"I'll call the Amsterdam office and have someone rush over some proper blood for Thomas," Wyatt assured her. "With any luck they'll have it there before he gets out of the shower."

"No, that's all right, Wyatt," she said in a panic. "I don't want to trouble you. I'll take care of it. Just give me the number and I'll call right away."

"Don't be silly. I'll handle it. It won't take me a minute to call."

Inez bit her lip. She hadn't foreseen this possibility, but should have. She thought frantically for a minute, and then said, "Oh, hang on Wyatt, there's someone at the door."

Inez pressed the phone to her chest and paced her room once, then twice, then lifted it to her ear and gave a laugh. "It seems I called you for nothing. That was the A.B.B. guy. Apparently he realized his mistake. We got the cooler meant for some place called the Night Club?"

"Ah," Wyatt said slowly.

Perhaps it was her paranoia, but Inez was positive she heard suspicion in his voice. The funny thing was she hadn't really lied about anything. Everything she'd said had happened, just not in the time range she'd claimed. Now she felt like she had to give him some kind of verification that she was telling the truth.

"Yes," Inez continued, hoping her voice didn't sound as stilted as it seemed to her. She had always been a rotten liar and felt like she was lying now, even if she wasn't really, well sort of not really. "He's replaced the blood, but I promised him I'd call and make sure he wasn't in trouble for the mistake. He didn't say who his boss was, though. Do you know?"

"Yes, yes, I'll take care of that for you."

"Thank you Wyatt," she said, relaxing. He'd call, find out everything she'd said was true, and take care of her promise to keep the delivery guy out of trouble too.

"It's not a problem, Inez. I know you two are busy

trying to locate Marguerite. This will leave you free to do that. Good luck with that by the way. Marguerite's a fine woman and I know Thomas is very fond of her. I hope you find her safe and sound."

"So do I, Wyatt," she said solemnly.

"Right. Well, I'll get off here and take care of that other matter for you," he said, then hesitated briefly before asking tentatively, "Will you be returning to work once you've found her?"

"Of course," Inez said at once, startled that he'd even ask the question.

"Good, good," Wyatt said at once. "I just worried that . . . well, Thomas lives in Canada and . . . Never mind. Good luck on your hunt. I'll see you when you get back."

There was a click as he hung up and Inez flipped her cell phone closed, but then just stood there staring at it, Wyatt's words ringing in her ears.

Thomas lives in Canada and . . .

That hadn't occurred to her. This lifemate business had seemed so perfect with the complete lack of a necessity to bother with awkward first dates and everything else, but it didn't resolve issues such as the two of them living in separate countries.

Surely, that wasn't really an issue though, Inez thought with a frown. She had a career here in the U.K. She was a vice president with an excellent salary and wonderful prospects while he just delivered blood in Canada and doodled music on a notepad.

No, it wouldn't be an issue, Inez decided with a faint smile at herself for thinking even for a minute that it might be. Thomas wouldn't have any problem moving here to be with her. Everything would be fine.

She was just borrowing trouble in her usual manner, spotting possible problems before they could become problems.

Shaking her head, Inez slid her cell phone into her purse and started out of the room, coming to a halt in the hall when she heard the muffled sound of a door closing in Thomas's room. Not the soft thud of the bathroom door closing, but a suction type sound, the insulation around the door to the hall had made when it opened and closed.

Frowning, she moved to his door and pressed her ear to it, disturbed by the silence beyond the wooden panel. The shower was now silent and Inez didn't hear him moving around or anything.

Biting her lip, she knocked lightly at the door. "Thomas?"

Inez waited a moment, but when she got no answer, opened the door and peered into the room. The lights were off. She flipped them on, her gaze moving over the empty bed and to the dark and equally empty bathroom.

Cursing, she started toward the door leading out into the hotel hall, but then realized she didn't have her purse and hurried back to her room to collect it knowing she might need her pass and the key to the hotel suite. She hurried out into the hall through her own door then, pausing abruptly when she saw the elevator doors closing.

"Damn," Inez muttered, sure that by the time another elevator arrived he'd be exiting the lobby and lost in the crowds out on the street. She didn't know her way around Amsterdam and even if she did, had no idea where he was going.

That thought sent her back to the hotel room door. She used the card key she'd received when they'd checked in and rushed inside, heading straight for the table in the living room and the notepad on it. A smile claimed her lips when she spotted the bold writing on it. He hadn't taken the note. A quick glance told her they were the latest coordinates for Marguerite's phone and no doubt where he was heading.

Inez ripped the top page off the pad and whirled away to rush for the door. She'd need a map of Amsterdam before she could find the spot, but she would find it and then she'd find Thomas.

He'd probably be annoyed that she'd come after him, but if he was going to be her lifemate, he might as well know right now that she didn't like to share. She wasn't going to leave the foolish man wandering around alone megadosed on Immortal Spanish fly. Especially not in Amsterdam.

Six

Thomas tapped his fingers impatiently against his leg as he waited for the tram. He could have walked the distance from the hotel to the city center easily, but the tram would be faster, and the faster he got there the better.

He'd hoped that once he was out of the hotel and away from Inez some of the need coursing through his body would ease, but it wasn't working out quite that way. It was a struggle for him not to turn around and march the twenty feet back to the hotel and back up to their suite. The only thing stopping him was his worry for his aunt and the knowledge that if he did march back in, he wasn't likely to stop marching until he reached Inez. And then he would probably still keep moving, just taking her with him, stripping away every bit of clothing she wore as he went. If they reached a bed or some other soft surface before he had her naked, she would be lucky, because the moment he had them both free of their binding clothes he was likely to crawl all over and inside her body.

Thomas knew he wouldn't be able to help himself. He was now sporting a killer erection and one that wasn't going away anytime soon. He'd never experienced need like this before. He'd thought the hunger was irresistible when he'd gone too long without blood, but in comparison, the effects of the Sweet Ecstasy were devastating. He felt like he was dancing on the edge of a knife, need lancing through him in pulsating waves.

His gaze slid around the few people near him waiting for the tram, gliding over one woman then another, noting their interested smiles with complete indifference. Horny as the Sweet Ecstasy was making him, Thomas knew they couldn't slake his thirst, it was Inez he wanted. Sweet Inez with her full, pouty lips, her curved body, and all her passion. He wanted her naked beneath him, her warm body embracing his, her need as hot and unbearable as his own.

Of course, she wasn't likely to have any need for him at all yet, let alone one as unbearable as what he was suffering. She hadn't had any Sweet Ecstasy. If anything, the woman was more likely to be screaming blue, bloody murder . . . or to be more literal, rape, as he bore her down to the carpet in their suite.

Grimacing, Thomas glanced up the road, relieved to see the tram coming. The further he got away from Inez and temptation, the better. When the tram stopped, he allowed the others to board before him, then retrieved his pass and followed. Despite the hour, the tram was busy. Tourists traveled around the city at all hours of the night, enjoying the pleasures on offer like naughty children who unexpectedly found themselves free of parental supervision for a weekend.

Thomas glanced over the seats still available as he slid his pass back into his pocket, then moved toward a pair of empty seats near the middle of the tram. He dropped into the aisle seat to discourage anyone from deciding to join him. They would have to be a bold person indeed, since they'd have to crawl over him to get to the window seat. Just to ensure none of the women smiling so prettily at him felt a sudden desire to do so, Thomas crossed his arms over his chest and glared around briefly, before turning his gaze out the window to wait for the tram to move.

It didn't leave the stop right away, but sat idling for a couple of moments. Thomas had just noticed this and glanced to the front of the tram when the driver opened the doors again. Realizing he must have been waiting for someone running for the tram, Thomas turned his attention back to the window, mentally reviewing the map he'd purchased in the hotel lobby. Marguerite's cell phone had last been tracked to the heart of the oldest part of Amsterdam, De Wallen. It was also known as Walletjes ("little walls") or Rosse Buurt . . . the Red Light District.

Thomas couldn't imagine what Marguerite would be doing there. Not that it was what one would expect from the title. It wasn't grubby or seedy. All in all it was a rather unique neighborhood with rows of buildings on either side of the canals. Bridges crossed the canal at intervals, and walkways ran along each side, lined with bars and night clubs along with sex shows and the infamous red-lit windows displaying scantily clad women inside. Most people would be surprised at how clean and attractive it all was.

Still, it just didn't seem the sort of place Marguerite would go. He suspected she'd been passing through the area on her way somewhere else, and would be gone by the time he got there, but he had to check it out.

Thomas blinked and glanced around with alarm as someone began to squeeze through the small bit of space between his knees and the back of the seat in front of him to reach the window seat. His eyes landed on black business pants and stayed fastened there as he recognized the shapely, upside-down heart of Inez's behind. His hands started moving of their own volition, reaching for her hips as if to catch her and draw her down onto his lap, and then Thomas regained control of himself and forced them under his arms as she finally finished squeezing past him and dropped into the window seat with a little sigh.

"Oh, my. I had to run for the tram," she said, flashing him a breathless smile. "You must have had to wait a bit for it or I never would have caught up to you."

Thomas simply stared at her, his brain slowly registering its horror, and then growled, "Inez. What are you doing here? You should be back in the hotel."

Inez frowned slightly as his obvious displeasure at seeing her, and then began to shift around in her seat.

Thomas winced and jerked his arm away as she brushed against him, leaning his upper body slightly into the aisle to prevent her touching him again as she slipped a hand into her pocket. It came out a moment later, holding a piece of folded paper that she silently held out to him.

He stared at the paper for a moment, and then carefully took it, avoiding any of his flesh touching hers. There was no way to keep her scent from drifting to him, however, and his nostrils flared as he inhaled her fragrance. Teeth grinding as every muscle in his body wound itself a little tighter, he unfolded the paper.

"You forgot the coordinates your friend Herb gave you," Inez said quietly as he glanced over his own writing. "I thought you might need it."

Folding up the piece of paper again, he tucked it in his jeans pocket, muttering, "I didn't need it. I remember."

"Oh. I didn't realize," she said, then shrugged and smiled. "Ah, well, better to be safe than sorry."

"Exactly," Thomas said grimly, "which is why when we get off this tram, you are going back to the hotel."

She stiffened at the suggestion, but then smiled and said, "Don't be silly. I'm here to help you. I'll come with you."

"You came to Amsterdam to hear the explanation about my people," he countered at once. "There's no need to help me here. I know my way around Amsterdam."

"Nevertheless, I'm here so may as well help out," Inez insisted.

Thomas turned a scowl on her, but his eyes landed on her lips and refused to go further. He found himself simply staring at her mouth, noting how full and soft it looked and recalling how good it had felt beneath his when he'd kissed her in the hotel. He'd like to kiss her again. He'd like to do more than that, he'd like to cover her mouth with his, and thrust his tongue between her lips even as he caught her by the waist and pulled her onto his lap so that she straddled him. And then he wanted to rip her top open and tug her bra off and bury his face between her full round breasts while he—

The ding of a bell, made him blink and glance around to see that the tram was stopping.

"Are you all right, Thomas?" Inez asked with concern, drawing his gaze back to her. "Your face is flushed and you've broken out in a sweat. Is that normal with Sweet Ecstasy? Are fevers a side effect?"

When she started to raise a hand as if to feel his forehead, Thomas lunged out of his seat, terrified that if she touched him he wouldn't be able to prevent himself from doing exactly what he'd just imagined, even with a whole tram full of people watching.

Noting the way her eyes had widened in surprise at his reaction, Thomas muttered, "We get off here."

He stepped closer to the door, silently begging it to open before she joined him and possibly touched his arm or innocently brushed against him. He was a vamp on the edge here, his mind running as wild as his body. Why the hell hadn't he read the label on that blood rather than just slapping it to his teeth?

When the doors opened, Thomas immediately burst off the tram, instinctively sucking in draughts of fresh air to try to clear his head, or at least to clear her scent from his nose. Damn, he'd never known a woman to smell so good.

"Thomas?" Inez was suddenly at his side, her scent filling his nostrils anew as she gently touched his arm.

Thomas hissed and jerked instinctively away as if she'd burnt him, then controlled himself and turned to face her. The stunned look of hurt on her face made him want to pull her into his arms and comfort her, but he didn't dare. Guilt now joining the barrage of other emotions swirling around inside him, Thomas frowned and glanced up the street, relieved when he spotted the tram coming up the street in the opposite direction to the one they'd just got off of.

"You need to take that tram to get back to the hotel," Thomas said grimly, pointing it out to her. When he glanced at her, she wasn't even following his gesture, but was staring at him with a silent determination that made him extremely nervous. Rather then try to take her arm, he gestured for her to start walking, saying, "I'll see you onto it."

Inez stood firm and shook her head. "I'm going with you."

"Inez," he began grimly.

"I know what Sweet Ecstasy is," she announced, and when he peered at her sharply, she shrugged and admitted, "I called Wyatt and asked about it. You presently have the equivalent of four to six cocktails running through your system. I'm guessing one or two would make you feel very . . . er . . . friendly. Four or six probably isn't leaving you thinking very clearly. I'm coming with you."

"That's not a good idea," Thomas assured her, knowing she really had no clue what state he was in or what he could do in this condition.

"I'm not leaving you wandering around alone while all hot and bothered, especially not in Amsterdam."

Thomas's eyes widened. Had that been a bit of possessiveness he'd heard in her voice? He'd known she was attracted to him back in the hotel in London, but that was before she'd known what he was. He'd worried since then over how she was accepting his explanations. Possessiveness was a good sign, though.

"Lead the way, Thomas," Inez ordered quietly, drawing him back from his thoughts. "Or I'll touch you."

Thomas blinked in surprise at the threat, but just shook his head and said, "Trust me, you don't want to do that."

On that note, he gave up trying to send her back and turned to head toward a dimly lit alleyway. He moved slowly at first, until she fell into pace at his side, and then picked up a little speed to stay a step ahead of her scent and discourage talking. Thomas was hoping that if she didn't touch him and he couldn't smell her and she didn't talk, he could pretend she wasn't there and his body might settle down a little. Every nerve in his body had been buzzing since she'd appeared on the tram.

It didn't work, of course. Inez wasn't one to be easily ignored.

"Where are we going?" she asked.

Thomas glanced over the people walking around them. It was a busy alleyway, the street cobbled and people both heading in their direction as well as walking the same way they were going. Other than the occasional light overhead being electric rather than oil lamps, it wasn't much different than it had been when he'd first come here one hundred and seventy-five years ago.

"Thomas?" Inez prompted.

"The Red Light District."

* * *

Inez was very glad that she'd decided to come after him. The idea of his wandering the famed prostitution area of Amsterdam in the state he was in was not a happy one.

Her gaze slid over him as they passed from shadow to light. She had been surprised to see him boarding the tram when she'd come out of the hotel. Inez had been positive she'd have to find him by finding the location on the note he'd left behind. She hadn't looked a gift horse in the mouth, however, but had immediately burst into a run to get to the tram before it moved off. Fortunately, the driver had seen her and waited.

Thomas had looked tense and unhappy when she'd first spotted him on the tram, and that was before he'd even seen her. He looked just as tense and unhappy now, or perhaps a little more so. It seemed obvious to her the man was suffering. He couldn't bear to be touched, kept breaking out in a sweat every time she got too near, and seemed to be having a hard time even looking at her.

They turned out of the short alleyway and onto a street, or what she assumed was a street. One side was separated from the other by a wide canal with bridges crossing over it at either end. Inez found herself gawking around at their surroundings. Much to her surprise it was all quite pretty. The buildings were all pressed up tight against each other and all were at least three, and sometimes four or even five, stories high. Some were very narrow buildings with only two windows on each floor, others were wider with three, but every one seemed to have businesses on the ground floor and everywhere she looked, lights twinkled out at her. Even the bridges had lights running in arcs on the arches over the water.

They passed bars, clubs, and sex shops at the outer fringe of this area and then—

Inez stopped dead and gaped at the row of windows lit up in red. Some had their curtains pulled, the cloth glowing red from the light beyond and one or two held empty chairs with signs that said be right back, but most had women in them, all dressed in lingerie or some other scanty bit of cloth. It was like a glass candy display case with the women as the candy. Bemused by it all, Inez began to dig in her purse.

Thomas turned back when he realized he'd lost her. Returning to her side, he frowned and asked, "What are you looking for?"

"My cell phone," Inez answered, checking the side pockets when she didn't find it in the middle pocket. Feeling it at last, she pulled it out triumphantly. "Ah, ha!"

"Who are you calling?" Thomas asked with bewilderment.

"I'm not." She flipped the cell phone open and started to raise it. "My phone has a camera built in. I want to take a picture."

Much to her amazement, Thomas stepped in front of her, blocking her view of the windows.

"No pictures," he said quietly. "It isn't allowed."

"What?" Inez asked with surprise and then glanced around. Spotting a man not three feet away with a huge honking camera in hand that he was focusing on the windows, she pointed him out. "Look, he's—"

Her words died abruptly as a shriek rent the

air. Glancing toward the windows, she saw a fully clothed, short, skinny older woman pushing her way past one of the young women in the windows to rush out of what turned out not to be a window at all, but a windowed door.

Inez's eyes widened incredulously as she went after the man with the camera, berating him for trying to take pictures. The man was backpedaling away, his eyes wide and horrified.

"Move," Thomas growled.

Inez drew her gaze from the dispute on the street and glanced toward Thomas. The moment she was looking his way he began to walk again, forcing her to either follow or lose him in the crowd. Sighing, Inez set out reluctantly after him. She'd really rather stay and see what happened here, but didn't want to lose him.

"Why won't they allow pictures?" she asked, glancing back over her shoulder where the man with the camera was offering money to the upset woman. Both Inez and the man flinched when the woman smacked the money away and continued to rage at him.

When Thomas didn't answer, she glanced around, and spotted two large men now coming out of the open windowed door to join the little woman. She was suddenly very glad that Thomas had prevented her taking a picture. It looked to her like the man with the camera was about to be in even more trouble.

Realizing that Thomas was continuing forward without her, she hurried after him. "Thomas? Why are they so upset about his taking pictures?"

"Privacy," Thomas said through gritted teeth as she caught up. "The women don't want to be photographed, and neither do most of the men who visit them. It's bad for business. Who would want to visit a prostitute if there was a chance his picture will be taken?"

"Oh, yes, of course," Inez said quietly as she slipped her phone back in her purse. For a moment there she'd forgotten what the women did in those little rooms when the curtains closed. Somehow it's all being out in the open like that had made it seem more like some sort of attraction at a fair than what it really was: prostitution. It was the atmosphere that did it, she realized as she glanced over their surroundings again. The area was well lit, and the setting almost romantic with the lights reflecting off the canal. The walkways were neat, the buildings tidy. There was no garbage lying around, no graffiti, all the buildings appeared well maintained and tidy in this light, and the people they were passing were mostly tourists, groups of men, couples, and groups of couples, all dressed in casual but nice clothes, laughing and talking as they walked along the street, peering in the windows with more curiosity than lecherous intent.

Despite the fact that they passed sex shops and peep shows, or live erotic shows interspersed among the window women, the atmosphere was almost that of a carnival rather than . . . well . . . a Red Light District.

Thomas stopped walking suddenly and Inez glanced at him curiously. "What is it?"

"This is the spot," he answered, his head turning slowly as he surveyed the area.

"Here?" Inez asked doubtfully. They were standing in front of a sex shop with red-lit, women-filled windows spreading out on either side on both the ground and second floors. Hardly a place she'd expect to find Marguerite Argeneau.

"Herb said that she'd be no more than fifty feet away," Thomas said with a frown as he glanced around.

Inez glanced one way and then the other, trying to judge how far fifty feet would be in each direction. There were no bars or restaurants in this little stretch, however, only the sex shop and red-lit windows.

Movement caught her eye and Inez glanced to the second-floor window in front of her as a pretty young blonde in white lace panties, bra, and stockings drew the curtains open. A man stood in the room with her, his belt undone and hanging open, his pants zipped up, and he was rushing to do up the buttons of his shirt. He was an average-looking man; average height, a little too thin, a little awkward looking. He also appeared pretty flustered about the woman having opened the curtains before he was dressed and gone, and Inez found herself embarrassed for him. She turned away, facing Thomas to give the man in the window privacy.

"She must have just been walking past here when they tracked her," she said. "Call your friend and have him track her phone again."

Nodding, he pulled out his phone.

Inez glanced around as she waited for him to make the call, her eyes sliding over the windows on the street, noticing that the women on the second floor all seemed to be just that little bit prettier than the ones on the ground floor. Most on the second floor also wore more expensive-looking lingerie, or leather compared to the women below, and she wondered if there was a price difference between the ones on the ground floor and the ones higher up.

Thomas began to speak next to her and Inez listened absently as he talked with his friend, Herb, and asked him to track the phone again. When he finished, she glanced his way in question as he flipped the phone closed.

"He'll call back when he has the location," Thomas explained, slipping the phone into his back pocket.

Nodding, she stepped out of the way of a large group of men gamboling down the walkway, singing some bawdy song. Once they were past, she turned to Thomas and suggested, "Why don't we go find a pub up the street while we wait?"

Thomas hesitated and then shook his head. "If we go in the wrong direction, we'll just have that much farther to backtrack."

"Right," Inez said on a sigh. She was exhausted. Her feet were sore and her ankles still swollen from the flight. She was also hungry again despite the fact that she'd eaten twice that day. And she couldn't complain about any of the above since he'd wanted her to stay at the hotel in the first place. Grimacing, she walked over to lean against the railing that ran along the canal to keep the unwary and just plain drunk or stoned tourist from stumbling into the canal.

"You look tired," Thomas said with a frown and when she merely shrugged, turned up the street. "Come on. It could be as much as an hour before he calls back. We may as well have a drink and maybe something to eat."

Brightening at once, Inez fell into step beside him,

finding a little energy at the prospect of a seat and drink in her future.

They hadn't gone far when they had to move to the side to make way for another large group, this one a bit rowdy and most definitely drunk or stoned or both. Thomas instinctively took her arm to move her out of the way of the group, having to pull her right into the mouth of a short narrow alley to get out of the way.

Inez tripped over the uneven path and though Thomas caught her, he was pulled somewhat off balance as well. They stumbled like a couple of drunks until she came up against the wall, her back slamming into it.

Grimacing, Inez lifted her head and found Thomas frozen before her, his face carved from stone, his eyes flashing silver in the dark alcove. Her own eyes widened and she found herself holding her breath as she peered up at him. It felt like a very dangerous situation to her, though she couldn't have said why, and then his head lowered and his mouth covered hers and she knew exactly why. The need pouring off the man and evident in his demanding kiss was almost shocking. This kiss was nothing like the one in the hotel in London. That had been commanding and seductive, this was wild and out of control, an explosion of desperate need that was frightening in its intensity.

Shocked, Inez remained completely still under the initial onslaught. Like a computer overwhelmed with information, her brain blanked out briefly and then restarted as his hands caught her by the behind and lifted her up, pressing her against his hard need. Regaining her senses, Inez reached up to catch him by the hair and tugged viciously, trying to make him stop. When that didn't work, she bit down on his tongue, not enough to do real damage, but enough to warn him off.

Thomas broke the kiss at once and she felt a moment's relief, but then his mouth simply slid across her cheek to her ear.

"Thomas," she hissed in a whisper, aware that the street was only a few feet to her left and not wanting to draw the attention of passersby, "you have to stop. Someone will see us here."

When he lifted his head and let her slide back to her feet, she felt a moment's relief, but then he simply urged her farther back in the alcove.

"What—?" Inez asked with confusion and then felt the wall press into her back again as he pressed her into the shadows. "Thom—"

His name died on a gasp of surprise as his hand suddenly covered one of her breasts through her blouse, then his mouth was on hers again, his tongue sweeping out to rasp against her own. Inez closed her eyes, trying to fight off the sensations awakening in her, but the man had had two hundred years to practice his technique and was good at it. Still, she tried one more time, twisting her head to the side to break the kiss so she could gasp, "Thomas you have to—"

Her eyes shot open in surprise as his head ducked and he closed his mouth over the breast he'd been caressing. Inez stared down in shock as she saw that he'd somehow opened her blouse without her realizing it, nudged her silk bra aside and was now suckling on one naked nipple, drawing it into his mouth and flicking it with his tongue so that the tender nub hardened with excitement.

"Thomas." She'd meant it as a reprimand, but it came out a breathless moan. Even worse, the hand that had been tugging at his hair, now cradled his head, urging him on.

When Thomas's teeth scraped against the excited flesh he was suckling, Inez moaned, and clutched her fingers closed on the strands of his hair again, this time not trying to make him stop so much as trying to pull him up to kiss her again. Thomas did at once, his tongue immediately sweeping out to dance with hers as he caught her by the behind and lifted her again. This time when he urged her against the hardness at his groin, she groaned and caught her arms around his neck, pressing her breasts against his chest so that she was plastered to him from top to bottom.

Thomas stepped closer, pinning her to the wall with his body so that his hands were free to roam. Inez gasped and shuddered and sucked furiously at his tongue as his hands slid over her. When he caught her under the thighs and urged them up, she instinctively wrapped her legs around his hips, slightly changing the angle of their contact as he ground into her.

"I need you," he growled, breaking their kiss again and leaning back slightly so that he could close both hands over her breasts. One was bare, but the other was still covered by her bra. Thomas fixed that quickly enough so that he could caress her naked flesh.

Inez covered his hands with her own and leaned her head back against the wall, moaning as she shifted her hips to grind against him and then one of his hands slid away and the cool night air caressed her breast as she felt him fiddling at the waist of her slacks.

"Why aren't you wearing a skirt?" he muttered with frustration.

"I will from now on," Inez promised and then the material at her waist gave and his hand slid inside and between her legs. Inez bucked against him and cried out as his finger brushed against her slick flesh, a sound that he cut off by covering her mouth again with his own.

Inez kissed him back frantically, slipping one of her own hands between them to press it against his erection, and squeezing firmly. When Thomas growled into her mouth, she released him and worked at the button and zipper of his jeans, opening both so that she could slip her own hand inside to find him, and then his cell phone rang.

Seven

Thomas and Inez both pulled apart slightly and then froze, their eyes locking on each other as his cell phone continued to ring. When he didn't react, Inez slid her hand in the back pocket of his jeans, retrieved his phone and held it up between them.

Sighing, Thomas allowed her to slide to her feet and took the phone. Opening it, he barked, "Hello."

Herb immediately began nattering in his ear, but Thomas wasn't paying attention. His gaze as well as all his focus was on Inez as she began to straighten her clothes. Thomas watched her tucking all that delectable flesh away, hard-pressed not to drop his phone and simply rip every stitch of material off of her. That was foremost in his thoughts despite the fact that one very tiny part of his brain was telling him he should really drop to his knees, apologize, and beg her forgiveness. The Sweet Ecstasy in his system might be driving him wild with need, but there was still one portion of Thomas's brain functioning and it was enough to throw a bit of guilt on the mixture of hunger and desire presently swirling in his brain.

It was a very tiny portion of his brain, but it was telling him that he had pretty much dragged Inez into the alley and attacked her. While he knew it was true and had even realized it as he'd done it, Thomas hadn't been able to help himself. A shock of excitement had gone through him the moment he'd taken her arm to steer her out of the path of the drunk and rowdy group moving toward them, and that was just from touching her elbow.

He'd feared that would happen. That's why he'd avoided touching her since the light brush of her arm against his on the tram. He'd known it would simply ramp up the need swirling through his body like a tornado. However, he might have resisted then, but when she'd stumbled and they crashed into the wall, their bodies briefly pressing together, he'd been lost, overwhelmed by the sudden surge of desire inside him.

A flash fire had gone through him, bursting to life at every point where their bodies had met and Thomas had attacked her. There was no other description for it and he knew it. He'd jumped her like a slavering animal, forcing himself on her despite her struggles. It was only when she'd said his name and pulled at his hair that he'd regained any sense at all and then it had only been enough for him to drag her farther into the shadows and shift to a lower gear, switching from taking what he wanted to a determined coaxing. But it *had* been determined. He would have taken her right there against the dark alley wall if not for Herb's phone call. Only the fact that she was wearing slacks instead of a skirt had slowed him down, and only the ring of the phone—a piercing reminder of the need to find Aunt Marguerite—had made him stop.

"Thomas? Did you get that?"

Blinking, Thomas forced himself to look away from Inez and concentrate on the voice on the other end of the phone.

"Herb. No, I'm sorry, could you repeat that?" he asked.

"I said you were right. She appears to be on the move. The coordinates are different this time. Are you ready for them?"

"Yes," he assured him, forcing himself to attention. "Go ahead."

He had Herb repeat them twice to make sure he had them fixed in his memory and then thanked him and signed off. Thomas closed the phone with a sigh and slipped it in his back pocket, then quickly straightened his own clothes before retrieving the folded map in his other back pocket and heading for the light at the mouth of the alley.

As he'd expected, Inez quickly fell into step beside him. Trying to concentrate on what he had to do, Thomas found it difficult not to yell at her to go back to the hotel and leave him in peace. The only reason he managed to control that urge was because he wanted her there with him as much as he wanted her gone. He was trying to fight the effects of the Sweet Ecstasy, but they were fighting him right back.

"What are the new coordinates?" Inez asked as he stopped on the lit path and opened the map.

Thomas peered at the tentative smile she was offering and shook his head slightly, amazed that she wasn't railing at him for what he'd just done. The woman was very forgiving, but obviously had no idea how precarious his control—and therefore her position—was. If she did, he was sure she'd be heading for the airport and the first plane back to England, or at least back to the hotel to lock herself in her room. Not that a locked door was likely to stop him if he lost control completely.

Turning his gaze back to the map, Thomas glanced over it, finding the new coordinates and comparing them to where they presently were, then glanced around as he quickly refolded the map.

"This way." Back to avoiding touching her, he led the way up the street as he slid the street map back into his pocket. They were headed back the way they'd come, and he frowned as he wondered if they'd somehow passed Marguerite on their way out without his noticing her, or if she'd already moved to where she now was before he'd headed out. That was more likely. He couldn't imagine Marguerite would have had any reason to be at the first spot. He just couldn't imagine her stopping in at a prostitute's windowed room.

Unless it was to feed, Thomas thought suddenly, realizing that without knowing where she was, Bastien had no way to send her blood. It wouldn't be that big a problem for her over here. As Bastien had said, the council in Europe had some different laws than those in North America. Biting mortals was allowed over here, although most immortals he knew tended to prefer the safety offered by bagged blood. They simply didn't want to give up the choice of fresh, warm blood from the source on occasion.

Marguerite might very well have been visiting one of the prostitutes in the window . . . to feed.

Thomas found the idea disturbing. He'd never known his aunt to choose people over bagged blood. But why *hadn't* she contacted Bastien and had blood shipped out? The longer she was missing the more worried he became. Something was obviously wrong, and he was the one in charge of finding out what that was. It was a task he couldn't fail, not just because he didn't want to let down the rest of the family, but because he himself needed her to be safe and well. She was the central focus of family to him. He loved Jeanne Louise and Lissianna as sisters, but Marguerite was stability and the very embodiment of home and family for Thomas. He had hardly cared that Jean Claude, Marguerite's husband, had died except that it meant he wouldn't be around to make the wonderful woman miserable, but losing Marguerite would be a crushing blow.

The red-lit windows had thinned out as they walked, separated more and more by bars and shops. When they reached the new coordinates, Thomas found they were standing on a walkway that was a little wider than the one they'd just left. On their right was a row of bars and restaurants, on their left was a row of outdoor tables with large outdoor umbrellas sporting various beer logos.

No doubt they had stopped here to eat. While Marguerite was over seven hundred years old and no longer ate, Tiny McGraw was mortal and did. If that was the case, they might still be here. Surely it would take some time to cook a meal and eat it.

"Is this the spot?" Inez asked, her gaze sliding over the tables.

Thomas nodded and they both began to move slowly along the walkway between the tables and buildings, their eyes moving carefully over the patrons seated outside.

"Maybe she's inside one of the restaurants or bars," Inez suggested as they drew near the end of the tables.

Thomas nodded and frowned as he glanced toward the front of the buildings, unsure what to do. He was afraid that if they started going into the restaurants, Marguerite might come out of one while they were in another and leave without them seeing her.

"I could wait out here while you check the restaurants, that way we would be sure not to miss her," Inez suggested.

Thomas glanced at her, grateful for the suggestion his own brain was in no shape to come up with, but he asked, "Do you know what she looks like?"

"Yes. I met her when I was in New York."

Relieved to have the matter settled, he glanced around and then suggested, "Why don't you have a seat at one of the tables on the end here so that you can watch all the doors. I'll be as quick as I can."

Nodding, Inez moved to the nearest table, settling herself in a seat that put her back to the rest of the path but gave her a view of the entrances of the row of restaurants and bars.

The moment she was settled, Thomas headed for the door of the first bar.

Fifteen minutes later, Inez watched Thomas walk into the last bar in this little area and sighed to herself. Obviously, he hadn't spotted Marguerite in any of the other bars, and she suspected he wouldn't find her in this one either. No doubt they'd missed her again. She probably hadn't stopped here at all, but had been tracked in the area as she was passing through again. They'd probably have to call his friend, Herb, and have him track her phone once more and Inez was beginning to fear they would spend the whole night hurrying from spot to spot chasing after her until near sunrise when she'd settle into whatever hotel she was stopping at. Inez was too tired for this nonsense.

A burst of laughter drew her gaze to a group of men seated at the tables of the next bar over, and she smiled faintly when she recognized the stag party group from Britain. They were laughing and having a good time, but the groom was looking a little the worse for wear. His wig was lopsided, he had several runs in his stockings, the makeup on his face—garish to begin with—was smudged as well as bleeding down his face with sweat. He still appeared to be having a good time, though; his smile was bright and beaming.

Shaking her head with amusement, Inez started to glance back toward the doors, but paused as her gaze landed on a man seated alone at a table two over from the stag party. He had short, spiky black hair above a thin face and looked vaguely familiar to her. Inez only peered at him for a moment, and then decided he too must have been on the plane with them. Amsterdam was a small city and every one seemed to go to the Red Light District at some point, if only to tour through and gawk. If she sat there long enough, she'd probably see every single person from their flight pass by, Inez thought as she glanced back toward the restaurants.

It should have been a boring business, sitting there watching people enter and exit and gambol by, but it really wasn't. It was a lovely night, with a clear sky, a light breeze, and the sound of gently lapping water to her side from the canal. Inez had always enjoyed people watching and it was hard not to in this setting.

"Hello, beautiful lady."

Inez glanced around with a start as three men suddenly took up the extra seats at her table. She'd seen them approaching, but had assumed that they intended to claim a table of their own, not join her. Now, she glanced wide-eyed from man to man to man; a blonde, a brunette, and a man with a shaved head. All of them were about her age and all of them wore a half-drunk, half-stoned, we're-here-to-have fun smiles.

"Can we buy you a drink?" the blonde asked in a rather slurred British accent.

"No, thank you, I've ordered one . . . and I'm waiting for someone," Inez added stiffly. This wasn't a situation she was used to dealing with. In fact, it had never happened to her before. Work kept her busy enough that she rarely went out socially, but when she did, it was with her girlfriends, Lisa and Sherry. They lived in the neighboring flat. She'd met them the day she'd moved from Portugal to London. Lisa wrote a column for a national magazine and Sherry worked in IT for the same magazine. They were both gorgeous model types; Lisa, a tall blond, and Sherry, a tall redhead, and always drew all the attention when the three of them were together, leaving Inez free of having to fend off advances.

That was part of the reason Inez did occasionally agree to go out with the pair. Going out with them was like going out with shields. In their presence, she disappeared into the surroundings and wasn't forced to socialize with the opposite sex. While Inez had a lot of confidence at work, was excellent at what she did, and could handle any crisis, in her personal life she was decidedly lacking in self-confidence.

Inez was short and—in her opinion—twenty pounds overweight. She was top heavy, her lips were too full, her hair too wild and unmanageable, insisting on curling in the damp English air. None of which was considered attractive by today's standards. Hairstyles today were all nice, flat helmets, and no matter how many creams or hair flatteners she used, her glossy black curls would not be beaten into submission. As for the rest of her, unfortunately, there was no cream to make her shoot up about six inches and give her a svelte figure.

"Oh, don't be like that, love," the one with the shaved head said. "We're just trying to be friendly."

Inez had a sudden, overwhelming urge to tell them to bugger off. She had Thomas, a lifemate chosen by nanos or God or both and dropped into her life without any effort on her part and no need to try to pretend to a confidence, beauty, or social skills she didn't have. She didn't feel awkward or unsure around him, didn't feel the least uncomfortable . . .

Blinking at her own thoughts, Inez suddenly sagged back in her seat. It was true. She didn't feel self-conscious or out of place with Thomas as she did with most men. She felt completely comfortable with him, even at her worst as she was right now. And she was definitely at her worst. She was tired, hungry, and while she'd had a bath at the hotel in London, she was still wearing the wrinkled clothes she'd tugged on that morning, hadn't had even an elastic to pull back her unmanageable hair, or any makeup to put on afterward other than the lipstick she'd had in her purse, and yet it didn't seem to matter to Thomas. He'd still kissed her in the hotel, and then gone at her again just moments ago in the dark alley.

Of course, he was a bit horned up right now on account of the Immortal version of Spanish fly, Inez reminded herself. Still, that didn't mean he had to jump *her*.

"Look, love, while its fascinating sitting here watching you nod and talk to yourself under your breath it might be more fun if you talked to us," the blonde said, forcing himself into her recollection again. "We'll buy you that drink and you talk to us, right?"

Knowing it wasn't advisable to be rude to sotted men, Inez was just opening her mouth to ask them politely to leave her alone when Thomas was suddenly there, looming beside her. She peered up at his face, surprised to see that his features were rigid and his eyes glowing silver. She'd seen his eyes turn that way before, both times when he'd kissed her, but somehow she didn't think it was passion making them silver right now.

"She said 'no, thank you,'" Thomas said coldly and Inez bit her lip, her gaze sliding worriedly between the men. She'd lived in Britain for almost eight years and knew the last thing you did was piss off a drunken Brit. They were considered all stiff upper lip and conservative by the world at large, and they were that, but she'd also never seen a group more likely to start swinging their fists than Brits when drinking. She suspected it had something to do with that very conservativeness that they were known for. All those emotions they bottled up so much of the time, had to come out at some point and when they were drinking seemed to be the point. She couldn't recall an evening out with Lisa and Sherry where a fight or absolute brawl hadn't broken out at the end of the night.

Inez knew Thomas wasn't your average guy, that he was faster, stronger, and could control minds, but she wasn't sure he could control three at once, or how much stronger and faster he actually was. Slinging her purse strap over her shoulder, she stood and murmured, "Thomas, I think we should move on and call Herb for another set of coord—"

"No, no, love. Sit down. We want to buy you a drink." The words were accompanied by a sudden sharp tug on her hand that sent her dropping back into her seat. Her eyes shot to the first man as he turned his attention to Thomas and said with a shrug, "I don't see a ring on her finger. She's free to sit with us."

Inez never saw Thomas move, but suddenly the blonde was dangling in the air, held there by Thomas's hand at his throat.

"Thomas," she said anxiously, standing up and catching his free arm with her hand. He jerked as if she branded him, his head whipping around, eyes blazing silver fire. Inez caught her breath and stared back for a moment and then glanced around sharply and cried out with surprise as she saw the brunette approaching Thomas from behind. Her warning came too late, even as the sound slipped from her lips, the man flicked open a knife and plunged it into Thomas's lower back.

He stiffened, his back arching slightly, then dropped the blonde and whirled on his attacker, baring his teeth and hissing. Inez saw the brunette's eyes widen incredulously as he shrank back, but she was already stepping between the two men.

"Thomas," she said in low warning.

For a minute, Inez thought he'd knock her aside and go after the brown-haired Brit, but a shout and the sound of pounding feet made them both glance around to see two uniformed members of the Amsterdam police force rushing toward them. Thomas growled at the sight of them, and then Inez suddenly found herself caught under one arm like a football as he charged up the walkway away from the police.

Inez was aware of their passing from light to darkness to light once more, and thought they were on the main street again. She heard people gasping and exclaiming in surprise as he whizzed up the street, dodging the crowds of pedestrians and knew this couldn't be a good thing. That was when Inez realized just how much the Sweet Ecstasy was affecting Thomas. She'd assumed that the concentrate would just affect his body, but now she knew it had to be affecting his mind as well. He'd bared his teeth in public, for heaven's sake and now was drawing attention to them with this superhuman rush up the road.

The good thing was that at the speed he was moving, it was doubtful anyone was getting enough of a look at either of them to be able to describe them later. Still, staying hidden was a creed among his people. They spent most of their lives trying not to draw attention to themselves. She knew he shouldn't be doing this. Inez had barely realized this when Thomas turned a corner and slowed so abruptly her stomach lurched. In the next moment she found herself upright and able to breathe again as he set her on her feet.

Inez stumbled, her legs not quite ready to support her, but Thomas simply held her upright with a hand under her arm and urged her forward, and into a building. They were halfway across the lobby before she realized they were back at the hotel. Inez supposed she shouldn't be so surprised, he'd certainly moved faster than the tram and it really hadn't been that long a ride on the tram in the first place.

They were on the elevator and the doors were closing before she glanced out and noticed the startled looks the few people in the lobby were giving them. Frowning, she glanced to Thomas, afraid he was still flashing his teeth, but he wasn't and then she glanced down and noticed the knife still sticking out of his lower back.

"Oh God," she breathed, feeling the blood rush out of her head.

Thomas didn't even look her way. His eyes remained fixed on the lighted numbers over the elevator doors. Biting her lip, Inez reached toward the knife, thinking to pull it out without warning so that it would—hopefully—hurt less, but let her hand fall back before she touched the handle. She simply couldn't bring herself to do it and didn't think she'd be able to do it even with his knowing.

The elevator dinged as it came to a halt, and she glanced around as the doors opened, then followed quickly when Thomas stepped out and started up the hall. She was so distracted staring at the knife sticking out of his back that Inez didn't notice that his steps were unsteady until they'd nearly reached their suite.

"Are you all right?" she asked anxiously, moving up to his side to peer at his face. Her alarm only increased when she saw how pale he was. "Thomas?"

"No, Inez, I'm not all right. I have a knife in my back. Unlock the door, please. I can't reach into my back pocket to get my card key."

"Oh." Realizing it would probably cause him excruciating pain to even attempt to retrieve the card key, Inez quickly dug hers out of her purse and unlocked the door, then rushed in and held it open for him, her concern deepening as he lurched through the door. She pushed the door closed and slid the chain on so they wouldn't be disturbed, and then turned in time to see Thomas sink to his knees and then fall flat on his face.

"Thomas!" she cried, hurrying to his side and dropping to her knees to peer at his face. He was as white as a sheet and unconscious.

Inez sat back on her heels, her gaze sliding reluctantly to his back and the knife protruding there. He had said that the nanos repaired all injuries, but supposed they couldn't do that while the knife was still in him. She'd have to remove it. The very idea made her groan and close her eyes, but they popped open again when a muffled chirping sound caught her ear.

In the state she was in, it took Inez a moment to realize that it was his cell phone. She glanced at the back pockets of Thomas's jeans, but while his wallet was in one and the map was in the other, there was no sign of the phone. The fact that the sound was muffled and very faint told her that Thomas must have put it in his front pocket since the last time she'd seen him use it.

There was no way she was going to turn him over to answer it, the man had a knife in his back. Obviously, she had to get it out. Ignoring the constant buzz of his phone, she considered the knife, noting now that his T-shirt was glistening with blood and that it had made a large, dark patch starting at his waist directly below the wound and spreading out and down to almost his knees. He'd lost a lot of blood.

She had to get the knife out, and then fetch the blood from the cooler and somehow feed it to him. Inez didn't know how she was going to do that, but she could only handle one problem at a time.

She leaned forward and reached for the handle of the knife, then suddenly straightened and launched to her feet instead. Towels. She had to have towels. She couldn't have him bleeding all over the floor. She was in the bathroom, grabbing up every towel there was in the room when her own phone began to ring.

Inez glanced down at her purse with surprise, only now realizing she still had it slung over her shoulder. Dropping the towels, she dug out her phone, and flipped it open.

"Is this Inez?"

She frowned at the clipped voice, not recognizing it. "I . . . er . . . yes. Who is—?"

"This is Herb Longford," the man answered, his English accent very thick. "Thomas gave me your number when he last called. He said his battery on his cell phone was running low and if I couldn't reach him to try your mobile."

"Oh," she murmured with a little sigh, thinking that at least she knew who the caller had been.

There was a moment of silence, and then a pointed, "I'm calling to give Thomas the new coordinates."

"New coordinates?" Inez stalled, wondering what to do. She had a feeling Thomas wouldn't want anyone knowing about the incident at the restaurants, feared he might even be in trouble if anyone found out about it. She suspected flashing his teeth in public and then exhibiting his incredible speed might be big no-nos among his people.

"Yes," Herb said impatiently. "He said he was checking the bars in the area of the last coordinates but there was no sign of his aunt. He wanted me to track her cell again. I have and if you'll put him on the phone I'll give them to him."

"Oh, I—he's . . . er . . . in the bathroom," she lied finally. "If you give them to me, I'll pass them along."

"Right. Do you have a pen and paper?"

"Yes." Inez dug in her purse one-handed in search

of the small notepad and pen she always carried with her, and then lifted the phone back to her ear. "Okay, go ahead."

Herb rattled off the information, and then said, "Give those to Thomas and I'll go ahead and track her again in case she's still on the move. I'll call back if she's at a different location."

"Yes, thank you," Inez finished the last word on a sigh as he hung up. Shaking her head, she put the phone away and then knelt to scoop up the towels. She had to remove the knife from Thomas's back, feed him blood, and then go out and find the latest location and search for Marguerite on her own. It was what she was here for, to help find Thomas's aunt, and it was what she would do, just as soon as she'd made sure that he was all right.

"You can do it," Inez told herself as she walked back out to the living room, but her voice sounded doubtful even to herself.

Thomas still lay exactly where she'd left him. Inez set the towels on the floor beside him and then examined the knife in his back, trying to judge how deeply in it was. She decided it appeared to have gone into his back at least a couple inches and then realized her hands were trembling.

She peered at them with a frown and then moved to the bar fridge. Inez examined the contents, then pulled out one of the tiny bottles of alcohol and began to open it. She was in Amsterdam, about to pull a knife out of a man's back, Inez couldn't think of a better time to reach for Dutch courage.

She downed the bottle quickly, grimacing as it

burned its way down her throat, then set it on top of the mini fridge and opened another. This one went down easier than the first, but didn't taste any better. Inez started to reach for another, but then changed her mind. She wasn't much of a drinker as a rule, and suspected the two would be more than enough. Three would probably have her unconscious on the floor next to Thomas.

Slamming the refrigerator door closed, Inez straightened and turned to approach Thomas, pleased to find that while the alcohol couldn't possibly have hit her blood stream yet, she at least *felt* a little steadier. It was psychological, she supposed.

She eased to her knees and surveyed the knife again. It still made her queasy just to think about pulling the knife out, but it had to be done.

Inez stared at it for the longest time, trying to come up with a way to avoid having to do it herself. Perhaps she could order more blood and make the delivery guy do it. It was all his fault Thomas was in this state to begin with. If he hadn't left the wrong blood here, Thomas never would have consumed a bag and been so out of control that he got himself stabbed. At least, Inez didn't think Thomas would have acted as he had if he hadn't been affected by the concentrated Sweet Ecstasy. He just didn't seem to be the jealous, head-banger type. He was too considerate and . . . well . . . sweet for her to believe he would have behaved like that under normal circumstances.

Inez seriously considered the blood order idea until it occurred to her that she might get a different delivery guy, and then someone else would know about what had happened tonight and instinct was telling her that wasn't a good idea.

"Just do it," Inez muttered to herself impatiently.

Taking a deep breath, she reached out and wrapped both hands carefully around the handle, trying not to jar it as she did. She then closed her eyes, counted to three, tightened her grip and jerked the knife up and out of his body, blinking her eyes open and glancing sharply toward Thomas's head when he groaned in pain. Unfortunately, Thomas's head was turned to the other side and she couldn't see if he was awake. However, when he didn't make another sound, she dropped the knife on the towels, and then had to move that towel aside so she could retrieve another one.

Turning back to Thomas, Inez tugged his T-shirt quickly from his jeans and peered at the wound, grimacing at the sight of the blood seeping out. It seemed to be flowing from him rather quickly. Biting her lip, she covered the wound with the towel and pressed down firmly, holding it there for a few minutes before lifting the now bloody towel away to see what was happening.

Thomas had said the nanos repaired and regenerated, but apparently it wasn't instantaneous like the vampires on television. The wound was still there, though it did seem as if the bleeding was slowing down. She pressed the towel to the wound again, waiting another few moments, and then lifted it for another inspection. The bleeding had definitely slowed down now.

Letting her breath out on a sigh of relief, Inez set the used towel aside and grabbed another, laying this one lightly over the wound, just to make sure the little bit of blood still seeping out didn't run down his side and drip on the floor, then she stood and moved to the cooler to retrieve a couple of bags of blood. Inez carried them back to Thomas and knelt beside him again, only to stare at him uncertainly. She had no idea how she was supposed to get the blood into him. If he were on his back, she'd just pop a hole in the bag and let it run into his mouth and hope he swallowed it. However, he was on his stomach.

Inez considered the problem for several moments and then sighed and simply laid the bags of blood beside his head so that he'd find them when he woke up.

If he woke up, Inez thought and frowned, but then recalled his saying that immortals couldn't be killed by most injuries. Not even a stake through the heart could kill them if it was removed quickly enough.

He'd wake up, she reassured herself. But now she had to go out and check the latest coordinates to see if she could find Marguerite. She didn't want Thomas's friend Herb calling back and wondering why they hadn't checked them out. Besides it was what they were there for. She started to stand and then knelt again as she recalled his phone. There was a good possibility Bastien might call to check on their progress and she thought it best if she had the phone if he did.

Gritting her teeth, Inez snaked her hand under Thomas's body, feeling around for his pocket. The knife was no longer in his back, but she still didn't want to jostle him too much and possibly worsen his injury. Finding his pocket, she slid her hand inside, caught the phone in her fingers with some difficulty and eased it out, her breath exhaling on a gust of relief when she had it free.

Inez dropped it in her purse, and then slid the map out of his back pocket and put that in her purse as well as she got to her feet. She hesitated then, feeling awful about leaving Thomas lying there. After a moment, she dropped to her knees again and slid one of the folded towels under his head as a pillow, then stood and headed for the door.

Eight

It didn't take Inez long to find the new location on the map. The next spot was a lot closer to the hotel than the others had been. It was only a few minutes walk away. Inez set out at a quick clip, eager to get this over with. She ended up on Rembrandtplein, directly in front of a huge night club with a ridiculously large queue of people in front of it. Judging by the number of people waiting outside, there must be a colossal number of people inside. It would be loud, dark, crowded, and impossible to find Marguerite.

Closing her eyes briefly, Inez prayed for strength, or at least a little energy, and then stiffened as a phone rang. Digging quickly in her purse she found her phone, pulled it out, and opened it.

"Thomas?" Herb asked.

"No, it's Inez," she answered, having to speak loudly

to be heard over the noise around her. Before he could ask where Thomas was, she quickly said, "The last coordinates are outside a large club called Escape. There's a huge queue out front waiting to get in and we're checking it out now."

Her eyes slid over the people in line, looking for the tall brunette as she continued, "But if she isn't in the line up, which she probably isn't since she could control the doorman's mind and make him let her go in, then we'll have to move the search inside. But this place is really big. I'm guessing it holds well over a thousand people, and it will be dark and noisy and crowded inside and she'll be impossible to find. Please tell me the new coordinates are somewhere else and she was just passing by here."

"They are," Herb answered.

Inez let her breath out on a sigh of relief and scrambled to find her pen and notepad to write down the coordinates as he rattled them off.

"Tell Thomas I'm going to check her coordinates again while you two head over that way. If she's still at the new location, fine. But if she's moved on again, I think it might be smarter to leave it until morning. Once the sun rises she'll stay in one place."

"All right," Inez murmured with relief. She was tired and didn't relish the idea of running all over Amsterdam tonight in search of a woman who was proving to be a ghost.

Inez said goodbye and hit the off button and then glanced down at her purse as the sound of ringing came from its depths.

Thomas's phone, she realized and knew it would be Bastien checking on what was happening. Sighing, she grabbed Thomas's phone, dropped her own in the purse, and opened Thomas's.

"Hello?"

"Inez?" Bastien sounded startled that she was answering Thomas's phone and Inez grimaced, knowing she was going to have to lie. She hated lying.

"Thomas is in the bathroom," she said abruptly. "We've been running all over Amsterdam following Marguerite's phone and are about to check one more spot. If she isn't at this new stop, we're going to call it a night and wait until morning to try again. Hopefully, she'll settle in one spot then and we'll be able to catch up to her."

"Oh," Bastien said, sounding somewhat startled.

Inez grimaced, knowing it was her terse tone that had set him aback, but she couldn't help it. She was a rotten liar. She hated doing it and didn't do it well.

"All right then. I guess that makes sense," Bastien murmured finally. "Tell Thomas to keep me informed."

"I will. Good night," Inez murmured and quickly pressed the button to end the call before he could say anything else. Muttering under her breath then, she slipped the phone in her purse and then opened the map to figure out where she had to go to get to the next location. It appeared Marguerite was heading farther away from the town center and into quieter residential streets. Curious about that, she headed out to the next spot.

Ten minutes later, Inez found herself standing in a circle of light cast by a streetlamp on the edge of a dark, public park.

Shifting uncomfortably, she peered into the dark

tree-filled park, noting that a trio of young men were sitting on a bench near the center, laughing uproariously. They were loud, English, gregarious, and obviously drunk and she was reluctant to draw their attention by entering the park alone.

Having Thomas here would come in handy right now, Inez thought and wondered how he was doing. Had he woken up yet? Had he found the bags of blood she'd left lying beside him? Had he healed? The only way to find out was to call the hotel, but Inez didn't have any idea what the hotel number was. Exhausted as she was, it seemed a lot of trouble to her to figure out the number for information in Amsterdam, call, get the hotel phone number, and then call the hotel. It would be easier just to get this over with and head back. Besides, she knew she was just stalling about going into the park alone.

"Coward," she muttered under her breath, took one step out of the circle of light and halted again. Dark, empty parks weren't exactly on the top of her list of safe places to go. After hesitating another moment, Inez suddenly pulled out Thomas's phone. It was extremely quiet here away from the noisy town center and, other than the three men, the park looked empty to her, but if she were to call Marguerite's number and her cell phone was anywhere around here, Inez thought she'd probably hear it ring and be able to follow it. She searched Thomas's digital phonebook for Marguerite's cell phone number, and was about to press the button to call it when she heard a scuffling sound behind her.

Turning nervously, Inez found herself staring at an approaching man dressed all in black. For one minute she hoped it was Thomas, but then he stepped into the circle of light with her and she saw that he was the thin faced, dark-haired man she'd noted at one of the tables outside the restaurants earlier, the one who had looked familiar. She'd thought at the restaurant that she must have seen him in the airport, and she had, Inez suddenly realized, but not on the way to Amsterdam. He was the man who had stolen the taxi she'd hired to follow Thomas that morning after he'd left her standing in the airport, she realized suddenly and felt alarm begin to creep up her back.

Surely it couldn't be coincidence that she kept seeing the man? Inez thought, stepping back as he continued forward. And then her mind went blank.

The ringing phone forced Thomas back to consciousness. The first thing he became aware of was pain. It was a pain he recognized, the full body agony of the hunger for blood, the acid sensation of the nanos infiltrating organs and tissue in search of what they needed. He then opened his eyes and saw red. Literally. Thomas's vision was filled with red. It took a moment for him to realize he was staring at a bag of blood lying directly in front of his face. The moment he did, he felt his teeth shift and shot his hand up to grab the bag and shove it into them.

A slow, relieved sigh slid around the bag in his mouth as he felt the blood rushing up his teeth and into his system. His pain began to ease at once as the nanos rushed back into his blood stream to collect the fresh blood entering. Thomas just lay where he was, ignoring the phone as he waited for the first bag to empty. The moment it did, he pulled the bag free and replaced it with the second bag lying there.

It was as he waited for the second bag to empty that Thomas's brain began to function properly again. His first thought was to wonder how the bags had got there, and then to wonder where "there" was, and what he was doing wherever he was. It only took a quick glance around what he could see of the room to recognize the hotel suite. He was lying on his stomach on the floor, seriously depleted of blood. The second bag was nearly empty when he recalled the rest of the night and how he'd ended up where he was.

His own bloody stupidity was how he'd ended up there. No one had ever claimed horny men thought with their heads. Thomas could now verify this was true. He didn't think he'd used his head since realizing he'd consumed a bag of S.E.C. Attacking Inez in the alley, and then attacking three drunken idiots in a fit of jealousy . . .

First, he'd displayed his unnatural strength by lifting the blonde off his feet with one hand, and then he'd actually *flashed his fangs!*

Fortunately, Thomas didn't think anyone but the brunette had seen and no one was likely to believe the account of a half-drunk, half-stoned idiot.

Now that he was beginning to think again, Thomas was concerned about other things. Like, where was Inez? And was the knife still in his back? All it took was a quick glance over his shoulder to see that the knife was no longer protruding from his lower back. He then saw it lying on top of a towel next to a stack of three or four more fresh towels and a small pile of blood-soaked ones.

Obviously, Inez had removed the knife from his back and staunched the flow of blood, then retrieved a couple of bags for him, but where was she now? In her bed was his guess. She'd been exhausted and beginning to flag before they'd reached the small bevy of restaurants and bars where he'd had her sit at one of the tables to watch the entrances while he checked inside each.

Sighing, Thomas pulled the second, now empty, bag from his mouth and got carefully to his feet. There was only the slightest twinge from his back, telling him it was mostly healed. And the acidy cramps that had been attacking him from head to toe were much eased by the two bags, but he'd probably need another couple of bags at least before they were gone entirely. Moving to the cooler on the table, he retrieved a third bag and popped it to his teeth and then stood there with another bag in hand as he waited for this one to drain. He was about to switch bags when the hotel room phone began to ring.

Recalling that a phone's ringing was what had woken him, Thomas tore the empty bag from his teeth and moved to the end table beside the sofa to answer it before it woke Inez.

"Thomas!" Herb sounded relieved to hear his voice. "I was getting worried. I couldn't reach you on your cell phone or Inez's and was beginning to think the two of you had disappeared right alongside your aunt."

"No," Thomas assured him quietly and reached into his pocket for his cell phone, only to find that it was missing from his pocket. Startled, he felt each of his pockets in turn, wondering if he'd put it in one of the others, but there was no phone.

"Obviously you aren't at the park anymore. Did you find your aunt there?"

Thomas gave up looking for his phone and straightened, confusion flowing through him. "The park?"

"I checked a map, the location I sent you both to after the Escape night club should have been a park," Herb explained. "Did you go to the wrong place? Maybe Inez misheard what I said. It sounded like it was noisy where you were."

Thomas stood still for a minute and then barked, "Hang on."

Setting the phone down on the end table, he turned and strode into Inez's room. He didn't bother to turn on the lights, his night vision was exceptional and he could see the bed was still made and unslept in. Cursing, Thomas whirled to hurry out of the room, but froze as the bedroom door leading out into the hotel hall suddenly opened. Pausing, he glanced to the door. His breath came out on a sigh of relief as he recognized Inez's petite figure stepping inside, then the door closed again. Thomas immediately moved to flip on the light switch in the room. Light exploded around them as he turned to peer at Inez, and then he saw her face and froze. It was completely blank, no expression at all and her eyes were empty.

"Inez?" he said, approaching her carefully.

She didn't respond to either his presence or his voice until he was standing directly in front of her and then she simply moved around him, saying expressionlessly, "I'm very tired and have to go to bed now."

Thomas turned slowly and watched her walk to the bed. She immediately began to strip, apparently uncaring that he was there. He watched her undo and shrug out of her blouse, but then turned and left the room, his expression grim with concern as he returned to the living room and picked up the phone again.

"Herb, tell me everything that you know after I called you from the restaurants," he said grimly.

There was a moment of silence and then Herb said, "But you know what happened. I gave you the next location. It turned out to be a night club called Escape and—"

"You told me? Or you told Inez?" he asked quietly.

"Well, Inez. You were in the bathroom or something," Herb said and then fell silent for a moment before saying, "You weren't in the bathroom were you?"

"No. I was here at the hotel."

"But you didn't answer the first time I called. What—?"

"It doesn't matter now," Thomas interrupted grimly. "Just tell me what happened."

Herb explained about the Escape club and then sending Inez to the next spot in the park, ending with, "I checked the location again while she was on the way there, thinking that if your aunt had moved on again, we should call it a night and try at sunrise when she should stay in one spot, but it came back as the same location. However, when I tried to call you back on Inez's phone to tell you that, she didn't answer. So, I tried your phone again, and then I thought to try the hotel."

Thomas was silent for a moment, and then asked, "Is this your second try calling the hotel or your first?"

"First," Herb answered, sounding curious.

"The other call must have been Bastien, then," Thomas muttered.

"Inez didn't find Marguerite at the park, did she?" Herb asked.

"No, I don't think so," Thomas said, though he wasn't sure at this point that she hadn't.

"Do you want me to check her location again and—?"

"No," Thomas said quickly. He had no intention of leaving Inez alone to go looking for his aunt. At least, not until he was sure she was all right. It seemed obvious to him that someone had taken control of Inez. But why?

"No," he repeated. "We'll try again in the morning, at sunrise if that's all right with you?"

"That's fine," Herb assured him.

"Good. Thanks, Herb. I'll talk to you in the morning, then."

Thomas hung up quickly, eager to return to Inez to be sure she was all right, but he'd barely taken a step away from the phone before it began to ring again. Knowing it would be Bastien, and that he'd have to tell him what happened, Thomas grimaced as he picked up the phone and said hello.

"Thomas." Bastien sounded relieved and Thomas supposed he'd tried both cell phones before resorting to the hotel phone and—like Herb—had worried when he wasn't able to reach them. "Was she there at the last spot?"

Thomas hesitated, and then admitted, "I don't know if she was or not."

"What do you mean you don't know?" Bastien asked with confusion. "Either she was or she wasn't."

"I don't know," Thomas repeated and then explained the night's events to his cousin, ending with, "Inez was blank-faced when she came in and all she said was she was very tired and had to go to bed now, and then she started to strip right there in front of me, her expression still blank."

"Someone took control of her," Bastien said sounding grim.

"That would be my guess," Thomas agreed.

"You don't think Mother would have . . . ?" He didn't finish the question.

"I don't know, Bastien. I don't know what the hell is going on. Why isn't Aunt Marguerite answering her phone? She obviously has it on her. It isn't walking around Amsterdam on its own."

His older cousin was silent for a minute and then said, "I don't know, I'm too tired to even think right now."

"You should go to bed and get some rest," Thomas said quietly. "You haven't slept since I left Canada, have you?"

"No, but—"

"I don't want to leave Inez alone right now. Not until I'm sure that coming in and going right to bed is the only order whoever controlled her put in her mind."

"I wish you could read her memory to see what happened," Bastien muttered.

"If she has any memory of what happened," Thomas said quietly. "It may have been tampered with too. In fact, it probably was."

"Yes," Bastien agreed on a sigh. "Okay, I guess I'll go to bed, then, but call me as soon as you find out anything."

"I will," Thomas assured him and the two men said good night and both hung up.

Thomas finally slapped the fourth bag of blood to his teeth, and then a fifth. The bad news was he'd lost a lot of blood from the wound to his back. The good news was he'd lost a lot of blood from the wound to his back. Thomas was pretty sure the worst of the S.E.C. was out of his system. He certainly wasn't feeling horny right now, or if he was feeling a little, it was easily overcome by his worry for Inez.

Pulling the last bag from his teeth, he closed the cooler, and then quickly cleaned up the mess in the room, removing the knife and bloody towels. He'd have to toss the towels to prevent upsetting housekeeping, Thomas supposed. He retrieved the small clear garbage bag from the garbage can in his bathroom, put the towels and empty blood bags in, and then put his cooler on the upper shelf in his closet. Once assured that there was nothing left lying around to upset housekeeping, he went through the suite, locking all three doors leading out into the hall, the one in his room, the living room door, and finally hers.

Thomas then moved to the side of the bed to peer down at Inez. She was sleeping peacefully and he peered at her for the longest time, his eyes just drifting over her face; from her closed eyes, to her sweet nose, to her full lips, and back, and then he eased onto the bed beside her, settling himself on top of the blankets next to where she slept under them. Thomas really wasn't comfortable leaving her alone knowing that someone had taken control of her mind. He wanted to stay near to make sure it didn't happen again, and also to be close by in case she needed him.

Turning sideways on the bed, he watched her sleep, awed by the fact that he was lying there peering at the face of his very own lifemate. Despite the fact that Lissianna was four years younger than he and had found her own lifemate some years back, Thomas had expected to have to wait another century or so before finding his own lifemate. His male cousins had all been older when they'd finally found theirs. In fact, he was the youngest male Argeneau to find his lifemate that he knew of. And yet there she was. Inez Urso.

Thomas smiled faintly at the name. Urso was the one word he did know in Portuguese. It meant bear. He knew that because he'd had a friend with the same surname almost two centuries ago. A mortal friend, the only mortal friend he'd ever allowed himself. It was too hard to watch them age and die when you knew you yourself wouldn't. Thomas had grieved the man's passing, but now wondered if he might be an ancestor of Inez's. Whether he was or not, the name Urso suited her. She was like a little she-bear when in a temper. He actually liked that. He'd found it adorable when she was babbling away at him in Portuguese, her little finger waving. Mind you, he doubted he'd have found her quite as adorable if he'd understood what she was saying.

Reaching out, Thomas brushed a strand of hair away from her cheek thinking she reminded him of an old painting he'd once seen, and that he'd be happy to wake up to that face every morning for the rest of his life. Thomas actually liked everything about Inez so far. He liked her feistiness and her intelligence. He even found her shyness adorable, and she *was* shy. He hadn't realized that during their first meeting in New York. Inez had been the very personification of efficiency and command then, and she'd seemed to be pretty much in command and confident with him as well since he'd arrived in London, but he'd been coming out of the last bar when those three Brits had sat themselves at her table that night and her reaction hadn't been what he'd expected.

Thomas supposed any woman might have felt a little leery of having three drunks pester her, but Inez had been more than leery. At first, she'd seemed completely shocked that they'd chosen to bother her, as if she had no confidence in her attractiveness. And then she'd shrunk back in her seat as if trying to make herself disappear from view. He hadn't liked seeing her so obviously scared and uncomfortable, and that had been part of the reason he'd reacted as he had, that and the fact that she was his.

Of course, the S.E.C. probably hadn't helped, it certainly hadn't left him clearheaded enough to control himself and handle the situation as he should have. Or maybe he was fooling himself. Maybe his rage had been purely and simply because she was his lifemate. He had waited two hundred years for her and hadn't liked seeing any other man trying to chat her up.

Grimacing, Thomas ran a finger lightly over her cheek, smiling when Inez shifted sleepily and instinctively turned her cheek into the caress. It was something else he liked about her, her response to him. He liked the passion she'd revealed both times he'd kissed her; when he'd kissed her the first time in London and when he'd pretty much attacked her here in Amsterdam. Inez had more than met his passion. It boded well for their future . . . as long as he didn't screw it up and scare her off with he-man outbursts at bars or attacking her in alleys. So far, Thomas didn't think he was doing a very good job of wooing the woman. That was something he'd have to work on. She obviously had some issues when it came to her attractiveness and he'd work on that as well, he decided as his eyes slipped closed.

Inez shifted in her sleep and murmured a grumpy protest as she bumped against something, and then sighed and snuggled into the warmth offered as that something wrapped around her. It was the scent tantalizing her nose that finally forced her out from under those last veils of sleep. She blinked her eyes open and peered at the black before her with confusion until she realized it was a black T-shirt, and then glanced up to find herself peering at Thomas's sleeping face.

Inez sucked in a startled breath, her body stiffening with surprise, but not alarm. Alarm was curiously absent considering the circumstances, and the circumstances were that she had no idea how he had got there. In fact, she had no idea how *she* had got there either.

A glance around showed they were in her bedroom in the suite in Amsterdam, a glance down showed her that while Thomas was still completely dressed and sleeping on top of the covers, she was naked under the sheet and blankets covering her. However, she didn't recall going to bed. The last thing she remembered was heading out to search for Marguerite after . . .

Inez's gaze shifted to Thomas, looking him over with new concern as she recalled his being stabbed and her removing the knife from his back. He didn't look pale anymore, and obviously he must have recovered enough to get up and walk in here because there was no way she could have carried him. Still, she wanted to see the wound to be sure.

Easing away out from under the arm he had wrapped around her at some point in the night, Inez pressed the sheet and blankets to her chest and rose up slightly to bend over him and try to peer at his lower back where the knife had protruded. Thomas's T-shirt covered the spot. Biting her lip, she glanced to his behind and legs, noting the large blood stain darkening them, then reached out and gently tried to lift and move the bottom of his shirt. Unfortunately, it was stiff with blood and stuck to his skin and she glanced toward his face nervously as she lifted it away, afraid she'd wake him.

When Inez saw that his eyes were still closed, she finished shifting the material out of the way and peered at the spot where he'd been wounded the night before, her eyes widening as she saw that there was absolutely no sign of the injury anymore. Not even a tiny scar. The skin was completely unmarred, as smooth and unblemished as a newborn baby's behind.

"It's healed."

Inez jerked her head to the side to see that Thomas's eyes were now open, they were alert and it made her wonder if he'd been playing possum and been awake the whole time. Letting the T-shirt drop back into place, she eased away and then hesitated. Her first instinct was to get out of the bed, but she was naked and rather trapped there unless she wanted to flash Thomas. Inez was pretty sure she didn't want to do that. They may be lifemates and all that, but that didn't mean he'd see her through rose-colored glasses that would show him a long, leggy figure rather than her own imperfect one. At least, she didn't think it would.

"How are you feeling?" he asked, his voice having a slightly gravelly quality first thing in the morning.

"Me?" Inez asked with surprise. "I'm fine."

"Are you?" Thomas asked solemnly, his hand sliding soothingly up and down her upper arm.

Inez swallowed as she noted the sudden increase of silver in his eyes. Her body responded to it like a flower opening to the sun. She could feel her nipples hardening and a slow, warm liquid pooling in her lower body. Her eyes also reacted, taking on a sudden laziness that left them at a sleepy half-mast. Inez knew she wasn't the only one to notice the changes taking place when a slow satisfied, male smile curved his lips.

"I love the way you respond to me," Thomas said quietly. "I love your scent as you do."

Inez fought off the sudden urge to sniff her underarms and simply stared at him, unsure how to respond, and then his fingers slid from the outside of her upper arm to the inside, gliding perilously close to her breast. Her skin tingled as his fingers brushed lightly over it, and despite his not touching it, her breast did as well in a sort of anticipation.

"Your heart is racing," he whispered, his fingers gliding over the inside of her elbow and Inez knew he was right, it had sped up along with her breathing which was now shallow and rapid. "You want me."

Her eyes dilated at the simple words and embarrassment almost made her deny it, but instead she managed one short, slight nod. Thomas's smile widened with approval at her honesty as his fingers slid up her arm, but this time when they slid down, one finger shifted to tug at the top of the sheet and blankets she held to her chest. Unprepared for the move, she lost her hold on the material and it slipped out from under her fingers, pooling around her waist. Her breasts were suddenly bare and then his hand was there in place of the cloth, closing warm and firm around one.

Inez bit her lip and closed her eyes as Thomas caressed her and then opened her eyes in surprise when he suddenly sat up and replaced his hand with his mouth, his tongue hot and wet as it swirled around the nipple. He laved and teased her, alternating between sucking, licking, and nipping and sending little arcs of electricity shooting through her until she moaned aloud, and then let it slip from his mouth and raised his head to kiss her instead.

Inez kissed him back, her mouth opening to welcome him, her body leaning instinctively forward to press against his chest and then he was easing her back onto the bed, his mouth becoming more demanding before pulling away to slide to her cheek, and then her neck. Thomas followed her vein down to her collarbone, nipping teasingly as he went, and then lifted his head.

Inez blinked her eyes open to find him simply looking at her, his eyes blazing silver fire as they traveled over flesh suddenly covered with goose bumps. She stiffened and bit her lip to keep back a protest as he used one hand to sweep the sheet and blankets lower until they rested below her belly button so that he could see more of her. Her head was filling with all the flaws he must be seeing and how imperfect she was when he said, "Beautiful."

Inez's eyes widened incredulously at the pronouncement, but then he suddenly caught the hem of his T-shirt and lifted it off over his head and she was distracted by her first sight of his chest unclothed. Thomas, she decided, was the one who was beautiful. A work of art.

Reaching out tentatively, Inez ran one hand over the muscles of his chest as he tossed the stained T-shirt to the floor and then he turned to peer at her and caught her hand against his chest with his. Watching her face, he raised her hand to his lips and pressed a kiss to her fingers before slipping one into his mouth and suckling at it lightly.

Inez gasped lightly at the sensations that suddenly jolted through her as he drew the finger slowly out. He then released her hand and bent to kiss her again. He used one hand and arm to hold his weight off of her, but the fingers of the other hand moved over her body, caressing first one breast and then the other before sliding over her rounded stomach.

Inez clutched at his shoulders and moved her legs restlessly as his hand slid beneath the sheet and blankets and across her lower stomach to one hip as he kissed her. His hand paused there, fingers tightening slightly on the outer side of her hip as his thumb ran along the sensitive flesh on top and then it continued down along her outer leg, smoothing over skin she hoped to God wasn't stubbly.

When was the last time she'd shaved her legs? Inez wondered a bit frantically and realized it hadn't been for two days at least. Damn! There would be stubble. It would give a whole new meaning to her last name, which she thought was perfectly apt because—like a bear—she seemed to have a lot of hair. Honestly, she seemed to even grow it in her sleep. During the day was the worst, though, she sported a five o'clock shadow on her legs after shaving them in the morning. Why had she been cursed with this body? She should have been a tall, leggy blonde with—

"Aiyeee," Inez cried out, her eyes opening with shock as Thomas's hand suddenly closed over the very core of her. She'd been so distracted with her self criticisms she'd hadn't noticed that his caresses had stopped going down her outer leg and had started up the inside. She'd missed the whole upward journey . . . also missing that he'd broken their kiss and was now nibbling on her ear. She wasn't distracted now, however.

"Are you back with me?" Thomas asked with amusement as his hand glided over her warm core.

Inez nodded breathlessly, her hands digging into his shoulders as he caressed her.

He chuckled against her ear and then asked in a whisper. "Where were you? What were you thinking?"

Inez would have swallowed her own tongue before telling him the truth. Unfortunately it was impossible to come up with a lie with him doing what he was doing. Much to her relief she didn't end up having to, because the hotel phone chose that moment to begin ringing.

Thomas stiffened above her and cursed. Inez closed

her eyes and silently thanked God for the intervention and making sure Thomas would never know how close he'd come to getting whisker burn on his hands from her legs. Releasing his shoulder, she reached out swiftly and snatched up the phone to draw it to her ear.

"Good morning?" Inez said with a cheer that made Thomas jerk his head up with surprise.

"Good morning, Inez," Bastien said, sounding crisp and well rested. "How are you feeling?"

Her eyebrows rose at the sudden turn in his voice. The question had sounded solemn and concerned, but she had no idea why he'd be concerned about her. That had been Thomas's first question too, she realized now and frowned to herself.

"I— What happened last night?" Inez asked with sudden apprehension as she searched her memories and found she had no recall of going to bed last night.

Bastien hesitated and then asked, "Don't you remember?"

"No," she admitted, feeling suddenly sick. Taking the phone from her ear before he could say anything else, she handed it to Thomas and then scooted off the bed, dragging the sheet and blankets with her and nearly rolling Thomas to the floor as she did.

Wrapping them around herself toga style, Inez hurried into the bathroom and slammed the door behind her. She stood there in the dark for a moment, trying to calm down. Her stomach had always reacted to her upset, and if she didn't calm down she was likely to be kneeling over the toilet retching in a minute.

Closing her eyes, Inez concentrated on her breathing, forcing herself to breathe more slowly. When she thought she had herself at least a little calmer, she felt along the wall beside her until she found the light switch and then flicked it on. Inez blinked in the sudden explosion of light and then peered at herself in the mirror. The sheet and blanket were gathered around her in a lopsided collection, her hair was wild about her head, and her eyes were a little wild and a lot scared.

"Why don't I remember coming back to the hotel and going to bed last night?" she asked herself silently. The answer she was afraid of was that she didn't remember because someone had taken those memories away . . . and the only people she knew who could do that were immortals, but who and why? The fact that she'd landed back here in her own bed in their hotel with Thomas lying beside her worried Inez. If she'd found Marguerite, the woman could have controlled her, but why? Why would any immortal want to control her and put her in her bed with Thomas? Except maybe Thomas. He'd been suffering under the effects of the Sweet Ecstasy Concentrate last night. Had he . . . ?

Inez killed the thought before it was fully formed, but she was terrified that the truth was that Thomas could read and control her after all. Maybe they weren't lifemates at all.

Nine

"Is Inez all right? She sounded upset."

Thomas forced his eyes away from the bathroom door and turned his attention to the phone in his hand. Pressing it more firmly to his ear, he said, "I think she realizes she's been controlled."

"That usually only happens if they don't put in a replacement memory," Bastien said slowly.

Thomas grunted acknowledgment. "I wonder why they wouldn't have?"

"Maybe they wanted her to know."

Thomas stiffened at the suggestion. "Why would they want that?"

A long silence passed as they both considered what might be behind Inez being controlled, but it seemed obvious neither of them could come up with a reason.

"We won't be able to solve this," Bastien acknowledged unhappily.

"No," Thomas agreed. "At least not until we find Aunt Marguerite."

"Speaking of which," Bastien murmured. "I know I was supposed to wait for you to call me, and I have been waiting most patiently. But when it got so late, I thought maybe—"

Thomas cursed as his eyes hit the bedside clock and he saw that it was well after ten A.M. He'd slept longer than he'd intended.

"Thomas?"

"I slept in," he admitted unhappily as he sat up. His gaze slid to the bathroom door as he heard the shower come on, and then he assured him, "I'll call Herb right now and head out as soon as he has coordinates for me."

Hanging up, he quickly punched in Herb's number. The immortal had always kept odd hours, working well into the morning at times if he got into his programming. Fortunately, this was one of those days and he didn't have to apologize for waking him.

After hanging up, Thomas stood and paced around the room as he waited for Herb to call back with coordinates. With nothing else to distract him, his mind immediately turned to Inez in the shower. She would be naked and wet in there, warm water spraying down over her body as she ran the soap over herself. He'd like to do that for her. Actually, he'd rather build up a lather between his own hands and then run them over her soft skin, across her breasts, along her sides, over her behind, between her legs . . . Thomas managed to get himself quite worked up with his imaginings and was on the verge of rushing into the bathroom to turn them into reality when the phone rang.

Shaking the seductive thoughts aside, he hurried to the phone to answer it.

Herb gave him the new coordinates at once and then asked, "Are you heading out right away?"

"No," Thomas admitted slowly, a little startled by the question. "I have to shower first and dress. It probably won't be for another ten minutes. Why?"

Herb hesitated and then said, "Because I want to call and check the coordinates again when you leave."

"Again?" Thomas asked, his eyebrows rising. "Why? She should be sleeping now and staying in one place, that's why we left it until morning."

"I know, but I checked these coordinates on a street map of Amsterdam that lists buildings in the area and it's not a hotel, it's a strip of cafés."

"That's not right." Thomas dropped back on the bed with dismay. "Aunt Marguerite isn't a day person. Why would she be out at this hour?"

"You said she was over here in Europe on a case, maybe that's forced her to work during the day," Herb suggested.

"I suppose," Thomas said with a frown. "I don't know much about being a private detective, but they might be checking records and so on and those offices would hardly be open at night—. Could you double check the coordinates, Herb?"

"I did," he assured him. "I actually triple checked them before calling you."

"Oh," Thomas said unhappily.

"I know, it doesn't feel right," Herb muttered. "But if they are having to work during the day . . . You said her partner was mortal. They may have stopped to feed him."

"Yeah, that's possible," Thomas agreed.

"Right. Call me just before you leave and I'll track it again to double check. That way, if she isn't there when you reach the coordinates, you can just move on to the next set I come up with."

"Right. Thank you, Herb. I appreciate all your help with this," Thomas said, but he was still frowning as he hung up. Something wasn't right.

His gaze slid to the closed bathroom door with new concern as his wonder about Inez being controlled and having her memory erased collided with the game of hide-and-seek they were playing with Marguerite. Why hadn't his aunt contacted her family? She had to still have her phone on her to be moving around constantly. Had Inez found her at that park? Was Marguerite the one who had erased her memory? What the hell was going on?

Standing, Thomas crossed the room to the door, tapped lightly, and when he got no reply, eased it open.

"Inez?" he called, stepping into the room. His gaze slid to the small shower room at the end of the bathroom, and shower room was the proper term. Showers here were not enclosed little cubes like those back home, they were small ceramic-tiled rooms with a floor with a drain in the center. The showerheads were huge, dropping water down like a rain cloud. Thomas had always liked showers here. Now he peered at the closed beveled glass shower door, his eyes swimming over the flesh-colored blur that was Inez.

"Inez," he repeated, moving to stand in front of the

door when he realized she hadn't heard him over the water.

She heard him this time. He saw her whirl to face him and saw the shape of her blur change as her hands instinctively covered the important bits. Thomas smiled faintly, imagining the startled, alarmed look on her face. A day would come when she wasn't so self-conscious around him in the nude. He would see to that. She had a beautiful body, short but shapely and would probably keep most of that shape after her turning, thank God. He'd never been attracted to stick-thin anorexic types and couldn't understand men who were. A woman was supposed to have curves and a little meat on them that could offer comfort to a man. At least, that was his opinion.

"Thomas?" Inez said uncertainly. He knew she wasn't questioning whether it was him or not. Who else would be in their suite? What she was asking was what he was doing in here.

"Inez, can you tell me what happened last night?" he asked, and then added solemnly, "It's important.

Another moment of silence followed and then she said, "You collapsed when we got back to the hotel room. I removed the knife from your back, went through a couple towels putting pressure on the wound until you stopped bleeding, then fetched a couple bags of blood, but couldn't figure out how to feed them to you. I didn't want to turn you on your back to lay on your wound, but couldn't feed you the way you were, and then Herb called with new coordinates."

"You didn't tell him what had happened," Thomas pointed out.

"No. I didn't know if you'd be in trouble for flashing your teeth in public and then giving away your strength and speed," she admitted.

Thomas grimaced at the knowledge that she'd seen him flash his fangs, but said, "Thank you."

"Anyway, he had new coordinates and so I put the two bags of blood beside you to find when you woke up and went out to the new spot. It was in front of a night club and I knew there was no way I could search it by myself, so it was a relief when he called again with new coordinates. Bastien called right after him, and I just told him we were still tracing Marguerite's cell and headed out. I walked a couple blocks farther on to a park."

"And then?" Thomas prompted when she fell silent.

"And then I woke up naked in bed with you beside me," Inez said.

Thomas frowned at the tone of her voice. She sounded uncertain and even frightened. He understood why when she spoke again.

"You didn't control me and wipe my memory, did you Thomas?"

"No," he said firmly, wishing she could see his face and see the truth there. "I already told you I can't either read or control you."

There was a moment of silence and then she asked, "So we really are lifemates, then?"

Thomas stiffened, his eyes straining to see through the beveled glass. "You know about that?"

He saw her shoulders rise and fall in a shrug. "The guy who delivered the blood explained it to me. I kind of blackmailed him into it," she admitted.

Thomas shifted from one foot to the other, his

hand raising toward the handle of the shower door and then dropping away. Finally, he asked, "Are you upset?"

"About what?" Inez asked with confusion, and he supposed there were several things to be upset about here. Being controlled and having her mind wiped, being his lifemate, waking up to find him in bed with her uninvited.

"About being my lifemate," Thomas explained and then held his breath as he waited for her answer.

Inez stared through the beveled glass at Thomas's outline. She could see that he was still bare-chested, wearing only his jeans as he had when she'd left him. She couldn't see his expression, but could hear the worry in his voice and that surprised her. She must be misunderstanding the tone of his voice, Inez decided. Perhaps the noise of rushing water and the shape of the bathroom were distorting sound. She bit her lip and then said tentatively. "You sound worried."

"I am," Thomas acknowledged.

Her eyes widened at the prompt, unselfconscious admission. "Why? You're handsome, intelligent, and sweet. Women must flock to you in droves. What do you care if—"

"Inez," he interrupted solemnly. "None of those other women matter. I can control them and read their thoughts. They're like pretty little blow-up sex dolls to me and every other immortal that can read and control them. They're puppets we can make do what we want.

"There was a time when that was enough," Thomas admitted. "I was young enough once to be pleased to have a pretty woman on my arm and in my bed even if she was nothing more than a puppet. But that passed pretty quickly. It was hard to be pleased to have a pretty woman on my arm when I could read her thoughts and knew she was thinking that I was cute enough, but the best thing was that I had money and could buy her whatever she wanted, or that while I was cute, she preferred blondes, or that she hoped to God I didn't expect her to ruin her figure by 'dropping babies,' or she hoped I was into S&M because she'd really like me to spank her, or . . . God, you wouldn't believe some of the things women think. Or men for that matter. They may just be passing thoughts, but it detracts quickly from their attractiveness when you can hear every one, and some of them can be hurtful even when they aren't meant to be.

"I've waited two hundred years for you, Inez. For a woman who's beautiful and intelligent and her own person, someone I can't read or control and who can't read and control me. A woman who can stir my passions like you do and whose passion I can enjoy without hearing her litany of worries about whether I think her butt is too big, or her breasts too small."

Inez bit back the sudden laugh that tried to burst past her lips as she recalled her own worries while Thomas had been caressing her. Despite her worries about being controlled and having her memory wiped and whether Thomas had done it, the first thing she'd done on getting into the shower was shave her legs and under her arms. Inez was terribly glad he hadn't been able to read her thoughts while she'd been worried about stubble on her legs, but was also glad to know she wasn't the only one who had worries like that in her head at such intimate moments.

"Yes, I'm worried. Actually, that's putting it mildly. Truthfully, I'm scared shitless. I'm afraid you won't find me as attractive as I find you, that my personality and lifestyle are too easygoing for a woman who is usually so competent and confident in business, that—"

"I'm not always confident and competent," Inez admitted, worried that he might lose some of his attraction to her when he realized she wasn't the perfect woman he was describing. Still, he would find this out soon enough and if they were to be lifemates. "I am at work, but socially I'm less so. I'm— I know I'm smart and good at what I do at work, but personally and socially . . ."

"I suspected as much when I saw how you reacted to those three men joining you at the table," Thomas admitted. "But most people aren't as confident as they may appear. Besides, that will change after the turn. The nanos keep you at your peak condition. You'll know you're the perfect you and have more confidence because of it."

Inez didn't hear anything beyond *that will change after the turn.* Those words reverberated in her head and when he fell silent, she asked, "After the turn?"

"If you agree to be my lifemate, Inez, you're agreeing to become an immortal, to live out your life with me," he said quietly. "Some immortals don't insist on their lifemate turning if she or he doesn't wish to. They spend what little time one lifetime allows because its all they can have. But I won't do that, Inez.

I don't want you for forty or fifty years. It will just hurt that much more when I lose you. I would insist on your becoming immortal too."

Inez just stood there, his words echoing in her head. She hadn't considered that he'd expect her to turn. Miss Details had missed that one. Actually, she hadn't even really thought about the fact that it was possible. She'd been too enraptured by the idea that here was a ready-made mate without the necessity for a long, drawn-out courtship that she could possibly bungle as she'd bungled so many relationships in the past.

The biggest complaint Inez had heard from past boyfriends had been that she was always working and hardly spent any time with them, yet she hadn't thought of work once since meeting Thomas, she realized. Perhaps she'd just needed the right man to distract her and she'd have to say Thomas was a great distraction. However, she'd have to become like him to have him; an immortal.

Inez considered the idea, trying to imagine living for hundreds of years . . . with Thomas. Oddly enough, the idea of living centuries was rather daunting until she added the "with Thomas" part. It was still daunting, but . . .

Who was she kidding? Inez thought grimly. It was more than daunting. Living centuries might sound like a great idea on first hearing it, but Inez instinctively looked for the problems inherent in any plan. It was why she was so good at what she did. She spotted possible future problems and did what she could to prevent them from being problems before they even cropped up.

Inez was seeing a lot of possible problems with being immortal. His people had to remain hidden, unnoticed by the mortals around them. She imagined that put a lot of restrictions on them as a whole.

There was also the fact that she would have to watch her own family age and die while she didn't. Inez knew instinctively that this would be difficult for her. While she didn't live close to her family at the moment because of her job, she loved them dearly and called and even visited often. Inez knew she would experience guilt and helplessness as they aged, and with her take-charge and fix-it attitude would want to fix things so they didn't. Somehow she didn't think she'd be allowed to turn her whole family, but could she not?

And then there was that whole blood deal. Inez had never really thought of herself as squeamish, but the idea of consuming several bags of blood every day for the rest of her very long life was just gross.

"Inez?" Thomas spoke so quietly she almost didn't hear him.

Her gaze focused on the blurred image beyond the glass and Inez almost sighed. Here was temptation; this beautiful man with his perfect face and perfect body and lovely silver blue eyes. Not to mention his tantalizing kisses and caresses. She wanted him, but knew it was like wanting the chocolate sundae without the calories. Unfortunately, the bad came with the good. But maybe she could have just a bite of the sundae while she considered whether she could stomach the calories that came with the rest of it.

"I don't expect you to make up your mind right now," Thomas said. "But—"

His voice died as Inez pushed the shower door open

so that they faced each other with nothing between them. Forcing herself not to drop into a huddle to try to hide her too generous figure, she said, "I think I need to get to know you better to make such an important, life-long decision."

Thomas's eyes flared silver as his gaze slid over her, and then he started forward, coming to an abrupt halt when Inez put out her hand to stop him. He frowned with confusion until she said, "Your jeans."

Glancing down as if he'd forgotten he was wearing them, Thomas reached for his belt buckle, but then stopped. He stood like that for a moment, his head bowed, hands still on his belt, long enough that Inez began to worry that he'd changed his mind and didn't want her. Finally, he raised his head and reached out to tug her to the lip of the shower so he could kiss her hungrily.

Sighing with relief, Inez melted against him, her arms twining around his head as she kissed him back. He ended the kiss slowly, raising one hand to run it over her wet hair and cup her head as she blinked her eyes open.

"I want you," he growled.

Inez nodded. She wanted him too. That was the one thing she was sure of.

"But Herb gave me new coordinates and we don't have a lot of time."

Inez drooped with disappointment as she realized he was rejecting her, but he continued.

"And I don't want our first time to be rushed, or interrupted, or while I'm distracted. I want it to be special and slow. I want to give you the attention and time you deserve."

Inez swallowed, feeling tears suddenly glaze her eyes at his words. He was such a sweet considerate man . . . and right at that minute she almost wished he wasn't. She didn't want consideration. Inez wanted hot sweaty sex in the shower. She wanted to know beyond a shadow of a doubt that this man wanted her as much as she wanted him.

"I want to do this so that I can give you so much pleasure that you can't resist agreeing to be my life-mate," Thomas added, and his words along with the grin suddenly splitting his lips made her own lips tip reluctantly into a smile.

So, okay, maybe he wasn't rejecting her. The man was plotting her seduction as carefully as she would plan the take over of a company. No one had said Thomas was stupid. Right at that moment Inez thought she might agree to being an immortal just to get his pants off. Probably not a smart way to make the decision, she acknowledged. Act in haste; repent at leisure as they said, so she wouldn't try to tempt him to change his mind. She'd accept his decision and spend some time getting to know him better and considering the pros and cons of becoming his lifemate . . . and an immortal.

Her thoughts died an abrupt death and she jerked in surprise as he suddenly slapped her wet behind.

"So finish your shower and get dressed. We have to get moving."

"I'm done in the shower," she said, straightening away from him as his arms slipped away. "You can take it over if you like. The water's already warm."

"I think I will," Thomas said and then glanced around and frowned. "You have no towels in here."

"Oh." She tsked with exasperation at her lack of forethought. "I took them out to the living room last night. I'll go get them and bring one for you too—" Her words died and her eyes widened in surprise as Thomas suddenly urged her back under the shower.

"Stay there and keep warm. I'll fetch the towels," he said and closed the door.

Inez stared through the beveled glass as he zoomed out of the room and then shook her head and closed her eyes as the water rushed over her. He really was a very considerate man. That was very important. Of course, men were often more considerate when wooing a woman than they were once they'd landed her, but even if Thomas's consideration dropped in half later, he'd still be far more considerate than any of the mortal men she'd known in her life. Inez supposed she had Marguerite to thank for that.

Her thoughts turned to the missing woman and her hunt for her last night. Thomas had said that he hadn't controlled her or wiped her memory, but someone had. She was beginning to think there was a lot more going on here than any of them suspected.

Until now, Inez had half suspected Marguerite Argeneau had just got busy, perhaps following a hot lead on this case she was on, and forgot to call her family. After all, three days without contact wasn't really that long. These were her children, not a husband or life partner. Inez only called her own mother once a week, usually on Sundays because the rates were cheaper and she had to call all the way to Portugal. They were usually long phone calls and she made them religiously, but . . .

Of course, the Argeneaus probably didn't worry much about cost. Still, the woman was in Europe and they were back in Canada so surely three or four days without a call shouldn't send her family into a panic. Even if she lived in Portugal, Inez wouldn't worry if her own mother didn't call her for three days.

That had been what she'd been thinking before this, but now Inez was beginning to fear she'd been wrong in that assumption. She was beginning to suspect the woman might be in trouble. Someone had taken control of her and kept her from calling Marguerite's phone and finding her. She doubted very much if it had been Marguerite herself. That meant someone else had and she couldn't think of any good reason for an immortal to want to keep her from finding Marguerite and setting her family's minds at ease.

The shower door suddenly opened, breaking her train of thought and Inez smiled with gratitude when she saw Thomas holding up a bath towel for her. He held it open for her to step into, which she did.

"Thank you," Inez whispered as he closed the towel around her.

"Anytime, beautiful," Thomas said lightly, pressing a kiss to her forehead before stepping away. "Now stop standing here all wet and tempting and go get dressed so I can shower."

"Yes, sir," Inez said with a grin as she moved passed him to leave the room. At the door she paused and glanced back to ask, "You didn't want help getting those nasty jeans off, did you?"

Inez grinned as the silver flared in his eyes at the very idea, but Thomas shook his head and one finger at her at the naughty thought. "I'm going to start calling you apple."

Inez wrinkled her nose. "Why? Because I'm short and round?"

"No. Because you're the apple sent to tempt me," he announced and then added solemnly, "And you are tempting, Inez. If you knew all the things I want to do to you right now. . . ." He shook his head and then apparently decided to tell her. "Right now I'd like nothing more than to peel away that towel, lick and nibble away every drop of liquid I see on your skin, and then—"

"Okay, I'm going to get dressed now," Inez said a little faintly, her gaze dropping instinctively to his jeans and widening as she saw the bulge there. She wasn't the only one affected by the images he'd presented.

"Go," Thomas growled, the word almost a warning.

Nodding, Inez turned quickly away and hurried out into the bedroom. Her skin was covered with goose bumps and little shivers were licking down her back, and she suspected once they did get together, whether it was fast and desperate or slow torture as he did all he wanted to do to her, by the time it was over she'd be hard-pressed not to agree to anything he wanted.

Shaking her head, Inez moved to the closet and quickly selected a pair of dress slacks and a pure white blouse. There wasn't a pair of jeans or T-shirt in the closet, but that didn't matter, Inez didn't wear jeans, they made her butt look big. She didn't wear T-shirts either, feeling they emphasized her overgenerous bust.

Dropping the towel, Inez quickly dressed, listening to the sound of the shower as she did.

Thomas turned off the shower and opened the door to step out, stopping when he saw Inez at the bathroom counter. She'd brushed her hair and was pulling the damp strands back into a ponytail. He saw her eyes slide over him and then widen as they dropped below. Blushing furiously, she turned quickly back to the mirror.

Thomas smiled faintly as he reached for the second towel he'd brought in earlier and wrapped it around himself, but didn't say anything to increase her embarrassment. Her reaction was because he was still sporting a very healthy erection. He wanted to blame it on the S.E.C. he'd consumed last night, but knew that was out of his system now. She, however, wasn't and—judging by what he'd seen with other true lifemates—wouldn't be out of his system ever. Oh, there might come a time, centuries down the road, when he could look at her without wanting to pin her against the nearest surface and give her "a good seeing to" as the British liked to say. But he would still want her, just in a more gentle, mellow fashion without all the desperation presently claiming him.

Right now he couldn't even think of the woman without "little Thomas" perking up with interest. It was really rather disconcerting.

"I'm going to go get dressed," he said brushing his fingers lightly down her back as he passed and smiling when she shivered in response. That was one good thing about all this; at least he wasn't alone in his need. Inez wanted him just as badly, he knew. Thomas could smell her hunger for him in the pheromones pouring off her body every time he got near.

Thomas hurried from her room and into his own, passing through the door just as the phone began to ring. Turning to the bedside table, he snatched up the phone, saying a cheerful, "Yo?"

"Thomas?"

He stiffened at the urgency in Bastien's voice. "Yes."

"You have to get moving. You have to find Mother."

Thomas felt his hand clench around the phone. "What's happened?"

"We've been calling Mother on her cell phone," Bastien said grimly. "None of us have been getting answers, but Etienne got the idea of trying during the daytime when she would be sleeping and couldn't miss the call. He apparently checked the Internet last night and found out what time sunrise was in Amsterdam and then called fifteen minutes after that."

Thomas waited, trepidation creeping up his back. He knew bad news was coming.

"The phone was answered this time," Bastien said grimly. "But not by Mother. A man with a British accent answered. He cussed out Etienne for the constant calls we've all been making, told him to 'bugger off' and stop calling or he'd—I quote—'Kill the bitch' and then he hung up."

Thomas sucked in a breath of combined rage and worry and then snatched up the knapsack he'd left lying on his bed and began dragging out fresh clothes one-handed. "I'm dressing right now. I'll be on the street in three minutes. I'll find her Bastien," he vowed grimly.

Thomas didn't wait for Bastien to say goodbye or hang up, but slapped the phone back in its cradle and snatched it back right away as he punched in Herb's number.

"I'm heading out now," he announced abruptly, not bothering with a greeting. "Can you check the coordinates again and get back to me if they're different?"

The moment Herb agreed, Thomas said thanks and hung up.

"Inez!" he shouted as he whipped off his towel and dragged on a clean pair of jeans.

"Yes?"

He glanced up as she came rushing into the room, concern on her face.

"Are you ready?" Thomas asked, doing up his pants. "We have to move."

"I'm ready," Inez assured him, patting the purse hanging from her shoulder. "What's happened?"

"Etienne got through on Aunt Marguerite's phone," he said as he grabbed the T-shirt he'd pulled out and tugged it on over his head. "Some guy answered and said if we didn't stop calling he'd kill her. We have to find her before he does something to her."

Inez nodded solemnly and he could feel her watching him as he pulled on a pair of socks and slipped his feet into a pair of casual Merrells.

"Do you think this man who answered Marguerite's phone is the one who took control of me and wiped my memory?"

Thomas glanced sharply her way. Her voice had sounded vulnerable and she looked upset. He didn't blame her. It would be very upsetting to know that someone had taken control of your mind and then wiped the memory of whatever had happened from your thoughts. Anything could have been done to her and she wouldn't now know about it. Stepping in front of her, Thomas pulled her to his chest and rubbed her back soothingly.

"I don't know," he admitted softly and then said flatly, "But if he is, he'll be sorry."

Ten

"This is the spot."

Inez looked slowly over the five or six restaurants in a row. Each had a grouping of tables and chairs outside. They were presently filled with people enjoying a late breakfast in the sunlight, or under the shade offered by the large umbrellas over each table.

Mouth thinning, she peered over the sea of faces, and then glanced up toward the sky where the sun shone brightly down, and finally to Thomas beside her. Worry drew her eyebrows together. He'd binged on six bags of blood before they'd left the hotel. He'd also pulled on a hat, sunglasses, and a long-sleeved shirt that was now buttoned all the way to the top to protect him as much as possible from the sun's damaging rays, but she knew it wasn't enough. He really shouldn't be out here at all, but had refused to listen when she'd suggested going by herself.

Thomas's refusal to even consider the suggestion had left her both upset and relieved. Inez was upset because she knew he really shouldn't be out here, but relieved because after being controlled the night before, she feared it happening again and really didn't want to go anywhere alone.

"I don't see her," Thomas said with frustration, and Inez turned her gaze back to the crowd, running her eyes more slowly over them, searching each table for Marguerite Argeneau.

"I don't either," she said at last. "But then if she's being held against her will, they aren't likely to take her out in public."

"No," Thomas muttered, his mouth tightening. "But whoever has her has her phone, and he shouldn't be out here either."

Inez glanced at him, eyebrows rising. "Why not?"

"He has to be immortal too," he pointed out. "And most wouldn't sit out in the sunlight like this."

Inez opened her mouth to ask why it had to be an immortal, but then realized that with the whole mind-control thing, no mortal could keep an immortal where they didn't want to be. That suggested that either Marguerite was dead, badly injured and without the strength necessary to take control of a mortal, or she was being held by an immortal who had a mortal working for him, and it was the mortal who had the phone and was seated here in the sun, eating a leisurely brunch. She was hoping it was the last option.

"The person with her phone could be anyone . . .

If her phone is even still here," she pointed out as his phone began to ring.

Thomas tugged the cell out of his pocket, flipped it open, listened, grunted an "okay," and then slapped it closed.

"That was Herb. It's still here," he announced, slipping the phone back into his pocket.

Inez was silent, her eyes scanning the sea of faces, but she had no idea who she was looking for. "You're going to have to call and see who answers the phone."

"No," Thomas said at once. "He threatened to kill Aunt Marguerite if we keep calling."

"He can't kill her if she isn't here with him," Inez pointed out reasonably. "And after you call and figure out who he is, you can read his mind to see where she is and we can go get her."

"Not if he's an immortal," Thomas pointed out unhappily. "If he's older than me, I won't be able to read him."

"But an immortal isn't likely to be out here," she argued.

"Not likely, no," he agreed. "But not impossible. I'm here."

"Yes, but— Never mind," she interrupted herself. "We'll call him and if he's mortal, you read him and find out where she is. If he's immortal and you can't read him, we keep our distance and follow him back to wherever he's staying."

"What if he's inside one of the restaurants instead of outside?" Thomas asked, his eyebrows threaded with worry.

Inez hesitated and then sighed. "We'll have to take the chance."

Thomas turned on her sharply, eyes flashing with anger.

"Surely if he was inside, the coordinates would have been on the next street over where the restaurant fronts are," she pointed out quietly. "This is behind the buildings. And to safeguard things, I can call. My number won't be on her phone. He won't know it's a family member. He might not blame her for it." She let him think about that and then added, "It's either that or we follow the phone around all day again and hope he goes somewhere where he'd be completely alone and we can figure out who he is, but I don't think the chances of that are very good in a crowded city like Amsterdam."

Thomas blew a weary breath out and then nodded once, grimly. "Make the call. Maybe we'll get lucky and he'll think it's a wrong number."

Inez nodded solemnly and quickly punched in the number he rattled off, but didn't press the button to start the call, instead she glanced at Thomas and said, "I think you should take one half of the restaurant tables and I should take the other half. If we positioned ourselves halfway along our portion of the restaurant seats, it would give us a better chance of hearing where the ring comes from when I call."

Thomas nodded and abruptly turned away, only to immediately swing back. He gave her a quick, hard kiss and then growled, "Be careful."

Inez smiled faintly as she watched him walk to the other end of the groupings of tables until he was at about the three-quarter point. She then moved herself to the quarter point and glanced down at her phone. The air was full of the sound of people talking and the clink of dishes, but there were no phones ringing at that moment. Taking a deep breath, she pushed the button to dial Marguerite's number and then glanced up. A bare second later a phone began to ring, playing some sort of jazzy digital sound.

Eyes sharpening, Inez glanced quickly over the tables and was just skipping her gaze over one of the nearer tables when one of the young men seated there pulled something from his pocket. A cell phone. He peered at the caller ID, cursed and then muttered with disgust, "Stupid phone! It's always ringing."

"Why don't you toss it or change the chip or something?" one of his buddies suggested.

The fellow with the phone shrugged. "Because until they shut it down it's free calls for me, isn't it?"

Inez snapped her phone closed and the ringing immediately stopped. She watched grimly as the young man slid the phone back in his pocket.

"He's mortal," Thomas growled as he joined her.

Inez nodded, but remained silent as he concentrated his gaze on the young man. Knowing he was reading him, she waited patiently, but bit her lip worriedly when she saw his expression turn down with displeasure. He didn't like whatever he was learning. That couldn't be good for Marguerite.

She glanced toward the table of men, eyes widening when she saw the one with the phone suddenly stand and murmur something to his friends and then head away from the table and toward them. Inez felt her alarm increase with every step he took toward them. It wasn't the fact he approached so much as the fact that his face was oddly expressionless as he did. She suspected Thomas was controlling him.

"Thomas," she hissed, afraid he intended to do something to the man right there in front of everyone. She'd seen him lose control in public the night before, and didn't want to see it again. When he didn't respond, she glanced nervously back to the young man, blinking as she realized he wasn't approaching them at all, but walking past them.

"Grab us a table and order us both breakfast, please, Inez. I'll be right back."

"But——" She watched with concern as Thomas walked away around the corner after the mortal, then let her breath out on a sigh and turned to survey the busy tables. There were two available. One outside the nearest restaurant and one farther down by where Thomas had been standing when she'd placed the call. The farther one was in the shade, however, so Inez settled herself there. She took the seat that gave her the best view of the corner and then stared fixedly in that direction until a waitress appeared at her elbow, distracting her.

Inez took the menu offered, glanced over it quickly and ordered two full breakfasts and two cappuccinos and then returned to watching the corner as the woman left her alone. Thomas seemed to be gone a long time, but then that might have been just because she was worried. When she finally saw him coming back around the corner, he was alone and looked just as unhappy as he'd been when he left. He was also talking on his cell phone. To Bastien, no doubt, Inez thought as she watched him walk toward her.

Thomas finished his conversation and snapped his phone closed just as he reached the table.

"What happened?" she asked worriedly as he settled in the chair next to hers.

Thomas put his own phone away, even as he set a second one on the tabletop. "I got Marguerite's phone back."

Inez stared at it blankly and then glanced to Thomas to ask, "What about your aunt?"

"Good question," he said wearily and then explained, "The mortal and a friend mugged Aunt Marguerite outside the Dorchester a couple days ago. Apparently, there were two cell phones in the purse, a sizeable bit of money, and credit cards. He took one phone, the buddy took the other, and they split the cash."

"What about the credit cards?" Inez asked.

Thomas grimaced. "They're just small-time thieves. They had no idea what to do with them. They tried to get their girlfriends to go out and run them up, but they're obviously Canadian credit cards and both women are British, with British accents, and were afraid of getting caught. When they refused, the cards were tossed.

"Aunt Marguerite had about three thousand pounds in her purse," he added dryly and cursed. "I'm forever warning her about carrying around large sums of money, but she just laughs and says, who could rob her? Well now she knows."

"How *did* they rob her?" Inez asked. "Your people are supposed to be stronger and faster."

Thomas shifted impatiently. "We're stronger and faster, but even we can't outrun motorcycles. He and the buddy apparently had a good thing going, riding along the street until they saw a woman who looked like she had money and appeared distracted. His buddy would steer the bike up onto the sidewalk, he'd hook his arm through the strap, and away they'd go."

Inez stared at him wide-eyed.

"I gather they hurt one of the tourists they mugged, though," Thomas went on. "She either got tangled up in, or wouldn't let go of, the purse and got badly burned when they dragged her for a block or so before he had the sense to let go of it himself. A hurt tourist is a bad thing in London, a city where tourism is so lucrative. The police started hunting for them, so it seemed to him like a good idea to take the little windfall he'd got courtesy of Aunt Marguerite and split to Amsterdam for a while to mug tourists here."

Inez sat back in her seat with dismay. "You mean we came here for——"

"Nothing," he finished with a weary nod. "This whole trip to Amsterdam and playing hop-scotch across town tracking and chasing her cell phone has been a complete waste of time."

Inez shook her head in slow dismay, but glanced to the side and sat back as the waitress appeared with their cappuccinos and breakfasts.

"Thank you," she murmured, peering down at the breakfast before her. It looked and smelled delicious and despite her upset over what she'd just learned, Inez was positively starved. She hadn't eaten since the airport the day before, which really wasn't so long ago, but it felt like it was. A lot had happened in that time and between one thing and another, she'd used up a lot of energy since then as well.

Thomas closed his hand over hers and Inez glanced at him with surprise.

"Eat," he murmured giving her hand a squeeze. "Bastien is arranging a flight back to London for us."

Inez nodded and picked up her fork, relaxing a little when he picked up his own and dug in. Eating was also a sign of finding a lifemate, she recalled the delivery guy telling her, and Thomas was eating. He had also had a meal with her in the pub at the airport the day before; though, he'd only ordered breakfast for her when he'd arrived at the Dorchester—but, then, that had been an apology of sorts, she recalled and was amazed to realize this whole adventure had started little more than twenty-four hours ago. It felt like a lifetime had passed, Inez thought and then changed her mind. No, not really. It was strange, this day and a bit had passed quickly enough, but she felt like she'd known Thomas a lifetime.

"I take it you like cats."

Thomas glanced up from the black cat and two tabbies he was alternately petting, and smiled faintly. "I love them."

Inez nodded with amusement and said, "And they seem to love you in return. We've picked up a new cat to trail us in each room."

"Jealous?" Thomas asked with a grin.

Inez chuckled as he straightened and the three cats immediately began to twine around his legs, meowing plaintively at being abandoned. Shrugging mildly, she raised her gaze back to his face. Arching one eyebrow, she asked lightly, "Why would I care if you enjoy playing with pussy? I've only known you a day."

Thomas's eyes widened incredulously at the sally. When she then turned away and headed out of the room, he stepped carefully over the still-complaining cats and hurried after her. Thomas found Inez standing just inside the door of the next room, gaping up at the painted ceiling. Thomas didn't even glance up. He'd been to the Kattenkabinet before and thought it was charming, that was why when he'd learned that Bastien hadn't managed to book them on a flight until that evening, he'd suggested he and Inez tour around Amsterdam while they were here. He wanted to show her a bit of one of his favorite cities.

A night tour would have been better, of course. It wasn't really in his best interests to stay out in the sun long, but Bastien had had enough blood delivered to the hotel to last for several days in the normal course of things. Thomas suspected he'd use up most of it in this one day and was now carrying a black collapsible cooler filled with several bags, enough to keep him going until they had to go back to the hotel to collect their things and head to the airport. They'd headed back to the hotel after their breakfast, stopping in a luggage shop on the way when Inez realized she had nothing in which to pack away all the things Bastien had ordered, purchased, and delivered to the hotel for her.

Thomas had spotted the collapsible cooler while in the shop and had purchased it, as well as a good-sized suitcase for Inez. Thomas had consumed several more bags of blood while he waited for Inez to pack, then had put the rest in the cooler and slung it over his shoulder before setting out.

He'd considered taking Inez to the Rijksmuseum, but one could easily spend a whole day there and he'd wanted her to see more of the city than just a museum. So they'd utilized the shadier areas and walked here to the offbeat and much smaller Kattenkabinet in a leisurely fashion, enjoying the sights and sounds of this most unique city. Inez had peered around at the seventeenth-century houses with wide eyes and Thomas had been a little wide-eyed as well since he'd never actually walked the streets here in daylight. It had been nice.

"You didn't ask *why* I love cats," he commented finally when she continued to ignore him and began to move toward the window to peer into the gardens behind the house, dedicated to anything and everything to do with cats.

"Why do you love cats?" she asked indulgently.

"Because they're intelligent, independent, graceful, subtle, and mysterious . . ." Thomas tilted his head slightly and commented, "Rather like you in fact."

"Me?" Inez asked, glancing at him with surprise and then chuckled softly and shook her head. "I'm not the least mysterious."

"You are to me," he countered solemnly. "And I like it."

Inez met his gaze, and then glanced toward the window as one of the cats leapt up onto the sill and lay down in the sunshine. Reaching out, she petted the cat and said, "Well, I'm not subtle either."

"You are," he assured her.

She chuckled wryly, "I hardly think my berating you wildly when I arrived at the hotel was subtle behavior."

"No?" Thomas grinned. "You berated me in Portuguese. For all I knew you were telling me I was the sexiest thing you'd seen in your life."

"In your dreams," Inez chuckled.

"Yes," he agreed and, when she glanced at him in surprise, added, "And much about you is subtle. You are intelligent, but don't flaunt it, quietly confident in your business abilities, you're able to make refined distinctions and judgments, and then there is your beauty and sex appeal."

Her lips had parted slightly with surprised pleasure at his words until the last one, and then they pressed together firmly and Inez shook her head and assured him, "I am no beauty and sex appeal is not even in my vocabulary."

"You have both," Thomas responded solemnly. "But both are delicate and understated, not the bold brassy stuff some women flaunt. For instance, you have lovely, wild hair."

Inez grimaced with distaste. "I have wild hair, all right. I can't do a thing with it."

"But it's soft and sexy and makes you look like you've just climbed from bed after making love for hours . . . and it makes a man think of making love to you for hours."

Inez stilled, her head bowed, her hand unmoving on the cat.

"And your lips are full and soft and slightly swollen as if you've just been kissed. It makes a man think of kissing you," Thomas continued, and then reached out to run his fingers lightly over the sleeve of the blouse she'd changed into for the flight home when they were back at the hotel. "And you favor silk blouses, wearing them buttoned higher than most so that just the barest hint of cleavage shows, enough to make a man wish he could see more."

Thomas let his hand drop away, brushing it lightly

over her derrière as he added, "And well-cut slacks in a draping material that fall over the curve of your behind, making a man wish to follow that curve with his hand."

Inez finally turned marveling eyes to him and whispered, "Boy, you're good at this seduction business. A girl could fall in love with a guy like you."

Thomas caught her face in his hands and assured her sincerely, "Every word I've spoken is true, Inez. That's how I see you and how I'm going to make you see yourself. I promise."

Seeing the soft sheen of tears in her eyes, he lowered his head and pressed a gentle kiss to first one brow, then the other. He was about to press a kiss to her lips as well, when the tabby on the window sill suddenly stood and decided to join the party. Launching itself onto its back legs, it rested a front paw on his arm and head-butted his chin as if to say, "Hey, buddy! What about me?"

Thomas and Inez both chuckled at the demanding behavior and then she broke free with a laugh and said, "What was that you were asking me about jealousy? It looks to me like you were asking the wrong feline."

He grinned and collected the cat into his arms to scratch it under the chin.

Inez shook her head at his indulgence and said, "Now, it's behavior like that that has always made me a dog person."

Thomas glanced after her with surprise, following when he realized she was leaving to head into the next room. "Are you really a dog person?"

"Of course," she answered idly, running one hand along the built-in buffet in the dining room. "Dogs are loyal, affectionate, direct, kind, helpful, and playful. What's not to love?"

"I'm loyal," he informed her, watching her move around the room. "Affectionate too."

"You're also direct and kind," she agreed. "And even helpful and playful."

Thomas smiled as she walked to the door and then she glanced back and teased lightly, "You're definitely a dog."

Grinning, Thomas set the cat down on the floor and trailed her out of the room.

"Are you following me, mister?" she teased lightly when he entered the next room.

"Of course, it's what dogs do," he pointed and then added with a wicked grin, "They chase pussy."

Inez burst out laughing. "Oh, you're bad."

"You started it," Thomas said promptly and caught her hand to draw her against his side and steer her toward the door. "Come on. Let's go find a café, I'm hungry again."

"But there are two more rooms," she protested.

"I'll bring you another time," he assured her, urging her to the stairs leading to the main level.

"Promise?" Inez asked quietly.

"Most definitely." He hugged her to his side and then released her to descend the stairs.

They found a café with a few tables outdoors. Thomas settled Inez at one in the shade, took a quick glance at the menu, and waited for the waitress to take his order before excusing himself. He slipped inside to find the men's room, then fed on a couple of bags of blood.

Inez was smiling faintly when he returned. When he

raised his eyebrows in question, she gestured vaguely to the people passing by and said with a shrug, "People watching is just so interesting here."

Thomas glanced around at the people walking and biking by.

"Like, look at that," Inez said, pointing to a family riding by; mother and father, both with child seats on the back, occupied by young children. "And that."

Thomas followed her gesture to an approaching couple. A smile curled his own lips as a woman appearing to be in her early twenties pedaled passed, craning her head slightly to see around a man of about the same age perched on the handlebars.

"Definitely a modern couple," Inez murmured. "And look! A girls' day shopping."

Thomas turned his head again, his eyes twinkling as he saw three women riding together, shopping bags bristling from hands grasping their handlebars.

He glanced back to Inez to see her shaking her head in wonder as she said, "I think I love this city."

I think I love you. The thought ran through Thomas's head, startling him because it was true. He'd never met anyone like Inez before and while he hadn't known her long, he'd come to know her well because of the circumstances.

The woman was fearless; standing up for herself and berating him when she'd thought he'd ignored her at the airport after her rush to collect him. Then there was her removing the knife from his back, tending his wound and heading out alone in the middle of the night, in a strange city to hunt down his aunt when he couldn't accompany her. He admired that courage.

Inez was intelligent too. It shone in her eyes and slipped from her lips every time she spoke to make a suggestion or observation.

And while she could be businesslike and commanding, she also had a good sense of humor, and a quick wit.

Thomas also knew he could depend on her to step up to the plate and do what was necessary in difficult situations. Exhausted as she'd been last night, she'd accompanied him into the Red Light District to help . . . without either irritation or complaint. She simply did what had to be done.

Yes, she was a special woman. The fates had been kind and wise in choosing her for his lifemate. Now he just had to convince her of it.

"I've been thinking, if—"

Thomas focused his gaze on Inez, but she'd stopped speaking and sat back. Glancing to the side, he saw that the waitress was there with their orders and sat back himself for her to set them down. Once the woman was gone, he raised an eyebrow at Inez and prompted, "You were thinking?"

"Well, you said Bastien had checked Marguerite's credit card. Did he check this Tiny person's credit card as well?"

"Yes," Thomas said, his mood suddenly solemn as he was reminded of his missing aunt. "There is no activity on his cards either."

Inez nodded. "So, has he checked the cards of the guy she's working for?"

Thomas peered at her blankly. "What?"

"Well, either you or Bastien told me that the last place you knew Marguerite had been was the Dorchester Hotel? That she was there to meet with this Notte fellow who hired them to find his mother."

"Yes," Thomas said slowly. "She told Bastien they were hoping to get more information out of him, something useful to help them with their search."

"Well . . ." Inez shrugged. "Maybe the reason neither Tiny nor Marguerite have used their own credit cards is because this Notte guy has joined them in the search and is footing the bill."

"Jesus," Thomas breathed, staring at her. It was such a simple suggestion, but neither he nor Bastien, nor presumably anyone else in the family had come up with it.

"What's wrong?" Inez asked with a concerned frown. "You're staring at me funny."

"I'm staring at you thinking you're brilliant," he explained on a laugh and shook his head. "I can't believe you came up with that. Actually yes, I can. What I really can't believe is that not one member of our family came up with that. Christ, we're supposed to have nano brains."

Inez grinned and teased, "Would that be very tiny, little miniscule brains?"

"It would seem so," Thomas said wryly, reaching for his phone.

Inez shook her head. "That's not true, and you know it. You're all just too close to the situation and too worried. You'd have come up with it on your own eventually."

"Thankfully we'll never know if that's true because you came up with it," he said, pushing the speed dial button for Bastien and raising the phone to his ear.

Inez began to eat as he talked to his cousin and told

him what she'd come up with and Thomas found himself watching. His eyes followed every movement as she lifted the food to her mouth and slipped it in and he marveled at how dainty and sexy she was about it. As tidy as a cat, he thought and smiled to himself, then forced his attention back to Bastien's words. The man was both excited by the suggestion, and full of self-disgust that he hadn't thought it up himself and saved them this wasted time.

Thomas told him not to beat himself up, pointing out what Inez had said; that they were too close to the situation and their worry had clouded their thoughts somewhat.

"Does he have a way to trace Notte's credit card?" Inez asked as he slipped his phone into his pocket.

Thomas nodded. "We have friends everywhere. And if we don't, we can send someone in to make new friends."

"You mean control them," she said dryly.

Thomas nodded in acknowledgment, but they had both stopped smiling. He was thinking about the fact that she'd been controlled and had her memory wiped, and knew she was too.

"If Marguerite isn't even here in Amsterdam, why control me and erase my memory?" Inez asked suddenly.

Thomas frowned as he tried to reason it out. "Herb said the location turned up the same the second time he checked it while you were on the way to the park. He said you should have found Aunt Marguerite there."

"But it wasn't your aunt," Inez said quietly, picking up on his train of thought and then added, "It was that mugger who had the phone in the park. He couldn't have controlled me or wiped my memory."

"No," Thomas agreed.

"So who did and why?" she asked. They were both silent for a minute, and then Inez said, "You don't suppose someone was trying to keep me from discovering that the mugger had the phone, and not Marguerite."

Thomas was so startled by the suggestion, that he dropped his fork. "Someone here in Amsterdam?"

Inez nodded.

He frowned at the idea and then said slowly, "But that would suggest that— I mean it was all just bad luck that the phone was here. Happenstance. The mortal mugged Marguerite and we followed the phone here."

"And so long as we're chasing the phone here in Amsterdam, we were on the wrong track," she pointed out.

"Yes," Thomas agreed, his own frown returning. "But if that's why you were controlled and your memory wiped . . ."

"Then someone doesn't want us to find your aunt," Inez finished quietly.

Eleven

"Here we are." The bellhop pushed the door open and held it with one extended arm for Inez and Thomas to precede him.

Despite the sudden nerves claiming her, Inez smiled at the man and led the way inside. She set her purse on the end table beside the sofa and moved restlessly to the row of windows, tugging the curtain open, and then peered blindly out over the twinkling lights of London at night. Her attention, however, was on the sounds behind her as the bellhop wheeled her suitcase with Thomas's knapsack on top into the room. She heard Thomas thank the man and guessed by the bellhop's cheerful response that he'd probably tipped him well for escorting them up, and then she heard the door close.

Inez didn't turn around, but stood stiffly where she

was, feeling like a virgin on her wedding night. They were back at the Dorchester.

Thomas and Inez had been relaxing in Schiphol airport, waiting to board their flight out of Amsterdam, when Bastien had called with the news that he'd not only traced Notte's credit cards, but had called Christian Notte's apartment, and when he'd received an answering machine, had then tried the Notte Construction offices. It was the business where the immortal worked in Italy, fortunately, a family-run organization despite it being a multinational company. His aunt Vita had answered the phone and Bastien had learned from her that Christian was in England as was his father, though she wasn't sure exactly where the two men were. She also had no idea when they planned to return and hadn't sounded pleased about it.

Bastien had then arranged to have both men's credit cards tracked in England. He'd found a charge for two suites at the Claridge's hotel here in London the night after Marguerite had checked out of the Dorchester. He'd also found a charge for five train tickets to York, where several charges had subsequently been made, the last of them occurring just the day before.

Bastien had immediately called the hotel, hoping to verify that Marguerite had been one of the guests in the suites, but all he'd learned was that Mr. Notte had requested three of the bedrooms in the suites have twin beds.

Deciding she had to have been there, he'd then tried to arrange train tickets for Thomas and Inez to York, but their flight from Amsterdam arrived too late for them to catch a train. He'd apparently checked into flights, but that wasn't possible either, so he'd booked them into the Dorchester Hotel for the night, reserving them a two-bedroom suite. They were to take a train to the walled city early the next evening.

Thomas had passed on all of this information in solemn tones, but then his eyes had flared silver as he pointed out that it meant they had a free night to themselves.

Inez had been a nervous wreck ever since; contemplating what was to come with an anxiety that had grown with each passing moment as they waited to be called to board their flight, on the flight, and during the taxi ride to the hotel.

Now the time was nigh, Inez thought with more than a touch of panic. Really, the anticipation was horrible. She hadn't been sitting on the flight remembering what his kisses had been like and imagining what the rest would be like; Inez had spent the entire flight wishing she'd known this was coming a couple months ago so she could have chosen not to skip so many trips to the gym in favor of work. She also would have bypassed some of the muffins she'd had for breakfast, and . . .

The *and*s were endless; a manicure, pedicure, facial, body wax, body wrap . . . Anything that might make her look better while naked ran through her head as something she should have and would have done.

Once Inez had finished shredding any confidence she'd previously had in her body, she'd turned to her sexual technique, or lack there of. She was no virgin, but she really had neglected her social life in order to concentrate on her career, and while that had got her promoted to vice president, it had basically left her social life, or more specifically her love life, in the toilet. It had been a long time since she'd even dated anyone, let alone slept with them . . . A very long time. It wouldn't have hurt to pick up a book that could give her a quick refresher course.

Inez knew it was a ridiculous idea even as she had it. It wasn't like she'd forgotten what went where and so on, but perhaps there were new skills or techniques she'd never heard of. A secret spot, for instance that you could press on to make the man blind so he wouldn't notice your imperfect body.

She was grimacing at the likelihood of there being such a spot when something brushed her shoulders. Startled, Inez squealed, jumped, and whirled around, eyes wide as she saw Thomas standing there, hands raised, obviously to place them on her shoulders, eyebrows practically disappearing into his hairline at her reaction to his gentle touch.

They both stood still for a moment, and then Thomas cleared his throat and said, "Are you all right? I didn't mean to scare you."

"I'm fine," Inez said at once, wincing as her voice came out a high-pitched squeak that would have done Minnie Mouse proud.

"Hmm." Thomas eyed her thoughtfully, and then said, "Well, I was going to suggest we order room service. Are you hungry?"

"Yes," she gasped, grabbing at the suggestion. Anything to delay what was coming.

"Right," he said slowly, still appearing thoughtful. "Well, why don't you look at the menu and see what you want?"

Nodding, Inez moved swiftly across the room to grab up the menu. Thomas took her place at the window, peering silently out as she made her selection. It wasn't quick. Her decision was, but then she spent a good, long time perusing everything on the room service menu at least three times in an effort to delay things. By the time Inez closed the menu, she figured she'd gained herself a good ten minutes with her dallying. And then she felt a hand on her shoulder. Inez jumped nervously, but managed not to squeal like an idiot this time.

Thomas was good enough to ignore her reaction. His voice was light as he asked, "Decided?"

Forcing a smile, Inez turned to face him, managing to take a step back as she did, and nodded. She held the book out between them and asked, "Do you need the menu?"

Thomas didn't say anything, but she could have sworn his lips twitched with amusement as he took the book.

"Thank you," he murmured and then glanced at her and suggested, "You seem a little tense. Why don't you pick your room and take a nice relaxing bath. I'll wait to place our orders so you can have a nice long soak."

"Oh, yes. That's a good idea," Inez breathed with relief at the offer. It was yet another delay as well as a chance to shave her legs again and do various other little tasks that might boost her confidence. She could have kissed the man. Instead, she caught the handle of the rolling suitcase they'd bought in Amsterdam and promptly headed out of the room.

"Inez."

She froze in the door and glanced back warily. "Yes?"

"You have to tell me what you want so I can order it," he pointed out gently.

"Oh." She gave a nervous laugh, babbled what she wanted in a rush and hurried out of the room before he could stop her again.

Inez rushed into the first room she came to, hefted her suitcase onto the luggage rack, unzipped it, and began pulling out items willy-nilly in search of what she would need for her bath. The room looked like a tornado had hit it by the time she was done, but Inez didn't care. She was stressed and didn't think she'd ever been this stressed before in her life.

She shook her head at herself as she hurried into the bathroom and dropped everything on the counter. She'd handled mergers, hostile takeover attempts, and various other business emergencies with easy aplomb, Inez thought with self-disgust as she squeezed bubble bath into the tub and turned on the taps. And it wasn't like this was her first time. She'd had sex before and never been this distressed by it all, not even her very first time. But then it hadn't ever really mattered before. She hadn't cared for anyone else like she cared for Thomas.

"What?" Inez gasped the word as she met her reflection's gaze in the mirror. But even as she asked the question, she knew it was true.

Inez had dated lots of men while at university, and then when she'd first started to work, but they'd all seemed terribly immature or even boring to her so that she'd begun to avoid dates and the whole social scene. Work had been more interesting. In effect, she'd had a love affair with her career for the last decade and hadn't met a man who could compete.

Until now.

Thomas could definitely compete. And while she'd at first thought the most attractive part of being his lifemate was the complete lack of effort needed on her part, leaving her free to continue her affair with work, her feelings were changing on the matter. Work had never made her feel the exhilaration and excitement that Thomas could with a look or a light touch, let alone the passion she experienced with his kisses. Work had never made her laugh and feel as lighthearted as she had today as they'd toured Amsterdam. And work had never made her feel beautiful and sexy as Thomas had made her feel at the Kattenkabinet when he'd said all those lovely things to her.

Thomas could, and was, competing with work and winning hands down.

"I'm in trouble," she murmured to her reflection, because it certainly felt like trouble to her. Thomas was the first person who had touched the calculator that past boyfriends had claimed was her heart . . . and he could quite easily smash it. While he had talked about her being his lifemate, he'd never once mentioned love, and Inez feared she was heading down that dark, frightening path. It put a whole new light on everything. Before, she'd just had to decide if she could handle living centuries, now she had to decide if she could live centuries with a man she would no doubt come to love with every fiber of her being, but who might not ever love her in return.

Panic giving way to a solemn mood, Inez turned

off the taps, stripped, and slipped into the tub to consider the problem.

"Inez?" The soft question, accompanied by a light tap at the door brought her eyes open and had her sitting up abruptly in the water, and then quickly dropping back down until the few bubbles still remaining covered her to the shoulders.

"Oh, you're awake," Thomas said, peering at her through the door he'd eased half open. "I was afraid you'd fallen asleep."

"No," Inez said quickly, forcing a smile. "How long have I been in here?"

"Well over an hour," he answered. "The food has arrived."

"I'll get out now," Inez said and started to sit up, but came to an abrupt halt as she recalled she was naked.

Thomas smiled faintly and grabbed a towel from the rack. Holding it open, he stepped to the side of the tub. When Inez eyed the towel and hesitated, he said quietly. "Shy? You weren't this morning."

Her eyes flickered to his face at the way his voice had suddenly lowered and she saw that his eyes had that silver glow. Swallowing, Inez hesitated another moment, then stood, knowing her cheeks were blushing furiously even as she did. Much to her relief, he immediately moved the towel forward and she lifted her arms to keep them out of the way as he wrapped it around her. Inez's eyes widened in surprise, however, when he didn't then release her and step away, but lifted her out of the tub like a child. That child image died an abrupt death when he kept lifting her, bringing her up until their lips met.

Surprised, she clutched at his arms with every intention of putting some space between them. Inez hadn't been sleeping, she'd been thinking, and what she'd come up with was it was better if she kept her distance from the man and refused to agree to be his lifemate until she knew if he could come to love her. That grand plan flew out the window, however, when his tongue slipped between her lips, coaxing a response from her.

A little moan of defeat slipping from her lips, Inez gave up her hold on his arms and slipped her hands around his neck, blinking in surprise when she felt that his hair was damp. Obviously, he'd taken a bath too or perhaps a shower. She didn't know which, but in the next moment didn't care. He'd turned with her and set her on the edge of the marble counter and the moment he took his hands away, the towel dropped to pool on the counter around her hips, caught beneath her, but no longer covering anything.

Inez shuddered as Thomas took advantage of the lack and urged her legs open so that he could step between them as he kissed her. His hands slid over her naked back, pressing her closer until her breasts rubbed against the soft cloth of his shirt as he kissed, and she moaned, scraping the nails of one hand through his hair, while the other clutched at his shoulder, urging him closer still.

She felt one hand leave her back and slide around to her side, feathering lightly across the side of one breast. She shuddered and kissed him more eagerly, her upper body suddenly taking on a mind of its own and twisting slightly, pressing one breast tighter against his chest while making space between his body and her other breast.

Thomas accepted the silent invitation, his hand closing warm over the eager orb and Inez moaned and arched into the caress, and then cried out into his mouth as he plucked at the excited nipple. She groaned in protest, however, when he tore his mouth away from hers, but then gasped and arched even more as his head dropped so that his lips could fasten on the nub he'd been teasing.

Catching both hands in his still-damp hair, she held on tightly and shivered as he alternately laved and suckled at first one breast and then the other, gasping little half-phrases of encouragement and need in Portuguese. However, her ability to speak deteriorated even as the excitement he was stirring in her built and Inez was soon merely moaning and then tugging firmly at his hair, demanding he return to kissing her.

Thomas chuckled at the silent command and raised his head to kiss her again, pressing forward as he did so that his chest and groin brushed against hers as his arms enveloped her. Inez groaned into his mouth at the assault to her senses and reached between them to catch the hem of his T-shirt and begin tugging it up.

Thomas broke their kiss and leaned back, his arms rising accommodatingly so that she could remove the item, but when he started forward again to kiss her after that, she didn't let him. Her hands were now on his chest, holding him back as she explored the muscular surface. His muscles weren't unattractively bulky, but sleek and well defined and his shoulders and chest were wide, a veritable playground for her to explore. Inez ran her hands over all that male flesh with awe, and then leaned forward to press kisses to the firm surface, before stopping to lick and nip at one flat nipple.

Thomas sucked in a breath and immediately caught her head between both hands to force her face up. His mouth then covered hers in a kiss that was hungry and carnal. Inez smiled against his mouth. Emboldened by this small success, she trailed her fingers lightly down his chest until they reached the top of his jeans. She worked blind at his belt buckle, then at the button and zipper and then quickly pushed the heavy material down over his hips until the upper half of his behind was bare. Her hands stopped then for a brief foray over the taut flesh, before slipping back around to the front to find him hard and free of the encumbering jeans.

A sigh of satisfaction slipped from her mouth to his as Inez closed her hand around his arousal, and then she stiffened in surprise as a wave of keen excitement coursed through her. Thomas growled into her mouth and reached down to catch her hand and try to drag it away, but all he managed to do was draw it the length of his shaft and Inez cried out with startled pleasure as another wave of pleasure, this one larger and heavier, poured over her. Her eyes blinked open as she realized that her own cry had echoed a growl from Thomas.

Inez tried to break their kiss to ask what was happening, but Thomas wouldn't let her. He also wouldn't let her touch him again. He forced her hand away from him and brought it up over her head, catching and raising her other hand at the same time. He then switched his hold so that he had both wrists caught in the fingers of one hand against the mirror.

Realizing how he'd trapped her, Inez tried to protest, but it was hard to do with his tongue in her mouth, and then his free hand closed over one breast and she arched and shuddered and forgot all about it as he drove her wild with both his kisses and caresses.

Just when Inez thought she couldn't stand it anymore, Thomas suddenly released his hold on her hands. Gasping with relief, she reached to wrap them around his shoulders, but he wasn't there to hold. He'd broken the kiss to travel her body with his mouth, his lips brushing over her throat, her collarbone, her breasts, and continuing downward as his hands caught her by the hips and pulled her bottom to the edge of the counter.

Gasping breathlessly, Inez dropped her hands to the counter and braced herself to keep from falling back against the mirror, hardly hearing the skitter of the cosmetics she sent skipping across the marble. Her attention was focused entirely on what Thomas was doing as his lips burned a trail over her stomach. When the path continued down over her hip, Inez shook her head and tried to close her legs, but he held them open with his hands, and even urged them farther open to accommodate his shoulders as he dropped to his knees before her.

Inez knew where he was going and what he planned to do, but still cried out and jerked in surprise as his head bowed between her legs. She may have known what was coming, but nothing could have prepared her for the shocking jolt of pleasure that shot through her at the first rasp of his tongue over her sensitive flesh.

That cry was one that seemed to have no end. It became an ululating sound that rose and fell and dropped into breathless gasps, but then rose again as Inez struggled on the counter, her hips and pelvis fighting to rise into the caress or alternately to shrink away when the sensations became too intense. She was allowed to do neither. Thomas held her in place, his grip firm on her thighs as he drove her toward the edge of sanity. When he suddenly stopped and lunged to his feet between her legs, she didn't know whether to be relieved or disappointed. He didn't say a word, simply slid his hand under her bottom and scooped her off the counter.

"What—?" Inez gasped with confusion, quickly wrapping her legs around his hips and catching one ankle over the other to help hold her weight as he turned toward the door.

"We can't do it here," Thomas growled. "You might hit your head on the marble or the mirror."

Inez hadn't a clue what he was talking about, she'd been in no danger of coming to harm that she could tell, but then he took a step to carry her out of the room and froze as the movement made her slide against his erection where it was caught between them. She saw his face tighten, though it looked more like alarm on his face than excitement, then his mouth firmed with determination and he took another step only to pause again as they both groaned.

Shaking his head grimly, Thomas took one more step and this time she felt his shoulders ripple in reaction to the pleasure that shot through them both.

A growl of what sounded like despair and frustration slid from his lips and Thomas suddenly turned. The three steps had taken him to the doorway, his turning placed her back to the doorjamb.

"I'm sorry, this is as far as I can get us," Thomas growled as he lifted her slightly against his chest until his erection sprang free from between them.

Thinking he meant because she was too heavy, Inez felt her face flush with embarrassment and opened her mouth to tell him to put her down if she was too heavy, that she could walk, but the words died on a gasp as he eased her back down and his erection pushed into her.

Inez met his gaze. His eyes were almost silver white now, there wasn't a drop of blue left in them and she suspected her own were probably black, the pupils dilated to erase the color. She knew they'd gone wide with shock at what she'd just experienced. When she'd touched him earlier, she'd experienced a shock of pleasure herself, as if he'd somehow sent his pleasure out to her, but that had stopped when he'd forced her hands away. However, Inez had just experienced it again, a wave of pleasure riding on top of her own pleasure, somehow joining and doubling it.

"I was trying to guard you from it. I didn't want to overwhelm you, but I can't concentrate enough to keep my guards up anymore," Thomas said through gritted teeth.

Inez stared at him blankly, not really understanding what he was talking about, but suspecting she was experiencing his pleasure on top of her own.

"Will you be all right?" he asked with concern.

Inez just stared at him for a moment and then whispered, "Do it again."

Thomas peered at her uncertainly, but then pulled out slightly and drove back in and Inez cried out and tipped her head back as another wave of their combined pleasure rolled over her.

"Again," she cried, digging her nails into his shoulders.

Thomas let his breath out on a sigh that sounded relieved and began to move. Inez soon realized that he'd still been holding back somewhat even when he'd claimed that he couldn't concentrate enough to do so. Suddenly it wasn't just one wave of pleasure with each move, but that wave rolled forward to thunder through her, receded and then poured over her again even as the next wave arrived to crash over her as well.

Inez soon felt she was going to drown in the pleasure swamping her. She couldn't catch her breath, couldn't feel the doorjamb pressing into her spine, couldn't hear the sounds she knew she was making, and couldn't even think. All she could experience was their mounting pleasure as Thomas drove into her, and then suddenly something snapped and the pleasure exploded, blowing out every thought and feeling. Inez screamed, vaguely aware that Thomas was shouting out too and then her awareness was suddenly sucked away, caught in a fiery backdraft.

It was a constant and repetitive tapping on his cheek that woke Thomas. Frowning at the irritating sensation, he blinked his eyes open, the frown fading at once as he found himself peering up into Inez's worried face.

"You're alive," she said with relief, stopping her

tapping the moment he opened his eyes. "For a minute I was afraid I'd killed you."

Thomas chuckled, sending her bouncing about where she leaned on his vibrating chest and then he assured her, "I would have died happy."

A small smile curved her lips, but then she arched an eyebrow. "Would you mind explaining what exactly just happened?"

Thomas felt his eyebrows fly up. "Well, the choo-choo went into the tunnel and—" He stopped and laughed as she smacked his chest with exasperation.

"Smart-ass," she accused, her lips twisting, then looked more serious and said, "I mean the brain thing. What was that?"

"That, my dear," Thomas said, catching her by the upper arms and tugging her to lie fully on top of him, "was immortal sex."

"Yes, but— Stop looking so bloody satisfied," Inez ordered on a laugh.

"I can't help it. I *am* satisfied." He wiggled his eyebrows at her and lifted his hands to slip them into her hair.

"What are you doing?" she asked as he ran his hands over her head, and then down her back, moving lower with every sweep.

"Checking for wounds. You didn't hurt yourself when we fell did you?"

"I don't think so," she said with a frown. "Nothing hurts."

"Good," he murmured, his hands slowing as he reached her behind. He couldn't resist cupping and squeezing the round cheeks. They fit perfectly in his hand and felt so soft and smooth . . . Little Thomas approved wholeheartedly of the foray and began to lift his head beneath her, making Inez's eyes widen.

"Thomas," Inez said in warning tones. "Don't even think about it. I want answers. What just happened? I could feel— Well, I think I might have been feeling what you were feeling. And I've never fainted in my life, but just now . . ." She made a face, showing her disgust for what she considered her weakness.

"I did too," he assured her, continuing on with his search.

"Hey!" Inez stiffened on top of him as his fingers slid between her legs.

"I have to be thorough in my examination," he said innocently, smiling as her eyes darkened and her breathing hitched and then settled into a fast, shallow pace.

"Thomas," she begged, squirming a little on top of him and making Little Thomas grow harder. Shaking her head, she tried to shift off of him, but couldn't, his wrists and lower arms were bands across the backs of her upper thighs. Giving up, Inez gasped, "Please. I want to understand what just happened."

Thomas stopped tormenting her and shifted his hands to her waist as he explained, "That is what it's like between lifemates. While they can't read each other or control each other's minds, they can share what they're experiencing while having sex and can eventually share thoughts and feelings without speaking."

Her eyebrows rose at this news, but then she frowned and said, "You said you were guarding me from it at first. What did you mean?"

Thomas hesitated, and then suddenly tightened his

hold on her waist and rolled so that she was beneath him, his hips nestled between her legs. Leaning his weight on his elbows to keep the worst of it off of her, he concentrated on keeping up the walls in his mind and ground himself against her. Thomas clenched his hands as pleasure shot through him and Little Thomas grew a little harder even as Inez gasped and shuddered beneath him. He then let the walls drop and did it again, closing his eyes as both her pleasure and his own charged through him, filling every corner of his mind and body.

"Oh, Deus," Inez moaned.

Thomas opened his eyes as the last of it passed and said, "I love it when you talk dirty."

A breathy laugh burst from her lips, and she informed him dryly, "I said, Oh God."

Thomas grinned. "No. I'm not God, but I can understand how you'd mistake me for Him after the mind-blowing sex I just gave you."

Inez snorted.

Expression growing more serious, Thomas peered down at her and said solemnly, "I've never had a lifemate before. I've heard about the sex, though, and how overwhelming it can be. I was afraid it might scare you, so I tried to keep my guard up as long as possible. And then I realized how foolish I'd been starting it in the bathroom like that. I was afraid one or both of us would be hurt when we fainted so tried to move it to the bed, a nice soft, safe surface to faint on."

"But I was too heavy for you to carry me that far," she said with an unhappy nod.

Thomas stared at her incredulously. "What?"

"Well, that's what you meant when you said it was as far as you could get us . . . isn't it?" she asked uncertainly.

"Inez," he said patiently. "You saw me lift up that blond guy one-handed in Amsterdam. He had a good eighty pounds on you. You aren't too heavy for me. You aren't heavy at all."

"Oh . . . right," she murmured, obviously recalling the incident, but then she frowned and asked, "Then what did you mean by 'it was as far as you could get?'"

"I meant that I couldn't wait any longer," Thomas said dryly. "I was all out of self-control. I couldn't walk one more step with you rubbing against Little Thomas and driving him crazy. I—"

"Okay, okay, I get it," she interrupted with a laugh and then arched an eyebrow and said, "Little Thomas?"

"Hmm." He shifted, nudging Little Thomas against her. "He says hello, and wants you to know he's very enamored of you."

"He is, is he?" Inez asked with amusement and then said softly, "Well, I find him very interesting too, almost as interesting as Big Thomas."

"Do you?" he asked with a grin, and then said, "Well, that's a shame, because the smells coming from the food cart in the living room are driving me crazy."

"You can smell it from here?" Inez asked with surprise.

Thomas nodded. "Yes. And I fancy eating in the traditional immortal fashion."

"What is the—" Her question was interrupted by a gasp of surprise as Thomas launched himself to his feet, pulling her up with him. Once upright, she finished—"traditional immortal fashion?"

"Oh, that," Thomas said lightly, retrieving both of the fluffy white hotel robes supplied with the room. He slid into his own as he walked back to her, then helped her into hers before scooping her up in his arms and heading for the door.

"Thomas?" Inez prompted as he carried her into the living room where the food cart with their meals waited. "What is the traditional immortal fashion?"

"Eating it off your naked body," he answered.

"It is not!" she protested with disbelief, and then asked uncertainly, "Is it?"

"No," Thomas admitted with a grin. "But we can always start a new tradition."

He wiggled his eyebrows and leered.

Inez laughed and said, "I love—"

Thomas felt his heart stutter as she suddenly hesitated. A full minute passed before she finished in more solemn tones.

"Being with you."

That's a start, Thomas told himself, and hoped his disappointment wasn't showing. For one moment he'd hoped . . . But it was early days yet, everything would work out. She was his lifemate, after all, he reassured himself, and tried not to think about the fact that he'd known times when it hadn't worked out. When the mortal lifemate refused to be turned and become immortal as well.

Twelve

"This is it."

"A terraced house?" Inez asked with surprise as Thomas urged her up a short walk to one of many such houses on a residential street in York. Her gaze slid over the stone façade and she wondered if it looked less grim in daylight. They'd caught the seven P.M. train from London, arriving in York just after nine.

"Terraced house?" Thomas asked with surprise as he looked it over. "We call them townhouses in Canada."

"But why a whole townhouse for just the two of us?" Inez asked.

"Bastien said all the hotels inside the walls of the city center were booked," Thomas said with a shrug as he removed the arm around her shoulders to take the paper out of his right hand and leave it free to knock on the door. "He thinks Aunt Marguerite, Tiny, and the Nottes will be staying inside the walls and wanted us to as well. He figures they probably had to rent a townhouse too on such short notice. That would explain why there's no hotel charge on the credit cards. Some of these places aren't set up to accept credit cards. They might have paid by check."

"Are we paying by check?" Inez asked, glancing curiously around the quiet street and wondering if one of the other townhouses on the street held Marguerite Argeneau.

"No. Bastien wired the money into the owner's account this morning."

"Oh." Inez smiled faintly as she watched Thomas knock again, wanting to brush aside the bit of dark hair that had fallen over his forehead, but not comfortable enough to do so.

She supposed that was ridiculous after the night they'd spent together. They hadn't gone to sleep until dawn, but had spent the night starting their meal, interrupting it to make love because Thomas insisted on eating portions of his off of her, and then making love again and so on. This had been interspersed with quiet moments of conversation, and Inez had learned that while Thomas had a light and carefree outer shell, there was a very serious and deep thinker under it all.

Her thoughts were disturbed by the sound of a door opening and Inez glanced to the entrance of the adjoining townhouse as it opened and a gentleman leaned out to peer at them. He was old with grizzled hair sticking out from his head, gray stubble shadowing his wrinkled face, and half his white shirt untucked from dark trousers. He also clutched a steaming teacup in one hand.

"Tom?" the man asked, eyes slightly narrowed.

"Thomas Argeneau, yes," Thomas said, turning now to peer at the man as well.

Nodding the fellow turned back into the townhouse and slammed the door.

When Thomas turned surprised eyes her way, Inez shrugged and murmured, "Northerners."

"Oh," he said blankly and she chuckled softly.

"Southerners say that whenever someone from the north does something inconceivable or odd," she explained with a grin. "I haven't figured out what it's supposed to mean yet, but give me another eight years here and I'm sure I will."

Thomas smiled faintly and then glanced to the adjoining townhouse again as they heard the door open once more. Both of them watched as the man hurried out, rushing from the step in his stocking feet, clutching a piece of paper in his hand . . . and a key, Inez saw, as the man opened his hand to offer both to Thomas.

"There's the key, son. My number's on the paper if you need aught. Show yourselves in and enjoy. I'm missing my *Baywatch*." On that note, he whirled away and rushed back inside his townhouse, slamming the door closed again. This time the sound of a lock clicking into place followed.

Thomas turned disbelieving eyes to her. "*Baywatch?*"

"We get reruns of all your best shows," she said dryly.

Thomas shook his head as he turned to unlock the

door. "I am Canadian. We're not responsible for *Baywatch*. You can not blame that on us."

"Just the Pamela Anderson part," Inez suggested with amusement.

"Only partially, I'm sure her implants are American," Thomas assured her as he opened the door and stepped back for her to enter.

Inez grinned and shook her head as she passed into the townhouse, flipping the switch to turn the lights on as she went. "I suppose we shouldn't make fun. *Baywatch* is probably the only excitement the old guy gets on a night."

"Old?" Thomas echoed with a wry laugh as he set her suitcase inside the door and followed her in. "He's a baby compared to me."

She must have had a stunned expression on her face because he frowned. "You knew that Inez. I told you I was born in 1794."

"Yes," she breathed and nodded her head. "I guess I just— It's so easy to forget. You don't seem old."

"Because I don't look old," Thomas said with a shrug and moved forward to rub his hands up and down her arms. "Are you all right? You aren't regretting—?"

"No," Inez interrupted quickly and gave her head a shake, not even really sure herself why the realization that he was older than the man next door had startled her so. She supposed 1794 had just been a number to her until now. Forcing herself to relax, she managed a stiff smile and teased, "I'm sure I'll adjust to dating an old fart."

"Oh!" Thomas groaned and clutched his chest. "That one went straight to the heart. You're a cruel woman, Inez Urso."

"And don't you forget it," she said, her smile becoming more natural.

"I won't," he assured her.

"And I have a temper too," Inez announced, turning away to peer into the living room beside them. It was a very neutral room; carpeted and painted in beige, the furniture all gray, and not a lick of decoration in it unless you counted a television as a work of art.

"A fine temper," Thomas agreed, glancing over her shoulder into the room. His hand curved over her bottom and he added, "And a fine behind too."

Inez slapped his hand away with a chuckle. "Behave, we have work to do."

"Yes, ma'am," he said agreeably, following as she walked up the hall to the kitchen. They both stood in the kitchen doorway, peering over the cream and brown room with a distinct lack of excitement.

"It looks clean," Inez said, trying not to be too critical.

"Yes, it does," Thomas agreed with amusement, turning his back to the hall wall so that she could precede him back up the hall and to the staircase. She understood why he wanted her to lead the way when she felt his fingers brushing down the backs of her ankles, tickling the spot he knew was sensitive as he followed her upstairs. Pausing, she turned a scowl over her shoulder. "I'm mortal. You really don't want me falling down these stairs and breaking my neck."

"I'd catch you," he assured her solemnly. "I'll always be there to catch you, Inez."

Swallowing, Inez turned forward again and continued upstairs.

There were two small bedrooms on this floor; one with twin beds and one with a double bed. There was also a rather large bathroom. Inez suspected the bathroom had been another bedroom before indoor plumbing became popular.

After testing the mattresses, she and Thomas settled on the room with the twin beds and retrieved their luggage to stow it there, then went down to check the kitchen for tea. Bastien had promised to have groceries delivered and apparently the old man had let the delivery guy in and put everything away. She supposed he'd forgotten to mention that in his eagerness to get to his *Baywatch* babes.

"Do you want tea in, or shall we go out and have a drink while everything is still open?" Thomas asked as they finished checking the cupboards.

"Let's go out. Maybe we'll get lucky and run into Marguerite while we're out."

Nodding, Thomas waited for her to grab her purse and ushered her out of the townhouse.

"I know you've never been to London before this trip," Inez said quietly as they walked. "But have you ever been to York?"

"Actually, I have been to London before," he informed her and then added, "But that was back in . . ." Thomas glanced skyward as he tried to remember. Finally he shrugged and said, "It was early eighteen something. I was in my twenties."

Inez glanced at him curiously. "And you never returned?"

Thomas shook his head solemnly. "My uncle, Jean Claude, pitched such a fit I didn't dare. He freaked if any of us even talked about going to England. He hated the place. I never figured out why," he added with a frown, and then went on. "Marguerite was born here and it's where they met. They spent a lot of time in England for the first couple of centuries. But . . ." He shrugged. "I don't know what happened, just that some time before I was born he got a hate-on for the country, wouldn't go near it himself, and tried to dissuade everyone else from going too."

Eyebrows rising slightly at this news, she asked, "And he was so scary that no one disobeyed him? I mean, even for an immortal, twenty must be considered an adult. Surely, if you'd wanted to go . . . ?"

"I wasn't afraid of him, Inez," Thomas said and then added, "At least, not for me. I no longer lived with him and Marguerite and could do what I wanted, but he'd take it out on her and Lissianna if I crossed him."

Inez frowned as she digested this. She already knew that Lissianna was Marguerite's daughter and Bastien's only sister, but had never heard much about Jean Claude. He was dead by the time she started working for Argeneau Enterprises.

"Was he physically violent?" she asked quietly, wondering if Thomas had been an abused child growing up. If so, he'd come around well, but she supposed he'd had a lot of time to do so.

"No." Thomas slid an arm around her waist and hugged her against his side. "Not physically. He was a drunk and mean as hell. The man could be vicious and could make everyone's life miserable with little effort and absolutely no remorse." Thomas sighed. "Marguerite and Lissianna were pretty much trapped at home with him. He wouldn't let Lissianna move out until she found a lifemate, and he refused to allow Marguerite to work. And he wasn't above using mind control to keep her there."

"Mind control?" Inez asked with shock, coming to an abrupt halt. "You said lifemates couldn't control each other."

"Marguerite and Claude weren't lifemates," he said quietly. "He turned her, but he could read and control her from the start and used it like a weapon. Against all of us."

"It must have made it hard for you growing up," she said quietly as they started walking again.

"There are worse things," Thomas said with a shrug and then glanced at her out of the corner of his eye and asked, "But I'm more interested in you. What was your childhood like?"

Inez smiled faintly and shrugged. "No one's life is perfect, is it?"

"Mine is. Right this minute my life is absolutely perfect," he assured her, and then frowned and added, "Except for the fact that Marguerite is missing."

"Yes," she said quietly.

"So," Thomas said after they'd walked half a block. "What was your childhood like? Were both parents there? Or was it a single parent home?"

"Both parents were there, and I had an older brother. He was a pain as most older brothers are; bossy, superior, protective," Inez said, and then commented, "You have one sister, right?"

"Jeanne Louise," Thomas said with a nod, and then added, "I love her a great deal, but Lissianna and I are closer. We were close in age and grew up together."

Inez peered at him curiously. "How old is Jeanne Louise?"

"She'll be one hundred next year."

"Only one hundred?" she asked with surprise. "God, you were over a century old when she was born. No wonder you're closer to Lissianna."

Thomas smiled faintly. "Immortals are only allowed to have one child every hundred years."

"You mean the woman only ovulates once every hundred years?" Inez asked with amazement.

"No." He laughed at the idea. "It's a law, not a biological thing."

"Oh," she said, but then asked, "Whose law?"

"We have a council that makes our laws and that is one of them."

Inez was curious about that, but figured she could learn more about it later. Right now, she wanted to know more about his family. "If Jeanne Louise is only a hundred years old, then your parents are still alive?"

"My father is, but my mother died when I was four. That's why Aunt Marguerite raised me. Father didn't have a clue what to do with a toddler."

Inez relaxed a little. She'd wondered why—if his parents were alive—he'd been raised by his aunt. "So Jeanne Louise is your half sister? Your father found a second lifemate after your mother died?"

"Well, no, actually he didn't," Thomas admitted with a wry smile and then said, "It's kind of complicated. Basically, my father seems to be cursed when it comes to wives. They just kept dying on him . . . Not an easy thing when they were all immortals," he pointed out and then went on quietly, "After Jeanne

Louise's mother died, he just sort of gave up. He's a recluse now and doesn't see anyone. Jeanne Louise doesn't even know what he looks like."

"How sad," Inez murmured quietly.

Thomas shrugged. "He has to deal with it in his own way. I can't imagine how hard it must be to lose a lifemate. It's something I don't even want to contemplate," he added, squeezing her a little tighter against his side.

Inez didn't know what to say to that. She couldn't promise he would never lose her, since she wasn't sure he had her. She was growing more and more sure of her own feelings with every passing hour, but it just made her more certain that she couldn't be his lifemate if he couldn't love her back.

Deciding a change of topic was in order she said, "Tell me about your music."

Thomas came to an abrupt halt, his head whipping her way. "How did you know about that?"

"Your binder was open when I brought the phone out to you the first morning," she admitted solemnly. "You write music?"

Thomas blew his breath out and started to walk again. "Yes."

She bit her lip at the reluctance behind the word and was debating whether to change the subject again when he began to speak. He told her about Marguerite teaching him to play, about Jean Claude's jeering response to it, and his decision to keep his efforts to himself after that. And he had all these years. It seemed the man she was coming to love had a stubborn streak, at least about things that mattered to him. But that was all right, Inez decided. She could be a bit of a bull herself.

"How about this place?" Thomas asked suddenly, and Inez glanced around to see that while she'd been thinking they'd left the quiet residential area and entered the shopping section. The road around them was full of stores and restaurants, but the one Thomas was gesturing to was a small café on a corner. It was two floors, with glass windows running along both sides that looked out onto the street. Inez could see that it was a popular spot, even at this hour there were few empty tables.

"It looks promising," she commented and they went in.

"Why don't you tell me what you want and go find a table while I order?" Thomas asked as they reached the counter.

Nodding, Inez glanced over the menu on the boards on the wall behind the counter and said, "A latte and lemon muffin."

"Not tea?" Thomas asked with surprise.

"I never have tea away from home. They never steep it long enough," she informed him.

"Okay," he said with a laugh, and then pressed a quick kiss to her lips and urged her away. "Go hunt us up a table. I'll find you."

Smiling, Inez headed for the stairs to the second level. There weren't many tables on the main floor and the few there were taken. The second floor wasn't much better. As she'd noted from the street, it was quite busy, but Inez managed to find an empty table by the window and settled there to watch the stairs for Thomas.

It wasn't long before he appeared. His gaze swept the second level until he spotted her and then he headed straight over. Inez couldn't help but notice the glances cast his way by the other women in the restaurant as he passed them. She had the most juvenile urge to stick out her tongue at them. He was hers and no matter how beautiful, smart, or accomplished they were, those other women could never be anything more than blow-up dolls, or pretty puppets to him. It was good to know, but didn't keep her from wanting to pop the dolls with a pin, and cut the strings on the puppets.

"What is that expression about?" Thomas asked with amusement as he set the tray on the table.

"What expression?" Inez asked innocently.

"I'd have to describe it as gentle malice," he informed her as he passed her a latte and her muffin.

"Malice?" she asked with surprise. "Never."

"No?" Thomas asked mildly as he set his own drink and muffin in front of the chair opposite her, and then set the tray out of the way on the window sill beside them.

"No," Inez assured him. "I was just noticing that the women all eye you like candy and that I'd have to hurt them if they were foolish enough to try something."

Thomas had been in the process of taking his seat when she said that, but stilled, his eyes widening incredulously at her words.

"I assure you there was no malice in the thought at all," she said with a shrug.

A burst of laughter slipped from his lips and Thomas finished settling in his seat, then shook one finger back and forth at her. "Naughty, naughty. And here I thought your eyes were brown, not green."

"I'm not jealous," Inez assured him solemnly as she began to doctor her latte, adding sugar to it.

"No?" Thomas asked doubtfully and said, "I am."

Inez glanced at him with surprise. "What have you to be jealous of?"

"Of every guy who gives you the up and down look."

Inez laughed as he showed her the look; squinting his eyes and running them up and down what he could see of her figure above the table. Shaking her head, she protested, "No one does that."

"They do," he assured her. "Mr. Ginger-hair behind the counter downstairs was doing it."

"Well, I've never noticed it."

"I know," Thomas said with amusement. "And I think it's adorable that you're completely oblivious to how attractive you are. It makes me glad I'm not a mortal. I think a normal man would have to hit you over the head before you'd notice they were attracted to you."

Inez shook her head. "Men preferred leggy blondes and sexy redheads. I'm just boring me."

"Inez, love, there's nothing boring about you," he said dryly.

She stared at him silently, wishing he meant that. She wanted to be his love. Swallowing the sudden lump in her throat, Inez glanced down at her latte, took a sip, and then asked, "So how are we supposed to look for Marguerite here in York?"

Thomas blinked at the sudden change of topic, then allowed it and grimaced. "Well, we can't trace her phone."

"No," she agreed on a sigh.

"Or her credit cards," he added and then shook his

head. "In truth, I haven't got a clue where to start. We already know she isn't in one of the hotels."

"That leaves flats and rental houses," Inez said.

Thomas nodded. "But nothing has shown up on the Notte credit cards."

"They paid by cash or check, then," she said thoughtfully.

"It looks that way. Unfortunately, we can't go around knocking on every door in town."

"No." She frowned, and then asked, "What kinds of things does she like?"

"Music," Thomas said at once, and then added, "and reading."

"Music and reading," Inez said thoughtfully. "Would she be likely to go to concerts?"

"She might, but she's here to work."

Inez blinked. "Right. I forgot about that. She's looking for Christian Notte's mother."

Thomas nodded. "She and Tiny spent three weeks going through church and city archives searching for any mention of his birth."

"His mother was married to his father then?"

Thomas opened his mouth and then closed it again and finally just shook his head as he admitted, "I don't know. They might have just been looking for any mention of a child born named Christian. I doubt it was a popular name."

Inez nodded agreement. "You're probably right."

"I know they were in London to meet with Christian in the hopes that he could help them narrow the search or give them a possible clue."

Inez was silent for a moment, and then asked,

"Couldn't the father just tell them who the mother is and where to find her?"

When Thomas stared at her blankly, she pointed out. "Well, obviously Julius was here in England. The hotel suites were on his credit card. He must know who the mother is, why did he not just tell him?"

Thomas shook his head slowly. "I don't know. Maybe he did and they're now just trying to find the woman."

"Would it be that hard?" she asked curiously.

"Christian is over five hundred years old. Immortals change their names, move around . . . And few have social insurance numbers or other paperwork to trace them through, at least not under their own name." He shrugged. "It can be harder than finding a mortal."

"Okay, so Marguerite and Tiny traveled to London to meet with Christian in the hopes of getting more information, and his father, Julius, joined them there and presumably told them something that led them here to York," she commented, and Thomas nodded. They were both silent for a minute and then Inez pursed her lips and said, "You know there's something that's been kind of preying on my mind."

Thomas raised an eyebrow. "What's that?"

"Well, there were seven people in the party in London and then only five traveled on to York. What happened to the other two?"

"Seven people?" Thomas asked with confusion.

"Bastien said Julius requested two suites at Claridge's, with two bedrooms in each, and that three of the rooms were to have twin beds," she pointed out. "Three rooms with twin beds, that's six. The last didn't really matter so either it was another two who could share a bed, or it was only one."

"You're right," Thomas said with surprise.

Inez nodded solemnly. "So who were all these people?"

"Well . . ." Thomas considered the matter. "Two would be Marguerite and Tiny. Christian Notte and his father were also apparently there."

"And the other three?"

Thomas thought for a minute, and then said, "I don't know."

"Do you know anything about this Christian Notte?" Inez asked.

Thomas shrugged. "He's related to someone who works for my cousin Vincent. He and some other family members flew to California when my cousin had trouble out there. They stayed at his place. My aunt did too; that's how she ended up getting involved in his case." He scowled and then shrugged helplessly. "I have no idea who the other three people in the party could be. Or why only five of them continued on here to York."

Inez sat back in her seat and sighed. "It probably doesn't matter anyway. It was just bugging me."

They fell silent, both concentrating on their drinks and muffins, and then Inez glanced around.

"What is it?" Thomas asked, noting at once.

"I was just wondering where the ladies' room is," she admitted.

He glanced around the upper floor, and then said, "I don't see one up here, but there's one downstairs next to the stairs."

"Thank you. I'll be right back."

Grabbing her purse, Inez stood, and walked to the stairs. She descended them slowly, finding them a bit steep for her comfort. Relieved once she'd reached the ground floor, she glanced around for a sign for the ladies' room.

"Can I help you, miss?"

Inez glanced toward the speaker with a start, her eyes widening as she found herself peering at a tallish man with ginger hair. He wore the same green apron as the girl behind the counter had worn. Mr. Gingerhair really did exist, she realized with surprise.

"Miss?" the man asked with concern. "Are you all right?"

"I—Yes," Inez said, suddenly flustered. "I was just looking for the ladies' room." They tended to be called toilets here in England, but even after eight years, Inez couldn't bring herself to say that when looking for a restroom. She preferred the polite euphemism to the literal word.

"Oh, they're right over here." He led her to the right and Inez smiled and thanked him when she spotted the recessed sign reading "Toilets." She went into the ladies' room, finding herself in a small room with a booth in the corner and a sink to her left. With the number of patrons in the place, Inez wasn't surprised to find she had to wait and was just glad there weren't a couple of women already waiting before her.

Moving to the sink, Inez peered into the mirror and scowled at her hair. Knowing there was no use trying to tame the wild curls, she reached into her purse for her lipstick. She'd bitten or eaten off the lipstick she'd put on earlier and that, at least, was something she could repair.

As she ran the color over her lips, Inez found her mind returning to the matter of the hotel suites at Claridge's, but knew it was a waste of time even as she pondered it. She didn't know the people involved well enough to know who the other three people might have been. Obviously it was someone connected to Christian Notte; family members or friends maybe.

Inez had barely had that thought when the hand holding the lipstick stopped moving. *What if the other three were Christian's mother and her people? Her family or friends?*

The thought had hardly crossed her mind before she gave a small shake of the head and finished with her lipstick. No. If Christian's mother had been in the party then the case would have been over and Marguerite would have returned home.

Inez stilled as another thought struck her. Straightening, she peered blindly into the mirror as she considered that it might not have been his mother, but it could have been someone who could lead them to Christian's mother. Marguerite might have found someone who was around at the time that he was born and who could lead them to the woman who gave him life. In which case, they may have come here, found his mother, and then . . . Then what?

If Julius was one of the ones who left the party when they left London, they might have felt it was necessary to meet back up with him after finding the woman to ensure they had the right one. In the normal course of events they could have just snapped a picture and sent it to him by cell phone or email to have him confirm or deny the woman's identity, but this wasn't a normal case. From the sounds of it, the father didn't want Christian to find his mother. He might make things difficult. They might have to fly back to Italy or wherever he was and see his reaction to the woman to know if they had the right one. If so, they might not even be here in York anymore.

On the other hand, Inez admitted, they may have found the woman and still be here for some reason. Their being in Italy was a slim chance, especially since Bastien had called the day before and was told they were in England. Still, they could have flown home since then and a phone call only took a couple of moments. There was no harm in checking was there?

The door opened beside her, and Inez glanced toward it, hoping it wasn't someone who would try to hop in line before her when the woman in the booth finally came out. She really had to go.

Fortunately, it was a man and he was obviously in the wrong bathroom. Inez offered a wryly sympathetic look as she waited for the tall, fair-haired man to realize his mistake, offer embarrassed apologies, and back out. But he wasn't doing that. He was staring straight at her with grim determination and continuing into the room.

Thirteen

Having grown up in a house with two women, Thomas knew how long they could take in the bathroom, so he moved to a table holding a stack of magazines and newspapers, searching for something to read while he waited for Inez. He'd just settled on the local newspaper, when he saw her returning. Eyebrows rising at how quick she'd been, he dropped the newspaper and headed back to the table.

Her head was bowed and she was peering down into her cup when he sat down. When she continued to sit like that, he frowned with concern. "Is everything all right?"

Inez glanced up, a questioning smile curving her lips. "Yes, of course. Why?"

Thomas smiled in return, and shook his head. "I just wondered."

She smiled and then took her last bite of muffin, and drank down the last of her latte. Thomas followed suit and then raised his eyebrows. "Ready to go?"

Inez nodded, collected her purse and stood. "Where to now?"

Thomas grimaced and admitted, "Well, the only thing I can think to do is keep walking around with an eye out to spotting Aunt Marguerite. York isn't that big a city, at least its center isn't large, and it doesn't appear too busy at night. Maybe we'll get lucky and spot her. In the meantime, we'll try to think of places to look for her. We might check the book stores to-morrow evening. It's too late tonight, but we'll have to check the hours and see if they're open later than five o'clock."

"They might be," Inez said as they walked to the stairs. "This is a high-tourist area, so they might stay open later to cater to tourists."

"Well, if we come across the store, we can check their hours," Thomas said as he followed her down the stairs. "But for tonight, we'll just walk around and try to come up with ways to find her. I'd suggest checking anywhere they might have archives, but those definitely won't be open at this hour. I suspect Tiny would have to do those kind of searches."

"Which makes Marguerite rather de trop," she said wryly.

"Yes," Thomas agreed. "And she wouldn't like that. I'm sure she'd have found some way to go with him, either going during daylight or finding a way to get in at night."

Inez nodded as she stepped off the bottom step.

She took two steps forward and then stopped and glanced around.

"What is it?" Thomas asked, stepping off the last step and moving to her side.

"I was just wondering where the ladies' room is," she answered with a grimace.

"You have to go again?" Thomas asked with surprise before he quite realized that if she had, she should know where they were.

"Again? I haven't been since we left the hotel," Inez said on a laugh. "Oh, there it is. I'll be right back."

Thomas stared after her with bewilderment, watching until she disappeared through the door labeled toilets. Turning away then, he moved to the counter and peered absently at the goodies in the glass display, but his mind was with Inez.

Again? I haven't been since we left the hotel, she'd said, but she'd excused herself to find the ladies' room earlier.

"Women."

Thomas glanced up from the display to find himself peering at Mr. Ginger-hair who had taken such note of Inez earlier.

The fellow grinned and shrugged as he nodded toward the door to the bathrooms. "They're forever in the bathroom, aren't they?" he said wryly and then asked, "Did you want something to go?"

Thomas stared at the man, but rather than answer, he slipped into his mind. It was a quagmire of dissatisfaction with his job, his life and his love life, but Thomas eventually plucked out the memory of Inez coming below earlier and his showing her where the

bathrooms were. He also picked up a couple of rather
x-rated thoughts the guy had enjoyed at the time about
following her in there and—

"I'm ready."

Thomas quickly withdrew his mind and glanced to
the side to find Inez there, smiling at him brightly.

"Shall we go?"

Thomas nodded and gestured for her to lead the
way, taking the time to cast a scowl at Mr. Ginger-
hair before following her. He waited until they were
outside and walking again before saying, "Inez?"

"Yes?" She glanced at him quizzically.

He hesitated and then said, "Tell me what happened from the time we entered the coffee shop until
we left, please."

"Tell you what happened?" she echoed with surprise.

"Yes. I know it sounds an odd request, but it might
be important."

Inez stared at him with bewilderment for a minute and then apparently decided to humor him and
shrugged. "Okay . . . well . . . we walked in, went up
to the counter, you suggested I tell you what I wanted
and leave you to order while I went to find a table.
There were no free tables on the main floor, so I went
upstairs, spotted two, picked one by the windows and
sat down. You came up a minute later with our order.
We drank, ate, and talked, and then came down to
leave. I went to the ladies' room, joined you at the
counter, and we left." She raised an eyebrow. "Now,
tell me why I just said all that."

Thomas glanced away to hide his troubled expression. He couldn't read her mind to tell if she was
lying, but there was no reason to. She had absolutely

no recall of the first trip she'd made to find the ladies' room. A trip that should have been successful because he knew the coffee shop guy had pointed it out to her and had seen in his memory that she'd gone through the door marked toilets, but apparently something—*someone*, he corrected himself grimly, an immortal, had stopped her from going to the bathroom because she'd still had to go on the way out.

Inez had been controlled again and her mind wiped.

"Thomas," she said, grabbing his arm with a laugh. "Why did you want me to tell you that?"

Thomas opened his mouth to answer and then hesitated as he recalled how upset and vulnerable she'd appeared after realizing she'd been controlled in Amsterdam. He didn't want to see her upset again. In fact, at that moment, he wanted to grab her up and rush her back to the townhouse and keep her safe from being controlled again.

Halting, he suddenly peered quickly around, taking note of the few people on the street. No one seemed to be paying them undo attention or following them, but he suspected someone was.

"Thomas?"

He glanced down to her again, noting that she was starting to look worried. Inez wasn't a stupid woman. She would realize something was wrong. Forcing a smile, Thomas slid his arm around her shoulder and urged her to walk again as he lied, "I just like to hear the sound of your voice. You have an interesting accent; Portuguese with an overlay of British. It's quite charming."

Inez laughed and the relief in her voice made him

glad he'd lied as she said, "I'm not the one with the accent. You are."

"No. I have no accent at all," he assured her, glancing —nonchalantly, he hoped—around the street again. Now that he was aware that someone must be following them, his back was creeping as if it could sense eyes on it, though he couldn't really, he just knew they must be there. "You are the one with the accent."

Inez just shook her head and said, "Maybe we both do. Now, we should really talk about Marguerite and try to sort out ways to find her."

Thomas nodded solemnly, but his mind was on why she might have been controlled again. She hadn't been controlled long enough on either occasion for anything untoward to have been done to her. She'd only been gone ten or fifteen minutes the first time and maybe a little more than five in the coffee shop.

Had she seen or heard something someone didn't want her to? Perhaps she'd seen Marguerite, he thought and then suddenly recalled that this had been his first thought when he'd realized she'd been controlled in Amsterdam, but Marguerite hadn't even been the one with the phone in the first place.

Frowning, Thomas recalled that Inez had suggested that perhaps someone hadn't wanted her to realize that they were chasing the mugger with the phone, not Marguerite. Thomas reconsidered the idea now.

"You've gone suddenly silent and grim," Inez murmured, bringing his attention away from his thoughts. "What are you thinking about?"

Thomas hesitated, but finally admitted, "I was

thinking about the first time you were controlled in Amsterdam."

Inez stopped walking abruptly. "The *first* time?"

Thomas cursed himself for the slip of the tongue.

Light suddenly splashed over them and the street was filled with the sound of voices and laughter as a door opened behind them. Thomas glanced around to see they were standing outside a pub. It seemed fortuitous, he suddenly needed a drink and suspected Inez was going to need one too.

"Come on," he said, taking her arm to urge her toward the door, "we'll have a drink and I'll explain everything."

"So you think someone controlled me again," Inez murmured, peering down into the glass of ale she'd barely sipped at since the waitress had set it before her. The pub was a small, crowded affair with people sitting around tables, or standing around in groups talking. It was the real deal, a true English pub, not one of the ones opened for tourists.

Thomas had just finished telling her his version of their stop at the café. It was quite similar to her own except for the part about her getting up in the middle to go find the ladies' room. She believed him, but had no recall of that whatsoever.

Thomas reached out and squeezed her hand comfortingly. "Yes."

She nodded a slow acknowledgment. "Okay. Well, either I saw someone or something I shouldn't have when I went to the ladies' room, or . . ." *Or what?* she wondered helplessly.

"Back in Amsterdam, you suggested you were controlled and your memory wiped because someone didn't want us to realize that the mugger had the phone, not Aunt Marguerite," he reminded her. "I think you might be right about that now. So long as we thought Aunt Marguerite was in Amsterdam, we would have stayed there searching for her. But finding out the mugger had the phone and not her made us immediately head back to England. And it turns out she was here in York the whole time."

"So you think I was right and whoever controlled me just now might have done so for a similar reason?"

He nodded.

Inez peered into her glass again, and then raised her eyes and said, "That would suggest that this last time I was controlled because I either saw or was about to see something that might lead us to Marguerite."

Thomas nodded and sat back in his seat, irritation on his face as he said, "But this time we don't have any idea what."

"No," she agreed and then added, "But it tells us we might be on the right track now."

"Yes, it does," he said with surprise and smiled at her.

"So, let's try to put together what we do know," Inez suggested and reached into her purse to pull out a notepad and pen. Setting the pad on the tabletop, she pushed the button to eject the pen nib and wrote at the top of the first page, "Things we know."

She glanced up at Thomas. "We know she drove to London with Tiny and stayed at the Dorchester."

Thomas sat forward as she wrote that down and

added, "And we know Notte rented two suites of two rooms, requesting three have twin beds."

Inez nodded as she wrote that down, commenting, "That has kind of bothered me since I heard it."

"I know. You said," Thomas murmured, sounding distracted.

Inez glanced up with surprise, but he was looking thoughtful, obviously considering what the next point should be. Shrugging to herself, she glanced down to the notepad, muttering, "I didn't realize I'd mentioned it to you."

"What?"

Inez raised her head again surprised to see the frozen look on his face, but told him, "I said I hadn't thought I'd mentioned it to you."

Thomas sat forward, leaning on the table as he said, "We talked about it in the café."

Inez was silent, her mind now chasing the memory of such a conversation, but there was no memory to be found. In fact, she just had some vague recollection that they'd chatted amicably but couldn't say what about. When she told him that now, Thomas sat back again, his expression thoughtful.

"Why would our conversation be removed from my memory?" she asked uncertainly.

"Maybe we were getting too close to figuring something out," Thomas said slowly.

That seemed a good possibility, Inez supposed. "What did we say?"

"You said that even though there were only five tickets to York, the two suites of two rooms with the request that at least three of them have twin beds sug-

gested there were seven people in London. We tried
to figure out who they were, but don't know enough
and came up three short."

"Who were the four we came up with?" Inez asked
and then said, "Marguerite, Tiny, and Christian and
his father?"

"Yes, but we couldn't come up with anyone else
and then you got up to go find the ladies' room."

"I was probably still thinking about it then."

"Yes," Thomas agreed and then said, "I think Bastien mentioned Christian having a couple of cousins
with him in California. They might have been among
the group."

Inez reached for her drink to take a sip as she considered this, and grimaced as the flat, tepid beer filled
her mouth.

"Bad huh?" Thomas asked with sympathy. "Mine
has gone warm too." He glanced around and then grimaced. "The waitress probably won't return so long
as our glasses are full. I'll go up to the bar and get us
a couple more drinks. Keep thinking about this and
try to come up with what you might have thought
of the first time. They can take away the memory of
figuring it out, but not the reasoning skills that got
you there and you have excellent reasoning skills," he
added encouragingly, then patted her hand and stood
to move to the bar.

Inez smiled faintly as she watched him go. He always knew the right thing to say. And she enjoyed
just looking at the man, she acknowledged, her eyes
dropping over his tapered back to his derrière in the
tight jeans.

A little sigh slid from her lips as she wished that

they had time just to be together. She'd really rather be back at the hotel Dorchester making love with him than here trying to sort out what had been stolen from her memory.

Unfortunately, until they found Marguerite, they didn't have the time for what she wanted, Inez reminded herself and set her thoughts on the matter of who the others in Marguerite's party might have been. Bastien had said that there had been only five tickets to York, so the party had dropped in number. She doubted Marguerite and Tiny had left the group, they were the ones who were supposed to find the mother. Christian would have been one too, and probably his father, but since she had no idea who the others might have been, she had no idea who had left the party.

Inez considered the cousins Thomas had mentioned being in California with Christian and wondered if Bastien had thought to try to contact them. If it was one of those men who had dropped out of the group when it moved on to York, they might be able to lead them in the right direct—

Inez thoughts died abruptly as she suddenly found herself standing up and turning away from the table. She wasn't doing either thing herself, it was simply happening, as if a puppet master were directing her movements.

That thought sent a wave of panic through her as she recalled Christian's description of most mortal women being nothing better than blow up dolls or puppets to immortals. She was being controlled again, Inez realized, and wondered if the first two times it had happened she'd been aware and felt the panic now claiming her. And Inez was most definitely feeling panic. Her heart was thumping wildly in her chest, her mind racing with desperate ideas to end this. She tried to take back control and force her body to stop, but couldn't even manage to slow her steps. Inez then tried screaming or even whispering, but her mouth was tight closed, not a sound coming from her throat.

Don't panic, she ordered herself. It will be all right. So what if your mind is erased again? You haven't been hurt by it before, she told herself, but the thoughts had a hollow ring to them. The previous two times she'd been controlled she'd been returned to Thomas, the first time back to the hotel in Amsterdam, and just an hour ago in the café she'd been sent back to their table—but now she was being led away from Thomas. Surely if they just wanted to erase her mind, they didn't have to take her away to do it!

Inez had no idea, she didn't know how it was done, but for some reason this time felt different. She didn't think the intention was to just erase her memory and let her go again.

She was walking through the middle of the pub on a path to the door, weaving her way around groups and individuals and no one seemed to notice the least little problem. Surely her eyes showed her panic?

Inez tried to find Thomas with her eyes. He at least would realize something was wrong, he would see her fear, she thought, but couldn't find him in the crowd. She couldn't even see the bar for the people between her and it. Inez kept trying, though; right up until she reached the pub door and her hand rose to push it open. As she stepped out into the cool night breeze, Inez knew she was lost.

The area around the bar was thick with people waiting their turn. The man pulling the draft was being worked off his feet, but was cheerful despite all that. Thomas waited, trying to be patient. It was always difficult to wait when you knew that, ultimately, you didn't have to. He could easily have taken control of the man and had him serve up their drinks in front of the others, and then could have stopped anyone who took issue with his being served before them, but he didn't. At least, he didn't until he saw the waitress who had served them on their arrival, slip behind the bar to collect drinks.

Pursing his lips, Thomas glanced at the long line still in front of him, and then slipped into the waitress's mind, deposited his order there for her to bring to their table, and then headed back to Inez. Crowded as it was, Thomas was almost back at the table before he realized Inez was no longer there.

Surprise flickered through him, but was quickly followed by alarm when he saw that her purse was still at the table, sitting out in the open for anyone to take. In fact, someone was approaching now and reaching for it, he realized and narrowed his eyes on the woman.

"I wouldn't if I were you," Thomas growled as he reached the table.

The woman snatched her hand back, saying quickly, "I was just going to take it to the bar. I thought the girl forgot it when she left."

Thomas didn't bother to argue with the mortal

woman. Lips twisting, he snatched up the purse and started to turn away, but then frowned as he realized what she'd said. Swiveling back, he stabbed her mind with his own, entering swiftly and found a vision of Inez walking stiffly out of the bar, her expression blank.

Cursing, Thomas whirled away and hurried for the door, Inez's pursed tucked under his arm like a football. It never occurred to him that he might look like a mugger fleeing the scene of a crime until a man stepped in his path, snarling, "Give it 'ere ye lousy t'ief."

Thomas nearly mowed the man down, but then quickly slipped into his mind and moved him aside instead. It was rare enough others troubled themselves to stop a criminal; and while the man had misunderstood the situation, he thought he was stepping up to help a lady in distress. Thomas thought he should be rewarded, not plowed down.

No one else got in his way, and Thomas crashed through the pub door and out onto the street without further hindrance.

A slight breeze had kicked up outside. It sent his hair ruffling as he glanced first one way and then the other. Thomas didn't see Inez in either direction, and panic became a living beast in his chest, clawing at his heart. He couldn't lose her now. He'd waited two hundred years for Inez, he simply *couldn't* lose her.

Spotting a crossroad just a little ways up to his left, Thomas hurried toward it, thinking that surely that would have been where she'd been taken. He hadn't been away from the table long, whoever was controlling her would have wanted to get her off this street in case Thomas came looking, and this was the nearest corner.

Pausing at the crossroads, he glanced left and right again, freezing when he spotted a bit of brilliant white in the distance. Despite his exceptional eyes, it took him a moment to realize that it was a figure in a brilliant white blouse and dark slacks being led off the sidewalk and down what must be steps by a dark figure all in black. Thomas couldn't be sure from this distance, but by the size difference between his petite Inez and the figure with her, he'd guess her captor was a man.

God Bless her penchant for wearing white blouses, Thomas thought as he set out up the street at a dead run. If she'd been wearing black like himself and the man with her, he never would have spotted her before she disappeared from view.

Thomas crossed the distance quickly, uncaring that anyone might see the speed he traveled at and wonder. He slowed when he thought he was drawing close to where Inez had been led off the sidewalk, and soon spotted a set of stone steps just before the bridge that crossed the river. They led down to a lower level with a stone path that ran along the river.

Thomas stopped at the top of the stairs and peered down, spotting Inez and her captor at once. The dark figure was most definitely a man, tall, and wide and built like a warrior of old. An immortal that was older than he, Thomas surmised, but couldn't care less. He wasn't giving Inez up without a fight, not even if it killed him.

He was about to start down the step when he saw

the man bring Inez to a halt. Thomas frowned as he watched him turn her so that she faced the water, placing her back to him, but when he then raised his hands placing one on her shoulder and one around her face, Thomas recognized that he was about to break her neck, then probably drop her in the river. He roared with fury and hurled Inez's purse like a missile.

Thomas didn't wait to see if the purse hit its target, but immediately charged down the stairs at a speed he didn't think he'd ever reached before. Still, he did see the purse slam into the man's head and send him stumbling a startled step to the side, dragging Inez with him. Regaining his balance, the man glanced up the path to where Thomas was just hurling himself off the last step and racing toward them. The immortal hesitated, and then shoved Inez off the edge and into the river even as he turned to race away.

Heart lurching in his chest, Thomas put on another burst of speed, raced to the edge of the path, and dove into the water after Inez. The River Ouse was cold, dark, and murky. It was impossible to see anything.

Silently cursing, Thomas waved his arms around, searching blindly for Inez. He was beginning to despair of finding her when the tips of his fingers brushed against something. Moving in that direction, he waved his arms again and this time caught something in the crook of his elbow. Grabbing at whatever it was with his other hand, he felt his fingers close around an arm and immediately pushed off the riverbed toward the surface, tugging her along with him.

The impetus of his push sent him whizzing through

the water. Thomas was still moving at speed when he hit the surface and rose out of the water up to his waist, before receding back into it. He glanced toward Inez as he started to slide back into the water, realizing only then that he had her by the calf, not her arm as he'd first thought.

Kicking his feet to stay above water, Thomas quickly shifted her around, drawing her head out of the water as he caught her by the upper arms. Her head was tipped back and the moonlight glowed down on her face. Thomas's jaw tightened as he noted the blue tinge to her skin. It was most noticeable around her lips.

Thomas drew her closer, pinched her nose and blew air into her mouth several times, then kicked toward shore, crossing half the distance before stopping again. He breathed into her again before continuing on to the embankment where he once again took a moment to breathe air into her.

Thomas managed to get them both out of the water, lifting Inez out first and then following. He crawled to her side and peered down at her face in the moonlight, frowning at her poor color. Swallowing back the fear tickling its way up his throat, he promptly set to work. Thomas tilted her head back and lifted her chin, then bent to listen for breathing. When he didn't hear anything, he pinched her nose closed, breathed into her mouth twice, and then placed the heel of his hand on her breastbone, placed his other hand on the first and pressed straight down fast and hard thirty times in a row before stopping to breathe into her mouth again, watching her chest rise as he blew in, then fall as he stopped.

"Come on, Inez," Thomas muttered as he switched back to compressions. "Don't you die on me. Come on!"

He bent to breathe into her mouth, jerking away when she suddenly began to cough. Turning her swiftly on her side, Thomas made sure her head was tilted back so her throat wasn't blocked and then simply rubbed her back as she continued to cough and began to spit up the water she'd swallowed.

When Inez finally fell back with a moan, Thomas reached down to brush away the damp hair plastered to her face and breathed out with relief.

Noting that her color was much better now, he took a moment to run his hands over her neck. Thomas was sure the other immortal hadn't got the chance to do an injury to her, but he checked anyway, relieved when her neck seemed fine.

Sitting back on his heels, he glanced up and down the path, but there was no one around. The immortal was long gone, and while he could see a couple of people walking across the bridge at the end of the path, they were far enough away they didn't even seem to notice he and Inez. Certainly no one appeared to have noticed them in the water and rushed to help.

Another moan from Inez drew his gaze back and Thomas leaned over her again. "Love?" he said quietly. "Are you awake?"

Inez's eyes fluttered open. They were full of confusion and pain until she recognized him and then relief filled her expression and she whispered, "Thomas."

"Yes, love. I'm here. You're safe now."

Her fingers clutched weakly at his hand, her eyes

solemn as she gasped, "Thought would die before could tell you—"

Thomas felt his heart tighten as she broke off into a deep, painful sounding coughing fit. Slipping his arm behind her back, he lifted her into a half-sitting position, and then rubbed her back, trying to help her through it.

"Have to tell you," she gasped once it was over.

"Don't talk, love. Just rest," he insisted worriedly.

She shook her head with frustration and tried anyway. "I want you to know, I lo—"

Thomas rubbed her back again as she went into another coughing fit. He was sure she was trying to tell him she loved him, and while he wanted to hear those words more than anything in the world, he didn't want them at the expense of her health.

"You can tell me after," he assured her, scooping her into his arms once this fit ended. "When you're feeling better."

When she merely moaned and sagged weakly against his chest, Thomas held her a little closer and turned toward the stairs. He stumbled over something on the path and glanced down. Spotting her purse, Thomas stooped and rested Inez's legs on his knees as he picked it up. Fortunately, it was a zippered purse and hadn't burst open on impact. Slinging it over his shoulder, he slid his arm under her legs again and straightened to walk to the stairs.

Inez remained still and silent in his arms as he mounted the stairs. Thomas kept glancing down at her, his attention torn between the steps and his concern for her.

"Hang in there, Inez. I'll take you to a hospital. You'll be okay," he murmured.

Inez's reaction to the words was almost violent. Jerking in his arms, she raised panicked eyes to him.

"No. . . . No hospital," she protested, her voice hoarse and weak.

Thomas frowned at her upset, but said, "It's for the best, love. You nearly drowned."

"He'll find me," Inez cried, and the fear in her voice made his heart hurt. It also told him that the immortal hadn't bothered to wipe his taking control of her from her memories, but then, why would he bother? Thomas was sure the man had intended for her to die. He'd stake his life that he'd been about to snap her neck when he'd intervened.

Perhaps the hospital wasn't such a good idea, Thomas acknowledged. He didn't want her out of his sight for a minute from now on and couldn't guarantee they wouldn't try to separate them at the hospital or try to keep her overnight. The immortal might very well get his hands on her again and Thomas wasn't allowing that.

"No hospital," he assured her soothingly as she moved restlessly in his arms. "I'll take you back to the townhouse now."

A little sigh of relief slipped from her lips and Inez closed her eyes and went still in his arms, but her expression was still tight with fear. Thomas felt a slow rage begin to burn in him as he peered down at her.

No woman should have to live in fear, and he'd be damned if his was going to, Thomas thought grimly as he started up the stairs. The moment he had Inez back to the townhouse he was going to turn her. The immortal would still be able to read her until she was taught to put up—and keep up—guards, but she would be harder to read and control . . . and definitely harder to kill. At least she'd have a fighting chance.

The streets were relatively quiet. Thomas only past a few people on his way back to the townhouse and had little trouble wiping the memory of their passing from their minds. The last thing he needed was someone calling the police and telling them they saw a man carrying an unconscious woman through town center. Still, he was so relieved to reach the townhouse that he didn't notice that the lights he'd turned off on the way out were on again as he struggled to unlock the door and get Inez inside.

Thomas had just kicked the door closed and turned to carry Inez upstairs to the bedroom when that realization struck him. He stopped, one foot on the bottom step as adrenaline began to rush through him, then jerked his eyes to the top of the landing as the sound of a door opening upstairs reached his ears.

When no one appeared at the top of the stairs and he heard movement in one of the rooms, Thomas whirled and hurried silently across the hall and into the living room. He set Inez out of the way on the couch, then turned back and crept toward the door, slowing only long enough to snatch a lamp off a table and jerk the cord out of the wall, before continuing out into the hall.

Fourteen

"You can't turn Inez without her permission."
Thomas scowled as Etienne repeated that refrain and wished he'd never mentioned his plans, but simply gone ahead and done it. Actually, he wished he'd koshed his cousin over the head rather than stop himself at the last minute when he'd realized who had just walked out of the bedroom.

After leaving Inez in the living room, Thomas had crept upstairs, the lamp at the ready to batter some immortal butt. He'd been on the landing, just approaching the only closed door—the one with the double bed—when it had suddenly opened and Etienne had walked out.

Thomas had lowered the lamp with relief and then the two men had hugged in greeting and Rachel had come out of the bedroom as Etienne explained that he'd met his deadline and she'd managed to get some time off work and they'd come to help in the search.

The crotchety old man next door had let them into the townhouse when they arrived. He hadn't been pleased to be rousted from his bed in the middle of the night, but Etienne had slipped into his thoughts and erased the whole event from his mind before sending him back to sleep. When he woke up in the morning, the man would think he'd slept peacefully through the night.

When Rachel had then asked what they'd come up with so far, Thomas had recalled Inez and rushed back downstairs and into the living room with them on his heels.

Rachel had taken one look at the unconscious woman lying pale and soaking on the sofa and sent Thomas upstairs to fetch a nightgown or something for her to change her into. Thomas had rushed upstairs, opened Inez's suitcase, peered at the sexy black negligee that had been purchased and sent to the hotel in Amsterdam, and promptly closed the suitcase. He'd be damned if Etienne was seeing her in that. He'd then gone to his own knapsack and retrieved one of his shirts, sure that—short as she was—it would hang well past her knees. He'd taken it down to Rachel only to find both he and Etienne banished from the room as Rachel stripped the unconscious woman of her wet clothes and replaced it with the shirt.

The two men had waited in the kitchen until she was finished and then Thomas had given them a quick rundown of what had happened and the deductions they'd come up with before heading upstairs to change. On the way to the stairs, he'd looked in the living room to see that Inez was asleep and tucked under a throw on the sofa.

Etienne had approached while he was staring at her and had said quietly, "Bastien says she's your life mate."

Thomas had nodded. "She is and I'm turning her as soon as I finish changing."

"She's agreed to it already?" Etienne had asked with surprise.

"No, but I'm doing it anyway," Thomas had announced and turned to head upstairs.

Sucking in a sharp breath, Etienne had immediately chased after him to argue the point as he changed. By the time Thomas had finished and started out into the hall, the argument had been getting pretty heated. Only the sight of Rachel in the hall had calmed them both down. Unfortunately, it hadn't made Etienne shut up.

"You can't," Etienne repeated firmly, following him when he started downstairs.

"You turned Rachel without getting her permission first," Thomas growled with resentment.

"Rachel wasn't conscious. I couldn't get her permission," Etienne pointed out, on his heels. "And she was dying; it was the only way to save her."

"Well, Inez nearly died tonight," Thomas argued as he stepped off the last step and started across the hall toward the living room door.

"But she didn't," Etienne growled, losing some of his patience.

"Only by pure luck," Thomas said in a soft hiss to avoid waking Inez as he reached the side of the couch where she was sleeping. He peered down at her sleeping form with worry.

"Don't be so bloody bullheaded. When she wakes up you can ask her and if she agrees you can turn her."

Thomas stiffened and then wheeled around, his heart thumping with alarm at the suggestion. "And what if she refuses?"

Etienne halted and peered at him silently, obviously uncertain what to say to reassure him. It was Rachel who spoke. Following them into the room, she slipped her hand into her husband's, presenting a united front as she asked quietly, "Have you not discussed it with her at all?"

Thomas glanced away. "She knows she's my lifemate, and a little about the turning, but she hasn't agreed to either be my lifemate or be turned." His mouth twisted with displeasure as he admitted, "I wanted to give her time to consider it."

"Well, she's had some time to think," Rachel said slowly. "Maybe she won't refuse."

"But what if she does?" Thomas persisted and admitted painfully, "I don't want to lose her, Rachel, and if I turn her now, I won't."

"Are you sure?" Rachel asked quietly. "Turning her without permission might actually make you lose her. I wasn't happy to be turned without my permission, but when it was explained that Etienne had done so to save my life, I understood. Inez would be a different matter entirely. She might resent having her choice taken away and might never forgive you for it."

Thomas sagged and let his breath out on a sigh, knowing she was right, but . . . Raising his head he admitted, "I'd rather lose her from my life, but know she was alive and well than lose her altogether to death."

Rachel's eyes widened slightly and then slid to the side and back before she clarified, "You'd be willing to live alone and without a lifemate for the rest of your life just to insure Inez was well?"

Thomas nodded grimly.

"Then you must love her a great deal," she said quietly.

"She's the woman I've been waiting for all my life."

A sound to the side made Thomas glance to the sofa. He stiffened as he saw that Inez's eyes were open and she was struggling weakly to sit up, her eyes wide as she peered at him.

"Inez." Stepping quickly to her side, he lifted her in his arms and then settled on the sofa, settling her upright in his lap. Holding her there, Thomas pressed her close and rubbed her back, his gaze worried as he glanced over her pale face. "How are you feeling? Are you all right? You look so pale," he added fretfully.

Inez peered at him silently, her expression solemn and then nodded and turned toward Rachel and Etienne as a rustle of clothing accompanied their moving farther into the room.

"This is my cousin, Etienne, and his wife, Rachel. Aunt Marguerite is Etienne's mother. They've come to help us find her."

Inez managed a small smile and nod, but didn't try to speak as she offered her hand to the couple in greeting. Recalling that her voice had been hoarse and weak when she'd tried to speak by the riverside, Thomas asked, "Is your throat sore?"

Inez nodded again and then tried to say "yes" but it came out a painful rasp.

"I'll see if there's any honey or something to soothe her throat in the kitchen," Rachel said as she released her hand.

"Thank you," Thomas and Inez said together, but his voice was the only one to be heard. He scowled and said, "Stop trying to talk. You'll just hurt yourself."

"So turn me and stop the pai—" Her raspy voice died as she was claimed by a coughing fit.

Thomas barely noticed that Rachel had stopped in the doorway and turned around wide-eyed. His heart had leapt in his chest and his gaze was fixed on the woman in his arms. He simply stared at her until her fit eased and she fell against his chest exhausted, then lunged to his feet and held her close as he headed for the door. "You heard her. She gave permission."

"Just a minute," Etienne said sharply hurrying after him and catching his arm to stop him.

Thomas paused reluctantly between Rachel and Etienne and turned so that he could see both of them. Eyeing his cousin impatiently, he asked, "What now?"

Etienne hesitated and then glanced at Inez and said, "Do you know what you're agreeing to here?"

She nodded solemnly.

"Vampires are forever, Inez," he said quietly. "Or long enough that it seems like forever."

"Thank you very much," Rachel said from the doorway in dry tones.

Etienne scowled at his wife. "You know what I mean."

When Rachel nodded slightly, he turned back to Inez. "Are you sure you want to do this?"

She nodded again.

"You realize you'll be his lifemate? Forever?" Etienne persisted.

Inez nodded once more, but when Etienne opened his mouth to speak again, Rachel tsked impatiently. "Just ask her what you really want to know."

Thomas raised his eyebrows as Rachel now moved in front of them and peered solemnly at Inez.

"I'm sorry, but I have to ask this. We love Thomas. He's a great guy and deserves to be loved. Do you love him? Is that love strong enough to last for centuries?"

Thomas glanced down at Inez, and despite the fact that he was almost positive she'd been trying to tell him she loved him down by the river, her found himself holding his breath. She didn't simply nod this time, but gave the question the consideration Rachel was demanding. She took a moment, her expression thoughtful, and then she turned a solemn gaze on him for another moment before turning back to Rachel and nodding.

Letting his breath out on a gust of relief, Thomas turned to head out the door. "You heard her. I'm turning her."

"Dammit Thomas, wait a minute," Etienne snapped, rushing after him as he started up the stairs. "You can't do this."

"The hell I can't. I can and *am* doing it right now."

"Stop thinking with your dick and use your head," Etienne snarled. "Do we have enough blood here for her to turn? And what about the pain?"

It was the second question that brought him to a halt at the top of the stairs. Frowning, he glanced at Etienne as the man squeezed past to get in front of them on the landing. Rachel followed, and Thomas couldn't help noticing she was biting her lip and looking worried now.

"It's painful," Etienne said grimly, his gaze focused on Inez's face as he spoke.

Noting the trepidation now growing on Inez's face, Thomas scowled. "Stop trying to scare her out of it."

"I'm not, but she should know it's not all happy, happy, joy, joy," Etienne said firmly and then turned to Inez again. "I'm not talking toothache pain here. I'm talking unbearable agony, drowning in a vat of acid that's eating you up inside and out, horrible, nightmare ridden, desperate pain that will make you wish someone would just put a bullet in your brain and end it all . . . or cut off your head since you'll be immortal and a bullet wouldn't kill you."

Thomas felt Inez shrink against him and snapped, "Shut up, Etienne. How would you know anything about it? You were born one and slept through Rachel's turning."

"I was unconscious," Etienne quickly corrected and then challenged, "And I know you were there for Greg's turning. Tell her it isn't true, if you can."

When Inez turned to him in question, Thomas sighed unhappily. He couldn't lie to her. From what he'd seen and been told it was a slow ride through hell.

"I'm sorry, "he said finally. "It is very bad. I wish I could go through it for you, but . . ." He shook his head.

"It doesn't have to be that way," Etienne said quietly. "Despite what you think I'm not trying to stop you, I'm simply trying to slow you down. Rather than do it now, why not call Bastien and have him arrange

for blood and drugs to be sent here so that she can
turn with at least a little less pain?" He glanced to
Inez then and said apologetically, "The drugs don't
stop the pain, but they ease it a little, enough, at least,
that it won't leave you insane at the end of it."

When her eyes went round, Thomas grimaced. He'd
forgotten about that little detail. There had been re-
corded occasions when turns had come out of it quite
mad, their minds snapped by the endless agony. Sure
she wouldn't want to be turned after this, and no longer sure himself that he could endure her suffering so,
Thomas turned and started back downstairs, growl-
ing, "Call Bastien, then, and get on it. In the meantime, I'm getting her some honey for her throat."

"You can put me down," Inez whispered when
Thomas carried her into the kitchen and tried to open
the cupboard door without releasing her.

"No. I almost lost you. I'm not putting you anywhere. You're staying with me until we catch this
bastard. And stop trying to talk," he muttered, finally
settling her rump on the counter and keeping one arm
around her waist as he opened cupboards and rifled
through them with his free hand.

Much to his relief, a jar of honey had been in the
groceries ordered and delivered to the townhouse.
Closing his fingers around it, Thomas slid his arm
under her legs, carried her out to the living room
and settled on the couch with her. Reaching his arms
around her to get both hands on the jar, he unscrewed
the cap and then hesitated as he realized he'd forgotten a spoon.

A glance at Inez showed her biting her lip, amusement twinkling in her eyes.

Thomas felt a laugh bubble up in his own chest at his ridiculous behavior and then sighed. "I'm going to set you on the couch and go get you a spoon."

Inez nodded. "You could do that," she whispered. "Or you could use your fingers."

Thomas eyed the challenge in her eyes, and then dipped one finger in the honey jar and scooped up some to hold out before her. Inez leaned forward, opened her mouth and closed it around his finger, slowly drawing her lips the length of the digit, her eyes meeting his the whole time.

"Damn," Thomas breathed as Little Thomas stirred to life beneath her bottom.

When his finger slid free of her warm, wet mouth, Inez smiled like a satisfied cat and licked her lips. Thomas watched her little pink tongue slide over those soft, full lips and felt Little Thomas come to gasping life. When she finished and raised an eyebrow, he quickly scooped up more honey and held it out.

"For heaven's sake, Thomas. Use a spoon."

Little Thomas fell into a faint as Thomas turned sharply to see Rachel standing in the door shaking her head.

"I'll get you one." Still shaking her head, Rachel headed off up the hall in search of a spoon.

"I used to like her," Thomas said sadly, staring at the empty doorway after she'd gone and then glanced quickly at Inez as she fell against him making alarming noises.

Promptly dropping the honey, Thomas caught her by the arms and urged her upper body away from his chest to see her face and figure out what to do to help her, but paused in surprise when he realized that she was laughing.

"What's so funny?" he asked with confusion, which just brought another round of the rather horrible honking sounds from her.

"Here. You can——" Rachel had started into the room, holding a spoon out before her, but suddenly stopped, her eyes going wide before she hurried forward. "Gees, Thomas, you've spilled the honey everywhere!"

He glanced down as she snatched the jar out of Inez's lap and noted that he had indeed spilled the honey. It was all over her lap, glistening on her bare thighs where the shirt had slid up, not to mention other delightful places that were still mostly covered.

"So I have," Thomas murmured and stood abruptly to carry Inez around Rachel and out of the room.

"Where are you going?" Rachel asked with surprise, trailing them to the doorway.

"I'm just going to see her cleaned up," Thomas called as he hurried up the stairs, bouncing Inez around in his arms. "We'll be back to hear what Bastien said later . . . Maybe a lot later. Inez is tired and needs a nap."

He'd reached the top of the stairs by then and hurried quickly into the bedroom with twin beds, kicking the door closed behind him. Inez was making those horrible raspy, honking sounds again, her body trembling with laughter in his arms, but Thomas didn't order her to stop laughing to save her voice. Instead, he simply kissed her to shut her up and didn't stop until the laughter died and a broken moan slid into his mouth.

Satisfied, he lifted his head to peer at her.

Inez opened her eyes and raised an eyebrow and said in a whisper, "I thought you were going to clean me up? Shouldn't you have taken me to the bathroom for that?"

"Oh no," Thomas assured her, moving toward the bed. "We don't need the bathroom for this."

Inez smiled quizzically. "You'll need at least a damp washcloth and towel, Thomas, I'm soaked with honey. It started on my upper legs but your bouncing me about sent it running in every direction."

"I know." He grinned. "And I will remove every last drop, I promise. I'm in the mood for sweets."

"Oh," Inez breathed, her eyes going wide as he laid her on the bed and turned his attention to keeping his promise.

"Good morning, Inez. I hope you're feeling better this morning."

Inez stopped just inside the kitchen door, her head turning sharply to find the man seated at the breakfast table. Her eyes widened with surprise as she spotted Bastien Argeneau, seated at the table looking thoughtful. He wore jeans and a T-shirt that made him look no more than twenty-six or -seven. She'd never seen the big boss of Argeneau Enterprises look so casual. It made her feel slightly uncomfortable in the dark slacks and red blouse she'd donned on waking. Inez didn't usually wear bright colors, but she'd dressed in the dark to avoid waking Thomas and had chosen her clothes by feel rather than color.

"Good morning, Bas— Mr. Argeneau," she corrected herself quickly. While Thomas, and now Etienne and

Rachel, kept referring to him as Bastien, and she'd started to think of him that way, he was still her boss and as such was Mr. Argeneau to her.

"You can call me Bastien," he said with a smile. "From what I hear, we're to be in-laws."

Inez blushed, but didn't know what to say. No one had said anything about marriage to her. All Thomas had said was that he wanted to turn her and that she was his lifemate. Marriage hadn't come into it.

Forcing a smile for Bastien, she shuffled her feet, and then asked, "Would you like some tea?"

"Thank you," Bastien murmured and then added, "I see you still have a bit of a scratchy throat. Did the honey not help?"

Inez's eyes went round with mortification at the question and she scrambled quickly to the teakettle on the counter, her mind racing. What had Rachel and Etienne told the man? She wondered as she retrieved the jug, removed the lid, and set it on the counter, and then moved to the sink to fill it with water.

"Is there something wrong?" Bastien asked, sounding concerned.

"No," she squeaked out as she shut off the water. Inez then turned to move back to the kettle, coming to an abrupt halt when she found Bastien there. They both gasped as the water in the jug sloshed over the lip and down his front.

"Oh!" Inez cried in alarm and hurriedly put the jug on the counter to snatch up a dish towel and mop up the liquid. Jabbering away in Portuguese, she pressed the cloth to his chest, patting him with it and following the large wet spot downward.

"Good morning."

Inez glanced, red-faced, to the door to see a lovely woman with long chestnut hair, an impish smile and wide, amused eyes. Bastien's fiancée, Terri Simpson. She was dressed casually in jeans and a T-shirt that said, "I vant to suck your blooood," Inez noted, and she had to bite her lip to keep from laughing. She'd met the woman in New York and liked her then. Knowing about their kind and seeing the T-shirt she now wore just made her like her more.

Continuing to mop at Bastien, Inez smiled and said, "Hello, Ms. Simpson, I was just—Oh!" Inez snatched away the hand holding the towel as she glanced back and saw that she'd continued blindly mopping at the water all the way to the man's groin.

Flushing with mortification, she stared down at the towel in her hand, afraid to lift her head and see the expression on her boss's face . . . or his fiancée's for that matter. *Stupid hand,* Inez thought with despair. How could she be so competent in business and so incompetent in social situations? For heaven's sake! She'd never done anything so foolish at work. Thank God for that. Surely, Bastien never would have agreed to her becoming vice president if he'd known what a twit she was when away from work. She was forever tripping over her own feet. He was probably going to fire her now that he knew what an idiot she was. He'd—

"Inez?" Bastien said gently, taking the towel from her hand. "It's all right. I don't think you're an idiot."

She glanced up warily to see amusement twinkling in his eyes as he peered down at her.

"No. He wouldn't ever think that," Terri assured

her, suddenly at her side, slipping her arm around her to steer her toward the breakfast table. "And we know you aren't a twit. Bastien has been ranting for days about your being the best damned employee he has in England and cursing Thomas for taking you away from him."

"He has?" she asked with surprise.

Terri nodded. "Now, you just sit down and relax. You had enough excitement last night. I'll make the tea while Bastien mops himself up."

"Thank you," Inez murmured as she sat down. She then sat watching the couple putter around the kitchen, moving in what almost seemed a choreographed dance around and near each other in the kitchen.

They worked together well, Inez noted. Terri refilled the jug while Bastien finished mopping himself up, then Terri slid by him, their bodies brushing and smiles exchanged as she set the jug back on the electric kettle's base while he spread the dish towel on the counter to dry. They then encountered each other again exchanging smiles and brushing against each other as she moved to retrieve cups and Bastien found the tea bags. He had the container open by the time Terri set the cups down, and then dropped the bags in each cup and resealed the container while she fetched sugar from the cupboard. And, finally, they brushed bodies again in passing as she headed to the drawer to retrieve spoons and he walked to the refrigerator to retrieve a carton of milk

A little sigh slid from Inez's lips as she wondered if she and Thomas would work as well together.

"I'm sure you will," Terri said as she carried the spoons to the table.

Inez stiffened as she realized the woman had read her mind, and then her eyebrows rose as she realized that both of them must have read her mind earlier to know she'd thought the words *twit* and *idiot*. They were poking in her head, she thought with dismay and not a little anger.

"We aren't poking," Bastien assured her as he set the cream and sugar on the table. "I'm afraid you're broadcasting your thoughts."

"He's right," Terri agreed as she returned to the counter to wait for the water to boil. "I haven't quite got the hang of reading thoughts yet unless they are broadcast like yours. It's because you're upset," she informed her kindly. "You're uncomfortable and flustered because you aren't sure how to act around Bastien now that you're involved with Thomas, and embarrassed by the whole drying-his-lap thing, so—in your upset—you're broadcasting your thoughts."

"Oh." Inez sat back in her seat with a sigh. She wasn't sure what broadcasting was, but believed she probably was doing it anyway.

"And just for the record," Terri added, picking up the jug as it began to boil and automatically shut off. "I liked you too when we met in New York, and still do, even if you aren't wearing a cool T-shirt."

Inez blinked at this easy announcement and then glanced to her boss as he chuckled softly.

"Isn't she wonderful?" Bastien asked when he noticed her looking his way.

Inez nodded at once, her eyes wide. She'd never seen this side of him before. At work, he was always cool and efficient as far as she knew. But the man obviously adored his fiancée . . . and was adored right back, she decided when Terri brought the three teas to the table and then kissed him. It started out a tender, affectionate brush of lips, but then started to heat up and Inez bit her lip and glanced away, wondering if she should leave the room. Also wondering if she and Thomas were this bad.

"I'm sure you and Thomas are just as bad," Bastien said wryly as he and Terri broke apart and took seats at the table. "And there's no need to leave the room. In fact, I wanted to talk to you."

"Oh." Inez sat up a little straighter in her seat, trying to present a businesslike front. Oddly enough, it was difficult. She hadn't even thought of work since Thomas had arrived in England and felt out of practice.

"It's not business," Bastien said solemnly.

"Okay." Inez relaxed a little, but then frowned and said. "I didn't realize the two of you were here last night too. I thought it was just Etienne and Rachel."

"It was." Terri raised her teacup to blow on the hot liquid lightly, before adding, "We arrived just before midday."

Inez nodded, but was surprised they had traveled during daylight. Thomas had gone through scads of blood the day they'd toured Amsterdam before leaving.

"We stocked up on blood," Bastien assured her, reading her thoughts again. "I brought enough on the plane with us to manage the journey and see to your turning too."

"Etienne got up and let us in," Terri added.

"Yes, and then we stayed up a while and talked before going to sleep."

"Where did you sleep?" Inez asked with a frown.

There were only two bedrooms and both were occupied.

"Both couches in the living room pull out," Bastien explained.

"Which is a good thing," Terri announced dryly and then explained, "We finally got a hold of Lucern and Kate and they're on their way here to help look for Marguerite. They should arrive sometime tonight."

"Lucern and Kate?" Inez asked uncertainly.

"Lucern is Bastien and Etienne's older brother," Terri said helpfully. "Kate is his lifemate. He writes romances and she does too now, though she used to be his editor. She's also my cousin."

"Oh. I think Wyatt has mentioned them," Inez said, but was thinking the townhouse was about to become very crowded.

"I hear someone moving around upstairs," Terri said quietly.

Bastien stiffened and looked almost alarmed as he glanced toward the ceiling. He sat stiff and still, listening for a moment, and then suddenly relaxed, saying, "It's Etienne. Thomas was always a late sleeper."

Inez felt trepidation creep down her neck at those words. They seemed to suggest that his tension was because it might have been Thomas. Why would it upset him if Thomas got up?

"Because we want to talk to you before he comes down," Bastien said quietly. "In fact, I'm afraid if you hadn't come below when you did, I would have slipped into your thoughts and brought you down."

Inez sat back in her seat, her eyes widening with distinct dislike at what she considered to be a threat. Having experienced being controlled, she wasn't likely to look kindly on anyone who suggested they might do it.

"It wouldn't have been anything like what happened to you last night," Bastien said quietly. "I would have eased your thoughts so you weren't frightened."

"It still would have been forcing me to do something against my will," she pointed out coldly.

"Yes, I know," Bastien admitted apologetically. "And we generally don't do it unless it's necessary. With most mortals that constitutes keeping them from learning something that could endanger our people or themselves."

"And with me?" she asked, her accent a little thicker with her upset.

"Because we needed to talk to you without Thomas," he said simply.

"Why?" Inez snapped the word, her wariness leaping back to full throttle.

"Last night Bastien and I came up with a way to find Mother," Etienne announced from the doorway. Walking into the room as they all glanced his way, he moved to the teakettle and began to make himself a tea with the just-boiled water as he continued, "But we knew Thomas wouldn't even consider it and we wanted to see what you thought of it without him there bellowing 'No!' and drowning us out."

"And before you ask, yes, we are certain he won't be pleased with our idea, because we wouldn't be pleased if it were Terri or Rachel we were asking to do this," Bastien said, his voice quiet. "In fact, I'm not too happy to ask you to do it, but we couldn't think of any other way."

Inez glanced slowly over each person in the room,

noting their grim expressions and thinking that they rather sucked as salesmen. All they'd managed to do so far was scare her silly, and they hadn't even yet said what they wanted her to do.

"You're right, of course, we aren't selling the idea well," Bastien said, a small wry smile briefly twisting his lips. "First of all, before we even mention it, I want you to know that you are completely free to say no. We won't be angry or upset and neither your job nor your acceptance into the family will be affected. We'd just have to brainstorm and hopefully come up with something else."

"It's just that this seems like the way most likely to succeed," Etienne added, joining them at the table with his tea.

"Oh boy, this gets better and better," Inez said dryly. "Please, just tell me what you want."

There was silence as Etienne and Bastien exchanged a glance and then Bastien faced her solemnly and said, "From what I understand, you've been controlled and mind-wiped twice and then controlled and nearly killed last night?"

Inez nodded slowly, that creeping feeling of trepidation turning into a fast march of all-out fear.

"He seems to have focused on you," Etienne pointed out.

"Probably because I'm the only vulnerable one," Inez said dryly. "He can't control Thomas or any of you."

"We're hoping he doesn't know the rest of us are here," Etienne said. "He was presumably trailing you and Thomas around when Rachel and I showed up, and it was daylight when Bastien and Terri arrived."

He shook his head. "He won't know we're here . . . which is to our benefit."

Before Inez could ask why, Bastien continued, "The point is that he's focused on you, and we're hoping to use that focus to trap him so that we can ask questions and get answers out of him. We hope to find out where Mother is."

"You want me to be bait in this trap," she said slowly.

"I'm afraid so," Bastien acknowledged. "And we need to do it right away, before he realizes the rest of us are here, which means you can't be turned until afterward . . . which leaves you somewhat vulnerable."

"Will you do it?" Etienne asked.

"No, she damned well won't!" Thomas said coldly from the door.

Fifteen

"I can't believe you talked her into this," Thomas growled, his eyes fastened on Inez in the coffee shop across the street. He'd walked her there from the townhouse, stopping in a bookshop along the way to pick up a couple of books to make it look like a normal outing, and then had escorted her to the coffee shop, ordered two cappuccinos, and sat with her for about ten minutes before looking at his watch as if just thinking of something he had to do or someone he had to meet. He'd then got up and hurried out of the shop.

Thomas had walked two blocks in the direction of the townhouse, and then had turned the corner and backtracked up the next street to join Bastien and Etienne on top of one of the few modern buildings in York. The roof of this building was the reason they'd chosen the coffee shop he and Inez had visited the day before. The three men could—and were—lying on their stomachs on the flat roof, peering down on the shop across the street. Its position and the glass windows that walled the coffee shop gave them a perfect view of every inch of the building and everyone in it. Not that it mattered. Thomas didn't care about seeing anyone else, he hadn't torn his eyes from Inez since dropping to lie between Etienne and Bastien several minutes ago.

"We didn't have to talk her into it," Bastien reminded him wearily from his right, his own gaze fixed on the coffee shop. "She listened to the plan, thought it was a good one and agreed to do it."

"Then I never should have let you tell her the plan," Thomas snapped. "I should have dragged her right upstairs and turned her at once."

"Why *did* you let her listen?" Etienne asked from his left. "I was rather surprised that you stopped yelling and bellowing, and settled down to let us explain what we were thinking of doing."

"Because I didn't want her to think I was a bloody dictator," he admitted with regret, and then added, "Besides, I thought she had the sense to say no." Shaking his head, he scowled at the woman under discussion and asked with bewilderment, "How could a woman who is as competent and accomplished in business as Inez is agree to this nonsense of a plan?"

"Precisely because she is competent and accomplished and saw that this was really a very sensible plan," Bastien said through gritted teeth.

Thomas was so angry he finally tore his eyes from Inez and turned sharply on Bastien. "Sensible? You've thrown a helpless bit of bait in the water without attaching a hook first and are hoping that when the shark shows up, you can dive in and chase after it before it eats the bait. That's not a plan, it's a suicide mission and you sent *my lifemate* on it," he said heavily and then added bitterly, "And without letting me turn her first which—at least—would have made her harder to kill and given her a fighting chance."

"I know," Bastien said, guilt joining the weariness in his eyes as he met his gaze. "I won't let anything happen to her, Thomas, I promise. But whoever this guy is, he seems to have focused on Inez for some reason. He has to be connected with Mother's going missing." He glanced back to the building across the street unhappily. "It's been seven days now since we've heard from Mother, we're . . . I," he corrected quietly. "I am getting desperate. We couldn't wait another day until she was turned."

"I'm worried about Aunt Marguerite too," Thomas said stiffly, his own gaze shifting back to Inez again. "But dammit, Bastien, I'm not willing to sacrifice Inez to find her. Especially if we'd just figured out what she figured out."

Bastien glanced at him with confusion. "What do you mean what she figured out?"

"Well, that's why he's focused on Inez," Thomas pointed out and then frowned. "At least I think it is. She must have figured out something. That's the only thing that makes sense." Thomas watched Inez brush her hair behind her ear as she read the book she held. "We were talking about who the seven people in the group might have been."

"The seven people in the group?" Etienne asked

with confusion, reminding Thomas of his presence. "What are you talking about?"

"With Aunt Marguerite," Thomas said and then explained the conclusions Inez had come to about the room request. "We were trying to figure out who the seven people were when Inez excused herself to find the ladies' room. I wondered if she hadn't kept fretting over the problem while away from me and came up with the answer. I thought maybe he had controlled her, and sent her back to the table with her mind wiped because of that. Hoping, perhaps, that removing the memory would remove the problem, but then when we talked about it in the pub afterward . . ." He shook his head. "We were trying to sort it out and I went to get us more drinks and came back and she was gone. That's when he tried to kill her."

"So you think because she kept coming up with the answer that he'd realized wiping the memory wouldn't suffice and that he'd have to kill her . . ." Etienne reasoned slowly.

"Rather than letting her identify these seven people . . ." Bastien continued.

"Which would lead us to Aunt Marguerite," Thomas finished with a nod. "Or at least put us one step closer."

A moment of silence passed and then Thomas cast a quick glance to both his cousins. Etienne and Bastien had their eyes on the coffee shop across the street, but they also wore thoughtful expressions and he knew they were probably trying to figure out what it was Inez had sorted out. Scowling to himself, he shook his head and turned back to the coffee shop. It was his opinion that they should have been thinking about this before dropping Inez out as bait. They should have made her talk out the matter of who it could be and not let her out of their sight to ensure the bastard couldn't get his hands on her again.

Thomas shifted his eyes to a woman with short spiky black hair as she walked past Inez, studiously ignoring her. He followed her with his eyes as she moved to the stairs and went below. It was hard to believe that was Etienne's redheaded wife, Rachel. The wig and goth clothes she wore made her completely unrecognizable.

He watched her stop at the counter on the main floor and place an order, and then lifted his gaze back to the second floor where Terri in a long blond wig and flowery dress was also at the ready. She too was hard to recognize in the get up.

Rachel returned upstairs with her drink and claimed a different table where she could still watch both Inez and the stairs. The moment she was seated, Terri stood and headed below to fetch herself another drink. Thomas wished they wouldn't, he'd rather both women not be more than five feet away from Inez, but knew they would be kicked out if they didn't have something to eat or drink.

Inez would soon have to refresh her cappuccino too, Thomas thought and glanced down at his watch, frowning when he saw that she'd been seated alone for more than half an hour.

"It's not going to work," he announced with relief. "If he was going to make a move, he would have done it by now."

"He's right, Bastien," Etienne said, but he sounded disappointed rather than relieved.

Bastien was silent for a minute and then said, "She's reading a book."

"As you instructed," Thomas said. She was reading one of Lucern's novels. She'd insisted on buying it so she wouldn't have to admit that she'd never read his work when Lucern and Kate arrived later that day. "You said to get her something to read so she wasn't sitting there thinking about the trap, unintentionally warning the guy off."

Bastien nodded silently and then said, "Call her."

"Why?" Thomas asked warily.

"You have to tell her to try to figure out who the seven people are. If she did work it out and that's what set him on her before, she might work it out again, and he might make a move," he explained. "After you call her, Etienne and I will call Rachel and Terri and tell them what's happening and not to let their guard down in case the long wait makes them think nothing's likely to happen."

Thomas peered unhappily down at Inez. He didn't want the guy to make his move. He wanted to take Inez back to the townhouse and keep her safe, not to mention turn her. When Bastien touched his arm, he turned reluctantly to peer at him.

"Please, Thomas, I promise I won't let anything happen to her. I'll jump off this building in full view of everyone, if necessary, to give chase and keep her safe."

That was a big deal. Bastien was the one constantly berating anyone for doing the least little thing to draw attention to their kind. For him to be willing to openly reveal what he was if it became a necessity to save her . . .

Sighing, Thomas slid the phone out of his pocket and called Inez.

Inez turned the page of the book in her hands, her eyes eating up the story of how Thomas's cousin Lissianna and her husband had got together. It was fascinating to read about people she'd met as well as those she would soon meet, and she was glad she'd picked it up. It was actually distracting her from the reason she was there, which was exactly why Bastien had said she should read.

Realizing that her thoughts were heading into an area she was supposed to avoid, Inez forced herself to concentrate on the story once more and reached blindly for her cappuccino, frowning and glancing down at it when she tipped it to her mouth and got nothing.

Her cup was empty she saw and wondered how long she'd been there. She was about to check her wristwatch when her cell phone began to ring. Leaning to the side, Inez picked up her purse and quickly dug out her phone.

"Hello?" she said as she placed the phone to her ear.

"Inez, I'm sorry to be taking so long," Thomas said quietly, and she presumed it was in case she was being read and then immediately tried not to think about that.

"That's all right," she murmured, managing not to look around and try to spot the men on the roof where they were supposed to be positioned to watch her.

"I shouldn't be much longer, but in the meantime, I

was thinking about that seventh person business."

Inez tilted her head, a frown plucking at her brow. "Were you?"

"Yes, and I want you to think who those seven people might be while you wait," Thomas said, his voice very solemn.

Inez stiffened, understanding at once.

"Can you do that?" Thomas didn't sound like he really wanted her to, but she wasn't surprised. He'd been angry with her ever since she'd agreed to be the bait in Bastien and Etienne's plan. In fact, he'd been short and stiff with her when he brought her here to the café. She'd almost been relieved when he'd left after sitting with her for ten minutes or so.

"Yes," she answered calmly. "I'll do that."

There was a long silence and she knew Thomas wanted to say something, but was hesitating. Finally, he simply said, "I'll see you soon."

"Yes," Inez whispered and closed the phone, and then slipped it back into her purse.

Leaving her purse on the table, she closed her book, but continued to hold it. She stared down at it, trying to do what Thomas had suggested and then glanced around as she heard a phone ring. Spotting Rachel pressing her phone to her ear, she glanced quickly away, cutting off the thought that Etienne must be calling to tell her what was going on. And then her gaze moved to Terri and away, as her phone too began to ring.

Forcing her mind away from the two women, Inez concentrated on focusing her thoughts. It took her several moments to manage it, however, but finally she found herself picking away at the puzzle of who the seven people in Marguerite's party could have been, but nothing happened. She wasn't suddenly controlled and forced to leave the café. Instead, half an hour passed and then her phone, Rachel's, and Terri's all rang at the same time.

"He's not going to make his move," Thomas said in her ear. "Something must have scared him off. Etienne and Bastien and I are coming down."

Inez felt her back and shoulders, and indeed, her entire body suddenly relax. She'd thought she'd been relatively calm about sitting there playing bait under the watchful eyes of five immortals, but now that it was over, Inez realized she hadn't been as relaxed as she'd thought, or even really distracted by the book she'd been reading. It had absorbed her conscious attention, but her subconscious had been as wound up as a clock.

"We'll be there in about five minutes," Thomas continued. "Why don't you order us both a cappuccino and we'll relax a bit and decide where you want to have your last meal as a mortal."

Inez wanted to smile at his words, he certainly sound cheerful saying them, but then he wasn't the one who was going to suffer the *unbearable agony, drowning in a vat of acid that's eating you up inside and out, horrible, nightmare-ridden, desperate pain that will make you wish someone would just put a bullet in your brain and end it all*. At least that's how she thought Etienne had put it. While she wanted to be with Thomas, the whole suffering-the-agony-of-the-damned part to do so kind of sucked.

"Yes," she said her tone solemn. "I'll go order us both a cappuccino and see you when you get here."

"I love you," Thomas said and then hung up before she could respond. Inez wasn't sure if she was glad or not. It suddenly occurred to her that she hadn't yet actually told him that she loved him. She'd nodded when Rachel had asked if she loved Thomas, but had never got the chance to actually say the words to him. She would do so the minute he got here, Inez decided . . . and then maybe she'd suggest they put off turning her until after Marguerite was found, or maybe longer. She loved him, but was not a great fan of pain.

"Inez? I'm going down to get another tea while I wait for the men to get here. Do you want anything?"

Glancing up, Inez smiled as she peered over at Terri in her wig and dress. She looked totally different in the outfit. Standing, she said, "I'll come with you, I have to order Thomas a cappuccino too."

"Okay. Don't forget your purse," Terri said easily.

Inez picked up her purse and was putting the book in her bag when Rachel joined them to descend the stairs.

"I swear, Terri, you look like a Stepford wife in that getup," Etienne's wife said with a light laugh and then added, "A gorgeous Stepford Wife, but still a Stepford wife. Did Bastien ask you to keep the wig for later?"

Inez laughed at the way Rachel was wiggling her eyebrows as she asked the question, but laughed harder when Terri blushed and nodded her head.

"Do they have a bathroom in this place?" Terri asked as they stepped off the stairs.

"Yes. Just there," Inez said helpfully, pointing out the door to the left of the stairs.

"Oh, thanks. I'll be right back."

Inez trailed Rachel to the counter as Terri moved off toward the door to the bathrooms.

"I wonder what their lemon muffins are like," Rachel murmured as they waited for an older woman to give and collect her order.

"They're quite good. Thomas and I had them the other day."

"Hmm, maybe I'll have one of those and a latte, then," Rachel murmured.

Nodding, Inez glanced over the board herself, trying to decide what she wanted. She was still looking when the woman at the counter claimed her order and moved on, When Rachel gestured for her to go first, Inez shook her head and waved her on. "I'm still looking."

Nodding, Rachel stepped up to the counter to give her order, and Inez turned to peer back to the board, but found herself continuing to turn until she faced the door, and then she was walking out of the café.

A silent scream immediately went off inside her head as Inez realized what was happening and that Rachel would be too distracted to notice until it was too late.

Inez had been so relaxed just then. Thinking it was over she'd dropped all her guards and hadn't been prepared for this sudden hijacking of her mind and body. Her memories of being controlled last night had been fuzzy and fractured when she'd woken up on the couch and heard Thomas, Etienne, and Rachel talking. Little bits and pieces and flashes of fuzzy scenes and faint feelings were all she'd been able to grasp at, but as the terror of it all struck her anew,

Inez recalled last night's events with stunning clarity.

The terror of being controlled and made to do someone else's bidding, the endless walk along dark streets in the cool night breeze, all the while wondering what her controller planned to do with her. The inability to do a single thing to stop what was happening or protect or defend herself in any way as he'd stopped and made her turn to face the river while knowing with every fiber of her being that he was about to kill her.

It was like that again now as she was made to walk once more up dark York streets to what she feared might, this time, be her death. As that thought struck her, Inez felt herself giving up and shrinking under the terror claiming her.

"Inez!"

Rachel's voice was like a lifeline in the middle of an ocean. Relief pouring through her, Inez immediately began to fight, trying to regain control and battle the mind controlling hers. It didn't work. There was no sudden stutter in her step, not even a miniscule movement of her mouth as she tried to cry out to Rachel. Instead, her body began to move more quickly, bursting into a run that sent her flying down the street at a speed Inez had never realized she had in her.

Rather than be alarmed at this, Inez took it as a sign that she might yet have a chance. Rachel must be in pursuit, and there was no way she could outrun her. The woman was an immortal and Thomas had said immortals had increased strength and speed. Inez was confident the woman would catch up to her quickly and she would be saved . . . so long as she didn't have a heart attack and die first by the effort being forced on her, Inez thought with reawakened alarm as her body began to move even faster. Her arms and legs were pumping at an unnatural speed that she was sure her body alone could never manage and would not be able to sustain long. Her heart was already racing in a way she'd never before experienced as it tried desperately to supply the oxygen this race required.

A man suddenly stepped out on the sidewalk in front of her, and Inez's eyes widened in horror as she recognized him. Tall, blond, bearded, and dressed all in black, he had a cold face without a drop of humanity or mercy in it. He had stepped out much like this last night, Inez recalled, though she hadn't been running then. He suddenly reached out with one arm and snatched her up.

Inez would have grunted in pain as her stomach crashed into his arm if she could have, but the blond man was now running, moving faster than her body had been able to accomplish. She was being carried along, her upper body leaning slightly forward over his arm, her head turned by the impetus so that she could just see Rachel out of the corner of her eye.

The woman was racing down the street behind them, grim determination on her face and Inez could have wept with relief to know she wasn't yet lost. A quick rage soon followed as Inez mentally balked at the unfairness of it all. Were the blond man not controlling her, she'd be kicking and screaming and clawing the skin off his arm. She'd have fought him with her last breath, but she wasn't being given that opportunity. Despite being bigger and stronger and faster, despite the fact that he was an immortal, impossible to kill since she had no idea how to, he was even now controlling her body and preventing her from defending herself. The man was a bloody coward, she decided, afraid to risk her puny struggles.

Much to her amazement, her captor suddenly stumbled in his step and she was sure his control on her slipped briefly, long enough for her to instinctively clench her fists in rage.

Realizing the man was still in her mind in order to control her, Inez thought she might have a weapon after all.

You really are a coward. I suspected as much when you cut and ran last night the minute Thomas showed up. But I just thought you were afraid to take on someone your own size, I never expected you to be afraid of little mortal me. What's wrong? When you were a little boy immortal did a little mortal girl punch or scratch you? I bet that's what happened, and I bet you cried like a baby.

"Keep it up. I shall kill you slowly and painfully and enjoy the doing."

Inez stiffened unsure if he'd actually spoken the words aloud as he ran, or if he'd somehow communicated them to her with his mind. Thomas had never said they could talk in your head, but they could alter memories in a mortal's mind, why not a thought?

I'm sure you will. And no doubt you'll control me the entire time so I'm completely defenseless. The big superior immortal, torturing a defenseless mortal female to death. Woo-woo! You should be proud. But then I bet that's how you get off. It's probably the only way you get off. Are you impotent? Inez asked in her head with interest.

I bet you are, she added. *I bet you have a really small penis too. I mean, I know nanos put you at your peak physical condition and all that, but some of you peak a little smaller than others, huh? And, I suppose, nanos can only do so much.*

Inez felt his control falter. Excited, she persisted, *Seriously, I want to know. Are you hung like a horse and just mean or did fate stick you with a mini tootsie roll between your legs that women stare at in horror and then say the dreaded, "size doesn't matter?"*

She'd definitely hit a sore point there, because a wave of rage poured through her mind and then died abruptly as the immortal's control over her suddenly collapsed. Knowing it wouldn't last long, Inez immediately kicked back one leg with all her force. She'd hoped to break his knee or something. Instead, she jammed her leg back as he was midstep, sticking it between one leg and the other like a wrench between the spokes of a fast-moving bicycle tire. Unfortunately, her leg wasn't as hard and solid as a metal wrench.

Still free of his control, Inez screamed in agony as her leg was mulched between both of his, one pushing forward against her calf bone, while his other leg swung back, snapping the bone with a thick cracking sound. She was still screaming as he pitched to the side and the ground rushed up toward her. While her leg had broken, it had also tripped him up. He was falling, some part of her mind realized and Inez had just enough time to hope she hadn't just killed herself before her head slammed into concrete. Stars exploded behind her eyes, along with the pain in her head and then they were rolling, the immortal still clutching her in the crook of his arm as they tumbled down what she thought were stairs.

"Inez!"

She barely heard Rachel's shriek as the lights behind her eyes began to fade and blessed unconscious took her away from the pain.

"What do you think warned him off?" Etienne asked with a frown as he, Bastien, and Thomas descended the stairs down from the roof of the building they'd chosen to watch the coffee shop.

"I'm not sure," Bastien said, sounding weary. "Inez may not have been able to keep all thoughts of what we were up to out of her mind."

"Don't blame Inez for this," Thomas said through gritted teeth as they stepped off the stairs and headed out the door into the alley between the rows of buildings. "I'm sure she did everything she could. She agreed to help, didn't she? Putting herself at risk for your stupid plan."

"It wasn't a criticism," Bastien assured him, soothingly. "And we do appreciate it. We also know how hard this has been on you, Thomas, and I'm sorry about that. We were just hoping to catch the bastard and find Mother."

"Well, I want to find her too, but . . ." Thomas paused in the alley, frustrated that he couldn't find the words to say what he felt. He was terrified of losing either woman, but Marguerite might already be lost to them, and he didn't want to lose Inez to find that out. Hell, he didn't want to lose her at all. Given a choice between saving one woman or the other, Thomas would rather die himself.

"But Marguerite is your aunt and Inez is your lifemate and you'd rather not lose either of them," Etienne said quietly, saying what he thought Thomas was trying and failing to verbalize.

"Marguerite is *my* mother too," Thomas snapped bitterly. "She's the only mother I know."

"You called her Mother as a child," Bastien said quietly.

"Yeah, well, Jean Claude soon put a stop to that," he muttered wearily, and then shook his head and turned away to continue up the alley. "Let's go. The women are waiting."

Bastien and Etienne hesitated and then fell into step on either side of him to walk out of the alley. They walked the rest of the way in silence, coming around the corner half a short block up from the coffee shop in time to see Terri come rushing out of the café, panic on her face.

"Something's wrong," Bastien growled and burst into a run.

His heart lurching with alarm because Inez was nowhere to be seen, Thomas raced past his cousin.

"Where is she?" he demanded, grabbing Terri roughly by the arms.

"I don't know," Terri cried with distress. "We all went down to get coffees for everyone and I went into the bathroom. But when I came out, Rachel and Inez were gone."

"Rachel's gone too?" Etienne asked with alarm as he reached them.

"Where did they go?" Thomas asked, ignoring him.

"Someone must have seen. Did you read the guy behind the counter? He had an eye for Inez and would have noticed her leaving."

"I tried, but . . ." She shook her head helplessly, guilt filling her eyes.

"It's all right," Bastien said as he caught up. Slipping his arm around her, he gave her a quick hug as he explained to Thomas. "She hasn't finished her training Thomas. Terri can't read mortals well yet. I'll do it now," he added, giving his fiancée a quick squeeze and then releasing her to hurry into the café.

Thomas whirled away from the woman, not angry at her but just plain angry as he peered up the road one way and then the other. There was no sign of either woman.

"Maybe we should split up, you go one way and I go the other," Etienne suggested anxiously.

Thomas turned cold eyes on his cousin. "The plan doesn't look so good when your own lifemate gets caught in it, does it?"

Etienne winced and briefly closed his eyes, then blinked them open and said, "I'm sorry, Thomas. I deserve that. We thought we had all the bases covered."

"The fact is, Etienne, that you can cover all the bases you want, but if you put a ball into the game, it's going to get hit by the bat at some point," he snarled.

"That way!" Bastien yelled, rushing out of the café.

Thomas glanced toward the man, and then burst into a run in the direction his cousin was pointing. The others were immediately on his heels.

Sixteen

Inez woke to the sound of, well it sort of sounded like sex—with grunts and moans and sighs and— Realizing she was making the sounds and definitely wasn't making them out of enjoyment, Inez forced her mouth closed and opened her eyes.

The good news was that she had control of herself again, or still, Inez supposed since she'd got it back just before the tumble they'd taken. The bad news was she was lying on a path at the bottom of a set of stone steps, bloody and broken . . . and she definitely felt broken. Pain was attacking her everywhere. Her leg, her back, her stomach, her head, one arm . . .

Gritting her teeth against the pain, Inez lifted her head and tried to peer at herself. She didn't see much before her head began to swim and she fell back, and yet it was more than enough. She was on her back, her lower leg bent to the side mid-calf in a most un-natural way, her left shoulder looked funny and she thought it was either broken or dislocated, there was some kind of wound on her lower stomach that seemed to be bleeding copiously, and the minute she'd tipped her head up, blood had poured down over her face from a head wound. Oh yeah, she was broken all right.

A furious growl caught her attention, and Inez shifted her gaze to the side, eyes widening slightly as she saw Rachel fighting with the blond immortal some feet away.

Inez watched, and soon realized she hadn't been the only one injured in the fall. The bearded blond was fighting with one broken arm hanging loose at his side. Rachel was taking every opportunity to boot or punch him in that injured arm, and when he cried out and grabbed it, she went for his groin or head.

Inez was truly impressed and wondered if the wom-an had taken self-defense classes before becoming an immortal. Although, there was nothing saying she couldn't. Rachel could have taken them *after* becom-ing an immortal.

A furious roar rang in the air and Inez frowned because she hadn't seen the blond immortal's mouth move. And she was quite sure the sound hadn't come from Rachel. That had definitely been a male sound . . . or perhaps the sound of a truck driving by, Inez thought vaguely and slowly turned her eyes to look up to the road.

A mild sense of surprised flowed through her when she saw Thomas frozen at the top of the stone steps. Inez could see his eyes glowing silver in the darkness and seriously hoped the man didn't think he was getting any sex in her condition. She loved him dearly, but really this wasn't the time for that sexy silver glow he always got when he was in the mood, she thought a little fuzzily.

It was getting harder to think and she hadn't really been all that clearheaded since the fall, but suspected the deteriorating state of her mind might have something to do with the blood gushing out of her from several spots.

The roar of fury and anguish that suddenly ripped from his throat caught Thomas completely by surprise. It pushed its way up from his chest and exploded from his lips when he saw Inez lying bloody and broken at the base of the stairs like a doll tossed from above. Launching himself forward, he scrambled down the stairs as if caught in a landslide, his body moving more quickly with each step until he leapt the last two to land on the ground beside Inez.

He was aware of Bastien and Etienne rushing past to chase after the blond immortal, but knew they wouldn't catch him. His roar had made both Rachel and the bearded man glance his way. The minute Thomas had started down the stairs, the man had burst into action, giving a still-distracted Rachel a shove that sent her flying onto her back before whirling away to flee. It had given him all the head start he needed.

Eyes roving over Inez's injuries, Thomas dropped to his knees and instinctively reached for her. Slipping his arms beneath her, he scooped her up against his chest, and then stilled when she moaned in pain. His heart began to beat again then. Thomas had been sure she was dead and had already begun to grieve, but as much as her pain-filled moan hurt his heart, it was also music to his ears.

"Inez," he whispered into her hair, his eyes squeezing closed against the tears of relief that tried to fill them. "It's all right, love. You're all right."

"No," she mumbled weakly into his neck. "No sex, Thomas. I hurt."

"She's delirious."

Thomas raised his eyes to see Terri at his side, concern clear on her face. He then glanced past her as the others now moved to join them. His eyes narrowed on his cousins and he opened his mouth to rip into them and then froze and glanced down at Inez with alarm.

"Her heartbeat's slowing," he said with dull horror.

"Lay her down, Thomas," Bastien ordered grimly, dropping to his knees beside him.

Thomas whipped his head toward him, wanting to smash him for causing all this with his stupid plan, but wouldn't release Inez to do it. Before he could at least tell him to go to hell, Bastien said firmly, "I know you probably hate me right now, Thomas, but believe me, it can't be more than I hate myself. Now put her down so Rachel can look at her. You might have to start the turn right away if we're to save her."

Thomas hesitated one moment and then eased Inez onto her back on the ground.

Rachel immediately knelt on her opposite side. While she worked in a morgue, she was a doctor, and that showed through as she moved her hands quickly over Inez, muttering as she went. "Broken leg, broken collarbone, broken ribs, fractured skull . . . She's

lost a lot of blood . . . too much." She glanced up at
Thomas and said, "You have to turn her. Now."

"It won't wait until we get back to the townhouse?"
Terri asked with concern.

"She'll be dead by the time we get back to the townhouse," Rachel announced baldly.

Thomas immediately raised his wrist toward his
mouth, intending to tear into it with his teeth, but an
open pocket knife appeared before his face.

Glancing at Etienne who was holding it out, Thomas
muttered, "Thanks," and then took it and sliced a four
inch gash up his wrist. Ignoring the pain radiating all
the way up into his shoulder, he immediately leaned
forward, only to stop when he realized Inez's mouth
was closed.

Rachel quickly used one hand on her forehead and
the other on her chin to pull her lips apart. Thomas
then pressed his wrist to Inez's mouth.

"Hey! Is everything all right down there?"

Thomas didn't even bother to glance around, leaving it to the others to deal with. He was vaguely
aware of Etienne moving away to do so, and then
raised his wrist to peer at it, frowning when he saw
that the nanos were doing their work and the bleeding had stopped.

"Did she get enough?" Rachel asked Bastien.

Thomas glanced over to see the frown on his face.
Knowing he was hesitating to say something, he
snapped, "What is it?"

"She's probably had enough to initiate the turn,"
he said slowly.

"But?" Thomas asked, knowing there was more.

"But if her condition is as bad as Rachel said, she

might not survive long enough for her body to repair itself and complete the change," he admitted and then added quickly, "But I've heard the more blood an immortal gives, the faster repairs can be made and the better the chance of a badly injured mortal surviving the turn."

He'd barely finished the words before Thomas was slicing himself open again. It made complete sense to him. The more nanos he poured into her, the faster they could work and they were definitely working against time here. Inez's heartbeat was still slowing with every passing moment.

Thomas sliced his arm open six times before allowing the others to convince him that he'd given her enough. He then scooped her into his arms and tried to stand, his heart lurching in alarm when he found himself swaying weakly and nearly dropping Inez.

"Give her to me, Thomas," Bastien said quietly.

Thomas scowled at the man, but didn't really have a choice. He wasn't at all certain that he could get back to the townhouse without help himself. He definitely couldn't manage the feat while carrying her. He reluctantly let Bastien take her, staggering after him when he turned away with her in his arms and then stumbling to a halt as the ground swayed under his feet.

"Let me help you." Etienne was at his side, drawing his arm over his shoulders. "We'll get you both back to the townhouse and give you blood. You gave up a lot and must be in pain."

Thomas was actually in agony, but didn't comment, his concentration was on staying on his feet as they moved to the stairs.

That walk was the longest of his life. Thomas was

fuzzy-headed and suffering pain from the blood loss, but he was also furious at the very people now trying to help him for putting Inez in this predicament and anxious over the agony she was soon going to go through—and, in fact, was beginning to experience. Increasing the amount of blood given might be good for speeding up repairs, but it also sped up the onset of the agony, and Inez was already moaning and beginning to thrash in pain as they turned up the short walk in front of the rented townhouse.

Terri rushed ahead to unlock the front door and light splashed over them as it opened. Thomas heard Terri exclaim in surprise, but didn't understand why until Etienne helped him in through the door and he saw Lucern and Kate in the hall, and Vincent and his lifemate Jackie in the doorway to the living room.

Thomas glanced at them, but couldn't muster up any interest in their presence. The pain had grown increasingly worse as they were making their way back to the house, while the nanos still in his system tried to replicate themselves, using up what little blood was left. They'd moved out of his bloodstream in search of blood and he was suffering, but when he realized Bastien was carrying Inez into the living room, he mustered up the strength to growl, "Upstairs. Our room."

Bastien didn't argue. He turned toward the stairs at once, asking Terri to bring up one of the coolers of blood they'd brought with them as he started up.

Etienne turned Thomas in that direction to follow, but before they could reach the stairs, Thomas was hit by a wave of pain that made him double over and his legs buckle. Whether Etienne managed to keep him from falling or not, he never knew. He lost consciousness.

When he woke up, Thomas found himself lying in one of the twin beds in the room he and Inez had chosen. An already half-empty bag of blood was stuck to his fangs and Etienne and Terri were leaning over him, worried expressions on their faces.

Terri looked relieved when his eyes opened, but Etienne just looked more worried and turned to announce, "He's waking up."

Thomas saw his lips move and wondered why it was so hard to hear his words and then realized a high, keening scream was rending the air. Turning his head sharply, he saw Inez thrashing on the opposite bed while Rachel and Bastien tried to hold her down.

Ignoring the pain still eating away at him, Thomas ripped the bag from his mouth. Blood immediately shot from the punctures where his fangs had been, splashing up and out like a geyser, but Thomas ignored that too and dropped it to the bed as he tried to get up and go to Inez.

"Dammit!" Etienne caught him by the shoulders, forcing him back on the bed with little effort as Terri scrambled to grab the spraying bag.

"Stay put," Etienne said grimly as Terri wrapped the bag in a towel and rushed from the room. "You need more blood. You'll be no good to her until you've got your strength back. Bastien and Rachel are helping Inez."

"Why haven't they given her drugs yet?" Thomas growled, giving up struggling against Etienne. It wasn't working anyway, the man was using only one hand to hold him down and didn't have to put much strength behind it to do it.

"They're in the other cooler. Lucern is getting them now," he explained and then added, "We just got you both up here. That bag was the first we put to your teeth."

"Here." Marguerite's oldest son, Lucern, rushed into the room with Kate on his heels. He was digging through the cooler he held as he moved. Stopping beside Bastien, he handed over an ampoule and syringe, and Bastien removed one hand from Inez to reach for it, but her good arm immediately jerked out of the hold his other hand had on her and plowed him in the face.

Thomas smiled as Bastien flew backward off the bed. That was what he'd wanted to do to him down by the river. It did his heart good to see Inez get the lick in for him.

"Bastien." Kate rushed around Lucern to kneel at his side and Vincent and Jackie appeared from somewhere, though Thomas wasn't sure from where. He hadn't noticed them in the room before this, but suddenly they were at the bedside trying to help Rachel hold Inez down. The combination of nanos and pain was making her strong and even with the three of them, they had trouble holding her in place.

"Give her the damned drugs!" Thomas bellowed, or tried too, his voice didn't have its normal strength. He really needed more blood.

Bastien's head suddenly appeared on the other side of the bed and he crawled forward. Ignoring his broken, bleeding nose, he stuck the syringe into the ampoule to draw out the drug. He pulled the needle free once it was full, squeezed it until clear liquid shot out the top, and then injected it straight into Inez's vein as Vincent held her arm out for him.

They all waited tensely, watching Inez. Her struggles and screams began to ease almost at once, the thrashing becoming restless writhing and the screams dropping to loud moans and then she stopped moving and fell silent.

A communal sigh of relief ran around the room like a wave and then every eye turned to him.

Etienne was the first to speak. "Open your mouth," he ordered, and slapped a bag on his still-protruding fangs before anyone else could speak.

Thomas suspected it was an effort on Etienne's part to keep him from saying any of the furious thoughts running around inside his head.

"Now," Vincent said dryly. "Does someone want to tell us who this young woman is and what the hell happened?"

Bastien's shoulders slumped as he replayed the night's events.

"You used Thomas's lifemate as bait?" Lucern asked with shock when Bastien was done. "His *lifemate?* While she was still mortal?"

Thomas closed his eyes with gratitude at Lucern's reaction, feeling vindicated in his anger. A lifemate was as precious to an immortal as life itself. Mortals could divorce and remarry and go through mate after mate if they wished, but for an immortal, a lifemate was a once-in-a-lifetime deal, or twice if they were lucky. And with an immortal that was a very long lifetime.

"Jesus, Bastien. What were you thinking?" Lucern

scrubbed one hand through his hair with disgust and said, "I'd have killed you for even considering something like that if it had been Kate. And I know damned right well that you never would have risked Terri like that."

"I wasn't thinking," Bastien admitted unhappily. "I was just so worried about, Mother . . . and I thought I could keep Inez safe. I thought I'd considered every contingency."

"*We* thought we'd considered every contingency," Etienne insisted grimly, determined not to let Bastien take the flack on his own.

Lucern's eyes skated to Etienne, and then away dismissively and Thomas saw the way Etienne's hands balled into fists. It suddenly occurred to him that he wasn't the only one the two older Argeneau brothers tended to dismiss as an immature young pup. Some of his anger with Etienne suddenly eased, replaced by sympathy. They were both in the same boat, he thought, and then glanced toward his older cousin as Lucern moved up the small aisle between the beds.

The man's gaze moved silently over the now quiet Inez, taking in her injuries with grim eyes before turning to Thomas.

"How angry are you?" he asked.

Thomas clenched his teeth as the question brought his rage stirring back to life and suddenly the bag in his mouth exploded, splashing the red liquid everywhere.

"I guess that answers that question," Lucern said dryly, wiping blood off of his face.

Terri hurried out of the room for more towels.

Ripping the burst bag from his teeth, Thomas tried

to sit up again, this time eager to get his hands around Bastien's throat as fury poured through him.

"Stay put, tiger," Lucern said, pushing him back on the bed. "You aren't strong enough to take on Bastien yet, you need more blood. Besides, Mother would never forgive you if you killed him."

Etienne immediately slapped a fresh bag of blood to his teeth as Thomas fell back on the bed. Terri returned then with a stack of towels and Etienne and Lucern both took one each to wipe themselves down.

"I'd better change," Etienne muttered, getting to his feet and moving away.

The moment he did, Lucern sat on the side of the bed next to Thomas. "You have to cut him some slack, Thomas. Bastien is a planner. It's an old habit from running the company so long. He thinks of things in bottom line terms. I have no doubt he considered the options, weighed the risks, and thought he had everything covered. I don't think he'd have gone ahead with this plan if he'd thought there was any real risk to your lifemate." He allowed a moment of silence pass to let him think about that and then added, "And there wouldn't have been if everyone hadn't let down their guard.

"That's always the most dangerous point," he continued with a grimace. "I can't tell you how many excellent warriors I've seen die *after* a battle is over. They let down their guard and relaxed and then *pow*, one of the enemy they thought was more seriously injured than they were suddenly reared up and killed them."

Thomas just stared at him, eyes wide above the bag

of blood in his mouth. Lucern wasn't much of a talker. In fact, this was the first time he'd heard him string more than a couple of words together. The immortal was over six hundred years old. He'd been a warrior, wielding a broadsword when he was younger, and still had the physical build needed to do it. He was also a writer, tapping out reams of words on paper, but when it came to talking it sometimes seemed as if he'd used up all his words in his books and had nothing else to say.

Lucern glanced to Bastien, considered him briefly, and then shook his head and glanced back to Thomas. "Bastien is suffering the guilt for it now. When he apologizes, let it go. We're all family and even immortals make mistakes."

Thomas hesitated, his gaze sliding to the next bed. Rachel and Bastien were hovering over Inez, Rachel cutting away her clothes and binding the wounds that were slowly closing, while Bastien held Inez slightly elevated with one hand under her neck and shoulders as he tried to feed her. Inez had no teeth yet and they had no IV to take care of the matter, so he was reduced to pouring blood down her throat straight from the bag.

Lucern patted his shoulder and Thomas glanced back to see that Etienne had returned and Lucern was getting to his feet.

"Kate and I are going to get out of the way. We'll be below if you need us. Just give a shout."

Thomas watched him go, noting that Kate, Jackie, and Vincent followed, leaving the other two couples to handle matters.

"I'm sorry, Thomas," Etienne said solemnly, drawing his attention again. "We really didn't think Inez was in any real danger. We thought we could keep her safe, otherwise we never would have suggested it."

Thomas hesitated, waiting for the familiar anger to rear up inside him, but this time it didn't. He just felt tired. Nodding wearily, he closed his eyes and waited for the bag of blood in his mouth to empty.

Thomas consumed five bags of blood before Etienne and Terri reluctantly let him get up. He immediately moved to hover behind Rachel, his eyes anxious as he peered over Inez.

"That's all I can do for now," Rachel said, drawing the blankets up to Inez's neck as she sat up straight on the side of the bed. "I've set her leg, bound her wounds . . . All we can do now is keep feeding her blood. It's up to the nanos to repair her."

They were all silent, peering down at Inez's pale face. She was resting quietly for now, but no one was foolish enough to think she would stay that way. There would come a stage when the drugs wouldn't be able to touch the pain and her mind would be filled with horrible images of fire, death, and blood. She would imagine she was burning up, or being rent apart. It was impossible to prevent that part of the turn.

"You look pale."

Thomas glanced at Etienne as he spoke, noting that he was peering at his wife with concern.

Rachel smiled faintly and leaned into his shoulder. "You don't look so good yourself."

"There's blood in the refrigerator downstairs, and lots of food too," Bastien said. "Why don't the two of you go grab a couple bags and make yourselves something to eat."

Etienne and Rachel exchanged a glance and then moved away from the bed. "Call us if you need us."

Bastien then turned to Terri. "You should go too, Terri. You're pale as well."

Terri glanced toward the departing couple with yearning, but then glanced back, her gaze skittering anxiously between Thomas and Bastien before she shook her head and said, "I'll stay with you."

Knowing she was afraid to leave the two of them alone for fear that he would attack Bastien the moment they were gone, Thomas opened his mouth to tell her it was all right, she should go, but Etienne spoke, cutting him off.

"We'll bring up something for all three of you," his cousin said as he ushered Rachel out the door.

Shrugging, Thomas moved to sit on the side of the bed and take Inez's hand in his.

"You should go take a shower and then catch some sleep."

Thomas glanced up at Bastien's quiet words. Terri was asleep on the twin bed he'd been lying on earlier, and had been for hours. Other than that, the two men were alone; one on either side of the bed Inez was in.

Shrugging, Thomas turned his gaze back to Inez. "You go ahead. I want to stay with Inez in case she wakes up."

It was well past sunset of the second night since Inez had been injured and then turned. It hadn't been an easy process for any of them. While the drugs definitely helped, there were times when they didn't seem to even touch the pain she was suffering and it had taken several of them to keep her in the bed. Rachel and Etienne had returned several times through that night and day as Inez turned, helping Thomas, Bastien, and Terri try to keep Inez still so she wouldn't reopen her healing injuries as she'd battled the pain as well as the demons filling her hallucinations, a side-effect of the turn.

Her screams had been the worst, though. Every single one had torn at Thomas's heart like a claw, ripping deep. But that had stopped hours ago and she had rested peacefully and deeply since then.

When Bastien had suggested Terri get some sleep earlier, she'd hesitated, and then had lain down on the opposite twin bed, telling them to just shake her awake if they needed her before falling into a deep, exhausted sleep. Thomas and Bastien had been alone since then, both of them working together to feed her the occasional bag of blood or give her another shot when she began to show signs of pain.

"It might upset her if she wakes up to find you covered in blood as you are," Bastien pointed out.

Thomas glanced down at himself and frowned. Neither of them had changed since returning to the townhouse and both now wore clothes that were wrinkled and blood stained. However, Thomas was pretty much soaked in a combination of Inez's blood and the two bags he'd spilled. It was dry now, crusty and unpleasant, and it would definitely upset Inez if she woke up to see him like that, he supposed.

He nodded, but hesitated, his gaze slipping back to Inez again.

"I'll stay with her," Bastien assured him solemnly.

"Thank you," Thomas murmured automatically as

he released the hand he'd been holding and got to his feet.

"It's the least I can do," Bastien said with a sigh and then met his eyes. "I'm sorry Thomas. I never should have put her in danger like that. I never would have had I realized this would happen."

"It's all right, Bastien, I know you wouldn't have," Thomas interrupted, waving away the apology. Lucern's earlier words flowing through his head, he added, "Besides, you're family and even immortals make mistakes."

"Thank you," Bastien said quietly.

Thomas shrugged and then added in hard tones, "However, I wouldn't have been so forgiving if she'd died."

"I know," Bastien said solemnly. "I would have lost you along with her."

Thomas didn't bother to deny it and simply turned away. He never would have forgiven either Bastien or Etienne if he'd lost Inez because of them. Never.

Grabbing his knapsack, he slipped from the room and crossed the hall into the bathroom to take a quick shower and pull on clean, or at least, mostly clean clothes. Thomas had run out of fresh clothes, but at least the ones he pulled on weren't covered with blood.

Returning to the bedroom, he nearly crashed into Etienne as the other man was leaving.

"The rest of us are going to go search York for any sign of Mother or the immortal."

"Rachel's the only one who saw him," Thomas pointed out with a frown.

"Yeah, but Terri did that sketch as per her description and Rachel says it's dead on. So each couple is going to take a third of the city center and go street by street."

Thomas nodded wearily. He'd forgotten all about the picture Terri had sketched in the bedroom between Inez's fits. Rachel had hovered, fussing over this and that, saying, "The nose was a little bigger . . . the eyes more squinty . . . the hair shorter.. . . ." until she thought Terri had it just right.

"Bastien and Terri are staying with you and Inez," Etienne continued, slipping around him to the stairs. "But call my cell if you need us."

Thomas watched him go, and then continued into the room.

Terri was still asleep, but Bastien glanced up as he reentered. The man had bags under his eyes from exhaustion, a very rare thing indeed with their constitution.

"You should sleep. You're exhausted," Thomas said as he dropped his bag, and moved back to sit on the side of the bed.

Bastien hesitated and then glanced down at Inez, before saying. "If we give her another bag of blood, I think it would be safe for both of us to catch some sleep."

Thomas glanced at Inez. He didn't want to sleep, but knew Bastien wouldn't if he didn't at least pretend he intended to, so he nodded.

Much to everyone's relief, Inez's teeth had come on around mid-afternoon. Aside from being a sign that she'd survived the worst of it and was nearing the end of her turning, it made feeding her easier and much less messy. Bastien bent to retrieve a bag of blood from the now almost depleted cooler, then took out another and offered it to Thomas. When he shook his head, Bastien hesitated and then popped it to his own teeth as Thomas grabbed one of the dry but blood-soaked towels and waved it back and forth under Inez's nose. Her teeth protruded at once and he popped the bag to her fangs with little effort.

It didn't take long for either bag to empty, and then Thomas crawled onto the bed next to her. He lay down on his side, leaving some room between them to keep from disturbing her in the small twin bed.

The moment he did, Bastien lay down and cuddled up to Terri in the next bed. His breathing soon became deep and even, telling Thomas that he'd fallen asleep.

Despite his intention not to sleep, Thomas soon found his own eyes drooping closed as he too drifted into sleep.

Seventeen

Inez woke and shot up into a sitting position, fear making her heart pound in a rapid tattoo. It took her a moment to blink away the remnants of the nightmare that had chased her from sleep and realize she was in one of the twin beds in the bedroom at the townhouse.

Sucking in a deep breath of relief as the fear began to slip away, Inez peered around the room, her eyes widening at the chaos evident. Bloody clothes and towels lay strewn everywhere, and an incredible amount of empty blood bags lay in a corner, tossed there with little care.

Her gaze slid to the man in bed beside her. Thomas. He was wearing different clothes than she recalled from the night they'd laid their trap and was asleep on his side, perched on the very edge of the twin bed.

She saw his face wrinkle with irritation in sleep as her movement allowed a circle of light to splash over his exhausted face and the sight made her smile.

Inez turned her head toward the bedside lamp between the beds with some vague idea of turning it off so it wouldn't wake him, but her eyes stopped and widened at the sight of Bastien Argeneau and Terri on the second twin bed in the room. She was under the covers, but he was on top. Unlike Thomas, Bastien still wore the same clothes he'd had on the night of the trap. They were now wrinkled and crusted with dried blood. Like Thomas, his face was exhausted and almost gray with it.

Reaching for the lamp, she switched it off, then lay back in bed. Unfortunately, she couldn't seem to get back to sleep. She wasn't tired, but she *was* hungry, and suffering mild hunger pangs with it, which made her wonder how long she'd been out of it. Long enough that Thomas and the others had gone through a lot of blood, she guessed, recalling the pile of empty blood bags in the corner.

And the bloody towels. She frowned and began to carefully move various body parts one at a time to see where she was hurt, but everything seemed fine. Other than the hunger pangs, she wasn't suffering pain anywhere, yet she distinctly recalled jamming her leg back between the immortal's legs as he raced down the street, and then the terrible wrenching pain. She seemed to recall thinking it had been broken, but now thought it must have just been dislocated or something, because it seemed fine and hadn't hurt when she'd moved it.

Everything after that was a blur, except for an explo-

sion of pain as her head had slammed into concrete.
That would have bled copiously she supposed. Head
wounds always bled badly. Her head felt fine now too,
though. It was only her stomach bothering her.

Inez slid her legs to the side and eased up into a
sitting position, her movements slow and steady to
prevent waking Thomas.

She sat still on the side of the bed for a moment,
waiting to see if she would be suddenly struck by diz-
ziness or pain. When neither happened, she got carefully to her feet, surprised to find her legs a bit shaky.
They held her up, though, and worked well enough,
she found, as she stepped away from the bed. Inez
had nearly reached the door, guided by the crack of
light seeping under it, when she realized she was buck
naked.

Grimacing, she tried to think where her suitcase
would be in relation to the door. Inez doubted Rachel
and Etienne would appreciate her traipsing through
the house starkers.

But the longer Inez stood there in the dark, the better she could see, at least enough to make out vague
shapes in the room. Supposing the slim line of light
creeping under the door was helping, she moved to
the suitcase lying open on the floor. Inez intended to
put on clothes, but came across the silk robe first and
allowed her hunger to convince her to slip it on instead and then stood and moved back to the door
again. Her hunger pangs were getting stronger with
every passing minute and she was eager to raid the
refrigerator.

The house was silent and empty when she descended

the stairs and Inez wondered if Rachel and Etienne were still sleeping, but the lights would probably be off if they hadn't already gotten up. *They must have gone out,* she thought as she walked up the hall to the kitchen.

The light in the kitchen seemed to be the only one not on in the house. Inez flicked it on as she entered, her feet taking her straight to the refrigerator. She pulled it open and looked over the contents with interest. There was a lot in there, but most of it needed to be cooked and she was too hungry to wait. Spotting some cheese, she picked it up and then grabbed a scotch egg, closed the refrigerator door, and carried the food to the counter. The kettle was half full, so she pushed down the button to start it heating.

Inez then grabbed a plate from the cupboard, opened the plastic wrapping on the Scotch egg and spilled it out. The moment it hit the plate, she set the wrapping down, grabbed the sausage-wrapped egg and took a bite out of it. Inez preferred them warmed up, but they were edible cold and she was too hungry even to take the time to microwave it.

Chewing and swallowing, she turned her attention to the cheese, but it didn't open as easily as the egg packaging. Scowling, she moved to the end drawer and pulled it open. Inez reached in to retrieve a knife, but paused when a slight breeze brushed against her cheek. She looked up, her heart skittering with alarm when she saw that the back door was cracked open.

Dropping the small paring knife she'd originally reached for, Inez grabbed a large butcher knife instead. She didn't pull it out of the drawer, but simply clutched it in her fingers as her gaze slid over the edge of the door, noting that the lock was broken. The door had been forced.

A shuffling sound from behind made her swivel slowly, her hand remaining in the drawer, still clutching the butcher knife as she turned to peer toward the archway leading into the hall. Some part of her wasn't terribly surprised to find the blond, bearded immortal standing there. Her gaze skimmed over his black clothes and overcoat.

"You healed quickly," he commented, his gaze sliding over her in the pink silk robe. "I was sure the leg was broken."

"I thought so too," she admitted, peering down at her legs hidden by the robe. She tugged the robe up slightly, with her free hand, revealing her perfectly healthy lower calf. Inez then turned the leg slightly, using it as an excuse to shift slightly to the side, enough that it hid her hand as she slid it out of the drawer, bringing the butcher knife with it. "I gather it was just dislocated, though."

His gaze slid back up to her face, one eyebrow raised. "And the head wound?"

"They always bleed a lot. Fortunately, it isn't troubling me much today," she said calmly, thinking how bizarre this all felt. She was having a perfectly civil conversation with a man who had repeatedly attacked her. Clearing her throat, Inez asked, "Was it you who controlled me in Amsterdam too?"

He shook his head. "That was someone else."

She nodded, but frowned. "Why?"

"I'd guess because the boss ordered it," he said simply.

"But why *me*?" Inez asked.

"I have no idea why *he* did it, but *my* orders were to keep you and Thomas here in York and off Marguerite's trail . . . to kill you both if necessary to accomplish it." He shrugged. "You keep thinking up other places to look."

Inez nodded slowly. "Marguerite's alive, then?"

"As far as I know," he answered.

Inez stared at him silently, waiting, but when he simply stood there, the tension of the passing moments began to get to her and she asked, "So you're here to kill me?"

He suddenly shifted one side of his long coat, revealing the sword that it had hidden. That and his answering smile made her blood run cold, and her fingers tightened on the knife behind her back.

"Why haven't you taken control of me?" Inez asked, suddenly eager to draw out the conversation and put off whatever he had planned for her.

"I wouldn't want you to think I was a coward, afraid of a tiny mortal female," he said, his mocking voice laced with anger. "Uncontrolled and with that butcher knife you're hiding behind your back, you have a fighting chance . . . don't you?"

Inez jerked with surprise and realized while he hadn't been controlling her, he must have been reading her. Either that or he'd simply been aware of what she was doing when she'd drawn the knife out. So much for the advantage of surprise.

"Are you done with your questions now? Can we get to the killing you part without your whining about cowardly behavior and so on? Or," he added with malice, "do you need to see the size of my penis to assure yourself I have more than a tootsie roll?"

"Er . . . no, I'll take your word on that," Inez muttered, her gaze slipping around the room, scoping out where everything was and looking for anything that might help her against him.

A soft click sounded behind her and Inez suddenly recalled the electric teakettle she'd set to boil.

"Good. Let's get to it, then, shall we?"

Inez glanced sharply back at the blond man as he withdrew the sword from his waist.

"That's a little bit of overkill, isn't it?" she asked, finally pulling the butcher knife from the drawer and bringing it around to her side. Much to her relief, his eyes moved to the small weapon. Taking advantage of his distraction, she reached back with her right hand to grab the teakettle.

"Perhaps," he admitted, turning his attention back to his own much larger blade. Holding it up, he turned it this way and that, watching the kitchen light shimmer off of it. "But it's my lucky sword and I haven't had much luck with you so far."

"Maybe it's your approach," Inez muttered, her fingers finding the handle of the kettle and her thumb settling on the lever that worked the lid.

"Do you think so?" he asked idly.

And then he was suddenly rushing her. Inez immediately lifted the teakettle and brought it around, her thumb pressing down on the lid as she sent the contents flying over him. She aimed for his face. The boiling liquid poured over one side of his scalp, face, and neck, bringing a startled roar of pain from his throat as he stumbled back.

Inez immediately whirled and made a run for the open

back door, but he caught her from behind. Screaming in frustration, Inez twisted in his arms to face him. The moment she did, he lifted her off the ground. Her eyes widened in horror as she saw his mouth open and his fangs glide out. Realizing he meant to bite her, she instinctively stabbed out with the knife, slamming it into the unburned side of his throat.

Blood began to gush out of the wound the moment she pulled the knife free and Inez was winding up for another stab when a funny thing happened. The hunger she'd been suffering, but had managed to ignore since the bearded blond had appeared, suddenly became unignorable and roared to furious life. It became an almost living thing in her body, as if a million bees were buzzing through her veins . . . and then Inez felt a strange shifting in her upper teeth and something pricked her tongue, making her mouth open with surprise.

"Jesus," the blond breathed. Freezing with her face inches from his, he stared at her mouth with amazement. "They turned you. Why didn't I pick up on that in your thoughts?"

Inez simply stared at him, her mind gone blank. She'd had no idea. She didn't recall being turned. The last thing she recalled was falling and bits and pieces of nightmares.

"You didn't know," he said with a disbelieving laugh.

It was the laugh that knocked her out of her shock. It rubbed her on the raw. Inez hated to be laughed at. She swung the knife again, ramming it once more into his throat.

The hands holding her tightened briefly in shock, and then he bellowed and threw her furiously away from him, hurling her across the kitchen. Inez slammed into the kitchen counter at the end of the room with such force she heard an ominous snapping sound from her back and then slid to the floor and simply lay there, unable to move. Her panicked mind was screaming that he'd broken her back and she was paralyzed, but Inez was having trouble believing it. She was supposed to be an immortal now. She had fangs. Surely you couldn't break an immortal's back?

Her eyes shifted to the bearded blond. He was still standing at the other end of the room, breathing heavily and glaring at her as he held one hand to the wounds on his neck. He stood like that for a moment and then withdrew his hand, and she noted that the bleeding had stopped. Inez was sure she'd hit the jugular vein, blood should be gushing from the knife wounds on his neck, but apparently he was already healing. Not that the gashes in his neck looked any smaller to her, but he'd healed enough that the bleeding had stopped. It made her wonder if her back would heal.

It might, Inez decided, but not quick enough to save her. The bearded blond had given up his position at the other end of the room and was now striding toward her. He looked pretty pissed, and she recalled his telling her that night he'd taken her from the café that he intended to kill her slowly and enjoy doing it. Inez suspected she was in for it now and he would doubly enjoy it.

The bearded man halted in front of her, dropped to his haunches and reached out, but he never laid another finger on her. As he lowered himself, Inez spotted Thomas behind him, his eyes glowing with silver fury. The sight of his head, neck, and then upper chest appearing behind the man as he dropped was as beautiful as the sun after a long night. Inez could have wept with relief as the immortal was suddenly caught by the back of the neck and jerked away. In fact, her eyes did fill with tears, obscuring her vision, and she couldn't raise a hand to wipe them away. She watched through blurred eyes as the two men struggled, blinking her eyes furiously in an effort to clear her vision, but the tears just kept coming.

When silence suddenly fell, Inez was in a panic, ears straining, desperate to know Thomas was all right, but it wasn't until he said her name that she even knew he was still alive. Then he was suddenly there, scooping her up into his arms.

"Inez?" he said with alarm when she lay limp in his hold.

"I think he broke my back," Inez admitted on a sigh. "I can't move."

"It's all right," Thomas whispered, adjusting her in his arms so that her head lay against his chest. He pressed a kiss to her cheek, and then started across the kitchen, assuring her, "It'll heal."

"You turned me," Inez whispered into his chest.

"Yes." His voice sounded uncertain. "You said yes to it. Did you not want—?"

"No, that's fine," she said quickly. "I just didn't realize—"

"Thomas? What's happened?"

Inez recognized Bastien's voice, but didn't try to lift her head to look around.

"I left you a gift in the kitchen," Thomas announced, continuing up the hall toward him.

"A gift?" Bastien asked with bewilderment.

"Yes," Thomas said as he carried Inez past him and then added, "I suggest you get in there and figure out some way to restrain him before he heals if you want to question him about Aunt Marguerite."

Bastien didn't bother to ask further questions, Inez heard his footsteps rush away up the hall and then Thomas was carrying her upstairs.

"Thomas." Terri's worried voice greeted them at the top of the stairs. "What's going on? I thought I heard a scream and Bastien went to check and— What is Inez doing up? Should she be up yet?" she asked fretfully. "Bastien wouldn't let me out of bed for a week after he turned me."

Inez couldn't help noticing those words made Thomas chuckle for some reason. Once the rumbling in his chest died, he asked, "Is there any blood left in the cooler, Terri?"

"A bag or two, I think," Terri answered. "Do you want me to get more from downstairs?"

"Yes, please," Thomas murmured as he laid Inez on the bed.

Terri hurried from the room as Thomas moved to the cooler and fetched the few bags left in it. When he returned to the bed, Inez glanced at the bags and just the sight of the blood made that strange shifting take place in her mouth. She opened her mouth to ask one of the million or so questions suddenly buzzing in her head about being an immortal and found a bag popped to her new fangs.

The bedroom was empty when Inez woke up. For one moment, she lay still in bed, afraid to try to move for fear she might still be paralyzed, but then she set her teeth and tried to raise her hand, her breath rushing out in a relieved sigh when she was able to do so. Thomas had assured her that she would be healed by the time they woke at sunset, but she'd feared something going wrong and finding herself paralyzed and forced to live that way for centuries. It was silly, Inez knew, but fears were rarely rational.

A shout from somewhere on the main floor of the townhouse made her stiffen and she listened tensely for a moment, but when several excited voices followed along with a couple of more soothing ones, Inez decided everything was probably all right. She'd feared for a moment that Blondie had gotten free and hurt someone, but judging by the tone of the muffled conversation she was now hearing, it didn't seem likely.

Sitting up, she glanced around and then leaned to the side to snatch up her robe from the floor. Inez slipped it on before letting the sheets and blankets drop away, afraid that someone might enter before she was properly covered. The townhouse was getting quite crowded with everyone here. Tying the sash of the robe, she got out of bed and moved across the room to her suitcase, but paused as she caught sight of her reflection in the mirror on the closet door.

Eyes locked on the image peering back at her, Inez

bypassed the suitcase to stand before the mirror. She hesitated briefly, and then undid the sash of the robe and opened it to peer at herself, curious to see what changes the turn had wrought.

Much to Inez's disappointment, her body didn't seem much different. She hadn't sprouted up six inches, and her breasts were still far too generous in her eyes. Still, she supposed she was a little firmer everywhere, her breasts a little higher, and her skin . . . Inez leaned closer to the mirror, running her fingers over one cheek with awe. Her skin was now flawless, as perfect as a baby's, and her eyes were now a beautiful golden brown, she saw, but her hair was still a wild halo of curls around her head.

Staring at herself, Inez marveled over the fact that after all the years of trying to diet and exercise her curves away she hadn't been far from her peak physical state after all.

The sound of the door opening made her jump guiltily. She quickly closed the robe and turned to see Thomas entering the room. The smile that started to curve her lips faltered when she saw the grim expression on his face.

"Oh," Thomas said when he spotted her by the mirror "you're up."

"Yes," Inez murmured, and then asked with concern. "What was all the excitement downstairs about? Blondie didn't have bad news when Bastien questioned him, did he? Marguerite *is* all right?"

"Blondie—as you so kindly call him—didn't say a word. He might have if we'd had more time, but somehow the European council got wind of what was going on and sent someone to collect him. They wanted to deal with him themselves. Our only hope was that they'd be able to get something out of him, but"— Thomas hesitated and then admitted grimly—"we got news a couple hours later that he and his escort were attacked and Blondie lost his head. It would seem someone didn't want him to talk."

Inez frowned over this news and asked, "Is the escort all right?"

"He'll survive but he was badly wounded."

Inez nodded silently and then said, "He said last night that his job was to keep us in York and off Marguerite's trail. He went after me because I kept coming up with ideas that would have led us out of York." She frowned and muttered, "I should have pushed for more information."

"Inez, the man was trying to kill you," he pointed out quietly. "It wasn't the ideal situation for gaining information. Besides, it doesn't matter now anyway."

"It doesn't?" she asked with surprise.

"Nope," Thomas said, some of the unhappiness on his face easing as he added, "Aunt Martine left a message for Bastien at his office, so he called her and— You have no idea who Aunt Martine is, do you?" he interrupted himself wryly as she stared at him blankly.

Inez shook her head.

"Right, well, she's Jean Claude's sister. She was—or still is I guess—Aunt Marguerite's sister-in-law. She lives here in York actually, but was out of town until a couple days ago. Bastien had called her, but she didn't get the message until today. Anyway, she got a call from Aunt Marguerite."

"She did?" Inez asked, eyes widening.

Thomas nodded with a grin. "And she had the number of where Marguerite called from. Bastien, Lucern, Vincent, and Uncle Lucian have gone to Martine's to get the number and then plan to head straight to where she is."

· "Uncle Lucian?" Inez asked with confusion.

"Jean Claude's twin brother," he explained. "He arrived with his lifemate Leigh while you were sleeping."

"Oh," Inez murmured and then asked, "Why go over there? Why didn't Bastien just call her to get the number?"

Thomas grinned. "He gave some lame excuse to Terri that she wouldn't even repeat, but I think the truth is he probably did call. I think the guys just wanted to look into it themselves without the women along. Which is why everyone is upset," he continued, "Etienne and the women are up in arms at being left out at this point."

Inez bit her lip as she considered all he'd said and what Blondie had said last night.

"You're not looking relieved or happy to hear that Aunt Marguerite is fine," Thomas pointed out, his own happiness slipping away.

"Is she?" Inez asked.

He stared at her blankly.

"Why hasn't she called any of her children?" Inez asked.

Thomas smiled wryly and said, "It's possible she has. Most of them are here right now, though, and wouldn't get her call."

"Bastien would have," she pointed out quietly. "He got Martine's message."

"Well . . ." He frowned, but then shrugged and said, "She called Martine. She has to be all right."

"Thomas," Inez hesitated, reluctant to be the bearer of bad tidings, but then sighed and continued, "Blondie was working for someone who was willing to kill to keep us from finding her and possibly interfering in their plans."

"Yes, I know. He's dead, though," Thomas pointed out. "He can't hurt her."

But the person he worked for isn't, Inez thought unhappily, but hesitated to say as much to Thomas. He was obviously relieved and happy to believe his aunt was all right, and she was reluctant to make him worry when everything might really work out all right.

"Inez?"

Letting her own worries on the matter drop for the moment, she met his gaze, noting that the grim expression was back and asked uncertainly, "Yes?"

"Terri tells me that in the coffee shop you were thinking that maybe we should put off the turning until after we found Marguerite," he announced abruptly. "She's worried that you might be upset about my turning you as I did."

Inez felt her eyebrows rise. It seemed like a long time ago, but she did recall having the thought. It had been a brief one brought on by her fear of the pain involved. Obviously she'd been broadcasting her thoughts at the time, because Terri claimed she couldn't read minds. And while she'd forgotten all about it after everything that had happened, Terri hadn't, and had found the thought worrisome, passing on that worry to Thomas.

"Inez, I'm sorry," Thomas said quietly, his expression earnest. "I had no choice. You were dying, and besides you agreed to the turn the night before. Didn't you?" He frowned and muttered, "Of course, it was right after you'd nearly drowned and you might not have really understood what was going on at the time. Do you even love me? You nodded to that too, but . . ."

He raised his head and said solemnly, "I'm sorry if you're upset about being turned, but I'm not sorry for doing it. Because whether you love me or not, Inez, I love you. You're strong, and brilliant and sweet and have a strength I've never seen in other women. This last week you've done whatever was required of you to help find Marguerite without complaint or allowing fear to stop you, even going so far as being the bait in the trap." He scowled and then admitted, "Though I have to say I thought that was rather foolish. I was really pissed at you for putting your life at risk like that."

"It sounds to me like you still are," she said quietly.

"I love you, Inez. It was hard for me to see you in such a vulnerable position," Thomas said, his expression solemn, and then rushed on, "Anyway, I'm not sorry I turned you. Even if you choose not to be with me, I'll not regret it. And I know we haven't known each other long, and you probably want time to get to know me better. I'm willing to give you that time. I—"

"Thomas," Inez interrupted, and he fell silent at once. "In ten hours I'll have known you one week."

"Well, really, we met months ago," Thomas said quickly.

She smiled faintly, but continued. "I'm usually slow and cautious in making decisions."

"I'm sure you've had to make snap judgments at work in critical situations."

"Our circumstances since we've met haven't been ideal, what with the worry about Marguerite, the need to find her, the attacks—"

"Inez," he interrupted worriedly.

"There has been a lot of pressure and stress. In effect, we've been living in a pressure cooker since your arrival."

"Yes, but—"

"In this week I've seen you worried, furiously angry, tired—"

"Inez," Thomas tried again with alarm.

"And despite all that," she continued, "you've made me laugh, and shown me more joy this last week than I've experienced probably in my whole life. You've been encouraging, and supportive, loving and caring, considerate and sweet to me."

"Well, except for that alley in Amsterdam," he pointed out guiltily. "And I'm really sorry about attacking you. I never would have if it hadn't been for the—"

"Thomas," Inez interrupted with exasperation. "I'm trying to tell you I love you."

"You do?" he asked, a smile spreading halfway across his face. "But then why did you tell Terri that you wanted to delay the turn?"

"It wasn't you. It was because of the pain involved," she said with a grimace and then admitted, "I don't like pain, Thomas. I mean I'm practically phobic about it. My whole life, I've avoided any situation that might involve pain. My dentist even has to gas me to fill a cavity." Inez shrugged unhappily. "I probably would have delayed and put it off as long as I possibly could if you hadn't had to change me to save my life. In truth, Blondie probably did us both a favor by precipitating the events that forced you to turn me."

"Precipitating the events?" he quoted, stepping closer to slip his arms around her waist and nuzzle her neck as he murmured, "God, I love it when you use big words."

Inez chuckled, her own arms slipping around his shoulders, as she reminded him, "Last time you said you liked it when I talk dirty."

"I do," Thomas assured her and scooped her into his arms, adding, "I also like it when you yell at me in Portuguese. I guess I just like to hear you talk."

Inez smiled wryly as he carried her to the bed. "That would be a good thing since you're going to be hearing me talk to you for a very long time."

"You say it like it's a threat," Thomas said with amusement as he set her on her feet beside the bed. "Trust me, it isn't. I look forward to spending the next countless centuries with your voice filling the silence."

"You're so sweet," Inez whispered, running one hand down his cheek, but glanced to the door as the muffled sound of the bathroom door closing reached them. "We should go down to join the others."

"No, we shouldn't. The turning is traumatic. Your body has been put through a lot and you need your rest," he assured her solemnly, his fingers beginning to work busily at the tie of the robe.

"Rest, huh?" Inez asked dryly as he finally got the knot undone and began to draw the robe open.

"Oh, yes." Thomas slid the robe off her shoulders and then bent to press a kiss to one breast as his hand closed over the other. His lips brushed against the quickly blooming nipple as he said, "Didn't you hear Terri last night? Bastien wouldn't let her out of bed for a week after her turn. There was a very good reason for that."

"I'm sure there was," she said, but his mouth had closed over her nipple, drawing on it lightly and the words came out a bit breathlessly rather than with the cynical tinge she'd intended.

Letting the nipple slip from his lips, Thomas straightened and kissed her again, his hands sliding over her body before he broke the kiss and said, "I, of course, shall keep you company to ensure you don't encounter any unforeseen difficulties."

"How considerate," Inez gasped as he caught her by the behind and lifted her to press her against the hardness suddenly straining his jeans.

"Marguerite raised me right," he assured her, bearing her down to the bed.

Her soft chuckle was muffled as his mouth closed over hers.

And now a sneak peek at

Vampire, Interrupted

Coming March 2008
from Avon Books

Marguerite's Story

Marguerite wasn't sure what woke her; a sound perhaps, or the crack of light from the bathroom being momentarily blocked, or maybe it was simply an instinct for survival that dragged her from sleep. Whatever caused it, she was alert and tense when she blinked her eyes open and spotted the dark shape above her. Someone stood at the side of the bed, looming like death. That thought had barely formed in her mind when the dark shape used both hands to raise something overhead. Recognizing the action from her youth when broadswords and weapons of its ilk were more common, Marguerite reacted instinctively, rolling abruptly to the side as the assailant's arms started their downward swing.

She heard the weapon sing by her head just before tumbling off the bed. Marguerite landed on the floor with a thump and a shout that became a frustrated curse as she found herself tangled in the sheets. Glancing up, she saw her attacker jump onto the bed to follow and swing the sword again. Marguerite promptly gave up on the sheets, snatched the lamp off the bedside table, and swung it around to block the blow.

Pain vibrated up her arm on impact, eliciting another shout, and she turned her eyes away from the flying sparks as metal met metal. Marguerite took a bare moment to be grateful that the Dorchester was a five-star hotel with quality—and fortunately metal-based lamps that didn't snap under a sword's blow, and then felt the weight taken off the lamp and glanced back to see her attacker winding up for another blow.

"Marguerite?"

Her shouts had apparently woken Tiny, she realized as he called out again, sounding closer. Her attacker realized it too and tensed briefly, then—apparently deciding against taking on two of them—turned away and raced for the balcony doors.

"Oh, no you don't," Marguerite muttered, dropping the lamp and lunging to her feet to give chase. She wasn't the sort to allow someone to sneak up and attack her in her sleep, then run off to do so again another day. Unfortunately, she'd forgotten about the sheets tangled around her legs, but was abruptly reminded of them when she crashed to the floor with her first step.

Gritting her teeth, Marguerite peered toward the balcony doors as the curtains were tugged open. Sunlight immediately poured in, illuminating her attacker. There wasn't much to see. The man was encased from head to toe in black; black boots, black pants, long-sleeved black shirt, and all of that covered by a black cape. He also wore black gloves and even a black balaclava covering his face, she saw as he turned to peer back at her. Then he slid out onto the balcony, allowing the curtain to drop back into place as the connecting door between her room and Tiny's slammed open.

"Marguerite?"

She swiveled her head to him, and then pointed toward the balcony doors, gasping, "He's getting away!"

Tiny immediately charged across the room, rushing for the doors leading onto the terrace. He wore nothing but a pair of gold silk boxers with a big heart on the backside, and the sight made her blink in surprise. The moment he disappeared through the billowing curtains, her surprise turned to concern. She'd sent the unarmed, nearly naked man after her attacker—who had a sword.

Cursing, Marguerite concentrated on the sheets wrapped around her legs. They fell away easily now that she was no longer under threat, and made her mutter to herself with exasperation as she scrambled around the bed and hurried to the balcony doors. She charged right into Tiny's bare chest as he stepped back into the room.

"Careful. It's daylight," he rumbled, catching her upper arms and moving her back away from the curtains. Releasing her, he turned to close and lock the doors.

"Did you see him? Where did he go?" Marguerite asked, trying to peer around his large frame at the brightly lit terrace beyond as he pulled one of the heavy panels of cloth into place. The action blocked out the worst of the sunlight and most of her view of the terrace.

"I didn't see anyone. Are you sure you weren't dream—?" Tiny paused mid-sentence as he glanced over his shoulder and caught a glimpse of her in the bit of sunlight still slipping between the gap in the curtains.

Marguerite raised an eyebrow in question at the sudden widening of his eyes.

"You're hurt," he said with a frown. Letting go of the curtain, Tiny caught her by the chin and tipped her face up and to the side so he could get a better look at her neck. He then cursed and released her chin, taking her by the arm instead to hurry her to the en suite bathroom.

Marguerite glanced down at herself, trying to see where she was injured. She couldn't see a wound, but there was a line of blood dripping down her upper chest and soaking into the satin of the pale blue nightgown she wore. Frowning, she felt around on her throat until she found the nick in her neck. Apparently the sword had caught her as she rolled away.

"Tell me what happened," Tiny ordered as he flipped on the bathroom light.

"I woke up to find a man standing over the bed. He had a sword. I rolled off the bed as he swung it," Marguerite said simply, her gaze shifting out toward the bedroom and the balcony doors through which the man had escaped. Her adrenaline was still pumping and she now found she had itchy feet. She wanted to be doing something to pursue the man who'd attacked her.

"Roll faster next time," Tiny muttered, drawing her mind back to their conversation. He'd been dampening a washcloth under the tap as he listened. Now he turned and began to wash the blood away from her skin. He scowled at the sight of the wound, and then said, "It isn't too bad. Not deep, I don't think. Just a nick."

"It will heal quickly," Marguerite murmured, moving away from him and back into the bedroom. She wasn't used to being taken care of and wasn't comfortable with it. She was more used to being the caretaker. Her feet took her to the curtained balcony doors and she shifted the cloth to peer out on the bright terrace. There was no one there, and no rope or anything else to suggest how he'd gotten onto her balcony either.

She scowled out at the skyline. They were on the seventh and top floor. Her attacker must have climbed down from the roof.

"He was aiming to cut off your head."

Marguerite released the curtain and glanced around at that comment. Tiny was at the side of the bed, examining the slice across the mattress right below her pillow . . . where her neck had been. But then she'd known that. She'd rolled to the side, managing to keep her head at the expense of a small nick to the neck.

She shifted on her feet, her thoughts starting to take order in her head. Her attacker had used a sword. That told her he was definitely an immortal. Mortals usually killed, or tried to kill, each other, with guns or knives. If they were trying to kill an immortal they went for the classic stake. Cutting off the head with a sword was the most efficient method of killing one of her kind.

"Do you have enemies here in England that you

forgot to mention?" Tiny asked suddenly, straightening from examining the bed to spear her with a frown.

Marguerite shook her head, her gaze sliding back to the damaged bed. "It must be connected with this case."

He raised a doubtful eyebrow. "Why? We haven't found out anything yet."

Marguerite grimaced, sharing the disgust he felt at their inability to unearth even a bit of information regarding Christian Notte's birth or his mother. That was the case they were on. They were there to help Christian Notte, a five-hundred-year-old immortal, find his birth mother. It had sounded an easy task on first hearing it, but she was coming to realize it wouldn't be. A lot of time had passed since his birth, and he had little information he could offer them except that he'd learned that his father had been in England until shortly after Christian's birth and had returned home to Italy with him barely two days old.

England being where the boy was born, that was where Tiny and Marguerite had gone in search of information. Since arriving in England, they'd spent the last three weeks searching through dusty church archives across the country looking for mention of his birth or even of the name Notte. They'd started in the southernmost part of the country, working their way north until they'd reached Berwick-upon-Tweed. It was there that Tiny had finally suggested they meet up with Christian and question him again to see if there wasn't some bit of information he could give them to help narrow the search to one area, or at least one half of the country.

Marguerite had promptly agreed. She'd expected private detective work to be much more interesting than it was turning out to be and was seriously reconsidering her decision to become one. But she'd promised to help Christian find out the identity of his mother and intended to do her best to accomplish that first. They'd called Christian in Italy and made arrangements to meet him in London, then rented a car and driven south through the night, arriving at the hotel shortly before dawn to find that his flight had arrived several hours earlier and he'd already checked in. They'd met briefly with Christian Notte, and his cousins Dante and Tommaso on arriving, but Tiny and Marguerite had both been exhausted from the long drive and it had nearly been sunrise so they'd merely made arrangements to meet at sunset to discuss the case, then had parted to go to their rooms.

As it turned out, the two-bedroom suite Marguerite and Tiny had been given was right next to the one Christian and his cousins were sharing. It would make it convenient for meeting up at sunset. Whoever was up and about first was simply to go to the suite of the other. Marguerite suspected the men would end up coming here to the suite she and Tiny shared to wait for her in the living room. Men were generally quicker about getting ready to face the day than women and she was a particularly slow starter. Seven hundred years as a housewife had not prepared her for the rush to dress and eat to get herself off to work.

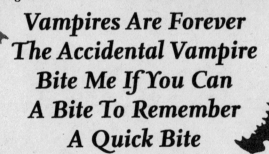